I0635049

THE NANCY DREW (TM) FILES

CAROLYN KEENE

THE NANCY DREW (TM) FILES
3 STORIES IN 1:

VANISHING ACT
BAD MEDICINE
OVER THE EDGE

AN ARCHWAY PAPERBACK
Published by SIMON & SCHUSTER

New York   London   Toronto   Sydney   Tokyo

VANISHING ACT, BAD MEDICINE and OVER THE EDGE first
published in Great Britain by Simon & Schuster, 1992
First published together in this combined edition in 1997 by
Simon & Schuster Ltd
A Viacom Company

Simon & Schuster Ltd
West Garden Place
Kendal Street
London
W2 2AQ

THE NANCY DREW FILES is a trademark of Simon & Schuster Inc

Simon & Schuster Australia
Sydney

A CIP catalogue record for this book is available from the British Library.

ISBN 0-671-00482-4

Printed and bound in Great Britain by Caledonian International Book
Manufacturing, Glasgow

VANISHING ACT

Chapter

One

"Nancy, get in here right away! The show's about to start!"

Nancy Drew glanced at her watch. "I'm ten minutes early, Bess," she called out through the open window of her car, smiling. Nancy slid out of her Mustang and started toward her friend. Bess Marvin was standing in the doorway to her house, almost dancing with impatience.

"Come *on,* come *on!*" she said as Nancy sauntered up the path. "George is already here. Do you want a soda or something? No, never mind. I'll get you one when there's a commercial. I don't want to miss even a *second* of this show."

"Well, you're certainly not going to," George Fayne commented dryly as Nancy followed Bess into the living room. George was Bess's first cousin, and she and Bess were Nancy's two best friends. "You have time to get fifty sodas if you want. I'm glad you're here, Nancy. It's too much for one person to deal with Bess when she's like this."

"I'm glad to be here, too," Nancy said. "I've been feeling lonely with Ned away."

Ned Nickerson, Nancy's boyfriend, had returned to Emerson College earlier that day after a long weekend at home. Nancy was delighted when Bess had asked her over. Now she wouldn't have to spend the whole evening missing Ned.

Bess wasn't listening to anything they were saying. "I just hope you programmed this thing right, George," she fretted, gesturing at the VCR. "This is one tape I *have* to have in my collection."

"Bess, no one can see if you keep standing in front of the TV," said George. "Just sit down and relax. It's all going to be fine. You'll have your permanent record of Jesse Slade to put in your hope chest. Not that it'll do you any good—unless he suddenly returns one day."

Bess sighed. "I still can't believe he's gone. My biggest idol—the greatest rock star in the world —gone. How could anyone have disappeared like that? Especially anyone so famous?"

"I wasn't as big a fan of his as you were, but I

do understand. It seems unreal to me, too," George said. "I can't believe three years have passed since he disappeared."

Three years, Nancy thought. It *did* seem impossible. Three years before, Jesse Slade had been on the way to becoming the biggest rock star in the country. He'd been only nineteen then, but he had already cut two albums—composing all the music, writing all the lyrics, singing and playing, and producing. The first had gone gold, and the second platinum.

Jesse Slade had also been the only rock musician in history to have six singles in a row reach number one on the charts. He'd won two Grammy Awards. And on top of that, he'd been gorgeous—with long dark brown hair, coal black eyes, and a sad, haunting smile that drove his fans wild.

"He was talented, Bess—I'll give you that," George was saying now.

"But I didn't like him because he was *talented!*" Bess protested. "And not because he was so cute, either. It was just— Well, there was something about him," she finished helplessly.

Nancy knew what Bess was trying to say. His talent and his looks weren't all that had made Jesse Slade so popular. He'd had a warm and intimate quality that made his songs seem as if they were a private conversation between each fan and himself. Jesse also made each fan feel as if he needed him or her.

3

Then, at the height of his popularity, Jesse Slade had vanished—without a trace.

No one knew *how* it had happened. Jesse and his band had been the main attraction at a huge outdoor concert on a beach in California. Jesse had been onstage for about forty minutes when he'd announced that he was going to take a short break.

He'd never been seen again.

The rest of the band was onstage when he'd disappeared. None of them had seen him vanish. Neither had anyone on the crew. And neither had any of the thousands of fans who'd been watching the concert. It seemed impossible—but he'd vanished and never come back.

But he'd never been forgotten—not by his millions of loyal fans, and not by the music industry. Both of his albums were still in the Top 100, and not a day went by that he wasn't mentioned in the music press. He might have disappeared, but the mystery of his disappearance had kept his career alive.

"It's even too much of a mystery for me," Nancy mused aloud. "I was just thinking about Jesse," she said in answer to George's quizzical look.

The show the girls were going to watch that night would kick off a week-long celebration of Jesse Slade on TV Rock, a cable music-video station whose nickname was TVR. "Who's hosting the segment tonight, Bess?" Nancy asked, her thoughts returning to the present.

"Dan Kennedy," answered her friend. "He's in charge of the whole week." Dan Kennedy was one of TVR's most popular veejays. "Tomorrow TVR's going to be interviewing the rest of the guys in Jesse's band, and the day after they'll go out to Jesse's hometown to talk to people who knew him when he was growing up. And they're going to play one of Jesse's songs every hour on the hour, and—"

"And they're going to have a seance to try to find Jesse, aren't they?" George put in.

"George!" Bess protested. "How can you joke like that?"

"Well, how can you make such a fuss about a guy you've never met and never will get the chance to meet?" George countered. "I mean, I know he was incredible, and I've heard of long-distance love, but don't you think this is a little *too* long-distance? Like so long-distance it's non-existent?"

"Oh, you're just—Wait, it's starting!" Bess said excitedly. She plunked herself down in front of the TV. "George, hand me that brush. I have to look my best."

"Right, Bess," George grumbled, but she gave her the brush anyway.

The TVR logo flashed on the screen. "TV *Rock!*" an echoing voice boomed. "Where the party never stops-ops-ops-ops-ops—"

"Oh, come on, get going!" said Bess. "We *know* it's TV Rock!"

Then Dan Kennedy strolled in front of the camera and sat down. "Hi, teen angels," he said with a grin, pushing his curly blond hair out of his eyes. "Like the shirt? A crazed fan just handed it to me on my way in." He pointed down at his T-shirt, which said "Evil Picnickers Unlock Secrets of the Pyramids" in huge black letters dripping with red. "I don't know exactly what it means," Dan Kennedy went on. "Maybe you do. Send your suggestions to me, along with ten dollars. When I have enough money, I'll retire!" he finished brightly. "Then I can devote my time to figuring out what my clothes are trying to tell me.

"Anyway"—Dan Kennedy's face became serious—"tonight marks the beginning of Jesse Slade Week. As most of you know, Jesse took off, or was taken off, or something, three years ago tonight. We're going to be remembering him at TVR this week—not that anyone who ever had anything to do with Jesse could really forget him. Tonight we're bringing you a very special tape of Jesse's last concert. TVR just uncovered it. It was thought to have been lost in a fire but was found mostly intact. We hope you'll be as moved by it as we were."

There was a burst of guitar music, and onto the screen flashed a picture of Jesse Slade bent over

6

his guitar. It cut to a shot of screaming fans leaping out of their seats at a concert, and then to another still of Jesse, vaulting through the air in one of the leaps that had been his onstage trademark.

"Jesse Slade—the man, the musician, and the mystery," came Dan Kennedy's voice-over. "Will we ever know what happened to him?"

"Nope," said George. Bess kicked her ankle.

"On this night three years ago, Jesse Slade played his last concert," Dan continued. "Tonight, we're bringing you that concert again."

The screen went to dark. At first Nancy wasn't sure what was happening. Then she realized that the screen was dark because the stage was dark. She could hear the occasional sounds of an expectant crowd—a catcall, throats clearing, a few bursts of applause. Then a tiny beam of light flashed onto the center of the stage.

A drum began beating—slowly at first, then fast. The beam of light grew larger—larger—larger. Now Nancy could see the huge outdoor stage that had been set up dramatically close to a cliff at the edge of the Pacific Ocean. Behind the stage, a fading sunset was a background for the black water.

Then Jesse Slade walked slowly to center stage —and the crowd went wild.

"Show the fans!" George said. "I love footage of fans."

As if in answer, the camera panned slowly over the crowd: a sweat-drenched boy waving a hand-painted sign that said "Jesse Forever"; a girl screaming hysterically and jumping up and down, tears of emotion streaming down her face; a forest of hands clapping rhythmically in the air as Jesse picked up a guitar and began the notes of his opening song.

For the next half hour the three girls watched the screen in total silence. Jesse stepped forward and held up his hand. Gradually the crowd grew quiet.

"I'm going to do one more," Jesse said, "and then I'm turning the stage over to my band for a while. They're pretty good, too, you know." There was a ripple of laughter from the crowd. "This one's from my first album," Jesse said, picking up his guitar. "I think most of you know it."

And he began to play the first bars of "Goodbye, Sweet Life."

Bess gasped, and a chill ran down Nancy's spine. "I'd forgotten that was the last song he played," Nancy said.

"Me, too," Bess answered. "It's creepy, isn't it?"

"Totally," said George. "It's almost as if he'd planned it or something. I wonder if . . ." Her voice trailed off, and the three girls fell silent again.

"Goodbye, sweet life," Jesse sang.

"You won't be missed . . .

"It's much too late to cry. . . ."

The crowd fell utterly silent for the next few minutes. Then, abruptly, the song ended. "See you in ten!" Jesse shouted jauntily as he strode off the stage to tumultuous applause.

"And that's *it?*" George said. "He doesn't come back?"

"No," Bess said sadly. "Well, I guess I'll get us a soda now. I don't care much about watching his band." Sighing, she pulled herself to her feet and went out to the kitchen.

Nancy picked up a magazine and began idly leafing through it as Jesse's backup band began to play. She wasn't really interested in them, either. She put down the magazine as Bess strolled back into the room carrying a six-pack of diet soda. On the television screen, Jesse's bass player was jamming with his guitarist. "How about switching channels for a little while, Bess?" she said. "This is getting kind of—"

Suddenly she broke off. What was that?

A strange flicker of movement in one corner of the screen had just caught her eye.

"What's the matter?" George asked.

"Something at the back of the stage," Nancy answered. "See, in that corner—there. Wait! What's going on?"

The back of the stage was dark and shadowy now. But Nancy was sure she wasn't imagining things.

She'd just seen what looked like it could have been a body. It was hurtling over the cliff beside the stage!

Chapter

Two

"BESS, STOP THE TAPE!" Nancy said excitedly. "Did you see that?"

"See what?" Bess asked. "What are you talking about?"

"I think I saw someone fall off the cliff! I have to check it again!"

"That's impossible! Why would something like that happen during a concert? Anyway, I didn't notice anything. Can't it wait?" Bess asked. "I want to watch the end. And I want the *whole* tape, not just part of it."

"Okay," Nancy agreed reluctantly. But she was so eager to check out what she'd seen that the rest of the show dragged for her. At last Dan Kennedy's face appeared on the screen again.

"We'll have more tomorrow night on Jesse," he said. "Same time, same place, same Dan. And now, take a look at the new video by the Same, ours exclusively on TVR—"

George leaned over and snapped off the TV. "Okay, Nan. What did you see?" she asked.

Quickly Nancy rewound the tape to the point where she thought she'd seen the body fall. At first she couldn't find the exact footage. Maybe it *was* just my imagination, she thought. I can't—

No. "There," she said breathlessly, pointing to the side of the screen. "See?"

"I don't know," Bess said. "It's awfully blurry."

For a second it looked as if the "body" teetered precariously at the cliff's edge. Then it plummeted and vanished into darkness.

George drew a long breath. "If it is a body, why didn't TVR notice it before?" she asked.

"I wouldn't have noticed it, either, if I had been really interested in the show," Nancy said. *"Anyone* watching would have missed it, I bet— the rest of the action's so distracting."

"But if it is a body, it's horrible!" Bess said. "What are we going to do about it?"

"What *can* we do?" George asked blankly. "It all happened three years ago, and if no one caught it then—"

"But three years ago—" Bess broke off. "That was Jesse Slade's last concert, and he was never seen after that. What if—"

"No!" George said. "That's impossible, Bess. If Jesse had fallen off a cliff, *someone* would have discovered his body."

"We don't know that for sure," Bess insisted. "Nancy, don't you think it could be Jesse?"

Nancy shook her head. "I think George is right, Bess. There'd have been no way to hide something like that."

"But it all *fits!*" Bess said. "I bet someone murdered him! Nancy, this is your next case, I just know it! You've got to get in touch with TV Rock right away!"

"Whoa!" Nancy said. "I can see it now." She picked up an imaginary phone. "'Hello, Dan Kennedy? I think I know what happened to Jesse Slade.' They'd never take me seriously, Bess. There's just not enough to go on!"

"Okay. Okay," Bess said, tense. "But if they *did* take you seriously—if they asked you to investigate this—would you do it?"

"I guess so," Nancy replied slowly.

"Then it's all taken care of," Bess said resolutely. "You just leave this to me, Nan."

Nancy couldn't help smiling a little. "Uh, Bess? How exactly are you going to take care of this?"

"Oh, TVR will take me seriously. You'll see,"

Bess answered. "Now, I think the best thing for you and George to do is go home and start packing."

"Bess, I have to hand it to you," Nancy said two days later. "You're very persuasive."

"I'll say," George chimed in. "If anyone had told me I'd be in Los Angeles today, I'd—well, it's hard to believe, anyway."

Twenty-four hours earlier Nancy had gotten a phone call. At first she'd thought it was a joke—that the guy at the other end was some friend of Bess's who'd been asked to play a joke on her. But soon she realized that the caller really was Dan Kennedy. And he really had been calling to find out whether she'd take on this case.

"I have to admit I'm intrigued by the whole thing, Mr. Kennedy," Nancy had said, "but I'm not totally sure there *is* a case to take on."

"Call me Dan," he'd answered. "You may be right, Nancy. But I agree with your friend Bess. Jesse Slade disappears at the same concert where a body mysteriously falls off a cliff—well, it's too much of a coincidence to be a coincidence. And I'm willing to fly you and your friends out here—and put you up at TVR's expense—if you'll agree to take a look around. I hear you're quite a detective. Bess told me about your work with Bent Fender, and I'm impressed."

Bent Fender was a rock group whose lead

14

singer, Barton Novak, had disappeared just minutes before a concert at Radio City Music Hall. The case had been one of Nancy's most challenging, but she had had more to go on then.

"All right, Dan. I'll give it a try," Nancy said. "But don't you have to get some kind of okay on this?"

"I'll get it okayed later. For now, I'll just put it on my expense account—and if there's a problem, I'll deal with it."

"Well, that's generous of you," Nancy said. "I'll come out with my friends, but I can't make any promises. In fact, I hardly know where to start!"

"Well, let me think about that. I'll try to come up with a few leads by the time you get here," said Dan. "And listen, Nancy—thanks."

That had been a day ago. Nancy had booked a flight for Los Angeles right after talking to Dan. She, Bess, and George had gotten on the plane that morning. They'd arrived just after lunch and rented a car at the L.A. airport. Now they were inching through a four-lane traffic jam toward the TVR studio.

"This is an incredible car," Nancy said. "I've never rented one with a cellular phone *and* super-Sensurround stereo! All this and traffic jams, too? I guess we really *are* in California!"

"If only I'd started my diet when I was supposed to," Bess said wistfully. "I mean, here we're going to be hanging out with rock stars—and I'm five stupid pounds overweight as usual. My one big chance, and I blew it!"

"Bess, you look fine," George said. "How many times have we been over this before?"

"Besides, I bet there aren't going to be a lot of rock stars hanging around TVR," Nancy put in, glancing into the sideview mirror as she carefully changed lanes. "Videos of stars, yes. Stars, no."

For a second Bess looked crestfallen. Then she brightened. "But the TVR veejays are almost like rock stars themselves. I can't wait to meet Dan Kennedy!"

"Whoops!" was all Nancy answered. Honking wildly, a flame-colored Jaguar had abruptly cut in front of the girls' rental car. "This traffic's going to take some getting used to! Let's hope it's not like this all the time."

An hour later Nancy pulled up in front of the three-story limestone building whose address Dan had given her. "Here we are," she said, climbing out and audibly sighing. "Boy, if that's how crowded it gets on the freeways, what's it like to drive on regular roads around here? Well, I guess we'll find out."

She pushed the glass door open into a lobby that was nothing like any other lobby she'd ever seen. It was painted hot pink, and filled with giant plastic palms. In back of the receptionist's desk was a huge screen showing a constant stream of rock videos without the sound. And next to her desk was parked a gleaming silver Porsche with a sign on it that said "Drive Me."

Even the receptionist looked perfectly suited to this place. No older than Nancy, she was wearing a hot pink rubberized dress, lime green stockings printed with tiny neon yellow polka dots, and electric blue high-top leather sneakers. On the black steel desk next to her typewriter was a tiny forest of palm trees just like the ones looming above her. She looked up expectantly as Nancy and her friends approached.

"What's the story with that car?" George asked before Nancy could say a word.

The receptionist smiled. "It belonged to the lead singer of the Slickboys. He gave it to us as a thank-you present when one of their videos went to number one. We didn't know what to do with it, so we just left it out here. Anyway, can I help you?"

"I'm Nancy Drew, and these are my friends Bess Marvin and George Fayne," Nancy told her. "We have an appointment to see Dan Kennedy."

"Have a seat," the receptionist said, gesturing toward a waiting area a few feet away. "I'll give him a call."

She picked up the phone and punched a few numbers. "They're here, Dan," she said. "Oh. Oh, really? Well, okay. I'll send her down."

She hung up and turned back to Nancy. "Dan says you're to see our president, Mr. Thomas, right away," she said. "Your friends can wait

17

here. Dan will be along in a minute to pick them up, and when you're done with Mr. Thomas you can come and meet them."

Uh-oh, Nancy thought. Why do I suddenly feel as if I'm being sent to see the principal? Aloud, though, she just asked, "Which way is Mr. Thomas's office?"

"It's down at the end of the hall. The office with the double doors," said the receptionist.

"See you in a little while," Nancy said, and headed down the hall.

The secretary's desk in front of the office was empty. I guess I'll have to announce myself, Nancy thought.

"Mr. Thomas?" she asked softly, peeking inside the double doors at the man speaking on the phone.

He didn't seem to notice her at first. "Okay. Book them for Friday. I don't care how, and I don't care what it costs—I just want it done!" he said into the receiver. "Now I have to go." Without saying goodbye, he hung up and turned to Nancy. "Yes, I'm Winslow Thomas," he said, "and you must be Nancy Drew." He jumped to his feet to shake her hand. "Please, have a seat."

Except for a huge, bushy ginger-colored beard, Winslow Thomas was the most correct-looking man Nancy had ever seen. He was wearing a navy pinstriped suit, a white shirt, and a navy checked tie. His wingtip oxfords had the burnished shine that could only have come from a professional polishing, and his short, wavy hair looked as though it had been trimmed five minutes ago.

What's he doing at a place like TV Rock? Nancy wondered as she sat down. He should be the head of a bank!

Before she could speculate further, Winslow Thomas cleared his throat. "I'll come right to the point, Nancy," he said. "Dan Kennedy told me this morning that you were coming to investigate the Jesse Slade disappearance." He had a slight southern accent, and his diction was so perfect that it almost sounded affected. "I have to say that I don't think it's a great idea," he continued. "And, frankly, I'm a little irritated at Dan for giving you the go-ahead without checking with me first. If he had, he'd have found out that I think a thing like this is definitely not in TVR's best interests."

"Why not?" Nancy asked, startled.

"A couple of reasons." Winslow Thomas leaned back in his chair. "First of all, the police have officially declared the case closed. It makes us look foolish to open it again with no more substantial evidence than a few seconds of film. Jesse Slade going over a *cliff*? How farfetched can you get?"

"I'll be honest with you, Mr. Thomas," Nancy said. "At first I thought it was a little farfetched myself. But don't you think we should explore any possibility if it could lead us to the right answer?"

"Not in this case," Winslow Thomas said. "I'll be honest with you, Nancy. The police don't think anything violent happened to Jesse. They suspect that he had reasons for dropping out of sight—reasons that wouldn't look too good if they became known. I'm afraid I agree with them. From the rumors I've heard—and I hear quite a lot in this business—Jesse Slade wasn't as perfect as his fans believed. But, what's the point of trashing his image now? What's the point of bringing the past to life if all it does is disappoint people?"

"I see your point," Nancy said slowly, "but I don't think that's a good reason for abandoning this case. What if those rumors you've heard *aren't* true? What if there *was* some kind of violence involved? I think it's more important to find out what really happened."

Winslow Thomas paused for a second. "Okay, I'll tell you what," he said briskly. "If you agree to work undercover in the record business—and to work as fast as you can—I'll agree to bankroll you for a reasonable amount of time. But I don't want any publicity. If the answer to this mystery turns out to be unpleasant, I don't want TVR getting a tainted reputation. We're a music station, not a muckraking business. And I don't want you getting my staff all fired up about this. They have jobs to do—and they don't include playing amateur detective."

Was that a dig? Nancy wasn't sure. "You

mentioned my going undercover," she said. "Do you have any suggestions what cover I could use so I could ask lots of questions."

"We use a lot of guest veejays at TVR. A contest-winner who was supposed to be our next guest veejay had to back out at the last minute. Maybe I could tell people that you're here to fill that slot. You could go undercover right here at the station. You'd have access to just about anyone you'd need to talk to."

"That sounds great," Nancy said.

"As long as you really pull your weight," Winslow Thomas added warningly. "As I said, I don't want my staff suspecting anything."

"Don't worry, Mr. Thomas," Nancy said. "I'll work hard. I promise."

"That's settled, then," said Winslow Thomas. "You can start tomorrow. I'll have my secretary call Dan, and he can start showing you the ropes. I've already told him not to let anyone know who you are, by the way. You can go up to his office now. It's one flight up—Room Two Twenty-four."

"Well, I will say one thing, Dan," Nancy said dryly a few minutes later. "Your boss is very efficient. Obviously he had decided to let me work here, but he made me convince him to reopen the case. Even with all of that, he had me in and out of there in five minutes flat."

"You don't have to tell *me* what he's like," Dan

said, wincing a little. "We've had our share of run-ins. I'm not too efficient. I'm kind of relaxed, myself."

"Yes, we'd noticed that," George said with a smile.

Nancy had arrived at Dan's office—a tiny cubbyhole of a place filled with wind-up toys, heaps of cassette tapes, and leftover pizza boxes —to find Bess and George chatting with him as if he were an old friend. She could see why. Dan was as easygoing and relaxed as Winslow Thomas had been brisk and formal. He had a mop of curly blond hair and laughing blue eyes, and he was dressed in black jeans, black running shoes, and a Bent Fender T-shirt—"put on in your honor," he'd told her. He was just as funny in person as he was on the air.

"I've got to do a taping before the end of the afternoon," Dan said, "so maybe I'll show you around tomorrow. But are there any questions you have now? I feel kind of responsible for you, since I brought you all the way out here."

"Well, I'd like to take a look at the site of the concert," Nancy said. "And I want to talk to someone on the crew that taped Jesse's last performance."

"Well, you're in luck. I've got a friend who worked on that tape," Dan said. "I'll give you her number."

"Great!" Nancy said. "And maybe you can help me make a list of the people I should talk to.

People who worked with Jesse, I mean. His manager, for instance. I don't even know who that was—"

"Tommy Road." Dan's voice was suddenly clipped and urgent. "Funny you should mention him. You know, since Bess's call I've been thinking a lot about Tommy Road. Did you know he vanished at the same time Jesse did?"

"That's strange," Nancy said.

"Very strange." Dan leaned closer. "I'd look into Tommy Road's disappearance closely if I were you," he said in a low voice. "If you want my opinion, Tommy murdered Jesse and hid the body before he disappeared!"

Chapter

Three

"Y<small>OU SEE,</small> N<small>ANCY</small>? I *told* you Jesse Slade was murdered!" Bess said triumphantly.

"Wait a minute," Nancy said. She turned to Dan. "That's quite an accusation, Dan. Where did it come from?"

"Shhh! Don't talk too loudly," Dan murmured. "After my conversation with Mr. Thomas this morning, I don't want him to think I'm taking time away from my job to work on this. Anyway, I don't have any hard evidence or even evidence of any kind.

"But I know that there were bad feelings between Jesse and Tommy Road before they disappeared," he continued. "I was a radio deejay then, and I interviewed Jesse a couple of times. I asked him something about Tommy once, and suddenly Jesse got really angry. I guess that's why I can still remember his exact words. He said, 'Tommy's done nothing to help me—in fact, it's the opposite. Off the record, I'm looking for another manager.' I asked him what he meant, but he wouldn't tell me anything more. Said it was nothing he could prove, and he'd appreciate my forgetting what he said. I did—until now."

"And Tommy Road vanished at the same time Jesse did?" George said slowly, thinking out loud. "I wonder why I never heard about it."

"It got some coverage, but Jesse was such a big star, Tommy's disappearance got buried."

"What was Tommy Road like?" Nancy asked.

"Kind of obnoxious," Dan answered. "I met him at a couple of parties. He was British, and he was always going on about how weak the American music scene was compared to that in England. I always wanted to ask him how he could complain when he was making so much money off an American like Jesse."

"What did he look like?" asked George.

"*Extremely* weird," Dan replied. "He shaved his head way before anyone else did, and he had tattoos on his face."

"Ugh! That sounds a little *too* weird." Bess shuddered.

"Yeah," Dan continued. "Two lizards, one on

each cheek. And he wore a long cape all the time." Dan shot a quick glance at his watch. "Look, I've got to go back to work. You'll be here tomorrow, won't you?"

"I sure will," Nancy answered. "I start work for you guys tomorrow!"

"Well, we can talk more then," Dan said. "Oh! Before I forget—that friend I was telling you about, the one who worked on the concert tape, works near here. She's over on Hollywood Boulevard." He picked up his phone book and handed it to Nancy. "Her name's Cari Levine. Here's her number."

Nancy jotted it down. "Can I use your phone to call her?" she asked.

"Be my guest. Okay, I'm out of here. See you tomorrow," Dan said and vanished out the door.

Nancy picked up the phone and began dialing the number Dan had given her. Bess sighed. "What a great guy."

"Really," George agreed. "Nan, can't you figure out some way to get us a job here, too?"

"Oh, I'll be keeping you busy enough. Hello, is this Cari Levine? My name is Nancy Drew. Dan Kennedy gave me your name. I'm doing some research on Jesse Slade." Nancy couldn't mention the fact that she was a private investigator. She didn't want to blow her cover. "I know this is short notice," she went on, "but I was wondering if you could spare a moment to talk to me and my friends about the night of his last concert."

"No problem," Cari said warmly. "Come right over."

"Hey! There's Melrose Avenue," Bess said as they drove toward Cari's office. "There are supposed to be incredible shops all along there. You know, I've been *needing* a little bit of L.A. to take back home with me. Like that stuff there." She pointed at a store window filled with peach-colored leather clothes being worn by mannequins turned upside-down. "Nancy, don't you think we could—"

"Not now," Nancy said firmly. "You'll get a chance to shop, I promise. But not now."

Cari Levine's office, which was on the ninth floor of a black glass skyscraper, was even messier than Dan's. Cans of film were everywhere, and snipped-off bits of tape littered the floor. The posters taped to the walls had all come unstuck on at least one corner.

Cari herself looked bright and energetic. She was wearing a scarlet jumpsuit with matching ankle boots, and from elbow to wrist her arms were lined with a mass of jangling silver bracelets.

"Sorry about the mess," Cari said. "I keep meaning to clean it up, but somehow every day goes by without my touching a thing. So, enough of my apologies. What can I do for you?"

Nancy explained. "We were wondering if

you'd noticed anything out of the ordinary that night," she said, finishing up.

"I was just a lowly assistant back then," Cari said. "I never actually talked to Jesse, but even I couldn't help notice that he was kind of edgy. He kept yelling at people while we were setting up—and that was the kind of thing that never happened with Jesse. Normally he went out of his way to be nice to camera crews and roadies and people like that."

"Did he say anything that seemed strange to you?" Nancy pressed.

"Well, it *was* three years ago. . . ." Cari thought for a minute. "And the main thing we were all paying attention to was the weather."

"The weather?" George repeated.

"Yes. We were all afraid it was going to rain. The sky looked incredibly dark and threatening, and you could hear thunder in the distance. As a matter of fact, there *was* a big storm right after the concert ended. Perfect timing! If the concert had been the next day, the whole stage would have had to have been rebuilt—the rain made half the cliff collapse."

Nancy looked up, suddenly alert. "Does that happen often?" she asked.

"Well, we do have a big problem with the coast eroding out here," Cari answered. "I'm sure you've heard about all the big beach houses on Malibu that have wound up in the ocean because the shoreline erodes so badly."

Nancy didn't answer for a second. "The timing . . ." she finally said. Bess, George, and Cari all stared at her, but Nancy didn't notice. "It's another case of the timing being too good," she said slowly. "Jesse disappears . . . the cliff he was performing on crumbles . . . and a body that may have fallen off the cliff is never found."

"You're not saying someone *made* the cliff collapse, are you?" George asked. "Nancy, that was obviously just—just nature! It can't have anything to do with Jesse's disappearance!"

"Oh, I'm not saying anyone engineered the collapse," Nancy said quickly. "All I mean is that the body might have been buried under the cliff when it collapsed. That might account for no one's discovering it!"

Nancy jumped to her feet. "Well, I wanted to see the site of the concert anyway," she said. "And there's no time like the present. Let's head out to the beach and take a look. It's not much of a lead, but it might tell us something. Can you give me directions to the site, Cari?"

"Sure," Cari said. "It's about an hour north of here. Now, if I can just find a map in all this mess . . . Forget it; I'll just tag along and show you."

"I can't believe how beautiful this is," Bess said half an hour later. "It looks like something from a movie!"

29

"From many movies," Cari answered. "This shot must be in hundreds of them."

The four girls were standing at the edge of a cliff that jutted out into the churning, white-capped ocean. Below them waves pounded relentlessly against glistening black rocks, and the air was filled with the cry of sea gulls.

"Where are the surfers?" Bess asked. She sounded disappointed. "This place is totally deserted."

"Well, look at the water!" George said. "No one could surf or swim here. It's much too wild, and those rocks would be horrible to crash into." Suddenly she shivered. "I feel sorry for Jesse if he did fall off this cliff. I don't see any way he could have survived."

"You're right," Nancy said. "It would have been almost impossible to investigate, too, especially once the cliff had collapsed.

"Let's see. The band must have been over there." Nancy gestured to a point about thirty feet away. "Right?" Cari nodded.

"And the taping crew was right where we're standing now," Cari added. "That means that the body I saw falling had to have been standing over there."

There was a spot at the edge of the cliff that overhung a huge boulder. Bess eyed it nervously.

"You're not planning to investigate *that*, I hope," she said. "Because if you are, I have to tell you I'd rather be shopping."

"Well, it would be nice to get a closer look," Nancy said. "I wonder what's the best way to get down to the beach."

Cari shrugged. "That, I don't know."

Nancy and Cari walked over to the spot and stared down at the shore.

"It's kind of windy, you two," Bess said fretfully. "Get back a little, will you?"

Cari inched back one foot, but Nancy kept looking down. "I guess I was expecting to *see* a collapsed cliff," she mused. "But, of course, that doesn't make any sense. Three years of tides moving in and out would smooth over the spot, wouldn't they? So there'd be no trace of a body now or of the rubble."

Bess's voice was edgy. "Nancy, Cari, you *know* I hate heights! Let's get out of here and go back and check into the hotel. I'm starving!"

"In one second," Nancy promised. "I'm just trying to fix this scene in my—"

Then she gasped. Under her heels, the cliff was starting to crumble, and the momentum shot her forward.

Instinctively Nancy threw herself back. Her arms flailed the air wildly—helplessly.

Cari made a lunge for her, but came up with nothing but a handful of air.

Nancy's frantic backpedaling only made things worse. Before she could draw a breath to scream, she was sliding down the rocky face to the treacherous boulders below.

31

Chapter

Four

NANCY SLID with her arms stretched above her head, grasping for any handhold. She held her breath, waiting for the terrible moment when she'd smash onto the rocks below.

Then a third of the way down, her shirt shredded and her back skinned, Nancy sped past a small bush rooted precariously in the rock. She opened her hand and clawed at it. Her fall was stopped, but the impact was terrible. Nancy hung, dangling by one arm, her shoulder wrenched and aching.

But she was alive!

She eased her toes down onto a narrow outcropping of rock—just a yard wide—jutting out from the cliff. Below her, the sea licked at the rocks as hungrily as ever.

Nancy lay there trembling. Every inch of her body was throbbing with pain, but she knew nothing was broken. Her shoulder was not dislocated. She ran a hand across her eyes and glanced back up at the cliff top. The others were staring down at her, ashen faced.

"H-hi," Nancy stuttered.

There were tears in Bess's eyes. She opened her mouth to return Nancy's greeting, but no sound came out.

"Don't move," George called. "I'll be right down to help you."

"No, I'm okay!" Nancy called back. "Just a little sore. And embarrassed," she added. "I can climb up myself."

Now that she looked, she noticed that the cliff was *covered* with scraggly bushes. Nancy slid along to the end of the ledge and pulled gingerly on the nearest one. It didn't move. She gave it a harder tug. The bush certainly seemed well rooted.

"I can use these bushes to pull myself up," she called up to the girls. "But keep an eye on me."

"We will," Bess said fervently as Nancy edged herself off the ledge and began her ascent.

"No, Ned, I'm okay. Really!" Nancy insisted. "A little bit scraped up, that's all." She felt the pain shoot down her arm when she eased her shoulder back and tried not to groan audibly. "It's sweet of you to want to fly out here, but I'm just not going to let you. Not with that big paper to finish . . ."

It was nine at night, and Nancy had just put in a good-night call to Ned at college. She still couldn't believe her good luck. She'd made it back up the cliff with very little trouble. Her knees and elbows were rubbed raw from the climb—but she would be okay soon.

"The fall did tell me something," she said to Ned. "It's entirely possible that whoever fell in that tape slid down just the way I did—because of the cliff's collapsing."

"So there might not have been any kind of 'foul play' involved?" Ned asked.

"Exactly. But I don't know what it all proves. It's just something to file away."

"Well, keep me filed away somewhere, too," Ned said. "I hate having you so far away."

"Me, too." Nancy sighed. "I'd better hang up. I've got a lot going on tomorrow—first day on the job, you know. I love you."

"I love you, too, Nancy. Call me again as soon as you can."

"Nancy, hi! You're right on time!"

Nancy turned to see Dan Kennedy striding toward her. "I'm starting to get the hang of driving around here," she said. "You just leave an hour earlier than you think you need to."

"That's about it," Dan said. "What have you done with Bess and George?"

Nancy hid a smile. Her friends would be delighted to hear that he'd asked about them. "They're working," she said. "I gave them their assignments last night. Before we left for L.A., I called Jesse's estate to find out who his accountants were. It's a firm called Lawrence Associates, and Bess is over there now trying to get permission to go through Jesse's financial records. George is at the library looking at old newspaper clippings of that last concert. Something might turn up—you never know."

"Well, tell them hi for me. Now, I'll take you around and introduce you to the people you'll be working with this week." Dan lowered his voice. "I've told them you're a guest veejay, even the receptionist."

Speaking normally again, he took Nancy by the shoulders and piloted her down the hall. "Let's go find out what a rock TV station looks like," he said.

"Here's the control room," he said, stopping beside one door. "There are three directors inside—the director, the associate director, and the technical director. The technical director's responsible for making sure the right tape's put on when it's time to show a video." Nancy pulled the door open a crack and peered in to see a man and two women sitting at a paneled board covered with what looked like millions of buttons.

35

On the wall in front of them were four television screens, each showing the set from a different angle. She eased the door closed again.

"And here's the sound room," Dan continued, indicating a room with a sliding glass door adjacent to the control room. "It's just what it sounds like—the technician here monitors the show's decibel level."

Dan stuck his head into the sound room and tapped the shoulder of a man wearing headphones. "Wake up, Ken! This is Nancy Drew," he said after the technician had turned around. "She's our new guest veejay. She'll be—"

"I have a lot of work to do," Ken said flatly, interrupting. "I'll talk to you later." And he turned his back on them.

For a second Dan looked bewildered. "Well, *he's* sure got something on his mind," he said. "Maybe one of the higher-ups has been giving him trouble."

They peeked into the makeup room, the editing room, and the preview room—a soundproof chamber where tapes could be played at all different sound levels to make sure the sound was undistorted. A bright red and white electric guitar was propped up against one wall of the sound room. "What's that guitar for?" Nancy asked.

"Oh, that! We had a demo band practicing in here a couple of days ago, and—if you can believe it—they forgot that. I don't think they're going to get far in this business."

Dan introduced Nancy to several more people. She couldn't understand it, but no one she met was very friendly—and a couple of people were even downright rude. As she and Dan continued on, Dan looked more and more confused.

"They don't know who you really are, do they?" he muttered.

"I don't see how they could!" Nancy whispered back. "And even if they did, why would they be *angry* at me?"

"Beats me," said Dan. "But something's going on, that's for sure. Here's the studio. They're taping now, so we'll just slip in the back door. Be very quiet. This is where it all happens."

The studio was an enormous room three stories high—the height of the whole building. The first thing Nancy noticed was that it was freezing in there. "It's so hot under all those lights that the rest of the room has to be kept cold so the veejays won't get too sweaty," Dan whispered.

Nancy looked up at the ceiling. It was hung with massive lights, each burning down onto the set.

"Why do they need three cameras?" she whispered to Dan, staring at the set.

"One's for the center, one's for closeups, and one's for the guest chair," he answered.

The center chair was where the veejay sat. One

was sitting there then in front of a large screen that was pulsing with color and weird shapes.

"What does he do when the video's on?" Nancy asked.

"Anything he wants—for as long as the video lasts. They run the tape in from the control room. Well, I've got just one more person to introduce you to, and that's Renee Stanley. I think she's in the dressing room. She's the veejay who'll be your boss this week."

"I've seen her on TV. She's great," said Nancy as they headed down the hall again. "But I thought my boss was going to be you."

"I wish I could be." Dan sounded genuinely regretful. "But all this Jesse Slade–week stuff's going to keep me too busy. I'll do everything I can to help you, though."

"Okay," Nancy said. She was trying to fight down the rush of nervousness that was rising in her stomach. I know this is just an undercover job, she thought. But if everyone's got a grudge against me, I'm going to need an ally. Maybe Renee will—

But one look at Renee Stanley and Nancy knew *she* wasn't going to be on her side.

The dressing room door was open. Three of the walls were lined with signed photos of rock stars, and the fourth was hung ceiling to floor with one huge mirror. Renee was sitting and brushing her hair, staring fixedly at her reflection when they walked into her office. She didn't stop brushing

—didn't even turn around—as Dan introduced Nancy. Then, very deliberately, she put her brush down and swiveled her chair around to face Nancy.

She was even prettier in person than on TV. She was wearing zebra-print tights and a low-cut sleeveless black T-shirt with a loose-fitting leather belt riding down on her hips. Tousled blond ringlets framed her heart-shaped face. Her eyes were a startlingly deep blue—almost violet—with lashes so long they cast shadows on her cheeks.

But there was nothing pretty about her expression, or about the silence that hung in the air as she stared first at Nancy and then at Dan.

Dan cleared his throat nervously. "I don't know whether you have time to talk to Nancy before you go on—" he began.

"Not really," Renee interrupted. "But I guess I don't have much of a choice, do I?" She glanced briefly at Nancy and picked up a hand mirror. "Well, you might as well sit down, Nancy," she said in a bored monotone. "Got a pad? I want you to take notes."

"Nancy, you look awful!" George said anxiously as Nancy walked slowly across the lobby of TVR. "I didn't find out much at the library—but I guess that had better wait. How was your day?"

Nancy tried to smile. "Not the greatest. I thought four-thirty would never come. If this is

39

the glamorous world of music television, you can have it." Wearily she ran a hand across her face. "Where's the car?"

George had dropped Nancy off that morning. Since Bess had been headed in a different direction, she took a taxi. "It's over there," George said, pointing across the street. "Do you want to go back to the hotel? You look as though you could use a rest."

"Not yet," answered Nancy. "We're going to see someone. I did get one lead today. Do you have the keys, George? I'd like to drive. Okay?"

"I don't know what I've done, but everyone at TVR is mad at me," she said as she pulled the car onto the freeway and headed toward the suburbs. "They must have been told something really horrible about me. But what? And by whom, I keep asking myself.

"Renee Stanley's *really* got it in for me," she continued. "All I did today was clerical stuff—that and errands. Renee treated me like a secretary. She sent me out to get her lunch. She made me type letters for her—thank-you notes for some birthday presents. She made me alphabetize some files. I wouldn't have minded—I mean, it's nice to help out—but she didn't say a civil word to me the whole day!"

"You should tell Mr. Thomas," George said indignantly.

"Oh, I can't do that," said Nancy. "I'm sure it would get out if I did, and then people would be angry at me for tattling. I'll just have to tough it out. But somehow I don't think I'll be learning a lot about the music business or meeting the right people to ask my questions."

"Say, where are we going?" asked George. "You said something about a lead?"

Nancy brightened. "Yes. I did get a chance to talk to Dan in the afternoon—he said to say hi to you, by the way—and he suggested that I talk to Vint Wylie. He was Jesse's bass player, and Dan thinks Vint probably knew Jesse as well as anyone in the business. So I made an appointment with him. He lives in a suburb called North Claibourne—we have two more exits to go."

"What's Vint Wylie doing now?" asked George.

"I don't know. Maybe he's playing in another band," Nancy answered. "Whatever he's doing, I hope he's nicer to me than the people at TVR," she added with a sigh.

They reached the exit and drove for a couple of miles before Nancy reached the right neighborhood. "This is North Claibourne. How gorgeous!" she exclaimed. "Look at all those beautiful gardens!"

They *were* beautiful. Every yard was lushly planted, every lawn an emerald rectangle. Flowering trees were everywhere, and their colors were nothing like those near Nancy's home—flaming reds, corals, and yellows. The houses were no less beautiful. Most of them were one story high, and most looked vaguely Spanish, with red-tiled roofs and stucco walls.

"It all looks sort of tropical," George said. "But so respectable, too. I can hardly believe a bass player would live around here. But I guess he has to live somewhere. Are we almost there, Nan?"

"*Right* there. Right now," answered Nancy as she looked at the address Dan had given her. "Wow! Vint Wylie's certainly done well for himself!"

At the end of a long, winding, flower-edged driveway, behind impressive wrought-iron gates, was a sprawling Tudor mansion—the only two-story house on the block.

The gates were open. "He's expecting us," Nancy said, turning carefully into the driveway and switching off the ignition. "He sounded very nice on the phone—said to come over."

There was no answer when she rang the bell. Nancy stood on tiptoe to peer in through the little lead-paned window in the door. All she could see was a dark, deserted-looking interior. There was no trace of anyone inside.

Gently Nancy tried the door. It was unlocked.

She and George eyed each other questioningly. "Should we go in?" George whispered.

"I don't know," Nancy whispered back. "Wait, why are we whispering?" she said in full voice. "Of course we should go in. He's expecting us. Maybe he's on the phone or something."

But no one was inside the dark, cavernous house with its carpets so thick the girls' steps were completely muffled. And the phone in the hall was off the hook.

Nancy stepped into the gleaming kitchen, which looked big enough to serve an entire restaurant. Through the kitchen window she could see the bright turquoise water of a swimming pool. "He must be out in back," she said, walking resolutely toward the kitchen's french doors.

She stepped outside—and gasped.

Sunlight was dancing on the little ripples in the pool, and a gentle breeze stirred the leaves of the trees overhanging the yard. It was a picture-perfect setting—except for one thing.

A man's body was lying facedown next to the pool!

Chapter

Five

"OH, NO!" NANCY CRIED.

As George looked on, horrified, she raced up to the motionless figure sprawled on the tiles and grabbed his shoulder. "Call an ambulance!" she ordered George. "There's a cordless phone on that table over there!" George dashed over to it.

Then the man stirred a little, groaned, and lifted his head. Now Nancy could see that he was very handsome, with a bronzed, appealingly craggy face. But he looked completely stunned.

His dazed eyes met Nancy's. "Wha—" he began.

"Mr. Wylie?" Nancy asked. He nodded. "I'm

44

Nancy Drew. It's all right. We're getting help," she reassured him. "You just take it easy."

"But I—" Vint Wylie groaned again and rolled over onto his back, raising himself up on his elbows.

Nancy patted his shoulder. "You'd better not move too much—just in case," she said. "Not until the ambulance gets here."

"But I'm okay," Vint Wylie said thickly. George had been dialing, but she stopped and stared at him. He gave an enormous yawn. "Sorry. I was just, uh, meditating."

"Meditating! You *look* as if you were—" George exclaimed. Nancy cut her off quickly. She knew George was about to say "asleep." And she was sure George was right. But there was no point in embarrassing Vint Wylie unnecessarily —he would talk more freely if he didn't feel self-conscious.

"Sorry if we startled you," she said. "We— well, obviously we thought there was something the matter. I guess I jumped to conclusions."

"It's sure lucky I hadn't reached the ambulance company yet," George said, a shade tartly. "It would have been embarrassing to have them get here and find out Mr. Wylie was okay after all."

"Call me Vint, you two. 'Mr. Wylie' sounds too weird. I don't think anyone's ever called me that before." He brushed the dark-brown hair out of his eyes and yawned once. He had meditated himself right into a deep sleep. Suddenly he grinned at Nancy, a slow, infectious grin.

"Great intro!" he said. "Shall we start all over?"

Nancy smiled back. "Sounds good," she replied. "Vint, this is my friend George Fayne. She's helping me on my—uh—research."

Vint gestured toward some teak chairs, and the three of them sat down while Nancy explained why they'd come. "Dan Kennedy said you knew the most about Jesse," she finished. "You two were pretty close?"

"Sort of." Vint bit his lip. "Jesse wasn't— wasn't that easy to get to know, really. He was probably the most private person I've ever known."

"No family?" Nancy asked. "No close friends?"

Vint looked away. He cleared his throat a couple of times, then sighed. "No. He did have a girlfriend," he said slowly. He drummed his fingers nervously on his knee. "I—I don't know about his family, though."

Why does he seem so tense? Nancy wondered. I'm not asking him anything to make him nervous. Aloud, she just said, "Do you know his girlfriend's name? Maybe I should talk to her."

"I—I don't know what her name was," Vint said quickly. "I can find out for you, though."

"That would be great. What about your band's

46

manager, Tommy Road? Did you know him well?" asked Nancy.

"That creep? I knew much too much about him," said Vint. He put his hands behind his head and stretched his legs out in front of him. In this elegant garden, his faded jeans and cowboy boots seemed out of place. "How much time have you got?" Suddenly he looked much more relaxed.

"Well, Dan Kennedy mentioned something about Jesse's wanting to fire Tommy Road. Had you heard anything about that?" Nancy asked.

"Jesse wanted to *fire* him?" Vint sounded astonished. "I can't believe it! He would never hear a word against him. I mean, *we* all knew what a loser Tommy was, but Jesse always refused to consider switching managers."

He scratched his chin thoughtfully. "Though there was some problem with money. Jesse was always short."

"Short of *money?*" George asked. "How could that happen? I mean, his records sold in the millions."

"I know. But it's true," Vint said. "He used to talk a lot about it. He paid me and everyone else who worked for him on time, but he was always grumbling about how he didn't have enough. That could be what finally came between him and Tommy. But as I said, I didn't know anything was up between them.

"I can tell you one person who might be able to

help you, though," he said, straightening up in his chair. "His name's Martin Rosenay. He lives out in Chelmsford—that's a town about twenty miles east of here. He really gets around in the music business—he's a dealer in rock memorabilia. And I hear he's done pretty well selling stuff related to Jesse. He probably has tons of photos, letters, and junk."

Vint stood up abruptly. "I guess I haven't been much help," he said. "I'm sorry. But I'm sure this guy Rosenay will be better."

It was definitely a dismissal. Nancy and George stood up, too. "Thanks, Vint," Nancy said. "Actually, you've been very helpful." Not *that* helpful, really, she said to herself. "Can I call you if I have any more questions?" she added.

"Sure! Any time!" Vint sounded a little too enthusiastic.

"Oh, there is one thing I forgot to ask," Nancy said. "What are you doing now? For a living, I mean?"

Now Vint looked troubled. "I'm in another band," he said. "You've probably heard of them. The Crisp."

"The Crisp! But they're—"

"Doing incredibly well," Vint finished for her. "It's true. But I'd trade it all in just to be able to play with Jesse again."

And this time Nancy was sure he was telling the truth.

"Well, what did you think?" George asked, when they were safely back in the car again.

"There's something going on," Nancy said, "but I'm not sure what. Did you notice it, too?"

"How could I miss it? When you asked him about Jesse's friends and girlfriend, he just about shriveled up."

"Yes, that's it," Nancy agreed. "But I was afraid that if I pressed him harder, he'd clam up altogether. I'll try again later."

She glanced at her watch. "It's almost suppertime. Let's go back to the hotel and meet Bess and hear how her day went."

The "hotel" where the three girls were staying was actually a group of small bungalows, each with its own kitchen and garage. "Boy, am I exhausted," Nancy said as she parked the car in their garage. "I feel so dirty, too. All I want to do tonight is—"

"Nancy!" Bess was at Nancy's elbow before Nancy was out of the car. "George! You're back! I've been waiting for you guys forever!"

She practically dragged Nancy out. "I've found out something *very interesting* about Jesse Slade," she said breathlessly. "A huge amount of his money is missing—and I'm sure Tommy Road was embezzling it!"

Chapter

Six

NANCY STOPPED on the path leading into the bungalow and stared at Bess. "We were just *talking* to someone who thought Jesse might have been having money problems," she said. "What did you find out?" All of a sudden she didn't feel so tired.

"Well, come in and sit down and I'll tell you," Bess said. "I just made some iced tea."

Her face was pink with excitement—and pride. "Now, are you ready?" she asked. "You're not going to believe I figured this all out on my own!"

Bess took a big swig of iced tea. "Well, I got to Mr. Lawrence's—the accountant's—office," she began. "It's a big, dark, and gloomy-looking place that looks like a men's club or something. I was a little scared, but I acted official and asked a secretary to see a computer printout of the general ledger Jesse's manager had kept—just the way you rehearsed me, Nan. I was told I could read it in this little conference room right next door to Lawrence's office. So I took this huge stack of computer paper and went in there and started looking through all the payments Tommy Road ever made while he was Jesse's manager.

"Most of it I could figure out pretty well," Bess continued, "but there were these huge payments to something called Bailey Promotional. That's where I started to get confused—because there were also huge payments to a public-relations place called Swang and Davis, and both companies were listed in the promotional category in the ledger. And public relations and promotion are pretty much the same thing, aren't they? Besides, the amount being paid to Bailey Promotional was really huge—I mean, hundreds of thousands of dollars. I don't know that much about this kind of thing, but I didn't see how *any* PR place could charge that much!

"*So*. I decided to call them up and just *ask* them about Tommy Road and Jesse. And guess what!" Bess was practically bouncing in her seat. "There was no Bailey Promotional in the directory! Isn't that fantastic?"

"But they could be unlisted," George objected.

"Oh, no. See, this is where I *really* got smart. I called the California Secretary of State's office. They have a list of all the businesses incorporated in the state. So I asked if they had a listing for a corporation called Bailey Promotional. And they did. It didn't have an address—just a post office box number. And it had been incorporated by a guy named S. Thomas *R-H-O-D-E.*"

"Tommy Road! Bess, that's great!" said Nancy. "He was sending Jesse's money to a corporation he'd set up! But how could the accountant have missed that?"

"Well, I finally worked up the guts to talk to Mr. Lawrence," said Bess. "He said that it wasn't his business to question payments that Jesse's manager had authorized. He just paid them. He also said there are lots of different kinds of promotional expenses. So what do you think?"

"I think you did a wonderful job," Nancy said sincerely, and George nodded her agreement. "I don't see how there's any other way to figure this—Tommy Road must have been embezzling, and Jesse must have found out. At last, a real lead! Now we have a motive—a reason someone would have wanted Jesse out of the way."

Then Nancy's face fell. "Oh. But it's going to have to wait," she said in a disappointed voice. "Renee told me that tomorrow's going to be completely crazy. She said I'd really have to buckle down—as if I haven't already been."

"How'd your day go, anyway?" Bess asked. "I forgot to ask."

"Don't ask," Nancy and George said in unison. Nancy grinned. "At least not until after supper," she said. "Let's go find a good Mexican place. Los Angeles is supposed to have millions of them."

"Perfect," Bess replied. "I was so excited about this embezzling thing that I didn't even notice how hungry I was—if you can believe that."

Without meaning to, Nancy and George spoke in unison again. "I can't," they both said.

"Nancy, why did you ever let me eat so much? I feel like a gorged boa constrictor!" Bess groaned theatrically as they walked back into the bungalow a couple of hours later.

Nancy laughed. "Bess, I refuse all responsibility. No one was forcing you to order that food, you know."

"I know." Bess sighed. "But I've got to blame *somebody*. Do you guys want to see if there's anything good on TV?"

"Not tonight," Nancy said. "I need a good night's sleep. I'm getting up at six tomorrow so I can go in to TVR early. I even arranged for a wake-up call."

"How? By telepathy?" George asked. "I've been with you ever since you left the office, and I haven't seen you go *near* a phone."

"I made the call from TVR," Nancy said, flushing a little. "I wanted to make sure Renee knew I was really trying hard."

Bess—who had heard the whole story of Nancy's day during dinner—leaned over and gave her a hug. "You'll show that Renee," she said comfortingly. "You just wait until tomorrow. She won't know what hit her."

Songbirds were going full-blast outside as the sun streamed in across Nancy's bed and landed directly in her face. Groggily she rolled over and looked at her watch. Then she sat bolt upright in bed.

The hotel management was supposed to wake her at six o'clock. Now it was after eight!

"They must have forgotten about me!" she gasped, throwing the covers back and jumping out of bed. "Oh, I'm going to be so late!"

A tousled-looking Bess peered in, rubbing her eyes. "You're still here?" she said, yawning.

"I sure am," Nancy said grimly, "and the second I'm dressed, I'm calling the hotel desk to find out what happened."

She hurried into a pair of acid-washed jeans and an oversize sleeveless orange shirt. Then she picked up the phone and punched the number of the bell desk.

"This is Nancy Drew. I asked to be woken at six," she said angrily when the clerk answered. "Why didn't it happen?"

"But, Ms. Drew, what about your note?" The woman at the other end sounded astonished.

"What note?"

"Well, I just got on duty, but there's a note on the desk canceling your wake-up call. It's signed with your name. I—I guess the clerk just assumed you had dropped it off. I mean, why wouldn't he?" The clerk sounded completely at sea. "Ms. Drew," she said, "there's obviously been some kind of mix-up. I'm so sorry—I don't know what to say."

"Oh, don't worry," Nancy heard herself answering. "It's not your fault, and anyway, it doesn't matter too much."

And that's really true, she told herself. I have to remember that my job at TVR isn't a real job. But *someone* left that note. Someone's trying to make me look bad at TVR. And I have a very good idea who it is. But I'm not going to give her the satisfaction of thinking she's getting to me.

"Where have you been, Nancy?" Renee asked an hour later. "I thought I told you this was going to be a big day."

Renee sounded offhand, but there was an undercurrent of anger in her voice. Nancy did her best to ignore it. She'd decided on her way over that the most professional way to handle this would be to act as though it had never happened. Renee had probably sent that note—

at least, Nancy couldn't think of anyone else at TVR who would have done such a thing—but on the off-chance that she hadn't, it would definitely be wiser not to confront her.

"I'm very sorry, Renee" was all Nancy said. "What would you like me to do first?"

"Well, I know you don't have any experience working with entertainers," Renee said, "but you're about to get some. A stand-up comic named Bonzo Bob is coming in today. He's been doing the comedy clubs recently, and I'd like you to talk to him to see if you think there's any way you can use him on your show. See what you think, anyway."

"Oh, that sounds like fun!" Nancy said, trying to hide her sarcasm. She could hardly believe her luck. She was supposed to be talking to people in the music business about Jesse, and she had to interview a *comic*.

It didn't take long for Nancy to realize that Bonzo Bob was not going to be on TVR. Nancy couldn't remember ever seeing anyone who made her feel less like laughing. And she'd never seen anyone with so little talent act so temperamental.

Bonzo Bob came bouncing into the little office where Renee had set Nancy up and shouted, "All right! Let's party! I'm a party dude!"

Oh, no, Nancy thought. What is he *wearing?*

Yellow-checked bicycle shorts, wingtip shoes

with gartered black socks, a red sleeveless tank top, and a white beret with a graduation-cap tassel were what Bonzo Bob obviously thought would make people remember him. But he doesn't look funny, Nancy thought—just dumb. Well, maybe he was nicer than he looked.

"I'm Nancy Drew," Nancy said, smiling. "I'm the guest veejay for this week. It's great to meet you, Bonzo—uh, I mean Bob."

For a long minute Bonzo Bob stared goggle-eyed at her. Then he opened his mouth and bellowed, *"Whaaaaat?* So TVR doesn't think I'm good enough for a *real* staff person to interview me, is that right? They think it's okay to send a lousy *guest?* Well, I've got news for you, Miss so-called veejay. Bonzo Bob is worth a lot more than that! Do you know how many people come to see my act at Attention Talent? A lot more than come to see *you!"*

Stay poised, Nancy told herself. You never have to see him again. "Please, won't you sit down?" she asked in as composed a voice as she could manage. "I promise to be as—as 'real' as I can."

"Sure you do," he answered bitterly. Nancy still couldn't tell if he was genuinely angry or if he thought he was being funny. "I believe that like I believe politicians tell the truth. And speaking of politics . . ."

It was all downhill from there. By lunchtime

Nancy's ears hurt from being screamed at, and she could count on one finger the number of jokes that had made her even smile. Bonzo Bob had spent the time alternating between insulting her lowly status at TVR and spewing out the worst humor she had ever heard. When he finally stormed out—again, without making it clear whether or not he was kidding—Nancy felt limp with relief.

"Well, I guess he's not right for us," Renee said briefly when Nancy described her morning's work. "Look, whip down to the commissary and get some lunch to go. I've got another job for you."

Not a word of thanks for all her wasted effort! Nancy was fuming as she walked down the hall toward the commissary.

When she came back with her turkey sandwich, she encountered Renee bent over a street guide. "See this intersection?" she said, pointing to a map. "There's a great bargain basement there called Kendall's. All the kids in the Valley use it—and today they're having a massive sale. I want you to head over there and find out what the scene's like. Take notes, buy a few things if they look interesting—TVR will reimburse you. We're thinking of doing a fashion segment."

Nancy tried to remain cheerful, but it was hard. All this running around wasn't answering any of her questions. It looked as though being undercover was going to be more of a hindrance than a help.

"The scene" at Kendall's turned out to be a huge store, all on one level, filled with long tables. All of them were heaped with jumbled piles of ultrafashionable clothes. The aisles were jammed with girls who were snatching clothes off the tables and trying them on wherever they happened to be.

Nancy took a deep breath and waded in. There was a table of tops in front of her. Curious, she reached out to pick up a leopard-print vest with skull-and-crossbones buttons, but just as she did, a lightning-quick hand snaked in from behind her and grabbed the vest. "I saw it first!" a girl squealed.

Too bad Bess isn't here, Nancy thought. *She'd* actually enjoy this madhouse!

It was almost four o'clock when Nancy finally got back to TVR. Tired but satisfied, she walked up to Renee's cubicle. In her hand was a shopping bag stuffed with clothes. She'd had to wait in line forty-five minutes to pay for them, but it was worth it. The clothes were some of the weirdest she'd ever seen, and she had decided that Kendall's would be a great place to feature on TVR.

Renee was in her office, bent over a pile of

fan mail. "Well, it's really a madhouse there, but I think you could get some—" Nancy started.

She never finished. "Where on earth have you been?" Renee shrieked. "You go on the air in five minutes!"

Chapter

Seven

NANCY DROPPED THE BAG of clothes to the floor. "What do you mean?" she said.

Renee was already propelling her down the hall in the direction of the studio. "I told you you'd be doing a live guest-veejay appearance at four!" she cried. "You're interviewing Carla Tarleton!"

"Carla Tarleton?"

"Yes. She's the lead singer for the Temple of Doom."

Nancy's heart sank. The Temple of Doom was a heavy-metal group whom she'd only seen on TVR once or twice. Nancy felt as if she were trapped in a nightmare. "I'm sorry, Renee, but you didn't mention anything about this!" Nancy panted as they raced along.

"I most certainly did tell you about it," Renee snapped. "Yesterday, just before you left. I remember it clearly."

Quickly Nancy reviewed the events of the day before. She was absolutely sure Renee hadn't said anything. This had to be another way she was trying to sabotage Nancy's work at TVR.

But I'm not going to give her that chance, Nancy vowed. I'll make good on this if it kills me!

"Well, there must have been some mix-up," she said in as calm a voice as she could manage. "Just fill me in on what I need to do, and I'll try the best I can not to mess up."

"It's too late to fill you in," Renee scolded her. "Just keep looking at the camera. Someone will cue you when they're about to switch over to a video. Here we are. No time to make you up— they'll have to do it during the first commercial."

They were at the studio door now. Renee pushed it open.

"Where was she?" someone hissed as Nancy and Renee rushed toward the set. "I'll explain later," Renee shot back over her shoulder. "Is Carla here?"

"Yes. I'm her agent," a dark-haired young woman answered. "We wanted some time for Carla to talk to the veejay first. It's really not fair to make a star go on without any warm-up, you know!"

To Nancy's intense relief, Renee didn't blame her for being late. All her energy seemed concentrated on making sure Nancy got on the air. "Sorry. A mix-up," Renee told the agent. "Can't do anything about it now. Okay, Nancy. Here's your chair."

She pushed Nancy into the anchor's seat in front of the camera. "Good luck."

Nancy's heart was pounding, and her hands were clammy. Face the camera, she told herself. And smile!

She looked up and stared into the camera. It was like staring into space. All she could see was the camera—everything else was black. Above her, the floodlights were beating down, but Nancy wasn't even conscious of how hot it was. Every nerve was concentrated on making this work.

A technician to the side of the camera waved to get Nancy's attention. He held up ten fingers— ten seconds to go. Nine. Eight. Seven. Six. Nancy felt as if she had a metal band being pulled tight across her chest. Five. Four. Three. I can't do this! she thought wildly. Two. One. She was on.

Nancy smiled into the blackness and was startled by the sound of her own voice. "Hello. I'm Nancy Drew, your guest veejay," she began, "and I'm brand-new at this. You have to bear with me for a little while because I'm so nervous I can hardly breathe, much less speak." There was a stifled laugh off-camera.

Now Carla Tarleton was slipping into the seat next to Nancy's. Nancy could hear her breathing fast and knew Carla was nervous, too. That realization made Nancy feel much calmer.

"Today we're going to be talking to Carla Tarleton, the drummer for the Temple of Doom," she said. "I mean, the *lead singer* for the Temple of Doom. Sorry, Carla!"

She turned to look at Carla, and for the first time noticed what her guest was wearing—a white leather T-shirt, a turquoise leather miniskirt with metal studs, and thigh-high boots entirely covered with yellow feathers. "Wow!" Nancy said involuntarily. "What incredible boots! Where did you get them?"

For an awful moment Carla just stared, openmouthed, at Nancy. Then she broke into easy laughter. "To tell you the truth, I wasn't ready for that question," she said. "Uh—Big Bird made them for me. No, actually, I made them myself. I bought the feathers at a warehouse and glued them on one at a time."

"But that must have taken forever!" Nancy exclaimed.

"Just about, but it was a perfect thing to do on the road. Gave me something to occupy myself on the bus. Some people do needlepoint, I glue feathers on boots. There's not much difference, really."

"I guess you're right," Nancy said. "But listen, Carla. You said you hadn't been expecting that question. What *were* you expecting, if you don't mind telling us?"

"Oh, something boring about what it's like being the only girl in the band. That's what people usually ask me."

"Well, we'll skip that, then," Nancy said. "What about—Oops! Wait, folks. One of the studio guys is giving me some kind of hand signal. I think—yes—you're about to see Temple of Doom's new video. Let's take a look."

"Okay, three minutes until you're back on, Nancy," said a cameraman. Everyone in the studio began talking at once.

The makeup woman rushed up to Nancy and began powdering her face. "Too bad we didn't get a chance to do this before," she said, "but I don't think anyone will notice. You're doing great."

Nancy was shaking all over. *"Great?"* she exclaimed. "All I did was goof up!" She turned to Carla. "I called you a drummer! I can't believe it!"

"Hey, it's okay," Carla said. "I'm having a good time. They'll see me sing on the video, anyway."

The makeup woman had finished, and now it was the hairdresser's turn. "Not much to do here," she said to Nancy. "We'll just mousse you up a tiny bit."

The cameraman was looking over the hairdresser's shoulder. "You're doing fine," he said reassuringly. "Very relaxed. Just make sure you don't turn away from the camera. Pretend it's a friend you're talking to."

"Carla, don't forget to mention the name of the new *album!*" came the frantic voice of Carla's agent.

"I will," said Carla calmly, "*if* it comes up. I don't have to talk about music *all* the time. If Nancy wants to talk about something else, that's fine with me."

"Okay, folks, back in places" came a technician's voice. "Nancy, keep up the good work."

The next twenty-two minutes passed in a blur. Nancy couldn't decide whether she was totally relaxed or more nervous than she'd ever been in her life. Whichever it was, she knew there was no point in trying to pretend she was totally comfortable in front of a camera—so she didn't try. And between commercials and switches to music videos, she managed to feel as though she were having a real conversation with Carla. They talked about everything, from what their high schools had been like to their favorite brands of ice cream.

When the show was over, everyone in the studio broke into applause—even Carla's agent.

All the lights came on, and Nancy looked out at the many faces that had been hidden by the dark. "Is that all?" she asked. "I don't get another chance?"

"You don't need one," the director said, walking up to her chair. "You came across completely naturally, and that's the most important thing."

"I hope Renee agrees with you," Nancy said, surprised and embarrassed when she started to yawn.

"It's perfectly natural," an assistant said. "It's the tension draining away."

Nancy smiled gratefully and peered around the studio. "Where is Renee? She was pretty upset with me just before the taping. I'd have thought she'd stick around to see how I did."

"She's probably tense because of the concert. In fact, she's probably *at* the stadium by now," a cameraman said.

"What concert?"

"The Crisp. They're at Featherstone Stadium tonight. I bet Renee left early to go with Vint."

"Vint Wylie?" Nancy asked. "She knows him?"

"Knows him! They've been going together for almost three years—ever since Jesse Slade disappeared."

"But I talked to—" Nancy stopped. She was supposed to be undercover and couldn't go around telling people she'd been talking to Vint Wylie!

The cameraman didn't notice Nancy's hesitation. "Renee doesn't mention it much around here," he said. "There's the thing about Jesse Slade."

"What thing about Jesse?"

"Well, you know that she was Jesse's girl before she started going out with Vint, right?"

"She *was?*" Nancy asked incredulously.

"Oh, yeah. They were quite an item. It didn't look too good when she started seeing Vint so soon after Jesse disappeared."

Suddenly he stopped. "Hey, what am I doing? I shouldn't be saying all this!"

"It's all right," Nancy assured him. "I won't tell anyone that you told me."

He seemed to perk up. "Okay," he said. "Anyway, I'm not telling you anything you wouldn't have found out sooner or later. Well, I've got to take off. Nice talking to you!"

Nice talking to *you,* Nancy thought. You've certainly added an interesting new angle to this case. And you've given me some pretty prime suspects, too.

No wonder Vint Wylie had lied about not knowing who Jesse Slade's girlfriend was. What if he and Renee had actually started seeing each other *before* Jesse died? Had they murdered Jesse?

Wait a minute, Nancy said to herself. Where's the motive? Could Renee and Vint be tied in to Tommy Road? Or did they have another reason to want Jesse dead?

Lost in thought, she walked slowly through the halls back to Renee's cubicle. She reached down

to pull her purse out from under Renee's desk—
and that's when she saw the note.

Please send Nancy Drew to my office
immediately.

Winslow Thomas

Instantly Nancy's heart began to pound. Had
Winslow seen her interview with Carla? Was he
angry?

When Nancy reached his office and saw his
grave face, she did not have her fears allayed.

"Sit down, Nancy," he said crisply. "I want to
talk to you. Hang on a second. I want Dan in
here, too."

Oh, no, Nancy thought.

Winslow picked up the phone. "Call Kennedy and get him in here," he ordered his
secretary. Then he hung up and turned to Nancy.

"You did a jolly good job interviewing Carla,"
Winslow said unexpectedly. Then he added,
"Considering your lack of preparation. You *were*
poised, but I think you'll agree that the whole
interview wasn't very, well, professional. I mean,
you certainly hadn't done your homework, had
you?"

What was Nancy supposed to say? She'd had
no time to do any "homework"—but she didn't
want to tell tales on Renee. Before she could
decide on an answer, Winslow spoke again.

"I also heard you were late this morning." He picked up a marble paperweight and began turning it in his hands, staring at it intently, unwilling to meet her eyes.

Finally he looked up. "What kind of progress are you making on your case?"

"Well, I—I have some leads, but—" Nancy knew she sounded as though she was floundering.

"But nothing definite," Winslow interrupted. "I thought that was what you'd say. Look, under the circumstances I can't justify having you here as a guest veejay any longer. I hate to say it, but I'm going to have to ask you to give up this case."

Chapter

Eight

BUT, MR. THOMAS, I've only been working for two days!" Nancy protested. "It always takes me a few days to start unraveling a case!"

"Be that as it may," Mr. Thomas said, "it's—well, disruptive having you here. Some members of my staff have started asking questions already. It hasn't escaped their attention that you came on as a guest veejay without coming through any of the normal channels. I can't fend off their questions much longer."

"But I—I don't understand why it would be bad if people knew who I was," Nancy said. "I'd think it would be good for TVR to get the credit for solving this mystery!"

"Not if the solution's unpleasant," Mr. Thomas countered swiftly. "And I'm afraid it will be."

"You wanted to see me, Mr. Thomas?" Dan Kennedy was poking his head into the room.

"Yes. Sit down. I've just been telling Nancy that I'd like her to stop investigating this matter with any help from us. I think it's doing the station a disservice. I wanted you to know, Dan," Winslow added wryly, "since you brought Nancy and her friends here in the first place."

Dan looked worried. Nancy couldn't blame him. Winslow wouldn't fire Dan because of her, would he?

She couldn't let that happen. She had to *prove* that Dan had been right in asking her to solve the mystery of Jesse's disappearance.

Nancy gathered up all her resolve. "Mr. Thomas," she said, "do you think you could give me another twenty-four hours here? If I don't have the case solved by then, I promise I'll forget it."

"I—I think that's a good idea," said Dan hesitantly. "I have complete confidence in Nancy, Mr. Thomas. She's been so busy since she got here that she really hasn't had any time to do much investigating."

Mr. Thomas met both of their eyes with his steely ones. Then quickly he stood, nodded his head, and said, "All right, Nancy. You've got your twenty-four hours. Use it well."

"Thank you," Nancy said with heartfelt relief. "Thank you very much. I do have an important lead I can follow up tomorrow morning." Last night she'd asked George to call Martin Rosenay, the dealer in Slade memorabilia, to set up an appointment with him for the next morning.

"I guess you'll be late tomorrow?" Mr. Thomas asked with a sly smile.

"I guess I will be," said Nancy, unconsciously holding her breath.

"Go ahead," said Mr. Thomas. "You can leave a note on Renee's desk and tell her I said it would be all right."

"I will. And thanks again, Mr. Thomas."

George and Bess were watching the evening news when Nancy walked into the bungalow and threw herself onto the couch. "I'm never moving again," she groaned.

"Can I get you a soda? Did you have another bad day?" George asked sympathetically.

Nancy sighed. "Yes, please, to the first question. Yes and no, to the second. It was interesting, at least." Quickly she filled George and Bess in on what had happened.

"At least you got to veejay. Do you have a tape?" Bess asked.

"Yes, they gave me one," Nancy said. "But I don't much feel like looking at it right now."

"I can't believe you didn't tell Mr. Thomas it was Renee's fault you weren't prepared!" Bess said. "Why are *you* taking all the blame for this?"

"Believe me, I *wanted* to tell him," Nancy said.

"But it just wouldn't be a good idea—especially now that she's a suspect. I don't want *her* to suspect that I suspect her, if you see what I mean. The nicer and more uncomplaining I am, the more relaxed she'll be around me."

"Well, you're just too much of a saint," Bess said. "But I suppose you're right."

"Did you two find out anything?" Nancy asked.

"Not that much," George said, "except that spending all day reading microfilm in a newspaper archive makes your eyes go crazy. I think I know every detail of the police investigation into Jesse's disappearance—"

"And I know every review of every song he ever released—" Bess put in.

"But nothing that looked like a clue," George finished.

Just then the phone rang. Nancy picked it up. "Hi, Nancy!" It was Dan Kennedy. "I just wanted to cheer you up."

"Well, I'm not feeling too great," Nancy admitted.

"Anything I can do to make you feel better? Are you free tomorrow morning after your appointment? Somebody canceled on me, and I've got a couple of hours open all of a sudden. I'd love an update on the case."

"Oh, Dan, I'm sorry. I'm going to be busy *all* morning," Nancy said regretfully. Then, from the corner of her eye, she saw Bess jumping up and down and pointing excitedly at herself and George. "But Bess and George are free," Nancy said. "Can they stand in for me?"

"Sure!" Dan said. "I'll take them to Fumetti's for breakfast. It's the latest hot spot. You know—mineral water and famous people."

"Sounds perfect," Nancy said with a laugh. "Should they meet you at TVR?"

"Sure. We'll go in my Lamborghini. It's my one luxury. I got it last year when my career took off. If it's worth doing, it's worth doing right—right?"

"Right. Thanks, Dan."

Nancy hung up and turned to her friends, smiling for the first time in hours. "We aim to please," she said.

The next morning Nancy dropped Bess and George off at the studio and stopped for a minute to admire Dan's car before heading to her appointment. She had just taken the exit for Chelmsford when her car phone suddenly began to ring. Astonished, she picked it up.

"Nancy? This is Lily, the receptionist at TVR. I'm sorry to bother you, but someone's just dropped off a package for you. There's a note on it that says it's urgent that you receive it immediately."

"A package? Who left it?"

"I don't know. I was away from my desk for a few minutes, and when I came back it was sitting here."

"Well, I'm on my way to an appointment that I really have to keep," Nancy said. "Could you possibly open it and tell me what it is?"

"Uh, gee, Nancy, I don't think I should," Lily answered uncertainly. "There's a sticker on it that says 'Private and Confidential.'"

"I see. Well, I guess I'd better come back, then," Nancy said. "Thanks, Lily."

Shaking her head in frustration, she turned and headed toward the freeway entrance that would take her back to the center of town.

She arrived at TVR, half an hour later, to find Lily looking terribly embarrassed.

"Nancy, you're not going to believe this," she said, "but I can't find the package. I was just on my way down to see if someone had taken it to Renee for you."

"I'll do that," Nancy said.

But there was no sign of the package in Renee's cubicle. And there was no sign of her package in the mailroom. Nancy checked on the off chance that it had been taken there by mistake. There was no sign of the package anywhere.

"I—I just don't know what happened," Lily said, faltering. "I went to the copy machine for a second to make some copies for Mr. Thomas, and when I came back, the package was gone! Do you think it was something important?"

"I hope not," Nancy said. She felt like screaming. A whole hour wasted, when she had so little time left! "Well, don't worry, Lily. It's not your fault." And she headed back out to her car.

Well, I've got to make the trip all over again, she thought to herself as she sat down in the driver's seat and switched on a classic-rock station. Then she headed out into the traffic.

She was just pulling into Martin Rosenay's long, gravel driveway when the radio suddenly stopped working—and the sound began.

A horrible, screeching, unbearably loud blast. A blast in full Sensurround blaring out through the car speakers, filling the car. And it grew even louder—and then unbelievably louder still.

Nancy had never felt a pain like the one assaulting her eardrums then. Black and red spots were dancing in front of her eyes, and her arms were shaking uncontrollably on the steering wheel. She fought desperately to keep the car under control, but the ear-shattering screech was finally too much for her. She doubled over in helpless agony—the steering wheel forgotten, her foot pressing down on the gas pedal.

The car swerved off the driveway, tossing up plumes of gravel before it crashed into the front of Martin Rosenay's house!

Chapter

Nine

WITH A BONE-JARRING CRASH, the car came to a stop. But with the impact, the terrible sound stopped abruptly. White-faced and trembling, Nancy crawled out of the car and collapsed on her knees on the ground.

"Are you crazy? What do you think you're doing? You idiot—you should be locked up!"

Shakily Nancy stared up at the person who was yelling so furiously from the doorway. She saw a plump little man whose face was red with rage and whose whole body was quivering as he glared down at her.

"Mr.—Mr. Rosenay?" she whispered.

"That's right. And who are you?"

"I'm Nancy Drew." Nancy took a deep breath and pushed herself to her feet. But her legs were too weak to support her. She sagged against the hood of her car.

"I-I'm sorry," she said with tremendous effort. "There was something wrong with the—the speakers. It hurt so much that I—"

Now Martin Rosenay's manner changed completely. He jounced down the front steps and rushed up to her.

"That sound was coming from inside your car?" he asked in horror. "I was way in the back of the house, and even there it shattered my eardrums!"

"I think it did shatter mine," Nancy said. Her whole head was throbbing, and Rosenay's voice seemed to be coming from far off, under water.

"Well, it's no wonder you lost control of your car," he said contritely. "I apologize for yelling at you."

"My car! How badly is it damaged? And what about your *house?*"

Her pain pushed aside, Nancy rushed to the front of the car. She couldn't see the front bumper at all. It was buried in the bushes that lined the front of Rosenay's one-story ranch house.

"I'd better check this," Nancy said with a sinking feeling in her stomach. She climbed into the car and held her breath while turning the key. Would it start? The engine turned over once and died. Once again and this time it caught. Nancy backed it up a few feet. Then she got out to assess the damage.

"Only a couple of scratches! Thank heaven for rubber bumpers!" Nancy said.

Then she remembered: the house. What had the collision done to *it?*

Hastily, she stepped forward and pulled back the bushes in front of the house.

Nancy could hardly believe her eyes. There were a few scratches in the siding, but that was all.

"Well, it looks like minimal damage," she said after a second. "I must not have been going that fast—even though I felt like I was flying." I've got to find out how that radio was rigged, she thought to herself. Whoever did it really wanted me out of the way!

"Let's forget about it for the time being, then," Rosenay said. "A little paint will cover it all. Come on in!"

He led her up the front steps and through the door. "Welcome to Rosenay's Rock Memorabilia," he said.

Nancy could hardly believe her eyes. Every available surface—tables, chairs, sofas, and the floor—was covered with mementoes and souvenirs. There were heaps of old 45s and autographed pictures. There were buttons and T-shirts and hats and stickers and posters and fluorescent paintings on velvet and even models of Elvis Presley's tomb.

"Where do you *sit?*" Nancy asked.

Rosenay laughed. "I try not to," he answered. "You're interested in Jesse Slade stuff, I understand."

"That's right. I'm investigating his disappearance, and I just wondered whether there might possibly be any clues here."

"I don't know if there are or not, but come into the kitchen. All my Jesse things are on the kitchen table."

The kitchen was just as cluttered as the living room. "I guess you try not to eat, either?" Nancy said.

"Take-out. All I eat is take-out. Here's the Slade stuff," said Rosenay, gesturing toward the kitchen table. "Have a seat—wait, let me move this stuff." He shifted a pile of magazines from the chair to the floor.

There was a surprising amount of memorabilia, considering that Jesse Slade had been famous for such a short time before he'd disappeared. "I wouldn't have expected so much," Nancy said thoughtfully as she sat down and began leafing through a pile of photos and articles.

Rosenay looked a little uncomfortable. "I've got a great supplier," he answered. "He's in touch with all the Jesse Slade fan clubs—there were about sixty, you know."

"How much of it do you sell?" asked Nancy.

"To be frank, not a whole lot—not yet," answered Rosenay. "I get a few letters a week or so, but mostly I think of this particular collection as an investment."

"Did you know Jesse at all?" Nancy asked.

"Pretty well. No, that's an exaggeration, I guess. Let's say I know people who knew him pretty well. Your friend said you were an investigator. Do you have any ideas about what happened to Jesse?"

"I've got a few. I'm not ruling anything out," Nancy said carefully. *"You* don't have any ideas about what happened to him, do you?"

"Oh, I have ideas. Everyone has ideas," said Rosenay. His chubby face suddenly became veiled. "I don't want to point the finger at anyone, but if I were you I'd ask Renee Stanley and Vint Wylie to explain a few things. Like why they were seeing each other on the sly before Jesse disappeared, and why neither of them seemed very upset once he was gone. It just doesn't seem quite right to me, that's all."

"Do you really think they plotted together to make him disappear?" Nancy asked.

"Off the record? Yes, I think that's exactly what happened," answered Rosenay.

"But is that a real motive?" Nancy put down the stack of photos she was holding. She'd been worrying about the motive ever since she'd first begun to suspect Renee. "I mean, if they wanted

82

to go out together, all Renee had to do was break up with Jesse. It might have been a little awkward —but not nearly as awkward as risking a murder charge!"

"Look, *I'm* not the investigator," Rosenay replied. "All I know is, I watched a local-TV news interview with Renee just after Jesse had disappeared. She didn't mention Vint—even though everybody in the business knew about him. And she kept referring to Jesse in the past tense. Now, why would she do that unless she knew he was dead?"

"Good point," Nancy said. She bent her head to a stack of photos. "I'd better start looking through this stuff. I'm sure you don't have all day."

"Make yourself comfortable," Rosenay said. "I'll be out back putting in my tomato plants."

For the next half hour Nancy sifted through the piles in front of her. There were lots of letters from Jesse to his fans—probably collected from the fan clubs, she thought—and dozens of pictures and fan magazines featuring him. But no clues leapt out at her.

At last she stood up and walked out back. "Mr. Rosenay?" she said. "I think I'm done."

He put down his trowel and stood up, brushing the dirt off his hands. "Find anything?"

"Not really," Nancy said. "But if it's all right, I'd love to borrow a picture of Jesse to take with me. I'll bring it back, of course."

"No need for that," said Rosenay. "I'll donate it to the cause. I hope you find out what happened to him."

"That's very nice of you," said Nancy. "Is it okay to take this one?"

It was a photo of Jesse Slade standing in front of his car. He was laughing at something off-camera, and he looked totally relaxed.

"He looks so happy here," Nancy said. "I guess that's why this is my favorite of all the ones you have."

"He does, doesn't he?" For a second the two of them stared at the picture in silence. "You're welcome to it," Rosenay said. "And give me a call if there's anything more I can help you with."

"I sure will. Thanks, Mr. Rosenay," said Nancy sincerely.

He walked with her to the front of the house and watched as she got into her car. "Careful, now," he said anxiously.

"Don't worry," Nancy replied. "Your house is safe from me!"

Feeling more cheerful than she had when she'd set out that morning, she headed back to TVR. This time, she kept the radio turned off.

Bess and George were waiting for her in Dan's office when she got back. "We were hoping you'd get here soon. Oh, Nancy! We had the greatest time!" Bess exclaimed when she saw her. "The restaurant was so good—and there were all *kinds* of stars having 'power breakfasts'—and Dan's the coolest guy in the world! Thanks so much for taking this case! Did you find out anything at that guy's house?"

"Well, nothing too specific," Nancy answered, "but he did give me a few ideas—and this picture." She took the picture out of its envelope and held it out to her friends.

"Nice," George commented. "Hey, that's a different color, but it's just like Dan's car."

Nancy went to George's side and stared at the picture again. Then she snatched it out of her friend's hands.

"Rosenay knows where Jesse is!" she gasped. "This picture proves it!"

Chapter

Ten

"YOU'RE RIGHT, GEORGE—it *is* just like Dan's car!" Nancy said angrily. "Dan bought his a year ago! Jesse's car is a Lamborghini, too, so this has to be *last year's model!*"

"Last year's model? But that means . . ." Bess began.

"Right, Bess," said Nancy. "It means Jesse was around last year. And *that* means he's probably still around now! Jesse could even be the 'friend' Martin Rosenay talked about—that would make sense. And Rosenay may be keeping his whereabouts a secret so that he can corner the market in Jesse Slade memorabilia. To think that I trusted him! And Jesse—why is he hiding out?"

"Are you *sure* about all this?" asked Bess.

"As sure as I can be without Jesse standing here. I can try to trace the license plate—too bad Jesse's standing in front of the second half of it. I'm sure that car is no more than a year old."

"Well, what are you going to do?" asked George calmly.

"I'm going right back there and tell Rosenay— No, wait. I can't do that." Nancy stopped pacing. "I've got to stay here. If I have only until tonight before I have to leave TVR, I'd better not waste any time. I'll go down and see if Renee's in and if she can use me for anything."

"What about us?" asked Bess.

"Let's see . . . I can't think of anything right now, guys. I guess you'd better take the afternoon off and go shopping."

But Bess was frowning. "Ordinarily you know I'd take you up on that like a shot, Nan. But don't you think you could use us for something around here? If it's your last day and all—"

Nancy felt very touched. Even if she never managed to solve this case, it was great to have such good friends. "That's nice of you, Bess," she said. "I really can't come up with anything at the moment, but why don't you two come down to Renee's office with me? I could use some moral support when I talk to her."

"Fine," George said. "And if she has any filing or something to do, *we'll* do it."

When the three friends got to Renee's office,

she wasn't there. "She's in the conference room down the hall," a man said as he walked by and saw them. "I just saw her in there."

Renee didn't notice them walk in. She was too busy watching a tape of some concert—and when Nancy looked more closely, she saw Vint Wylie on the screen. It must be the concert from the night before.

"Hi, Renee," Nancy said, plunking herself down next to the veejay. "What are you watching?"

"Oh! You startled me!" Renee whirled around with an irritable scowl.

"It's just a tape of the Crisp concert from last night," she told Nancy. "I was watching it to see—uh, to see whether we could use any of it."

"And to see Vint, right?" Nancy asked. Behind them, Bess and George silently sat down. "You two *are* going out, aren't you?"

"That's none of your business," Renee snapped.

"Well, I guess I should level with you. I'm a private investigator," Nancy said, and Renee's jaw dropped. "I didn't really come to TVR as a guest veejay. I'm looking into Jesse's disappearance." I don't have to mince words, she told herself. There's no reason why I need to stay on Renee's good side anymore. "I was surprised to find out that you and Vint are going out."

"Do you know Vint?" Renee asked cautiously.

"I talked to him yesterday," Nancy said.

"You *talked* to Vint?" Renee whispered.

"Uh-huh. But he didn't mention that the two of you had been together for three years. Didn't he mention that I'd come by?" Nancy continued.

Renee shook her head.

"I wonder why not," Nancy said thoughtfully.

"He—he probably didn't want to worry me."

"*Worry* you? About what?" Nancy asked.

"Well, he knows I get pretty upset whenever—whenever anybody asks about Jesse. I— He wouldn't have wanted me to know that someone was stirring the whole thing up again." Renee drew in a shaky breath.

"And is there any reason you didn't mention that you and Vint had been seeing each other?" Nancy continued implacably. "It's not a secret, is it?"

"N-no," Renee stammered. "But we never—" She cleared her throat. "I— Well, it's just a little bit awkward. That's really the only reason I try to downplay it. You know, a veejay and a musician going out . . . people might get the idea there were possibilities for—well, conflict of interest."

"I can see how they might," Nancy said. "I haven't had time to check Jesse's will yet, Renee. Is there anything in it I should know about?"

Renee was scowling now. "What is this—a firing squad? Oh, all right," she muttered after a second. "Yes. He left me some money."

89

There was a little pause. "Oh, I know what you're thinking, Nancy!" Renee burst out. "But Vint and I don't know what happened to Jesse. We really don't! You have to believe me!"

"Why?" was all Nancy said.

"Because—because—why would we do something like that?" Renee was twisting her hands together so hard that her knuckles were white. "It's true that we didn't tell Jesse we'd started going out—but that doesn't mean we'd kill him! And he wasn't going to leave me *that* much!"

"I didn't mention killing him!" Nancy said sharply. "Do you think he *was* killed?"

"Why, of course I do. I mean, what else could have happened? How could he still be alive?" Renee's eyes were enormous in her white face. She leaned forward and grabbed Nancy's wrist painfully hard. *"He isn't alive, is he?"* she almost shrieked.

"I'm not sure, Renee." Gently Nancy pulled Renee's clawing hand off her wrist. "But I never rule out anything."

"Oh, no," Renee said breathily. "It can't be!" She stood up on shaky legs. "I-I'm on in fifteen minutes," she said. "I don't want to be late." And she walked slowly from the room.

"If Jesse is alive, what's Renee worried about?" Nancy asked out loud. Unless—unless she thought she'd killed him herself—

Nancy gave herself a mental shake. "I'm wasting time sitting here speculating about all this," she said. "I bet Renee knows more than she's saying." She leaned forward to switch off the tape in the VCR, and then paused. "I can't resist watching Vint for a second," she said.

The Crisp was the kind of group that was really proud of being down-to-earth and unflashy. They never wore anything fancier than T-shirts and jeans, they never used any lighting effects fancier than a strobe, and they always sang songs about ordinary working-class people. Nancy didn't follow them much—she actually thought they were a little boring—but they'd been topping the charts for six months now. Vint certainly knew how to pick people to play with!

There he was in back, brandishing a two-necked white bass guitar and looking much more wide-awake than when Nancy had talked to him in person. He appeared to be unconscious of the camera—except that he had an uncanny knack for always facing it. Even when the concert ended and the band took a bow, Vint angled his body slightly toward the camera instead of the crowd. Very subtle scene stealing.

The audience screamed in disappointment when it finally became clear that the band wasn't going to do another encore. Once again Nancy leaned forward to turn off the tape—and once again she stopped. The tape had just cut to what was obviously a huge post-concert party at Vint's house.

"Hey!" said George. "Let's watch this for a second, too! Bess never got a chance to see what Vint's house was like."

As she watched, Nancy saw that all the trees on Vint's property had been covered with tiny hot-pink lights, and the swimming pool was ringed with potted tropical trees of all kinds. There was Renee on Vint's arm. He was wearing jeans, but she was in a skin-tight strapless leather mini dress.

The camera focused in on a waiter's tray next. It was full of tiny hollowed-out potatoes filled with caviar. As Nancy watched, a woman's hand with fluorescent green nails reached in and picked one up.

Then the scene shifted to Vint's front yard, where what looked like an entire precinct of private security guards was directing traffic and keeping out gate crashers. Behind a barricade was a crowd of people trying to get a glimpse of the party, and behind them was a mess of cars trying to get through.

Poor guys, Nancy thought. It must be really maddening to get stuck in the middle of party traffic.

But wait! What car was that?

The car Nancy noticed was nosing slowly up to

the edge of the crowd. It was impossible to see the driver, but the first half of the license-plate number looked awfully familiar. And the car itself was a white Lamborghini—last year's model.

"That must be Jesse!" Nancy gasped.

Chapter

Eleven

"THAT PARTY was last night!" said Nancy. "If Jesse was there, then that means he can't be that far away! We've got to find him!"

"Where are you going? What about Renee?" asked Bess as Nancy jumped to her feet.

"We'll worry about her later," said Nancy. "There's one person who I'm *sure* knows where Jesse is—and that's Martin Rosenay. Let's get out to his house right away!"

Nancy was almost out the door when she suddenly remembered something else. "Let's get all of Jesse's license-plate number from the tape," she said. "If Rosenay won't talk, we might still be able to track Jesse down. At least I hope so. We *can't* let him get away when we're this close to him!"

The three girls dashed out of the studio and into their car. Miraculously, the traffic wasn't too bad and they reached Chelmsford quickly to find a car in Martin Rosenay's driveway. With a screech of brakes Nancy stopped behind it and jumped out. "Come on," she said over her shoulder to Bess and George. "Let's get this over with."

The three girls stalked up the front path, and Nancy rapped loudly on the door. In a second Martin Rosenay appeared, wiping his mouth with a napkin. He was carrying a huge bowl of chocolate ice cream.

"Nancy!" he exclaimed. "And?" he asked, looking at Bess and George.

"These are my friends, George Fayne and Bess Marvin," Nancy said, making the introductions fast.

"Come in, come in! Wait, let me put this down somewhere. Let's see. Where?" Rosenay asked himself, looking for any place that wasn't piled high with memorabilia. "Don't want it to spill on anything—the fans would *not* go for that." He chuckled. "I can just see telling them the picture they wanted was—"

"It's the picture we're here about, Mr. Rosenay," Nancy interrupted. "The one of Jesse that you gave me."

He looked startled. "What about it? I said you could keep it, didn't I?"

"Yes, you did," Nancy replied. "But I'm surprised. Are you sure you wanted me to have such a recent picture of Jesse?"

"A what? What do you mean?" Suddenly Rosenay didn't look quite so cheerful.

"I mean that can't be an old picture. I mean that picture was taken only last year. I mean that Jesse Slade is still very much alive and living very near here."

Rosenay just stared at her.

"Let me refresh your memory," Nancy said.

She reached into her bag and pulled out the picture. "Whoever shot this must not have known anything about cars," she said, pointing to the Lamborghini in the picture. "This model is not three years old! You've been running a pretty good scam, Mr. Rosenay—but now it's time to stop."

"Let me see that picture," Mr. Rosenay said in a ghost of his usual voice. Slowly he reached out and took it from Nancy's hand. He stared at it for a second, then collapsed onto a pile of letters in a nearby chair.

"You could be right," he whispered. "Maybe he *is* still alive." Still staring at the picture, he absentmindedly took a spoonful of ice cream. "But who would have guessed?"

"You mean *you* didn't know?" Bess burst out.

Rosenay shook his head. "I didn't. I didn't think he was still alive. I thought some of my pictures might possibly be fakes—but I thought they'd been made with a Jesse Slade look-alike. Not the real Jesse!

"I know—I know what you're going to say," he said when he saw Nancy's expression. "I shouldn't have sold them if I thought they weren't genuine.

"But look at it from my point of view," he went on. "Jesse memorabilia may get really big one day. And when I suddenly started hearing from a supplier who could give me all kinds of stuff, including great pictures, I couldn't resist. Sometimes I did wonder if the pictures were fakes, but I didn't *know* for sure. Was I supposed to rock the boat?"

"Yes," George said bluntly.

Rosenay gave her a sad smile and a shrug. "Maybe," he said, "but you don't know what it's like trying to earn a living in this business. Also, I didn't want my supplier getting in trouble. I was thinking about protecting him—if you can believe it."

Nancy could almost believe it, but not quite. She'd liked Rosenay when she first met him, but now she wasn't sure how she felt. But one thing was certain—he was definitely out for himself.

"I'd like to believe you, Mr. Rosenay," she

said, "and I would like your help now. You can't protect your supplier any longer—not if he knows the truth about Jesse. It's our duty to inform the world if Jesse's still alive."

Nancy didn't mention the fact that she thought Jesse himself was probably the "supplier." That wasn't information she wanted him to have. "You can understand that, can't you?"

"Sure," he said after a minute. He stood up decisively. "Let me get this stupid ice cream out of my hands"—he took one more bite—"and I'll go and find the shipment that that picture came in. I haven't cataloged it yet."

"This is an incredible place," Bess whispered when Rosenay had left. "How can he give up his living room like this?"

"It's not just his living room; it's the whole house," Nancy whispered back. "The Jesse Slade things are in the kitchen. I hope he can *find* the shipment he's looking for."

From the sounds coming from the kitchen, Nancy decided Rosenay was having trouble. There were several thuds as though he'd dropped some boxes, an "ouch!" and then the unmistakable noise of a pile of papers slithering to the ground.

At last Rosenay reappeared, clutching a large manila envelope. "I think these are the ones," he said. "Let's hope so. I kind of tore the place up looking for them."

Eagerly Nancy took the envelope. It was

postmarked Los Gatos, California. "No address, I suppose," she said to Rosenay.

"No. Just a post office box—box forty-six. But Los Gatos is tiny—it shouldn't be hard to track someone down there."

"I hope you're right," Nancy said, taking a stack of photos out of the envelope and dividing them among the three of them. "Just look through these for a sec," she said.

"What are we looking for?" George wanted to know.

"I'm not sure. Background details, I guess. Anything that might tell us where the pictures were taken."

It was eerie seeing so many pictures of Jesse Slade and knowing that he must be alive after all. *I wonder who knows about him besides us?* Nancy thought. *Can it be possible that we're the only ones?* She shivered suddenly.

Bess must have been thinking along the same lines. She looked up from her stack of pictures and said, "I should think it would be lonely, having no one know you're *you.*"

"Maybe so," Nancy said. "Have you guys noticed anything? Because I haven't."

"I haven't, either," said Bess, and George shook her head.

"Then we'll just have to go out to Los Gatos and see what we can find," Nancy said. "And we'd better get going. The afternoon's going to be gone before we know it."

"And we haven't had lunch yet. . . ." Bess said plaintively.

"After that giant breakfast?" George asked, amazed that Bess was hungry already.

"We'll pick up something on the way," Nancy answered to keep peace. "Mr. Rosenay, thanks."

"No problem," he said a little sheepishly. "I hope you find him."

"What a gorgeous town Los Gatos is," Bess said gloomily half an hour later. "Really, Nancy, you do take us to the glamor spots!"

"Welcome to Los Gatos—Pop. 182," said the fly-specked sign just outside town. It was hard to believe such a dusty little place could be just an hour outside of Los Angeles. Los Gatos looked more like a ghost town in an old western movie than anything else—hot, dirty, and empty. There was even an old dog sleeping lazily in the middle of the road in front of the post office.

Carefully Nancy steered her car around him. "We might as well ask someone at the post office whether they can help us," she said, "since the gas station is closed."

A woman reading a magazine behind the counter looked up in mild surprise as the girls trooped in.

"Afternoon, ladies," she said. "May I help you with something?"

"Well, it's a little complicated," said Nancy.

"We're looking for the address of one of your boxholders. The box number is forty-six."

"Let's see." The woman put down her magazine, heaved herself to her feet, and ran her finger down a list of names on the wall. "Mr. Joplin, that is," she said. "Out on Horse Pasture Road. Take a right at the stop sign out front and drive for about a quarter of a mile. You'll see Horse Pasture on your left. It's a dirt road, and his house is the only one on it. You can't miss it."

"Thank you so much," said Nancy. "We really appreciate it."

"We're lucky this is such a small town," she said to George and Bess once they were safely back in the car. "In a bigger place I don't think she'd have given us the address like that."

"Well, we don't exactly look like dangerous criminal types," said George. "She probably knew she could trust us. Look, there's the turn. We're here at last!"

The modest gray house at the end of the road seemed to huddle forlornly in the shade of the steep hill behind it. Shades had been drawn across most of the windows, and the lawn had gone to seed.

Nancy's heart was pounding as she switched off the ignition and heard the refrain of a wailing guitar float out an open window. The three girls slid out of the car. Nancy couldn't place the melody. I know I've heard it recently, she said to herself. But when?

Then she remembered. It had been the night they'd been watching television at Bess's. It seemed so long ago now! The song was "Goodbye, Sweet Life," and it was turned up to top volume on the stereo.

The melody broke off in the middle, then started up again. It wasn't a record. *Someone inside was actually playing the song.*

Nancy pressed the front doorbell, and the music stopped in the middle of a measure. She heard footsteps move toward them.

The man who answered the door looked thin, and his jeans and grubby T-shirt were threadbare. He looked as if he hadn't shaved for a couple of days. But all three girls recognized him right away.

"You're—you're—" Nancy had trouble getting the words out.

"Yeah," said the man with the crooked grin. "I'm Jesse Slade."

Chapter

Twelve

So SOMEONE FOUND ME at last," said Jesse Slade. "I knew it had to happen sometime."

The face that had smiled out from millions of record covers was now staring suspiciously at the three girls. "Can I do something for you, now that you're here?"

Nancy found her voice. "I'm a private investigator. Could we possibly talk to you for a few minutes?"

"Depends," said Jesse. "What are you planning to do with whatever I tell you?"

"I—I don't know yet," said Nancy. "I haven't thought about that, actually. I guess it depends on *what* you tell us."

Slade shrugged. "That's honest, anyway. Come on in."

He led them into what Nancy guessed would have been called the living room if it had had any real furniture. There were two tattered armchairs, a television, an electric piano, a stereo and compact-disk player, and an amplifier.

"It's a little primitive in here," Slade apologized. "I hope you don't mind. Let's see—two of you can have the chairs, one can have the piano bench, and I'll take the floor."

Nancy took the piano bench. From there she could see most of the other rooms in the house. All of them were furnished, or not furnished, like the living room. The walls were bare, the floors were bare. There were no homey touches—it all looked as though Jesse Slade had just moved in.

"How long have you lived here?" she asked.

"Going on three years," Jesse answered. "Ever since—ever since I disappeared." He looked around as if seeing the place with an outsider's eyes. "It still needs fixing up, I guess. I just can't seem to get around to it.

"Well!" he continued. "What brings the three of you to my doorstep?"

"My name's Nancy Drew," Nancy said, "and I'm a private investigator. These are my friends Bess Marvin and George Fayne." Jesse nodded at them. Bess just stared, open-mouthed and wide-eyed. George did return his nod.

"We were watching a TVR special—you know

what TVR is, right?" He nodded again. "A TVR special about your last concert, and I noticed some movement, what looked like a body falling off a cliff just beside and behind the stage. We began wondering if maybe you had fallen off that cliff."

"So someone finally noticed that," Jesse said grimly. "It sure took long enough. I decided that maybe the cameras hadn't caught the actions."

"It was on the tape, but a good tape wasn't found until very recently," Nancy told him. "And it was just by accident that I saw the fall. It was very dark, and I only saw it because of the movement. Anyway, Bess called TVR, and they agreed to let me use the station as a base of operations while we looked for you. And—here we are.

"We thought you could have been hurt," she went on. "That's why we decided to investigate in the first place. If someone had hurt you—or even killed you—and there was some way to catch that person . . ."

"But I'm that person," Jesse said softly.

The three girls stared at him, not understanding.

"I *was* involved in that accident on the cliff." he said. "But I wasn't the one who fell."

Nancy's mouth was dry.

"*I* knocked *him* off. My manager, Tommy Road. We were yelling at each other. I took a step toward him—I guess I must have looked pretty scary—and he stepped backward. The cliff crumbled under him, and he went down." Jesse didn't speak for a long minute. "Did he die, do you know?"

His eyes were fixed on Nancy's with painful intensity. "I don't know," Nancy said. "No one knows. He never turned up after that night—he disappeared just like you."

Slowly Jesse let out his breath. "So I'll never know if I'm responsible for his death or not."

"Jesse," Nancy said gently, "maybe you'd better start at the beginning."

"Okay," he said after drawing in a ragged breath. "You probably know that my career was going pretty well before that concert."

That broke the tension in the room, somehow. All four of them laughed. *Pretty* well," George said.

"Yeah. Well, I guess that is an understatement. And a whole lot of the credit has to go to Tommy Road. He took a chance on me when no one else would. He practically never slept, trying to get someone in the industry to listen to me—and when Clio Records finally signed me, he got me just about the best deal in recording history."

He stood up and stared out the window at the drab view outside. "But after a while I began to suspect that Tommy wasn't being exactly straight with me. It's partly my fault, I know. I mean, I *let* him take control of my money, just the way he took control of my career. I didn't want to be bothered with financial details. I hate numbers and making boring phone calls to accountants and things like that. And he was great at it.

"But every now and then I'd wonder where the money was all going. He said he was investing it for me." Jesse gave a short laugh. "Funny way of investing it—funneling it into his own account."

"I found out about that, too," Bess put in timidly. "I checked your general ledger at Lawrence Associates."

"Yeah, that's what I finally did, too. And I figured it all out the day before that last concert. I was furious, as you can imagine. My own manager—the guy who'd been like my best friend for *years*—embezzling from me practically since day one!

"I didn't have a chance to talk to him about it until the night of the concert," Jesse went on. "That gave me a lot of time to decide what to say. When I took my break, I found Tommy and said that I was never going to perform again unless he returned every dollar. I figured that would scare him. You know—that he wouldn't want to lose his biggest client.

"But it turned out he'd been waiting for this," Jesse said savagely. "Tommy told *me* he didn't want to be my manager any longer! He said he was going to leave the country—*with* all my money—and that I'd never see a cent of what he'd taken. On top of that, he started insulting me for not having noticed what was going on before then. . . ."

Jesse's voice faltered. "So I took a step toward him. I don't know if I meant to punch him or what. He—he went down without a sound, just like something in a nightmare. I was terrified to look down over the edge. I was afraid of what I might see. It must have only been a couple of seconds, but it seemed like hours before I looked down." He closed his eyes as if the memory was too painful for him to stand. "Then I looked. There was his body lying down there, all crumpled up on the rocks."

Bess winced.

"I looked around the stage," Jesse continued. *No one had noticed a thing!* My backup band was still playing, and all the technicians were running around setting up for the finale. If I'd wanted to, I could just have gone back and rejoined the band, and maybe no one would ever have found out what had happened. But I couldn't do it. Even though he'd been cheating me, I couldn't leave him down there."

"So you climbed down after him?" Nancy said.

"Right. Boy, I had plenty of time to think about how he must have felt going down! It was pitch dark, and the wind was whipping around, and pieces of the cliff kept crumbling under my feet. . . .

"But when I got down to the bottom—down to where the rocks were—the body was gone. A wave must have come in and carried it out."

Jesse sighed. "So there I was. And right then I decided to take off for Mexico. No way could I go back up there without people realizing something had happened—and I couldn't stand the thought of facing a murder charge. I had about two hundred dollars in my pocket. I walked down the beach for about an hour, then climbed up another part of the cliff, found a road, and started hitchhiking. I crossed the border into Mexico the next day."

"No one recognized you?" George asked.

"Nope. You know, people don't usually recognize famous people unless they're expecting to see them. They usually just think, 'Gee, that sure looks like so-and-so.' Once in a while someone would say how much I looked like Jesse Slade"— he smiled—"and I'd just tell them I'd heard that before."

"But how have you been living since then?" Nancy asked.

"In Mexico things were pretty hand-to-mouth for a few months, until I got a job as a waiter. I scraped up enough money to buy a guitar, and when I could afford to come back here I started giving lessons. But I don't do that too much. Mostly I do odd jobs. I'm a caretaker for the big house back up the road. The owner's great. He lets me use the pickup parked outside."

Nancy happened to glance over at Bess, who looked as if she were wilting in her chair. Nancy was sure she was crushed that her idol had sunk so low. But to Nancy, it didn't sound as if Jesse was unhappy about the direction his life had taken.

"You don't seem to mind your obscurity and poverty too much," she commented.

Jesse thought about it for a second. "Nope. I guess I don't," he said thoughtfully. "It's a relief not having everyone look up to me—and not feeling as if I'm responsible for making a million fans happy. Having all those girls in love with me got kind of—kind of exhausting." Bess looked up, a little startled.

"Well, I've managed to fool everyone till now," Jesse said. "How did you finally find me?"

Nancy explained about Martin Rosenay, and Jesse grimaced. "Of course. Of *course*," he said. "I should have known that car would get me in trouble. It belongs to the guy whose house I take care of."

"Who took the pictures, by the way?" George asked.

"I did. I gave some guitar lessons in exchange for a secondhand Nikon. I cleaned myself up, set the timer, and started posing. Selling the pictures was an easy way to get cash."

"I wonder what did happen to Tommy Road," Nancy said thoughtfully. "Is it possible that he's still alive? It seems hard to believe that his body was never found. The police combed that whole site so carefully. What if he survived the fall? What if he slid down the cliff instead of falling?"

"I guess he could have gone underground like me," Jesse said. "And he was such a crook that he's probably managed to do a lot better for himself than I have," he added bitterly.

Silence fell. Suddenly the little house seemed as remote and forgotten as Jesse Slade himself.

"What are you going to do now that you've found me?" he suddenly asked.

Nancy stared at him. "I don't know. I just don't know," she said. "I don't blame you for what happened, and you're not a murderer. What do you *want* me to do? I'm sure that if you came forward with your story, people would believe you. The general ledger will bear you out—"

"No. I don't want to come forward," Jesse said in a strained voice. "I don't want to live in that fishbowl again. I'm all right where I am, and I'm not bothering anyone. Please, Nancy," he begged, "can't you leave this alone? Can't you forget you ever saw me, and not tell anyone where I am?"

Nancy looked from him to Bess and George. Almost imperceptibly they nodded.

"All right, Jesse," Nancy said. "We'll go back to L.A. And we won't tell anyone about you, except the people at TVR. I think I can promise that they'll keep it confidential, and I really owe it to them."

"Thank you," Jesse said. "Thank you more than I can say."

"You're welcome," Nancy said, getting to her feet. "I guess we'll be on our—"

Just then they heard a car door slamming, quickly followed by footsteps coming up the walk. Then there was a frantic knock at the front door.

Everyone froze. "You expecting anyone else?" Jesse muttered.

The knock sounded again, even louder this time. Jesse strode forward and opened the door.

A blinding burst of light exploded in his face!

Chapter

Thirteen

JESSE STAGGERED BACKWARD, his hands covering his face. Another strobe light went off, and another and another, as if someone had hurled a bunch of silent firecrackers into the house.

Now the three girls could see the reporter framed in the doorway, a cameraman at his back. He jammed a microphone into Jesse's face. "You're Jesse Slade, aren't you?" he asked. "I'm from Channel Six. What a story this will make! Hey, who are the girls?"

"Get out of here!" Jesse shouted, hurling himself against the door. Quickly he slipped the bolt shut. Then he leaned against the door, breathing hard.

"You didn't tell anyone you were coming here, did you?" he asked Nancy.

"No, except for—except for Martin Rosenay," Nancy said. All of a sudden she knew exactly what had happened.

So did Jesse. "Rosenay! Of course! He must have finally figured out that I was the supplier. He'd do anything to sell that junk of his. He must have called all the press in town, that little—" He stopped. "Well, there's certainly no reason for you to keep quiet *now.*"

"I guess not," Nancy agreed quietly. "I'm so sorry, Jesse. I hope you know I didn't expect things to turn out this way."

"Oh, I know," said Jesse. More cheerfully, he added, "It could never have lasted, anyway. I always told myself that. And maybe I can fend them off for a while, at least long enough for me to track down a lawyer."

"Good idea," said Nancy. "And speaking of tracking down people—I'd better call Mr. Thomas at TVR and let him know what's happened."

"Why?" Jesse inquired. "He's sure to find out soon enough, the way things are going!"

"Yes, but it wouldn't be fair to let this kind of news catch him unprepared," said Nancy. "He'll have every reason to be angry at me if the regular networks scoop him. I'm not saying he'll send reporters out here," she added hastily when she saw Jesse's face, "but he should know."

But Mr. Thomas's personal line was busy. It was busy a couple of minutes later when Nancy tried again, and a couple of minutes after that. At last she gave up.

"We'll just drive back and tell him in person," she said. "Is there a back door?"

"In the kitchen." Jesse led the way, but just before Nancy opened the door he put out a hand to stop her. "Do you three think you can come back later?" he asked almost shyly. "It would be nice to have some supporting troops around. I have a feeling this is all going to get pretty heavy."

"Sure," Nancy said immediately. "It's really the least we can do. Okay, Bess and George, when I open the door, run for the car. And don't answer any questions."

They were almost to the car when the reporter at the front door saw them. "Girls! Girls!" he shouted, racing toward them. "What were you doing in there? Where's he been all this time?"

"No comment," Nancy said firmly as they clambered into their seats. Frantically the reporter beckoned to the cameraman to come and join him in front of the car. "You'd better get out of the way when I start this thing," Nancy muttered under her breath.

To her relief, the reporter and cameraman scuttled out of the way once the engine turned over.

"Okay, we're off," Nancy said.

"You solved the case, Nan," Bess said. But she didn't sound too enthusiastic about it.

"Yes," Nancy agreed wearily. "And I'm not sure that's a good thing at all."

"And he's been living there all this time?" Winslow Thomas asked in amazement.

"That's right," said Nancy. "Giving guitar lessons and being a caretaker."

"Well, blow me down," said Mr. Thomas, and he really did sound as though someone *had* blown him down. He sat at his desk a moment, considering—and then stood up and shook Nancy's hand vigorously.

"Very impressive work, Nancy," he said. "As you know, I had my doubts, but you're obviously very good at what you do. Congratulations."

"Thank you," Nancy began. "I'm happy to have cleared up *one* aspect of this case, anyway. But Mr. Thomas, do you think you could possibly downplay this story for a few days? I know it's big news for a station like yours, but Jesse seems—well, he seems a little out of it. I think it would be unkind to make him talk now."

"I think you're right," said Mr. Thomas. "Let's be as kind as possible to the poor blighter." Where does he get these odd expressions? Nancy wondered irrelevantly. "I tell you what," Mr. Thomas went on. "I've got an appointment now, but before I go I'll have my secretary call a meeting of all the TVR executives so that we can decide how to handle this story. First of all, we'll schedule a press conference. When Jesse's feeling more on top of things—"

"Jesse who?"

It was Renee. She and Vint Wylie were standing in the office doorway—and both of them looked as though they'd seen a ghost.

"What are you doing here, Renee?" Mr. Thomas snapped. "I thought you weren't on today."

"I'm not," Renee said in a strangled voice. "Vint and I just stopped in to pick up something I'd forgotten. Mr. Thomas, wh-who are you talking about?"

"Well, I have to confess I wasn't going to tell the staff yet," said Mr. Thomas, "but it seems Jesse Slade has come back to life."

"Oh, no!" Renee put her hand to her throat. "I—I can't breathe!" she cried. "This is terrible!"

And she burst into tears. "I can't handle this!" she cried, and raced out of the office.

"Renee! Wait!" Vint called, rushing after her.

Mr. Thomas shook his head. "These temperamental stars!" he said with a chuckle. "Well, I'm off." He gave them a cheery wave as he disappeared down the hall.

"I wonder if Dan's around," Bess said hopefully. "He should hear about this, don't you think?"

"I definitely think so," Nancy said. "Let's go to his office and see."

Dan *was* in, and he was as amazed by their story as Mr. Thomas had been.

"The poor, poor guy," he said, shaking his head. "When you think of what he's been through—he's got to feel totally shell shocked. Look, Nancy, do me a favor. If he wants somewhere to stay until all the publicity dies down, will you give him my address?" He was scribbling it down as he spoke. "I won't call him and bother him, but tell him he can call me or come by any time he wants."

"That's great, Dan," Nancy said warmly. "I wouldn't be surprised if he takes you up on it. We're heading back there now, and I'll tell him first thing."

"What time is it?" George asked as they passed the sign for Los Gatos. "I feel as if we've been doing nothing but drive for about ten hours."

"It's six," Nancy replied. "We'll just check in with Jesse, and then we can go back to the hotel and call it a day."

"And get some supper," Bess interjected.

"And get some supper," said Nancy. "Oh, no. What's going *on?*"

She'd just turned onto the dirt road leading to Jesse's house. "I bet every camera crew in Los Angeles is here," Nancy said hopelessly.

It certainly looked that way. The little dirt road was crawling with people. Cars and camera trucks were parked all around the house. Reporters were thronging the front yard—and the hill in back was packed with spectators. The little house, all of its lights out, looked as though it was under siege.

"Oh, why can't they leave him alone!" Bess cried. "We don't have a chance of getting in to see him!"

"I'm afraid you're right, but we have to give it a try," Nancy said.

Just as the girls got out of the car, a roar went up from the crowd. Nancy turned quickly.

A light had just been turned on in Jesse's living room. Now the front door was opening a crack— and then all the way. And now Jesse was walking out onto the front step.

He stood there for a second, silent, making no attempt to shield his eyes from the glare of the flashes. "All right! All right! I'll tell you everything you want to know!" he shouted at the crowd.

At that exact moment a gunshot rang out— and Jesse Slade crumpled to the porch.

Chapter

Fourteen

ANOTHER SHOT ripped through the silence—and then there was instant noise and pandemonium.

"We've got to help Jesse!" Nancy shouted to Bess and George. But the screaming, panicky mob that was now rushing away from the house knocked her down before she could take a step. Dizzily she struggled to her feet and forced herself upright into the sea of elbows and knees. At last she pushed her way to Jesse's front steps, Bess and George right behind her.

Jesse was hunched over, covered with blood. When he lifted his head, the skin on his face was pulled tight with pain.

"Just—just my arm," he gasped. "Lucky. But get me inside."

Nancy was already moving. She, George, and Bess dragged him into the house and slammed the door. Just then a third shot rang out.

"Keep down, everybody!" Nancy ordered as she bolted the door. "Call the police, George—and tell them to bring an ambulance!"

She threw herself to the ground, slithered across the floor on her stomach, and lifted her head to peek cautiously out the window. On the road dozens of shrieking people were rushing to get into their cars. Nancy shuddered. Not all of them were driving away, but most of them were staying put, secure in their cars.

"Let's get you cleaned up, Jesse," she said briskly, turning away from the window. Quickly she tore his shirt open at the shoulder. Then she sighed with relief.

"You were right. It's only your arm," she said. "I can't get the bullet out, though—it's too deep. It must hurt incredibly."

"Burns," said Jesse through clenched teeth. "Who do you think is after me?"

"You'd know that better than I would," Nancy said as she hastily tied a strip of shirt around the wound. But Jesse just shook his head. She could tell that the effort of talking was too much for him.

"Nancy," said Bess in a trembling voice, "do

you realize we're trapped in here with a killer outside waiting for us?"

"Don't worry, Bess," said Nancy as calmly as she could. "The police should be here any minute."

"But what if he's right outside the door?"

"The door's locked. We've done everything we can. They'll be here before you know it," Nancy assured her friend. She only hoped it was true.

Jesse moaned. His lips were gray now, and his eyes kept rolling back in his head. Nancy checked his pulse. She could hardly feel it—and the bandage she'd put around his arm was already drenched in blood.

"They've got to get here soon," she repeated. "We've done everything we can."

But ten minutes crawled by before Nancy and her friends heard the welcome sound of the police siren.

"They're here!" Bess was almost sobbing with relief as she ran to the front door and yanked it open.

In just seconds the house was swarming with people. The reporters piled out of their cars and were furiously snapping pictures again. Two paramedics bundled Jesse onto a stretcher. They were pushing through the crowd to carry him out the door when Jesse whispered hoarsely, "Nancy," and stopped their progress.

"Here I am," she said, moving over to stand next to the stretcher.

"Where are you staying, in case I need to get in touch with you?" he asked, and Nancy told him the name of their hotel. "A friend of mine at TVR has a place where you can stay when you get out of the hospital," she added, "so you won't need to come back here if you don't want to."

He smiled. "I—don't," he whispered. His head was lolling sleepily to the side now.

"We'd better take him in, miss," said one of the paramedics. "You can call to see how he is later."

Jesse gripped Nancy's hand for a second, and then the paramedics carried him away.

Nancy felt tears stinging her eyes as she watched them load the stretcher onto the ambulance. What have I done to that poor guy? she thought. If I'd never come looking for him, this might never have happened! If only—

"Miss?" A police officer was standing at her elbow. "I'm Officer McIntyre. I wonder if I could get a statement from you."

When she'd told him everything, he shook his head. "Not much to go on in the way of suspects," he said.

"I do know of two possible suspects, though," Nancy said and told him about Renee and Vint.

"That's something, anyway," Officer McIntyre said. "I'll have someone track them down. But what about this Tommy Road? Do you really think he could still be alive?"

"I don't know. I just don't know," said Nancy.

Something flitted across her mind just then, but she didn't have time to identify it before it was gone. "That cliff was so steep I don't see how anyone could survive a fall from it. But I can't believe a body could disappear without a trace, either."

"Stranger things have happened," said the officer. He turned to a younger officer who'd just come in. "Yes, Rogers? What is it?"

"This, sir." The younger man held out his hand. "It's a spent rifle cartridge. We found it way up on the hill behind the house. No other signs of the gunman, though."

Or gunwoman, Nancy said to herself.

"Probably long gone," said Officer McIntyre. "But we'll post two guards here overnight, just to make sure." He turned to Nancy. "I'd like your number, in case I need to ask you anything more. Other than that, you and your friends are free to go."

In silence the three girls drove back through the dark to the hotel. Silent still, they parked the car in the garage, went into the bungalow, and sat down facing one another.

At last Nancy spoke. "We never got any supper," she said. "Anyone hungry?"

"I'm not, that's for sure," Bess said in a small voice. Then she burst into tears.

"I feel so terrible for Jesse!" she wept. "He's been through so much. And he's—he's not even like a real person any more. There's nobody inside. He's just a—a robot!"

"I feel bad, too," said George. "It was horrible to see someone who'd once been such a star living like *that*. I wish we'd never come here in the first place."

When Nancy spoke, it was as much to reassure herself as her friends. "Anybody would get a little strange living alone for so long—especially with that cliff scene in his past," she said. "He'll become himself again now that he's out in the real world again. He won't be able to help it. Someone that talented can't hide from things forever."

"As long as whoever's after him doesn't *get* him," George said darkly.

Nancy shivered. "That's the thing I do feel awful about," she said. "If we hadn't found him, the person with the rifle wouldn't have, either."

Then she squared her jaw and sat up straighter. "We'll have to catch that person, that's all," she said. "We started this, and we're going to finish it. But we need a good night's sleep first. I'd better call Ned. He'll be wondering what's happened to me."

"Hello?" came Ned's groggy voice after she'd dialed his number. She was using the phone next to her bed.

"Oh, Ned, I'm so sorry!" said Nancy, aghast. "I forgot about the time difference. I'll call you back tomorrow—"

"No, you won't. Talk to me now," said Ned. "I'm getting more awake every second. How's the case going?"

"Oh, Ned . . ." Nancy poured it all out to him, and when she was done she was almost in tears herself.

"This just isn't the way cases are supposed to go," she said in a wobbly voice. "I'm supposed to come in and solve them, and then everyone is happier and I can go home. But this time it seems as though I've only made things worse!"

"Not true," Ned said emphatically. "You've helped that guy, whether it seems like it now or not. And you'll catch whoever shot him—you always do, you know. I'm not even going to tell you to be careful this time. You just go out and *get* that gunman. But be careful," he added at the last minute.

Nancy giggled. "I love you, Ned. I feel a lot better now. I'm really glad I called—even if I did deprive you of your beauty sleep."

"Hey, I'm already gorgeous enough," Ned said lightly. "Now you go and get some beauty sleep yourself—not that you need it, either. And give me a call when you get a chance. I love you."

The phone woke her early the next morning.

"Nancy?" It was a man's voice, hoarse and hesitant, and for a second Nancy was too sleepy to recognize it.

"It's Jesse. I'm sorry to call you, but I didn't have anyone else to call."

"Hi, Jesse," Nancy said, struggling to sound alert. "How's your arm doing?"

His answer startled her. "The arm doesn't matter. Nancy, I'm in trouble. Really big trouble."

Nancy was wide-awake now. "What's the matter?" she asked.

"The matter is that there are two policemen standing at the foot of my bed right now. And they're here to arrest me!"

Chapter

Fifteen

Yes, I THINK we've finally got the proof we need," the police officer told Nancy. "It will be nice to see this case closed. I'm sorry for Slade, though. It doesn't look good for him."

Jesse had been so frightened by the sight of the police at the foot of his bed that he'd panicked. He hadn't been under arrest at all—the police had just wanted to ask him a few questions. But the direction the questions had led was all too clear to Nancy.

"Where's your evidence?" Nancy asked, controlling her anger.

When she'd finished talking to Jesse Nancy had woken George. Bess had been so sleepy that

Nancy had had to give up trying to rouse her. She'd left a note before she and George hurried into clothes and rushed off to the police station to see what was going on. Now they were talking to one of the men who'd questioned Jesse—Officer Squires, a tall, gangly man with an infuriatingly patronizing expression.

"We've got some very convincing evidence," he said. Nancy half expected him to add, "Young ladies." "Last night someone delivered us an anonymous package. I'm the one who opened it." For some reason he seemed quite proud of himself. "Inside there was a bloodstained T-shirt— and a note. Here's the note, if you'd like to see it. Careful not to touch it, though."

Nancy and George stared at the note. It had been scribbled in pencil on a torn sheet of notebook paper.

This shirt once belonged to Tommy Road, who was viciously murdered by Jesse Slade. I saw it happen and found the body. Slade's been hiding out all this time—but he can't get away from justice.

It was signed, "A Friend of the Law."

"But this is ridiculous!" Nancy protested. "There's no way to prove that the shirt is Tommy's—or that whoever wrote this note witnessed anything at all!"

"There's no way to prove it," agreed Officer

129

Squires. "But you may be interested in knowing that we did a lab check on the T-shirt. The blood type is the same as Tommy Road's. And the bloodstains are the right age."

He stared smugly at her, and for a second Nancy could think of nothing to say.

I know Tommy Road's not dead, she said to herself. I'm just sure of it. I've got to keep Jesse from going to trial for murder! But how do you explain a hunch to a police officer?

At last she found her voice. "As you say, that's interesting," she said. "But it can't be true—for a very simple reason. I know that Tommy Road is still alive." From the corner of her eye she could see George turning to stare at her, but she kept her gaze on Officer Squires.

"And just *how* do you know that?" he asked.

"I'm working on the evidence right now," Nancy replied. I'll find some, anyway, she thought. "And I'm sure that TV Rock will back me up. I'm heading right over to the station to bring one of their camera crews here."

To her secret satisfaction, Officer Squires was starting to look worried. "And now," Nancy asked, "where's Jesse? We'd like to talk to him."

"He's out of the hospital," the officer answered a little sullenly. "You can see him any time. He's waiting for you in there." He pointed to a door at the end of the room and turned his back on them. "I've got a lot of work to do," he muttered. "What a way to spend a Sunday morning."

Jesse was sitting on a bench, his head against the wall. He stood up when he saw them—and then winced. "I've got to remember to move more slowly," he said.

Under his shirt, his shoulder was bulging with bandages. "How's your arm?" George asked solicitously.

"Much better." He started to smile, but the smile faded instantly. "It'll have plenty of time to heal in jail, too."

"Don't talk that way!" Nancy said. "You're not under arrest. And we're going to beat this thing!"

"I'm glad to hear you say that, Nancy," George said, "and I can't wait to hear how. But let's talk about it outside. I don't want to turn around and find Officer Squires looming over me."

There was a little coffee shop next to the police station. Over coffee and doughnuts Nancy told George and Jesse about her hunch. Both of them looked at her doubtfully when she'd finished.

"It would be great if it were true," Jesse said, "but why are you so sure? Just because there's no body doesn't mean there wasn't a body once, if you know what I mean. Believe me, I'm not eager to face a murder rap, but I don't trust hunches."

"Nancy's hunches are *always* right," George said loyally. "And not because she's psychic or anything. She only gets hunches when she's noticed some little detail subconsciously. It's as if something trips her memory. That's why I'm sure she's right now. But how you're going to explain this to the police and Mr. Thomas, I just don't know."

"It's the shirt," Nancy said.

"Excuse me?" Jesse asked.

Nancy was frowning thoughtfully. "When you think about it, that bloody shirt doesn't make any sense," she said. "Let's just say it's true that there's a witness to the fight who doesn't want to get involved. Let's take it even further and say that the witness did hang onto the shirt all this time, hoping that when Jesse did turn up, he or she would be able to incriminate him. Okay, it's possible—barely.

"But it was a T-shirt! Can you imagine anyone who'd watch the fight, wade into the water to retrieve a body, take a bloody T-shirt off a *corpse,* and then decide just to leave the body in the water? It's not believable. It just doesn't make any sense! I don't think there was ever a dead body. I think Tommy Road survived the fall, kept his shirt, and only came forward now that Jesse's back."

"You know, you're right! That's just Tommy's style," said Jesse. He gave a giddy laugh. "I guess I'm not a murderer after all! Boy, I feel as though you've lifted a ten-ton weight off my head!"

"But we've still got to convince everyone else," Nancy said. She set her coffee cup down with a click. "Let's get over to TVR now. I'm going to call Mr. Thomas and ask him to meet us there."

"He's on his way," she said, returning from the pay phone. "He wasn't tremendously happy to be woken up this early on Sunday, but I told him it couldn't wait."

The TVR building was all but deserted. A sleepy-looking receptionist in the lobby winced when she saw them rushing in. "You look *much* too wide-awake," she said with a yawn. "Go on into Mr. Thomas's office. He's expecting you."

He was sitting behind his desk when they walked in, his fingers drumming the desktop impatiently. "This had better be good," he began —and then he saw Jesse.

His eyes widened. "Jesse Slade!" he exclaimed. "I thought you'd been arr—I mean, taken to hospital!"

Nancy was sure Mr. Thomas had been about to say "arrested." Now, how did he know that? she wondered. Did he find out about it on TV? But what news station could have gotten the story so quickly? Jesse had only been with the police for half an hour.

And why had he said "taken to hospital" instead of "taken to *the* hospital"?

The ghost of a suspicion was beginning to float around Nancy's brain. Could Winslow Thomas be British? Tommy Road had been British, too. . . .

Before she could think about it further, Mr.

Thomas jumped up with his hand extended. "I'm so pleased to make your acquaintance," he said rapidly. "On behalf of TVR, I'd like to welcome you back to the world."

"Nice to meet you," Jesse said. He was looking a little perplexed, Nancy thought. "We—we haven't met before, have we?"

"I wish we had," Winslow said regretfully. "But TVR hadn't really taken off when you—uh—vanished. I hope we'll have the pleasure of working together often from now on."

He turned to Nancy. "Was this why you had me come—to meet Jesse?"

"Not exactly," said Nancy. She took a deep breath. "Mr. Thomas, I've gone ahead and stuck my neck out on something. I hope you won't mind." And she described what had just taken place at the police station.

"You *what?*" Mr. Thomas asked, reddening angrily. "How could you involve this station in something so farfetched? That seems a little nervy to me, Nancy."

"I really had no choice." Nancy met his gaze steadily. "You see, I know I'm right."

Winslow Thomas's face was contorted with rage now. "I've never heard of such a thing! You wheedled your way in here, and now you're going to make a laughingstock of us! I should call the police and have you thrown out of here!"

What was happening to his accent? All of a

sudden it was British! Nancy looked at her friends and saw that they were as puzzled as she.

The hint that had been nagging her began to surface. Suddenly she realized it had to be true.

"Go on, get out!" he was shouting.

"You are Tommy Road!" Nancy whispered.

Mr. Thomas froze. "What—what are you saying?" he sputtered. *"You* really are crazy!"

"No, she's right!" Jesse gasped. "I *knew* I'd seen you before!"

"It's all starting to make sense now," Nancy said. "Your voice. The British phrases that kept popping out. Your weird-looking beard. And there was plenty of time for you to get over to Jesse's house last night, once I'd told you everything. You were the one who shot him. You must have been hanging around and watching to see what happened. You gave that shirt to the police. That's why you thought Jesse had been arrested!"

Mr. Thomas—Tommy Road—hesitated for a second. Then he gave her an ironic bow. "I must congratulate you," he said, his eyes full of hate. "I'm only surprised our friend Mr. Slade didn't recognize me sooner."

He wheeled around to turn his full fury on Jesse. "You tried to kill me," he spat out.

Jesse's face was white with shock. "I—I didn't! You know I didn't mean for you to fall off that cliff! It was an accident!"

"It may have been an accident," Tommy Road

said in a steely voice, "but you'll pay for it. When I'm done with you, you'll wish *you'd* been the one who'd slid off that cliff."

"You didn't even really manage to hurt me," he sneered. "I sprained my ankle, but that was about it. I watched you come down the cliff. I could tell it was too dark for you to see me. I swore I'd kill you when you reached the bottom. But when you took off down the beach, I thought —wait, this is my big chance!

"I assumed you'd report that I'd died. I hoped you'd be found guilty of my death. Whichever one happened, I knew no one would be trying to arrest Tommy Road for embezzlement. You can't arrest a dead man! It was my big chance to get away with the money and start a new life. I wouldn't even have to leave the country.

"Of course I saved my bloody shirt just in case it might come in handy someday," he continued. "And earlier that week—when I found out you'd been snooping around the accounts—I'd taken the precaution of switching the money in my account to a numbered Swiss account. No names necessary. All I had to do was grow a beard, wait until my hair grew in—and start life over. First I invested in record production. Then in music videos. And then I got my own music channel." He chuckled suddenly. "Of course I don't let any of the bands I used to handle perform on TVR."

Now he turned to Nancy. "You've obviously done a lot of thinking, Ms. Drew. It's a pity that you're so clever, because I'm not about to let *anyone* interfere with my plans. Not an amateur detective. Not a has-been rock star. Not *anyone!*"

And before anyone could stop him, he bolted from the room.

"We've got to catch him!" Nancy shouted.

The three of them dashed out of the office. Tommy Road was just disappearing into one of the preview rooms at the end of the hall. They pursued him to the door.

"It was this room," Nancy called, and they ran into it so fast that they piled up at the entrance.

The little room was pitch-dark. "Wait!" Nancy said. "He's not—"

There was a click—the sound of the door being locked.

Nancy whirled around to test the door they'd just come through. "He just locked it," she said.

Frantically Jesse rattled the knob of the door at the other end of the room. It was locked, too.

Then a light came on in the production booth on the other side of the glass wall. Tommy Road was sitting at the controls.

"Now that we're all gathered together, I've got a little number for your listening pleasure," he cooed into the microphone. "It's the first play of a song that I know will go gold. I know you're going to love it."

He smiled—and hit a switch in front of him.

A screeching blast filled the preview room. It was the same noise—the same unbearably loud

137

noise—that Nancy had heard in her car. But now it was magnified a hundred times.

Nancy clapped her hands over her ears, but it was no use. Nothing could protect them against that deadly shriek.

Jesse collapsed to the floor, writhing. George looked as if she was screaming, but the evil blast was drowning out her voice.

So he's the one who rigged the car stereo, Nancy thought dazedly. It was all she could do to hold on to that thought. George had fallen to the floor, and Nancy knew she also was about to collapse.

The sound was killing them!

Chapter

Sixteen

As she fell to her knees, Nancy could see Tommy Road laughing maniacally. She reached her hand pleadingly out to him, but all he did was wag a teasing finger at her. He'd gone mad. He picked his suit jacket up off the chair next to him and strolled leisurely out of the control booth.

He's leaving us to die! Nancy thought desperately.

The preview room was soundproof. If there was anyone in the building, he or she couldn't hear the sound that was slowly draining the life out of Nancy and her friends. Nancy hurt so badly she couldn't move a muscle.

But she knew she had to try.

The electric guitar, Nancy ordered herself. Someone had left it there—she couldn't remember who. It was still leaning against the wall across the room.

With torturous slowness Nancy set out to crawl across the floor toward it. She felt like a diver whose last bit of air was gone, but she made herself move until she'd reached the wall.

Pick up the guitar, she ordered herself. She reached forward—but her hand wouldn't close.

Pick it up! she screamed at herself. And this time she did. Staggering, she dragged the guitar over to the sound booth and hoisted it into the air. With all the force she had, she hurled it at the glass separating them from the sound booth. Then she grabbed the window ledge and pulled herself up into the booth.

Her brain was screaming instructions at her. What switch? *What switch?* It had to be that one—the red one right in front of her. Feebly Nancy reached forward and flipped it.

The sound stopped, and a miraculous silence filled the room.

Nancy let out a long, shaky breath and collapsed into a chair. All she wanted to do was let the quiet soak into her.

On the floor in the preview room, George and Jesse were slowly uncurling and sitting up. To Nancy, both of them looked as though they were just coming out of a long, wrenching nightmare.

"Thanks, Nancy," Jesse said. He cleared his

throat. "Sorry I couldn't be more helpful. I really think that if that sound had gone on for one minute longer, I'd be dead now."

"I know I would have been," said George, and quickly shuddered. "I can't believe you've had to go through this twice, Nancy." She looked around. "I suppose it's no good hoping that Tommy Road is still around."

"No. He left a few minutes ago," Nancy said. "I'm sure he didn't hang around, either. He's probably off to plan some alibi."

"Do you mean he's going to get away with this?" George asked in horror.

"No, he's not," Nancy answered firmly. "What we need to do is think up a way to trap him. And I think I've got a perfect idea. Tommy Road has never seen Bess, has he? Well, then . . ."

Winslow Thomas's press conference at the Wilshire Hotel was attended by everyone who *was* anyone. The dozens of reporters packed into the room listened attentively as he described his feelings about Jesse Slade's return.

"To put it simply, I couldn't be more delighted," he said, "both for the music world and for TVR. This is a bloke with a tremendous talent who hasn't even begun to tap his potential in music videos. We're going to do great things together."

"Do you know Slade personally?" one reporter asked.

The flicker of a frown passed across Mr. Thomas's face and quickly vanished. "Of course I do," he said sincerely. "He's a fabulous, fabulous person. It wouldn't be putting it too strongly to say I love him."

"What about his legal problems, Mr. Thomas?" another reporter asked. "Will he be charged in Tommy Road's disappearance?"

"As far as I'm concerned, that problem doesn't exist," Mr. Thomas said graciously. "Of course we'll do all we can to help him if he *needs* help, but we're not interested in dragging up the past here. It's much more important to—"

"He's dead! Jesse's dead!" came a heartbroken wail from the doorway.

There was a gasp of shock. Everyone turned to see Bess standing by the door. Her face was contorted with grief and terror, and she was shaking from head to foot.

"They're all dead," she sobbed. "I—I went over to TVR, and they were all lying dead in one little room! Oh, Jesse!" And she burst into fresh tears.

It was Winslow Thomas's finest hour. As he listened to Bess, he actually grew white. Horror seemed to shrink him in his clothes. He groped blindly behind him for a chair and sank into it.

"What—what happened?" he asked hoarsely. "What do you mean, he's dead? How can that be?"

Bess wiped her eyes. All the cameras in the room were focused on her now.

"I—I went to TVR to pick up two friends," she choked out. "I couldn't find them anywhere, so I started looking up and down the hall. And in one of the rooms at the end, I—oh, it was too horrible!" She buried her face in her hands for a minute while the cameras clicked avidly. "I saw my friends and Jesse just lying there in a pool of broken glass!"

"Mr. Thomas" was clearly stricken. He rose tremblingly to his feet.

"Because of the tragic circumstances," he almost whispered, "I'd like to end this press conference immediately."

There was a murmur of sympathy through the room. Mr. Thomas tried to walk toward the door, but shock had made his legs too weak. Two men sprang to his aid, and—leaning heavily on their shoulders, the very image of a broken man—he staggered toward the door.

"Hi, Tommy," said Nancy breezily as she, George, and Jesse walked in right in front of him.

"Jesse!" It was a strangled scream—and Nancy knew that this time Tommy's horror was real.

"You're not here. You're not," he babbled. "None of you. No one could survive a noise like that—I made sure of it. You're dead. You've got to be dead."

"Why, Tommy," Jesse protested in a syrupy

voice, "don't you know that it would take more than a little rock 'n' roll to kill *me?* What do you take me for?"

Tommy Road just stared at him, transfixed. Then, for the first time, he realized that all the cameras in the room were still rolling. Screaming, he turned to run.

But he wasn't quick enough. Nancy tackled him like a ton of bricks—and the reporters were there to catch every detail.

Chapter

Seventeen

So Tommy Road has confessed to everything?"
Dan Kennedy asked.

It was the day after the press conference.
Nancy, Bess, and George were entertaining a few
visitors in their bungalow. Renee Stanley and
Vint Wylie were sitting next to each other on the
sofa. Dan Kennedy was lounging comfortably on
the floor. And Jesse Slade was sitting in an easy
chair that supported his bandaged arm.

Even with the bandages, Jesse already looked
like a different person. It wasn't only that he'd
shaved and bought himself some new clothes. "If
I'm going to pick up where I left off, I need to
dress the part," he'd told Nancy. And Bess had

had a wonderful time helping him shop. It was more a change in his expression. He no longer seemed beaten, lost, and withdrawn. Now he looked calm, relaxed, and confident. As George had teasingly told him, his star quality was back.

"Yes," Nancy told Dan. "He confessed to everything. Including spreading rumors at TVR that I was a spy from a rival video station."

"I sure fell for that one," said Renee, wincing. "He came in the night before I met you, Nancy, and told me that he'd hired you as a guest veejay because he thought that would be the best way to keep you from finding anything out. In fact, he *ordered* me to keep you from finding out anything. He told me it was fine to give you a hard time on the job—and he also told me to keep him posted on your schedule. It wasn't my fault that you're so quick on your feet." She smiled at Nancy, and Nancy smiled back.

"I'd kept wondering why Mr. Thomas insisted on making me go undercover and made me promise not to tell anyone," Nancy said. "Now I know that it was because he didn't want anyone to notice that his story and mine were so different. And now I know why everyone seemed so unfriendly that first day!"

"Did he plant that phony package for you, too?" asked Bess.

"Yes. Mr. Thomas—I mean Tommy—

managed to drop it off without the receptionist seeing, and then picked it up when she was off making the copies he'd asked her to do. While I was trying to track it down, he wired my car stereo."

Bess shivered. "I can't believe how lucky you were, Nan. What if you'd been driving on the freeway when that noise started up? You could have been killed!"

"Believe me, I thought of that," Nancy said dryly. "So could a lot of other people—but Tommy didn't care about that. He's *really* charming."

"What happens to him now?" George asked.

"Well, he'll be charged with embezzlement, of course," Nancy said, *"and* attempted murder. You know, he's claiming there's no evidence linking him to that little scene in the preview room. He's so convincing that I'd almost believe him myself. It's lucky he spilled the beans in front of a roomful of reporters."

"What about TVR?" Bess asked, and Dan smiled.

"I got the news about that this morning," he said. "Winslow's—I mean Tommy's—second-in-command will take over. She's really great. And I've been promoted, too—to head veejay."

"Congratulations!" Renee said, and she sounded as though she meant it. "That's great. It will be fun to work for you."

She cleared her throat nervously. "Nancy, you

know I owe you an apology—but at least I behaved badly to you because I thought you were out to sabotage the station. But there's another person here who deserves an apology, too. Jesse—I don't know what to say."

"I don't, either," said Vint. "We're just really sorry, Jesse. We didn't mean to hurt you."

"That's why I freaked out so much when I heard that you were still alive," Renee said. "I couldn't stand thinking that you'd find out I'd started seeing Vint. It seemed like one of those horribly sad movies where the hero goes to war or something, and when he gets back his girlfriend has married someone else . . ." She took out a tissue and blew her nose.

"Don't think about it," Jesse said. "It's all past tense now. You're two of my favorite people, and I'm glad you're together. Besides, my life-style for the past few years hasn't exactly been the kind of thing I'd want to make a girl share.

"Anyway, now that I'm going back into the rock-star biz I'll have lots of money again. And I'll be able to date all kinds of incredible girls," he added teasingly—then dodged as Renee hurled a throw pillow at his head.

"What are you planning to do, Nancy?" Renee asked.

"Oh, we're heading home," Nancy told her.

"You know, you don't *have* to leave right away," said Dan. "I found out something interesting just before I came over here. It seems that guest-veejay interview you did was a big hit. We've been getting a lot of calls about it— everyone wants to see you on TVR again. Any chance you'd consider taking a job with us?"

"You're kidding!" Nancy gasped. "Me, a veejay? That's great! I mean, it's a great compliment. But, Dan, I'm a detective. I *like* being a detective. I like my life in River Heights. Thanks, though."

"Well, couldn't the three of you stay a little longer just for a vacation?" Dan asked. "As head veejay, I have an even bigger expense account now. I'd be more than happy to put you up at the hotel a little longer. And I could make some time to show you the sights, too."

Nancy looked at Bess and George. They all shook their heads.

"It's a tempting offer. Maybe we could take you up on it in a couple of months. But I want to go home for now," George said. "All I seem to do is sit in cars here."

"I'd love to come back here someday, but I want to go home, too," said Bess. "But I'll watch you every day, Dan. And Jesse, I expect you to write at *least* one song about all this."

He smiled at her. "It'll be dedicated to you, Bess," he said, and Bess giggled happily.

"I have to go home, too," said Nancy. "I miss Ned too much—and besides, there are sure to be other cases waiting for me back in River Heights."

"But they won't be as *glamorous* as this one was, will they?" Renee teased her.

"I hope not!" Nancy said fervently. "I've had enough of the glamorous music world to last me a lifetime. From now on, I'm sticking to plain, ordinary, uncomplicated everyday life."

But no one in the room believed her for a second.

BAD
MEDICINE

Chapter

One

T HE MAD DOCTOR bent over the young reddish-blond-haired girl strapped to his table. His scalpel glinted dangerously in the harsh glow from the overhead lights in the operating room. "You'll bother me no more!" he said with an evil cackle.

He lifted his hand high above her chest, ready to plunge the knife in.

Bess Marvin covered her eyes. "I can't look! Tell me when it's over!"

Nancy Drew glanced up from the television screen, amused by her friend's terrified look.

1

"Don't worry. The hero's about to come and save her."

"How can you tell?"

"By the music, Bess. It's definitely hero music," Nancy answered.

"Why can't she save herself?" asked George Fayne, Bess's cousin and one of Nancy's best friends.

"Because she's trapped with a maniac!" declared Bess, flipping her blond hair behind her ears.

At that moment the movie's hero threw open the door to the operating room and wrestled the doctor for the scalpel. The scalpel clattered to the floor, and the villainous doctor staggered toward the door. The heroine's eyes fluttered open.

"Oh, Robert . . ."

George jumped up from the couch and snapped the television set off, disgusted. "I can't stand a wimpy heroine."

"Me, neither." Nancy stretched and yawned. "I thought this movie would be better."

The three friends were seated in the Drews' den, eating popcorn and spending a quiet Saturday night at home.

"Since when are you interested in medical thrillers?" Bess asked as Nancy rewound the videotape.

"Since Ned decided to enroll in a week-long

seminar at Westmoor University Medical School," Nancy answered. Ned Nickerson was Nancy's steady boyfriend and a student at Emerson College. "All next week he'll be right here in River Heights, at the med school. He's going to be studying hospital administration."

"Hospital administration, huh?" George said. "Will he have any time off?"

"I don't know, but I hope so. I'm seeing him tomorrow night before the seminar starts, but I think he'll be pretty busy after that. His friend Trevor Callahan is a second-year resident at the school and hospital here, and I know Ned wants to spend time with him." Nancy hit the eject button, and the tape popped out of the machine.

"Trevor?" Bess asked. "I don't think I've met him."

"You haven't," Nancy admitted. "Actually, neither have I. Trevor's family has lived down the block from the Nickersons for a while, but Trevor's older than Ned and he's been off at medical school for years."

"He's a second-year resident? What exactly does that mean?" George asked, reaching for another handful of popcorn. "Is he still a student?"

"Well, yes—in a sense. But Trevor's a real doctor, too. He finished medical school, and now he's doing his residency."

3

"Well, Trevor won't take up all Ned's spare time, will he?" Bess asked. She pulled on her denim jacket. "You should still have some time for fun."

"I hope so."

Nancy walked Bess and George to the door, then locked up the house and climbed into bed, folding her arms under her head. She was eager for Sunday to come and for Ned to start his seminar.

"Trevor or no Trevor, you're going to spend some time with me, Ned Nickerson," Nancy said, staring up at the dark ceiling with a smile on her face.

"Are you sure you want to get involved in hospital administration?" Nancy asked Ned as she pulled against her seat belt to look out the windshield.

She was peering through the early-evening shadows, trying to get a good look at the prestigious medical school. The hospital, a huge gray stone building, stood in the forefront of the campus. A smaller building flanked it on the south. The dorms were clustered around the parking lot, and farther back, across a grassy parkway, stood an older ivy-covered brick building.

"Not exactly," Ned admitted, pulling into a parking spot near one of the dorms. It was four stories high, and a covered walkway extended from the front door to the parking lot. "That's why I'm attending this seminar—to see if I like the business end of running a hospital."

Nancy sent him a sidelong look. Ned was rugged and good-looking with an easy smile and an athletic build. She couldn't imagine anyone else being her steady boyfriend. She was thrilled to see him and spend time with him. "You know, I've always wondered what it would be like to work in a hospital."

Ned laughed. "Nurse Nancy, eh?" He tousled her reddish blond hair affectionately.

"Very funny. I was thinking more about *Doctor* Drew."

Grinning, Ned said, "Well, you're about to meet *Doctor* Callahan. Trevor said he and April, his fiancée, would meet us in front of this building. Then we're all going to dinner."

Nancy knew very little about Trevor except what Ned had told her. She knew he was specializing in cardiology, hoping to be a heart surgeon soon.

They waited in the car, but twenty minutes after they were supposed to meet, there was no sign of either Trevor or his fiancée. Eventually an attractive girl with blunt-cut shoulder-length brown hair pushed through the front doors of the dorm. She wore a blue dress, and what looked like a lab coat was tucked under one arm. She hesitated on the brightly lit stairs, peering through the covered walkway.

"Do you think that could be April?" Nancy asked.

"There's one way to find out." Ned climbed out of the car and called, "Are you April Shaw?"

"Yes," she answered. "Ned Nickerson?"

"The one and only."

April hurried toward Ned. "Trevor's going to be late. His shift was changed today, and he won't be off until after seven. I'm sorry. He tried to call but couldn't reach you."

Nancy opened her door and walked around the front of the car to meet April, who looked about twenty-three or -four. Though the evening was warm, her arms were wrapped around her waist, as if she felt cold. She kept glancing over her shoulder at the hospital building.

"This is my girlfriend, Nancy Drew," Ned said, introducing them.

Up close, Nancy could see that April had serious deep blue eyes and a small turned-up nose. "Hi," April said distractedly, shaking Nancy's hand. "I'm Dr. April Shaw."

"Doctor?" Nancy repeated, impressed.

April smiled faintly. "I'm in my third year of medical school. I won't be a full-fledged doctor until I'm finished, but we address one another as doctor as soon as we're admitted to medical school." She threw another look at the imposing gray building.

"Do you want to go to the hospital?" Nancy asked.

"Am I that obvious? Yes, I guess I do." She shook her head apologetically. "You see, Trevor's over there now checking on my father. He came to visit me last week, but three days ago he had a heart attack. Now he's a patient here, and I'm really worried about him."

"Oh, I'm sorry," Nancy murmured. Her heart went out to April.

They walked along a curving sidewalk to the hospital's main entrance. "My father is a doctor, too," April went on. She seemed anxious to air her problems. "Dr. Gerard Shaw. When I got accepted to med school here, he was the happiest man in the world. But then he got sick." She sighed heavily. "I didn't really want him to visit me. I was afraid the trip would be too much for him."

"You mean you thought he might have a heart attack?"

7

"He does have a heart condition," April admitted.

The hospital's main lobby was decorated in cool tones of gray and white. Several sofas were grouped around a rectangular glass table, and several magazines were fanned across the table's glossy surface. The reception hub took up the center of the room. Two women sat behind it, one greeting visitors and the other working the switchboard.

"Trevor's on seven—the cardiology floor," April explained as they stopped by the group of sofas. "He promised to check on my father. I won't bother him now; the doctors in CCU want him to rest."

"What's CCU?" Nancy asked.

"Cardiac Care Unit. The cardiac nurses staff it around the clock. I'm hoping my dad'll be well enough to be moved to a private room soon."

Nancy glanced at Ned. She didn't see how they could leave the hospital and go out to dinner. April was too upset. "Maybe we could eat in the hospital cafeteria," Nancy suggested out loud.

Ned grimaced. "Hospital food?" he repeated, clutching his throat as if he might gag. "How about going somewhere else? Anywhere else!"

"April might want to stay at the hospital," Nancy pointed out, nudging him in the ribs.

"No, that's okay," April insisted. "As soon as Trevor's through, I'd like to get away. I've been sick with worry all day." She looked at the clock on the far wall. "Do you mind waiting?"

"No problem," Nancy said, and they sat down in the lobby. Nancy started to ask April about being a doctor when a disembodied voice announced over the loudspeaker, "Dr. Trevor Callahan to Room seven fifty-five. Dr. Callahan. Room seven fifty-five. Stat."

"Now, what's that all about?" April muttered. "Nobody calls stat unless it's very serious. Come on," she added abruptly. "We'll meet Trevor on seven."

Nancy and Ned exchanged glances. They didn't want to get in the way of an emergency. But April had already ushered them to an elevator.

"The room's in the west wing," April said as they stepped off the elevator into a gleaming corridor.

A blond man in a doctor's coat was just pushing open the door to Room 755 when Nancy, Ned, and April approached. "There's Trevor now," April said, rushing forward.

Intent on his task, Trevor disappeared into the room. Nancy stood by the open door. Inside the room, someone was gasping wildly. Alarmed,

Nancy caught a clear glimpse of a middle-aged woman lying in bed, her face swollen and contorted, her fingers clutching at her throat.

"She's choking!" Nancy exclaimed.

But instead of helping her, Trevor just stood at the foot of the hospital bed, staring. Nancy was horrified. He was going to let her die!

Chapter

Two

TREVOR SUDDENLY LEAPT FORWARD and pulled the woman's hands from her throat. Quick as a flash, he bent her head back to clear her air passage. "Get more help!" he yelled over his shoulder to the nurse who had run in. "I need an intubation! Something's wrong. Quick!"

"Penicillin," the patient wheezed out.

Nancy realized that Trevor had been hesitating because he was diagnosing what was wrong. Apparently this was serious.

The nurse turned on her heel, going for help. Before Nancy could move, she was nearly knocked over by a distinguished-looking doctor. "What's wrong?" he demanded tensely, rushing past her into the room.

"Dr. Callahan's ordered an intubation, Dr. Rayburn," the nurse called over her shoulder. She was already hurrying toward a hospital paging phone posted in the hallway.

"Call a code ninety-nine!" Trevor yelled after the nurse.

Rayburn took matters into his own hands. He snatched up the phone in the room. "Code ninety-nine, stat. This patient's suffering from penicillin poisoning!"

Nancy and Ned stepped away from the door of 755. "What's an intubation?" Ned asked Nancy. She shook her head.

When Nancy posed the same question to April, she said, "They're going to insert a tube into the patient's windpipe because she can't breathe on her own."

"Is that what code ninety-nine means?" Ned asked.

April looked grim. "No, that means cardiac arrest."

The hospital staff that had responded to the code finally began to disperse. Nancy, Ned, and April stayed back from the action, not wanting to get in the way. Finally only Trevor and Dr.

Rayburn remained inside the room. The patient's lungs were being artificially filled with oxygen. Nancy could see the little blips on the screen, which she assumed indicated the woman's heartbeat.

Trevor slowly walked out of the room. Now it was he who seemed to be in shock. The look he sent April was dazed and bleak. Dr. Rayburn shook his head and studied the patient's chart as he slowly walked out of the room. "Something's wrong," he said, as if to himself. "There's got to be a mistake here."

Trevor glanced over Dr. Rayburn's shoulder at the chart. The blood drained from his face and he turned chalky white.

"I don't know how this happened," Dr. Rayburn said seriously. "This patient should never have been given penicillin!"

Trevor nodded dumbly.

"Trevor, what's wrong?" April asked anxiously after Dr. Rayburn left.

"Nothing." He seemed to shake himself, focusing on Nancy and Ned for the first time. "I'm—uh—almost finished. I'll change and meet you out front in fifteen minutes."

"Are you all right?" April was obviously very worried.

"Yeah, I'm okay."

As they headed down the elevator, Ned whispered in Nancy's ear, "Now what was that all about?"

Nancy shook her head. She didn't know, but she'd gained the distinct impression that something was seriously wrong.

"How's Dad?" April asked Trevor as soon as the four of them were seated around a table at one of River Heights's most popular Mexican restaurants. A basket of corn chips sat in the center of the hand-painted blue- and gold-tiled tabletop.

Nancy studied Trevor for the first time. He was quite handsome, with blond hair and gray eyes that had sunbursts of laugh lines at the outer corners. Ned had assured her he was fun-loving and casual, yet he seemed so serious that Nancy couldn't imagine his having a sense of humor.

Trevor looked blankly at April for several seconds. "Oh, your father was okay when I checked in on him. The same as when you left."

"He's no better, then?"

Trevor moved his hand over to cover April's. "Give him time."

April looked so downcast that Nancy decided to try to change the subject. "How did you two meet?" she asked Trevor. "At medical school?"

He nodded. "April was in her first year and I

14

was in my fourth. I'd already decided to specialize in cardiology, so I'd geared my studies in that
direction. When April was assigned to Dr. Rayburn for cardiology we bumped into each other."

"Dr. Rayburn's a cardiologist?" Ned asked.

"The chief of cardiology," April corrected
him. "He's got quite a reputation at W.U."

"He's one of the main reasons I decided to take
my residency here at W.U. rather than apply to
another hospital," Trevor admitted.

Nancy smiled, glancing at April. "I can guess
the other reason."

Trevor smiled back, and Nancy caught her first
real glimpse of the man who was Ned's friend.
Once he was relaxed, Trevor wasn't so intimidat-
ing and serious. It was clear he adored April.

"How long is a residency?" Ned asked.

"Six years in cardiology," said Trevor.

"Wow. You'll be an old man before you finish!"

"I want to be the best cardiologist around.
That takes time. By the time April is through
with med school, we'll be ready to get married."

April and Trevor looked at each other and
smiled. Ned slipped his arm around Nancy's
shoulders. Nancy felt warm and happy. Someday
she'd like to make plans as April and Trevor
were. From the sweet glance Ned sent her, she
could tell he was thinking the same thing.

After they finished eating, April and Trevor ordered coffee and seemed to be content to linger. "I wish my dad had stayed in Saint Louis," April said, revealing what was uppermost on her mind.

"That's where you're from?" Nancy asked.

She nodded. "My father was on staff at one of the most respected medical school hospitals in the country. He was head of cardiology there until his heart condition prevented him from working." She smiled wistfully. "But he's a consultant to the state medical board of examiners, so I guess he's still a pretty important guy."

"Do you have any other family?" Ned asked.

"My mother died when I was little," she said. "I don't have any brothers or sisters."

"Neither do I," said Nancy. "And my father's a widower, too."

April asked about Nancy's father, and Nancy explained that he was a lawyer in River Heights.

"Does your father want you to become a lawyer, too?" April inquired.

"Oh, I don't know. I'm pretty happy with what I'm doing."

"What's that?"

"Didn't I tell you?" Trevor broke in. "Nancy's a detective. According to Ned, she's solved more cases than most detectives twice her age."

Nancy laughed. "Well, I wouldn't go that far."

16

"A detective?" April perked up. "That's great! Tell us about some of your cases."

Nancy entertained them with several of her more fascinating investigations, and as they listened, April and Trevor both seemed to forget their problems at the hospital. "And then there was the time that Ned got engaged to another girl just so he could find out what she was into," Nancy finished, giving Ned a friendly jab in the ribs. "And she ended up trying to push me out of the picture—permanently."

"What do you mean?"

"We went skydiving, and she sabotaged my parachute so it wouldn't open!"

April shivered. "Luckily, you survived!"

"Well, she actually saved me at the last minute. She was just trying to scare me."

"Detective work is so dangerous," said April. "You could get killed."

"Don't I know it," Ned said with feeling.

Then slowly Trevor's good mood evaporated as he became distracted and quiet, staring off into space.

As they drove back to the medical school, Nancy turned to Trevor. "Do you have to live at the school when you're in residency?" she asked.

"No, I have my own apartment. But sometimes it's easier just to stay in a dorm. I've had to work double shifts when we're understaffed."

17

"Double shifts. You mean sixteen hours? Don't you get tired?"

"You bet." As if to emphasize the point he stretched and yawned. "Last week was a real stress test. I'm exhausted."

"What happened in Room seven fifty-five tonight?" April asked Trevor quietly as Ned pulled up in front of her dorm.

Trevor stiffened. "What do you mean?"

"Why did Dr. Rayburn say there'd been a mistake?"

Nancy tried not to appear to be too interested, but she was curious. All evening she'd wanted to ask him about the patient who had nearly strangled to death.

Trevor took his time answering. "That patient was allergic to penicillin. There was red tape across the chart warning against prescribing it."

April looked puzzled. "So?"

"So apparently I prescribed penicillin anyway. The order was right on the patient's file in my handwriting! The patient was given the medicine orally. Her throat swelled up instantly. Her windpipe closed off. If I hadn't arrived when I did, she would have died. And it would have been *my fault!*"

18

Chapter

Three

"Bᴜᴛ ʜᴏᴡ ᴅɪᴅ ᴛʜᴀᴛ ʜᴀᴘᴘᴇɴ?" April protested. "You must have seen the red tape!"

Trevor looked baffled and miserable. "I don't know how it happened. Mrs. Deverly, the patient, was admitted because of chest pains. She also had a slight infection, so an antibiotic was prescribed. I don't remember prescribing penicillin. But I know my own handwriting when I see it. And Dr. Rayburn saw it, too."

Nancy's mind was racing. She turned around to look at Trevor. "You were paged to Room seven fifty-five. By whom?"

"By one of the nurses." Trevor's eyes met

Nancy's. "I suppose Mrs. Deverly recognized her symptoms and called a nurse."

"Maybe the nurse or Mrs. Deverly can help explain the mix-up," Nancy suggested.

"And that's just what it is. A terrible mix-up," April declared. "No wonder you were upset."

Trevor shook his head soberly. "Mrs. Deverly was in shock and her heart stopped. Another couple of minutes and she could have died."

Nancy didn't blame Trevor for being shaken up. It was a serious mistake, and it appeared to have been Trevor's fault.

Ned dropped April and Trevor at the dorm. Both were quiet as they said good night to Nancy and Ned. April insisted that they all get together again while Ned was in town.

Afterward, while Ned was driving her home, Nancy was quiet and thoughtful. "What are you thinking?" he asked as they pulled into the Drews' driveway.

"That scene at the hospital was really scary tonight. Being a doctor sure means taking on a lot of responsibility."

Ned agreed. "What do you think about that prescription mix-up?"

"I think doctors can't afford to make that kind of mistake. It could be fatal."

"For what it's worth, Nancy, Trevor's not

irresponsible. I mean, I've known him a long time. All he's ever wanted is to be a good doctor. The best. He wouldn't prescribe the wrong medication. He would double-check."

Nancy nodded. Her impression of Trevor had been the same. He seemed conscientious, concerned, and caring. But there was always an element of human error in anything.

"Will I see you tomorrow?" Ned asked as he walked Nancy to the door.

Nancy laughed, gave him a quick kiss, and slipped inside the house. "How about noon at the hospital cafeteria? Maybe I'll treat you!" she threw over her shoulder.

"Some treat." Ned laughed, grimacing.

The sun was shining as Nancy drove up the winding road to Westmoor University Medical School. She pulled into the parking lot, searching for a spot near the main hospital entrance. The lot was nearly full, so she had to circle around toward the back entrance and squeeze into a narrow slot near the emergency room.

Once inside the hospital, Nancy found her way to the cafeteria with the help of red lines painted on the floor.

Nancy didn't see Ned, but she was hungry and decided to go ahead and order. "I'll take a

21

cheeseburger and fries," she told the girl behind the glass case.

Nancy was heading for a small table near a window when she saw April. She was standing and talking to a young man in a white lab coat. Nancy walked up behind the older girl.

"Hey, it's not my fault," the guy in the lab coat was saying. "Your old man got sick all on his own!"

Nancy had been about to speak, but the man's rudeness stopped her cold. She stared over April's shoulder at him.

"You had no business in CCU!" April replied in a shaky voice. "What were you trying to do?"

Nancy read the man's name tag: David Baines. He had no title so she assumed he was a volunteer or an orderly. He glared at Nancy through dark, angry eyes. "I was called in by the nurse, okay?" he snarled. "I was just doing my job."

"After that last incident, I told the nurse on duty to keep you away from my father. Don't you ever go near him again!"

"Fine, *Doctor* Shaw." He shouldered past April, knocking her into Nancy. Nancy scrambled to balance her tray, but some of her french fries tumbled to the floor anyway.

"Oh, Nancy," April said, flushing when she saw the damage. "I'm sorry. Let me help."

"No problem. I could do with a few less fries, anyway." She set the tray down on an unoccupied table, picked up the scattered fries, and disposed of them. Glancing at April, she asked, "Are you all right?"

April sighed and sank down into the seat opposite Nancy's. "You heard, huh?"

"Most of it."

"David Baines is a troublemaker," April declared angrily. "He's got a thing against doctors. You heard how he spoke to me! I don't know what his problem is, but I heard that he flunked out of med school and he resents anyone who's still in."

"I couldn't help overhearing you say something about 'that last incident,'" Nancy said, probing tentatively. "Do you mind my asking what happened?"

At that moment Ned called out, "There you are! Sorry I'm late." He appeared at their table, holding a tray piled with food. "My class ran over. Interesting stuff. I learned how each department in the hospital functions. It's amazing how many people work here. . . . Uh-oh, did I interrupt something?" he asked, apologizing.

"I just had an argument with one of the

hospital staff," April explained. She told Ned about David Baines, then added, "When my dad first came to visit, David must have seen us together. Apparently he knew my dad was a doctor. After my dad had his heart attack, David made a remark about how the 'eminent Dr. Gerard Shaw must be as mortal as the rest of us after all.'"

"How awful!" Nancy exclaimed.

"It really upset me," April admitted. "That's why I don't want him anywhere near my father."

"I don't blame you," said Ned. "What a jerk."

"Aren't you having lunch?" Nancy asked April.

"I'm not hungry. Too worried, I guess. You see, my father has a degenerative heart disease, and it's only a matter of time before he dies. There's nothing anyone can really do for him now. He was doing a little better for a while, but now . . ." She shrugged helplessly. "I just wish he could get better or that it would all go away! It's so hard watching him suffer."

They were all subdued during the rest of their meal. April's depression was catching, and after she left to return to her classes, Nancy and Ned were both quiet.

"I guess I should be getting back, too," Ned said. "We're getting a quick tour of the hospital pharmacy and medical labs this afternoon."

"Mmmm—"

"Nancy?"

"Hmmm?"

"What are you thinking about?"

"April. Trevor. David Baines. Medicine. Dinner tonight at my house. With you." She sent him an expectant look.

"I'll be there," he said, grinning. "As soon as classes are over."

Later that evening Nancy and Ned were settled down in front of the television set in the den. Nancy was nestled against Ned's chest, smiling to herself. It was good to have him around. "I'm so glad you're home for a while," she said, voicing her thoughts.

Ned gave her a squeeze. "Me, too. This seminar is really interesting, but I can't decide whether I want to specialize in hospital administration or not. It's fascinating. I mean, some of the jobs these people have. Can you imagine working in pathology?"

"Cutting up bodies? Yuck." Nancy grimaced.

"The medical school has a dissecting lab where they actually work on human bodies."

"Say no more," Nancy said. "I get the picture."

"And you wouldn't believe it. There are underground tunnels leading between all the buildings. They're kind of creepy and poorly lit, like something out of a horror movie."

"Don't tell Bess!" Nancy laughed.

"No way. She'd never set foot inside a hospital again!" Ned's grin slowly faded. "I saw Trevor today, but he was too busy to talk. He was discussing something with Dr. Rayburn and it looked serious."

The telephone rang before Nancy could ask Ned more about what he might have overheard. She answered it. "Hello?"

"Nancy? It's Trevor."

"Oh, hi, Trevor. Ned's right here, I—"

"No, wait, Nancy. I need to talk to you." His voice was low and shaky. "Can you come to the hospital?"

Nancy sat up straighter. "Sure. What's wrong?"

"Nancy, April's father, Dr. Gerard Shaw, died tonight," he said, his voice barely audible.

"Oh, no! How's April?"

"She's okay. At least she's putting up a good front. She'd been preparing herself for a long time." Trevor hesitated. "But, Nancy, it happened so unexpectedly. There's bound to be an investigation."

"Investigation? What are you talking about?"

"I was in the room just moments before Dr. Shaw died, and he was fine! But something must have gone wrong. Nancy, the hospital's blaming me for Dr. Shaw's death!"

Chapter

Four

HURRY, NED," Nancy called as she ran up the steps to the front entrance of the hospital.

"I'll be right there. Just let me lock the car!"

Nancy didn't wait. She yanked open the door, then stopped for a moment, looking around. The hospital lobby looked much the same as it had the evening before.

Trevor was seated in the lobby, and he looked really upset.

"Nancy!" he said, obviously relieved to see her. He jumped to his feet at the same moment Ned entered the building. "Ned. I'm so glad you're both here."

"Tell us what happened. From the beginning," Nancy said.

Trevor nodded. "Let's go to the doctors' lounge. It's more private."

He led them downstairs to a basement room that served as a lounge. They sat at a table, where Trevor collapsed in his chair. He ran his fingers through his hair in frustration. "Everything was normal. I just went in to check on Dr. Shaw. The cardiac nurse was there. April's father was doing fine."

"Where's April now?" Nancy asked worriedly.

"With Dr. Rayburn and the chief of staff and one of the other residents."

"Why are you being blamed?" asked Ned. "As I understand it, Dr. Shaw was really ill."

"He was. But Dr. Clemmons—he's the resident at the meeting—checked Dr. Shaw's chart, and he claims I ordered the wrong medicine for April's father. Dr. Rayburn checked it, too. And it's true!"

"You mean Dr. Shaw died from what you prescribed?" asked Nancy.

"No. The cardiac nurse knew her stuff. She knew the medicine prescribed was dangerous and took the chart to Dr. Clemmons. Clemmons was going to check on Dr. Shaw and then contact me. But April's father was dead by the time Clemmons and the nurse returned to the room. It

29

all looks really suspicious because I was the last person to see Dr. Shaw alive except for the cardiac nurse."

Nancy was thinking out loud. "Maybe I'm missing something. Couldn't Dr. Shaw just have died from his heart condition?"

Trevor turned hollow eyes on Nancy. "I hope so. But we need an autopsy to prove it. Maybe I ordered something else wrong. That's what Dr. Rayburn, the chief of staff, and April are discussing." He drew a long breath. "This can't be easy on April. And I'm scared, too. What if the autopsy proves I did something wrong? How can I be making these mistakes?" He leaned his head against the back of the chair and stared up at the ceiling, answering his own question. "I'm *not* making these mistakes. It's impossible! I would at least remember making them if I had."

"Then what's going on?" Ned asked.

"I wish I knew." Trevor sighed. He turned to Nancy. "Any way you look at it, I'm in real trouble. My reputation as a doctor is at stake." He swallowed. "Clemmons brought the word 'malpractice' up a couple of times. If I get blamed, I might as well kiss my entire career good-bye."

"Oh, no. It can't be that bad." Nancy tried to make him feel better.

"Can't it?" Trevor rubbed his hand over his face. Then he looked at Nancy, his expression brightening a little. "I asked you to come because you're a detective, Nancy. Do you think you could help clear my name?"

Nancy glanced at Ned, then back at Trevor. "I can try to find out how those prescription mix-ups happened."

"I'll need all the help I can get." Trevor smiled wearily. "Oh, by the way, I talked to Mrs. Deverly's nurse. Mrs. Deverly recognized her symptoms and realized that she'd been given penicillin; she'd been through it once before. She called the nurse, and the nurse in turn called me. Nothing more suspicious than that."

The door to the doctors' lounge opened, and April walked in. Her face was pale and drawn, her lips bloodless. Trevor stood up and tentatively took her arm. Nancy could tell he wasn't certain of his reception. After all, he'd practically been accused of causing her father's death!

April managed to pull herself together, forcing a weak smile for Nancy and Ned. "I don't want you to think I blame you," she said to Trevor. "I know it's not your fault."

Trevor gave her a big hug of relief. "Thanks" was all he said.

Ned cleared his throat as April and Trevor sat

down. "Trevor's asked Nancy to get to the bottom of this prescription mix-up," he informed April. "If anyone can do it, she can."

"Good," April said, distracted. "That's the important thing now."

The color was coming back to April's face, and Nancy could tell she was getting over the worst of her shock. Pretty fast, too, Nancy thought.

"I'm almost relieved it's over," April said as if reading Nancy's mind. "My dad suffered far too long. Now we can all get on with our lives. That's what he would have wanted."

"When's the autopsy to be done?" Trevor asked.

April's pretty face clouded. "I wouldn't grant permission for it. I know it's unprofessional of me, but I can't help it. We're talking about my own father's body."

Trevor stared at her in surprise. Nancy could almost guess what was going through his mind. If April didn't consent to the autopsy, Trevor's name would never be completely cleared!

"I think it's time to call it a night," Nancy said. "I'll start work on this first thing in the morning." She turned to Trevor. "How about if I meet you in the lobby around nine tomorrow?"

"Fine," Trevor murmured, but his gaze never left April's face.

* * *

The next morning Nancy arrived at the hospital promptly at nine. She wasn't certain what she could do to help, but she planned to ask Trevor's colleagues a few questions.

Trevor was waiting in the lobby, dressed in street clothes.

Nancy smiled. "I forgot you're not on duty at this hour. Sorry. We could have made it later."

"Forget it. I'm so anxious to clear my name, I'd work around the clock if necessary." He grimaced. "I ran into Dr. Rayburn this morning and he was pretty upset. I've made two critical mistakes in two days. I feel as if I'm walking on eggshells."

"Can you give me an hour-by-hour replay of your last few days? Since the day before Mrs. Deverly was given the wrong medication?"

"I'll try," he said.

They walked outside, taking a path through the park that separated the hospital from the cliff high above the river. Trevor was quite open and so detailed that by the end of a few hours Nancy was convinced that he'd accounted for every minute.

"Whew!" she said at last. "Most people wouldn't be able to account for their actions in such detail." Nancy realized that Trevor had an uncommonly good memory. How could someone like that make the kind of errors he'd been accused of? It didn't seem possible.

Back at the hospital Trevor went to the cafeteria in search of April. Though it was lunchtime, Nancy headed straight to the cardiology floor. She wanted to ask some questions about Trevor. Nancy stopped a young nurse on the seventh floor and engaged her in conversation.

"Oh, you want to know about Trevor." The nurse smiled knowingly. "Sorry, he's taken already. He's engaged to one of the medical students. I think her name's April."

"I've met April," Nancy said, hiding a smile. "I just wanted to know what Trevor's like to work with."

"The best. He's fun, and he works hard. And he doesn't order the nurses and staff around. He's really great." She looked a little wistful.

Nancy smiled to herself as she headed for the elevators. Well, Trevor had at least one loyal fan!

She took the elevator downstairs, and when the doors opened on the first floor, Nancy nearly stepped right into April and Trevor.

"There you are!" Trevor said, clearly pleased to see Nancy. "April's got only a few minutes before she has to be in class, but she wanted to tell you something."

"What?"

April looked down at her hands. "I thought

you should know that I've agreed to the autopsy after all. Not that I think there's any reason for it," she said quickly. "I'm sure my father died of natural causes. But if it'll help prove no one was at fault, then I guess it's necessary." She turned her gaze on her fiancé. "But I do hate the idea."

Trevor nodded understandingly. He looked at Nancy. "They're taking April's father's body from the morgue to the pathology lab. I think I'll check to make sure things go smoothly."

Nancy realized Trevor was trying to make April feel better. "May I come with you? I haven't seen the pathology department."

"Are you sure you're up to it?" Trevor asked.

"Lead on, Doctor." Nancy smiled.

Nancy and Trevor took the elevator down to the basement. The elevator doors clanged open, revealing a narrow cinder-block hallway painted off-white.

Trevor walked briskly, apparently as anxious as Nancy to get this over with. The words "Hospital Morgue" loomed ahead, painted in black letters on a door at the end of the hall. Trevor pushed against the door. Nervously, Nancy followed. Against one wall was a row of built-in steel cabinets. The morgue itself was neat, tidy, and cold. Only the stinging scent of formaldehyde and the low temperature reminded Nancy of where they were.

"Hi, Glen," Trevor said to the man seated at a desk in the corner. "This is Nancy Drew. Nancy, meet Glen Waters. Glen's in charge down here."

"Hi. What can I do you for?" Glen grinned widely.

"It's kind of delicate," Trevor admitted. "Dr. Gerard Shaw's body was brought down yesterday. He's my fiancée's father, and I promised I'd just check to make sure everything's okay."

"Yeah. That one's scheduled for a postmortem," Glen remarked. "I'm sending it over today."

He walked over to the row of steel cabinets. Nancy knew the cabinets held bodies. She drew in a breath as Glen grabbed the handle of a drawer marked "Gerard Shaw."

The drawer slid open. The cabinet was empty!

Chapter

Five

GLEN STARED IN AMAZEMENT. "But that's impossible!" he sputtered. "I put the body in here myself. Someone's taken it!"

"What?" Trevor demanded.

"I tell you, I put the body in this drawer last night!" Glen insisted.

"Well, then, where is it?"

"I don't know!"

"Who else works here?" asked Nancy, trying to calm them both.

Glen blinked several times. "Well, Sam Hughes works the night shift now. I just switched today to days, so I relieved him this morning. There's another guy on the afternoon shift. But he hasn't worked since Dr. Shaw's body was brought down. Sam's the only other person who could have moved it."

Glen reached for his desk phone and called Sam at home. It was clear from Glen's side of the conversation that Sam didn't know what Glen was talking about.

Replacing the receiver, Glen frowned. "Sam says nobody touched that drawer while he was working. And he only left the morgue once, to get a sandwich from the vending machine. He always does that. He locked the door when he left, as he always does."

Nancy shared a look with Trevor. "Could the body just be misplaced?" she asked Glen.

"No way. But if it'll make you feel better, I'll look in every drawer to make sure. Shaw's body *has* to be somewhere!"

"What will I tell April?" Trevor murmured as they headed back upstairs. "If Glen doesn't find Dr. Shaw's body, I'll have to inform the chief of staff."

Trevor left Nancy, intending to track April down in class and tell her the upsetting news. Nancy grabbed a sandwich from a vending machine, then rode the elevator to the seventh floor. She hoped to catch Dr. Rayburn. He might be able to explain more about what had happened to Dr. Shaw's body.

Nancy recognized Dr. Rayburn standing outside one of the patients' rooms, his nose buried in a chart. "Dr. Rayburn?" she asked.

He lifted his brows inquiringly.

Nancy introduced herself, adding, "Trevor has asked me to help clear his name. He's afraid a malpractice suit could ruin his career."

"Trevor's right," Dr. Rayburn said regretfully. "But I don't see how you can help, Ms. Drew. The medical board of examiners looks into these things. The decision about Trevor's future as a doctor is in their hands. After the autopsy's performed, I'm sure his name will be cleared."

Nancy had just about concluded her interview when a man in a guard's uniform approached her. "Are you Ms. Drew?" he asked.

"Yes."

"The chief of staff would like to see you in the conference room. I'll take you there now, if it's all right."

"Thank you."

Dr. Wicks, the chief of staff, was a white-haired gentleman with a deeply furrowed brow. Trevor was with him in the spacious oblong room when Nancy arrived. He shot her a nervous glance.

"Ms. Drew," Dr. Wicks began without preamble, "I understand you were with Dr. Callahan when he discovered that Dr. Shaw's body was missing."

"That's correct."

"I don't mean to be abrupt, but this is a confidential hospital matter. I'd like to keep it as such."

"I have no intention of talking to the press," Nancy assured him. "I just would like to help April and Trevor."

Dr. Wicks's attitude warmed somewhat. "I'm certain the problem will be resolved shortly. Please, sit down." He gestured toward the chairs tucked snugly beneath the polished table. "I've been informed you've been asking questions about Dr. Callahan, Ms. Drew, and that you've been working in an unofficial capacity to help him avoid a malpractice suit. You're not a member of the hospital staff, and it's highly irregular to have you asking questions at all."

Nancy opened her mouth to defend herself, but she had no time to follow through. Dr. Wicks leaned across the table and said, "I, for one, would be interested to hear what you've learned. Why don't you start from the beginning and tell me what's been going on?"

Two hours later Nancy and Trevor left the conference room. Trevor seemed dazed. "Well, he didn't say you couldn't help me," he said. "That's something."

"Yeah, but I've got to find a way to be less conspicuous," Nancy reminded him. "What do you think I should do?"

It was nearly time to meet April and Ned, so they headed directly to the cafeteria, where they'd agreed to rendezvous.

"How about becoming a candy striper?" Trevor suggested as they pushed through the door.

"A candy striper!" Nancy repeated and laughed.

"There you are," April called out, obviously relieved. White-faced, she hurried toward them, Ned in tow. "How could my father's body be missing?" she asked in a quavering voice. "What's happening at this hospital?"

Trevor put his arm around her shoulders. "I don't know. But it's clear to me that someone's out to get me."

Nancy didn't comment. She wasn't as convinced as Trevor seemed to be that he was the prime target. Whoever had moved Dr. Shaw's body was taking an enormous risk. If someone was trying to destroy Trevor's career, there were easier ways. "How do I become a candy striper for a few days?" she asked.

Ned cocked an eyebrow at her. "A candy striper? Oh, Nancy, I can hardly wait."

Nancy smiled, glad to have lightened the mood.

"I can tell the supervisor in charge and she'll sign you on," said Trevor. "We always need volunteers. Just go to Madeleine Creyton's office tomorrow morning."

"Where's that?"

"It's in the administration building," Ned explained. "The small building next to this one."

"You're sure learning the geography," Nancy teased, linking arms with him.

"Hey." He humbly lifted his palms. "Can I help it if I'm an A student? Go ahead, ask me anything."

"Where's the school's anatomy lab?" April asked, relaxing a bit.

"Ummm." Ned squeezed his eyes shut in concentration. "The medical school classroom building. The older ivy-covered building right above the river. It used to be the hospital before this structure was built."

"Pretty good. Which floor?"

"Fifth?"

April smiled. "The medical school is only three stories high."

"Oh."

Nancy laughed. "Two out of three's not bad. Come on, take me home and feed me or lose me forever."

"Are you sure there're only three floors?" Ned grumbled as Nancy tugged him toward the door.

"Positive," April called after him.

Nancy gave Ned a quick peck on the cheek as soon as they were outside.

"And what was that for?" he asked, drawing Nancy into his arms.

"For shaking off some of April's depression. And—because I like you."

"That's it? You just *like* me?"

Nancy laughed and pulled him toward her car. "What do you think?"

Wednesday morning Nancy was at the hospital promptly at seven, in time to work the first shift of the day. At Trevor's suggestion, she'd worn a pair of white tennis shoes. She'd also done her hair in a French braid.

She found Madeleine Creyton's office and was given a pile of forms to fill out as well as a candy striper uniform. "Dr. Callahan told us to expect you," the supervisor said with a friendly smile.

"Thanks."

"Report to the emergency room. Normally, we don't have candy stripers working there, but we're really shortstaffed this week. Dr. Callahan assured me you could handle it."

Nancy wasn't so sure. Emergency? She had visions of people coming in covered with blood. Sighing, she headed back to the hospital. She wasn't sure she wanted to be a candy striper. When would she find the time for detecting?

The emergency room was quiet when Nancy walked in. She introduced herself and was handed a clipboard and a stack of forms. "We need you to take down information as patients come in," the head nurse told her. "Don't worry. Most of the day cases are pretty minor. The late-night accidents are the worst."

There was no time during her break to do any investigating, but at lunchtime Nancy made a dash through the cafeteria, grabbed a sandwich, then headed for the double doors.

"Whoa!" Ned exclaimed when she barreled into him. "Where are you going? Aren't we eating together?"

"Sorry. I've got to use every spare minute to learn who's out to ruin Trevor's reputation."

"Well, where are you going?" His gaze swept over her. "You know, you look kind of cute."

"Thanks a lot." Nancy grinned. "Actually, I'd like to take a look at those patients' charts on which Trevor supposedly prescribed the wrong

44

medicines. Do you know where Dr. Shaw's chart would be now?"

"Uh, no. Ask the ward clerk at the seventh-floor nurses' station. She ought to know."

"Okay." A teasing light sparkled in her eyes. "You know, for someone who thinks hospital food isn't fit for consumption, I notice you're here in the cafeteria a lot."

"Hey, bad food is better than no food."

Laughing, Nancy headed for the elevators. The seventh-floor ward clerk wasn't sure where Dr. Shaw's file was. "I doubt it's down in medical records yet. Check with Dr. Rayburn. His office is down the hall and around the corner. He and Dr. Callahan and Dr. Clemmons were discussing the case."

Nancy headed in the direction the ward clerk had pointed; Rayburn's office was easy to find. Nancy rapped on the gray door, but there was no answer. Twisting the handle, she found it unlocked.

A woman was just rising from a desk, straightening papers. "Sorry," she said. "I was just finishing some work before lunch, and I didn't answer the door right away. Did you want to see Dr. Rayburn? He's not in, but you can leave him a message. I'm his secretary."

Nancy was in the anteroom of a two-room office. Plush pearl gray carpeting swept across the floor and into the adjacent room, Dr. Rayburn's office. Nancy glanced toward his open office door. "Will he be long?" she asked.

"I'm not certain."

"May I wait a few minutes? I'm on my lunch break, too. I'd really like to see him."

Hesitating, Rayburn's secretary finally shrugged her shoulders. "Okay. I won't be long." She discreetly closed Rayburn's office door before she went to lunch.

Nancy waited a few minutes, then grew anxious about all the time she was wasting. All she really wanted to know was if Dr. Rayburn had Dr. Shaw's or Mrs. Deverly's file.

She tried the door to his office. Locked. Seeing the keyhole in the knob, Nancy knew it would be an easy lock to pick. She pulled a hairpin from her braid and stuck it into the keyhole. The lock button popped open. Nancy noiselessly pushed open the door and slipped inside.

Rayburn's desk stood in the center of the spacious room. A brass coatrack occupied one corner, and one paneled wall was covered with an impressive display of medical diplomas and awards. Nancy's gaze zeroed in on a short stack of narrow three-ring binders—the kind used for patients' charts—sitting on a counter beneath the window.

Nancy quickly searched through the binders. Mrs. Deverly's was on the bottom. Aha! she thought excitedly, pulling it out.

Across the front of the binder was a piece of red tape with Allergic printed in white letters over and over again across its face. It was impossible to miss!

Quickly Nancy leafed through the papers clipped to the top of the binder. A shuffling noise startled her and she glanced over her shoulder. No one there.

Nerves, she thought, hurriedly scanning the pages. A smaller white page labeled Standard Orders was on top. "Penicillin" was handwritten on the sheet, plain as day, followed by the initials *TC.*

"There it is as big as life," Nancy murmured unhappily. She stared at the chart, wishing she knew enough about medicine to understand all the codes on the page. Trevor's initials appeared several more times.

Another creaking sound sent a shiver of alarm up Nancy's spine. She whirled around. Her eyes widened. Someone dressed completely in green surgical garb was charging straight at her!

"Hey!" Nancy screamed. Hands encased in plastic surgical gloves covered her mouth. Nancy tried to scream again.

To her horror she felt something jab into her upper arm. A hypodermic needle!

"Help me!" she yelled against the smothering fingers, but it was too late. Blackness descended over her. She slipped limply into unconsciousness, the binder dropping from her fingers.

Chapter

Six

"NANCY! NANCY! Please, wake up! *Nancy!*"
Nancy heard her name being called far in the
distance. Her ears buzzed and her tongue felt too
big for her mouth. She swallowed, then tried to
form words.

"Nancy? Look, she's coming around!" the
same voice cried in relief.

It was Ned's voice, Nancy realized. She
couldn't open her eyes. Her eyelids felt weighted
down.

"Give her this." Nancy heard Trevor's voice.

She was lifted into a sitting position, a paper
cup placed against her mouth. Some liquid

slipped between her lips, and she swallowed automatically. It was water. Slowly, she opened her eyes.

"Where am I?" she asked, confused, not recognizing her surroundings.

"You're in one of the patients' rooms," Trevor said. "A nurse found you in the stairwell. We were taking you to the E.R. when you started to stir, so we brought you here instead. What happened? Did you fall?"

Slowly Nancy focused on Trevor. He was standing at the foot of the hospital bed. Ned was holding her shoulders, his dark eyes worriedly searching her face.

"Fall?" Nancy repeated on a short laugh. "No, I didn't fall. I was attacked!" She turned her arm so the small red mark was visible where the hypodermic needle had pricked her skin. "I think I'm lucky to be alive," she added soberly.

"*What?*" Trevor grabbed hold of her arm, staring in disbelief at the small puncture wound. The color drained from his face. "Someone did this to you on purpose?"

"I was in Dr. Rayburn's office, looking at the Deverly file. Someone ran in dressed in surgical greens and mask. I've got to get that file!" Nancy struggled to her feet, remembering.

"Slow down!" Ned warned, gently pushing her

down onto the bed. "Someone just shot you with a hypodermic. You need to be checked out!"

"I know, but I need that file. I'm sure that's why I was attacked."

"I'll go back to Rayburn's office and get the file," Trevor said. "Ned, take Nancy down to the lab. I'll call and order some blood tests."

An hour later Nancy was pronounced fit to leave. She'd been injected with a common sedative, which had no serious side effects.

"I still think you should go home," Ned said worriedly.

"Trust me. I'm fine. Besides, you're the one who has to explain why you missed your class."

"Are you Nancy Drew?" one of the lab nurses asked as they were about to leave.

"Yes."

"Dr. Callahan just called. He asked you to meet him in the doctors' lounge in the basement if you feel up to it."

"Thanks."

"I'm coming with you," Ned insisted.

"No, Ned. You go back to your class. I'll talk to Trevor. I'm fine. Really." She squeezed his arm, heading for the door.

Grumbling under his breath, he muttered to the room at large, "There's no talking to her."

Trevor was seated at one of the tables, and April was with him. "I begged off my classes this afternoon," April admitted. "I can't concentrate right now."

Nancy smiled sympathetically. "What about—" she began, but stopped in midsentence when Trevor shook his head.

"The Deverly file wasn't in Dr. Rayburn's office. In fact, it seems to be missing entirely. Dr. Rayburn is really upset about everything. He's furious that you were in his office and that someone purposely sedated you. And he's fit to be tied about the missing file." Trevor grimaced. "The chief of staff's in a real state, too. We had to order a new file made up."

Nancy hoped Dr. Wicks wouldn't pull her off the case. It was certainly within his power. "Whoever attacked me didn't want me to see that file."

"Then it won't surprise you that Dr. Shaw's file is missing, too," Trevor added. "I told you, Nancy—it's a plot. Someone's trying to ruin my career!"

This time Nancy didn't argue. Someone *had* attacked her. And that meant someone thought she was a threat. "Who would want to ruin your career?" Nancy asked. "Have you got any enemies?"

April and Trevor quickly exchanged looks, but

neither responded right away. "Well, maybe," he said finally.

"Who?"

"Suzanne Welles," April answered for him. "She's an administrator here at the hospital, and she—uh—doesn't really like Trevor—or me."

Nancy asked, "Why?"

"Suzanne and I were dating," Trevor explained. "We were pretty serious for a while. Then she talked about getting married, but I didn't think I was ready. We broke up, and then right after that, I met April." He shot his fiancée a quick, affectionate glance. "The rest is history," he added softly.

"Do you think she would carry a grudge this far?" Nancy asked skeptically. "I mean, not only is Trevor's reputation suffering, but whoever's changing the patients' charts is also endangering their lives. That's criminal."

Trevor seemed to consider. "No, I don't think so," he answered. "Suzanne's angry, but she's not vindictive. She wouldn't risk patients' lives or her career."

April opened her mouth, then clamped it shut again; clearly she had wanted to disagree with Trevor. Nancy sensed the hostility April felt for Suzanne. She wasn't sure what to believe, but she made a mental note to find Suzanne Welles as soon as possible.

Nancy left a few minutes later to check at the administration building to find out where Suzanne worked. She learned Suzanne had her own office on the fourth floor.

Nancy took the elevator and stepped out into a hallway. A dark gray carpet deadened the sound of her steps. The lighting was indirect and tasteful. Unlike the hospital, which was designed for efficiency, the administration building—at least this floor—was decorated for comfort.

Suzanne's name was embossed on a bronze nameplate recessed in the oak door. Nancy knocked softly, and a young woman let her in.

"Yes?" she inquired politely, taking in Nancy's candy striper uniform.

"I'm looking for Suzanne Welles," Nancy explained. "My name is Nancy Drew. Are you Suzanne?"

"I'm Suzanne's secretary," the young woman explained. "Do you have an appointment?"

Nancy hadn't understood the importance of Suzanne's position. It was clear Suzanne was high up to be awarded such a luxurious office and her own secretary. "No. I'm a friend of Dr. Trevor Callahan's."

The young woman hesitated, then shrugged and lifted the receiver on her phone. She explained who Nancy was to the person on the other end.

"Go right in," the secretary said, her voice tinged with surprise.

"Thank you." Nancy opened the door to Suzanne Welles's office.

A woman in her twenties sat in a leather chair behind a massive oak desk. Her dark hair was swept up, and the suit she wore was simple and expensive.

"All right, Nancy Drew," she said. "What's your angle?"

Her directness surprised Nancy. "Angle?"

"I have a budget meeting in fifteen minutes with the administrative director. I don't have time to waste. What have you got to do with Trevor Callahan?"

"Maybe I should come back another time," Nancy murmured.

"Did Trevor send you?"

"No, I—" Nancy stopped to collect herself. Suzanne Welles certainly had a way of making her feel ill at ease! "Trevor said you're a friend of his," Nancy spoke up, deciding to fight fire with fire. She could be as direct and bold as Suzanne. "He's in trouble now, and I thought you could help."

"What kind of trouble? And how are you involved?" Suzanne drew her brows together.

Nancy quickly explained everything. Suzanne visibly softened.

"But Trevor didn't actually ask for my help, did he?" she guessed. Sighing, she said, "Okay, let me be honest. I thought I was in love with Trevor once, but I wasn't. That's over."

"You don't know anyone who might want to hurt him?"

Suzanne's face flushed. "Is that why you're here? Because you think I want revenge?" She rose, crossed the room, and opened the door. It was a clear invitation to leave, and Nancy reluctantly turned toward the outer office.

"If someone's making mistakes, it might be Trevor himself, you know," Suzanne said. "He's the most logical choice, isn't he?"

She closed the door behind Nancy with more force than was necessary.

It was late afternoon by the time Nancy returned to her post in the emergency room. Her head was swimming with thoughts of Suzanne Welles. She was certain Suzanne still had feelings for Trevor, no matter what she said. Why else would Suzanne have agreed to see her unless she hoped Trevor had sent Nancy as a way of breaking the ice between them again? When Suzanne had seen that Nancy was merely trying to help Trevor, her hopes had obviously been dashed, although she'd tried to deny her feelings.

She must still love Trevor. But how could she be involved in ruining his reputation? She had seemed genuinely concerned for Trevor until she found out why Nancy was there.

In the emergency room, a young girl in a softball uniform was slumped in a chair beside her mother. The sticker on her T-shirt said her name was Carla. Nancy smiled at her and asked, "Can you fill this form out?"

Carla lifted her left hand, pointing to her right one. "I can't," she said, heaving a huge sigh. Her right hand was wrapped in a white terry-cloth towel.

"We think Carla's finger is broken," the woman beside her said, taking the clipboard from Nancy.

"I might be out for the season!" Carla wailed.

"Maybe it's not that bad," Nancy said consolingly. She stared at the sticker on the girl's T-shirt, and something clicked inside her head. White sticker. Penicillin. "Excuse me," she said, striding toward the emergency room desk. On top of the counter were several patients' binders. Nancy opened one. A chart had just been started. A white paper marked Standard Orders lay on top, the patient's name typed across the page.

"Hey, Nancy! I thought your shift ended at three."

"Ned!" she cried excitedly, grabbing his arm, and dragging him toward an empty corner of the emergency room.

"Well, if I'd known I was going to get this warm a reception, I would have been here sooner," he teased.

"It gets better." Nancy's eyes sparkled. "I just figured out how someone tampered with Trevor's patients' files!"

Chapter
Seven

NED STARED AT HER in amazement. "You did? How?"

"I got a quick look at Mrs. Deverly's file this morning before I was attacked. On the doctor's Standard Orders page Mrs. Deverly's name was on one of those white labels stuck on the chart. Normally the patient's name is typed on. Don't you see? Someone *covered up* the real name. Trevor's orders weren't for Mrs. Deverly at all!"

Ned whistled.

"Those orders were for some other patient," Nancy went on. "That's why Trevor's handwriting was on it! Someone substituted those orders into Mrs. Deverly's file. Trevor had really ordered penicillin for another patient!"

"Wow." Ned shook his head. "But what about the red tape warning against an allergic reaction?"

"It had to have been ripped from the file and later replaced."

"But weren't Trevor's orders dated?" Ned asked, thinking fast. "They date everything around here."

"I bet the dates were altered, too. Those orders could have been for any patient since Trevor's been a resident. No one really looked at the dates. It was Trevor's handwriting on the file *ordering* the penicillin that put everything in an uproar."

"Nancy"—Ned gripped her arm—"if what you're saying is true, then some maniac is running around the hospital switching files!"

"Switching *Trevor's* files, and putting patients' lives in danger! He or she is after Trevor."

Ned nodded, his handsome face grave. "Why would anyone be out to get Trevor?"

Nancy thought of Suzanne. "I don't know," she said quietly. "And what about Dr. Shaw's body? Whoever took it must have had a powerful motive. I can't believe it hasn't turned up by now."

They headed for the seventh floor to look for Trevor in cardiology. As they rounded a corner, Nancy nearly ran into David Baines. The surly orderly was trying to follow Dr. Rayburn into his office.

"Excuse me, Mr. Baines," Rayburn said patiently but firmly. "I have work to do."

"Work to do. Right. Like in Saint Louis?" David asked, his tone nasty. He anxiously twirled a set of keys around one finger.

Rayburn just shook his head and strode into his office. David, noticing Nancy and Ned for the first time, said with a short laugh, "Well, if it isn't the girl detective and her flunky."

Ned bristled, but Nancy put a hand on his arm. "Who told you I was a detective?" she asked David.

"No one had to tell me. You're asking all kinds of questions about Trevor Callahan." He twirled the keys again before he walked past them.

"Did you see those keys?" Ned demanded. "Those were Porsche keys. I recognized them."

"Porsche keys," Nancy repeated, staring down the empty hallway where David had disappeared. "Tell me, how can an orderly afford a Porsche?"

"I don't know," Ned replied thoughtfully.

Ten minutes later they found Trevor in Room 721, speaking with a young boy whose chest was bandaged. Trevor was holding a soccer ball and smiling at his patient. "So, you're a soccer player," he was saying. "How long have you been playing?"

"A few years." The boy plucked at his sheets. "I won't play this year."

"Oh, you never know. You've got six months until fall season. You'll be as good as new by then." He glanced over his shoulder, spying Nancy and Ned in the doorway. "Be back later," he told the boy with a wink.

"What's up?" he asked, joining them in the corridor.

Trevor listened attentively while Nancy told him about her theory regarding the altered charts. "Nancy, you're fantastic! So *that's* how it was done!"

"We don't know for certain," Nancy reminded him. "It's just a theory."

"I'm going straight to the chief of staff to straighten this out," Trevor said, already in motion.

"Trevor, I—"

"Catch you later," he yelled, running through the closing doors of the elevator.

"Now what?" Ned asked.

Nancy pushed back a strand of hair from her face. The way Trevor jumped to conclusions made her uneasy. "How about food?" she suggested.

"You read my mind. But let's get out of this place, okay?"

"Okay."

They rode the elevator down to the first floor and headed for the exit. Ned held the door, and the cool evening air stirred Nancy's hair.

"You know, I should talk to April before we leave," Nancy said. "I want to know more about David Baines."

Ned clutched his stomach as if he might die of starvation.

Nancy laughed. "Bring the car around to the front of the hospital. I'll be right back. I promise."

"Okay."

Nancy walked quickly down the corridor toward the front desk. It was quite possible April had already left for the day, and if so, Nancy was going to have to call her dorm room.

"Could you page Dr. April Shaw?" she asked the woman wearing the headset.

Recognizing Nancy, the woman smiled and complied. Within moments a call came back through. "Dr. Shaw's in the cafeteria, Ms. Drew. She asked you to join her."

When Nancy entered the cafeteria, she found April seated in the corner, an untouched plate of food pushed aside. She was holding a photograph in her hands as Nancy sat down beside her.

"Hi," Nancy said, looking at the photograph. "How're you doing?"

"This is a picture of my dad." She handed it to Nancy. Tears suddenly filled her blue eyes. "It's all so terrible," she said, her voice cracking. Suddenly she covered her face with both hands and sobbed. All the emotion she'd been bottling up came pouring out. "I feel so guilty!"

"April, I'm really sorry about your father," Nancy murmured softly.

"No. No." She shook her head, sniffing. "I miss him, but his death was a blessing. Now it's Trevor I'm worried about."

"Listen, don't worry about Trevor. Everything will be fine as soon as I—"

"You don't understand." April dropped her hands, staring at Nancy through scared, tear-drenched eyes. "I think—I think . . ." She stopped, as if she couldn't go on.

"You think what?" Nancy probed gently.

"Nancy, I think Trevor's got serious problems. It *is* his fault that my father's body is missing! He's the one making the mistakes!"

Nancy stared at April in disbelief. "What do you mean?"

"These things that have happened—they're not coincidences. There's only one explanation that makes sense: Trevor arranged everything!

We only have his word that he didn't." April's eyes swam with fresh tears.

She's really distressed and not thinking clearly, Nancy thought. "April, listen to me. I think I know how Trevor's patients' charts were tampered with." Quietly and calmly she explained her theory.

But April shook her head. "Nancy, there's more." With a supreme effort, April collected herself. People at other tables were starting to stare, and she pulled a tissue from her pocket and dabbed at her eyes. "Nancy, the CCU nurse reported a conversation she overheard between Trevor and my father. My father was depressed, and he told Trevor it would be better if he just died. Nancy, he even suggested *ways* Trevor could arrange it."

"The CCU nurse told you this?" Nancy asked quickly.

April nodded. "Uh-huh. She reported it to Dr. Rayburn, too. What if Trevor did kill my father?" she asked in a low, shaky voice. "Oh, Nancy, what if Trevor thought he was doing me and my dad a favor?"

Chapter

Eight

Nancy wanted to cover her ears. She'd just seen what a wonderful doctor Trevor was. Could what April was suggesting be true?

"Maybe that's why he's hidden the body," April said, clapping her hand over her mouth in distress. "He's afraid an autopsy will reveal the truth!"

"You're talking murder, April," Nancy warned quietly. "A mercy killing is still murder."

"I know," she murmured miserably. "Why do you think I'm scared to death?"

Ten minutes later Nancy walked April through the cool spring evening to her dorm. She signaled to Ned, indicating through hand motions where she was headed. Ned turned on his lights and drove ahead of them toward the dorm.

April was like a zombie. "You don't have to baby-sit with me, Nancy."

"You're in no condition to be alone tonight. Are you sure you don't want me to stay?"

"No, there're a lot of people in the dorm. And Trevor will stop by later." She sighed heavily. "I don't know what I'm going to say to him."

Realizing April had half convinced herself of Trevor's guilt, Nancy saw it was becoming even more important to find out who had tampered with the files. I've just got to find them, figure out who did it, and *why,* she thought. Then Nancy remembered something she had wanted to ask April. "I ran into David Baines today," she said. "Does he drive a Porsche?"

"Umm. I don't know. No, wait a minute. Somebody said something about a red sports car. I think he does drive a Porsche." She stared blankly at Nancy. "Why?"

"Well, how can he afford one on an orderly's salary? Does he have another job?"

"I don't know."

Nancy tried another tack. "I overheard him say something about Saint Louis to Dr. Rayburn this afternoon. Didn't you say your father was from Saint Louis?"

"Oh, I know what that's about," April answered. "Saint Louis is where David flunked out of med school. He told one of the staff he got thrown out by mistake, but knowing David, I doubt it."

"Is that how he knew your father was a doctor?" Nancy was fishing, but she thought there might be some connection. "Could that be why David was so bitter toward him? Because your father taught at the med school that tossed him out?"

"Maybe."

They stopped in front of the door to the dorm. "Thanks, Nancy," April said with a small smile. "See you tomorrow."

On Thursday morning Nancy smiled as she parked her car near the emergency room entrance. The now familiar buildings of Westmoor University Medical School looked solid and secure, not like the home of the mad killers who had filled Nancy's dreams.

Spotting the reflection of her pink and white uniform in the hospital's glass door, Nancy made a face. She had to find time away from her candy striper duties to do some investigating.

She'd barely begun recording new patient information when Trevor appeared. He was in jeans and an open-collared shirt. "Nancy," he said. "Could I talk to you?"

"Sure." She gave him a quick look. His voice was strained, and he looked as though he hadn't shaved that morning. "You're here awfully early."

"I didn't sleep at all last night. What's wrong with April? She would hardly talk to me."

Nancy sighed. "Trevor, I need to ask you some questions," she said delicately, realizing he could easily take what she was about to say the wrong way.

"Ask away."

"Well, I was talking to April, and apparently one of the CCU nurses overheard a conversation between you and April's father."

"What kind of conversation?"

Nancy explained to Trevor what April had told her, finishing with "The nurse apparently reported the conversation to Dr. Rayburn."

At Nancy's abrupt silence, Trevor glanced away. "I remember. Lots of patients talk like that, Nancy. They get depressed. You have to encourage them, and as they get better, they get over their depression."

"But, Trevor, we're talking about a patient who suggested a mercy killing!"

A dark flush moved up Trevor's neck. "It

wasn't like that." His gray eyes fixed on Nancy's for the first time since she had made her suggestion. "You don't seriously believe I would perform a mercy killing, do you?"

"No. I don't."

"But someone else does, right? Who?" Trevor demanded, growing angry. "Who said that? Dr. Rayburn? He knows I'd never do anything like that!"

Nancy hardly knew what to say.

"No, wait. I get it. You talked to Suzanne yesterday, didn't you? She somehow found out about that conversation. She won't leave me alone."

"It wasn't Suzanne," Nancy admitted reluctantly, "although I do need to talk to you about her."

"Then who was it?" Trevor demanded, ignoring Nancy's attempts to divert the conversation. At Nancy's continued silence his face slowly changed. "Oh, no. Not April." He looked shocked.

"April's upset about her father," Nancy said hurriedly. "I think she's been hiding her feelings, trying to bury them. It didn't work and now she's a wreck. She said she even feels guilty."

"Nancy." Trevor's eyes were full of pain and disbelief. "Does April believe I killed her father? Is that why she was so distant last night?"

How do I get myself into these things? Nancy wondered unhappily. "She knows you love her, and she thought maybe, because you knew how much it hurt her to see her father suffer . . ." She trailed off, not wanting to hurt Trevor further.

Trevor stared at Nancy for several moments, then slowly climbed to his feet. He left without saying goodbye. Nancy felt terrible. She went back to work, but could hardly concentrate. When Glen Waters called from the morgue, she listened only halfheartedly.

"Hey, look, security really tore this place apart from top to bottom. Dr. Shaw's body just isn't here," Glen said. "But there is something kind of strange."

"What?" Nancy asked.

"Well, Sam Hughes, the night man at the morgue, remembered that his keys were missing for a while the other night. He couldn't find them the whole shift. Then just as he was about to leave—bingo—they were on the floor beneath the counter. Sam says he's positive they weren't there earlier. He looked."

"Thank you, Glen," Nancy said, excited. "You just solved one mystery for me!"

At lunchtime Nancy met Ned in the cafeteria. She told him about Glen's message. "I'm sure that's how the body snatcher got into the morgue. He lifted Sam's keys, made duplicates, then

71

replaced them. He waited until the morgue was deserted, then let himself in and stole Dr. Shaw's body."

Ned bit into his hamburger. "But why?"

"Maybe an autopsy would reveal something he doesn't want known," Nancy guessed. Recalling her conversation with Trevor, she sighed. "I really feel bad for Trevor."

"So do I," admitted Ned.

"The only thing to do is wrap this investigation up as soon as possible and prove his innocence."

As they left the cafeteria a few minutes later, a familiar feminine voice sounded somewhere ahead of them in the corridor. Nancy looked up, listening. "Ned," she whispered. "I think that's Suzanne Welles."

Before Ned could respond, Suzanne sauntered around the corner. Gone was the serious woman of yesterday. She looked happy and bright.

To Nancy's amazement Trevor appeared right behind Suzanne. Before either Nancy or Ned could react, Suzanne slipped her arms around Trevor and planted a long kiss on his lips. And Trevor didn't fight back a bit!

Chapter

Nine

NED MURMURED in Nancy's ear, "Talk about a lip lock."

Nancy was so surprised she didn't answer. Trevor finally surfaced from the kiss. When he saw Nancy and Ned, his face reddened. "Oh, hello. What are you two doing?" he asked, embarrassed.

"We just ate lunch," Nancy murmured.

The starry-eyed look on Suzanne's face made Nancy uneasy. What was going on? she wondered. The last she'd heard, Trevor didn't want Suzanne anywhere near him. But that kiss told a different story!

"Let's go, Trevor." Suzanne linked her arm through his. She seemed anxious to steer him away from Nancy and Ned. Trevor glanced back once, then disappeared around the corner.

"Now, what's that all about?" Ned wondered aloud, staring after them.

"I'm almost afraid to find out." Nancy made a face. "I didn't tell you before, but last night April said some pretty outrageous things about Trevor."

"You mean they're having a fight? What kind of things?"

"She thinks Trevor may have been responsible for her father's death after all. April's afraid he might have performed a mercy killing, because he knew how unhappy her father's illness was making her."

"What?" Ned's jaw dropped. "No way! Trevor would never do a thing like that. Not for any reason!" Nancy's continued silence prompted him to add, "You don't seriously believe her, do you?"

"No. But it is possible. Trevor admitted to me that Dr. Shaw asked him to end his suffering."

Ned stared at Nancy in shock. "And . . . ?"

"Trevor said he wouldn't even consider it," Nancy assured him. "A lot of people say things they don't mean when they're depressed."

"Like April herself?" Ned suggested, lifting a brow.

"Yes, like April. She's been under a lot of pressure too." Nancy shook her head. "I just can't seriously consider Trevor a suspect. He wouldn't take such a risk, even for April."

"If Trevor loves April," Ned said slowly, "why is he with Suzanne?"

"He was pretty upset when he found out what April had said to me. He might be with Suzanne because he's hurt." Another thought struck Nancy, and she felt cold inside. "Or maybe April's right, and he's with Suzanne because he's got a guilty conscience where April's concerned."

"Don't even think of it," said Ned, but the look on his face suggested he was worried, too. "I don't want to be around when April finds out about Trevor and Suzanne," he added quietly.

"Neither do I. Come on, let's get back to work."

They parted at the elevator. "I've got to race to the administration building," Ned said, holding her face between his palms and kissing her lightly. "Today's a late one. I won't be out until after six."

"Okay, that'll give me a few hours to do some detective work. I'll meet you in the lobby later."

* * *

The emergency room was a madhouse. An afternoon auto accident had the whole staff working frantically. Nancy raced around to help, filling out forms, directing patients into the examining rooms, and guiding them to the X-ray department whenever necessary.

While she worked, her mind kept turning over the riddle of this particular case. Who would want to ruin Trevor's career? Suzanne, for all her talk, was clearly still interested in Trevor. Would she have altered the files? *Could* she have? And now that Trevor seemed interested in Suzanne, would she change her tactics?

Then there was David Baines. He held a grudge against doctors in general and, it seemed, against the Shaws in particular. Nancy thought his bitterness might have something to do with having been expelled from medical school. And what had David meant by asking Dr. Rayburn about St. Louis?

The emergency room slowly cleared out. Nancy was surprised to see it was after four; she'd worked an hour overtime. Nancy finished up quickly and dashed for the door.

It was time to confront David Baines. He'd been underfoot during this whole investigation, needling April, talking to Dr. Rayburn. He'd even been on the cardiology floor just before Nancy had been attacked.

Thinking she might still catch him at the hospital, Nancy asked the switchboard operator to page him. The page went out over the loudspeaker, and Nancy waited over ten minutes, but Baines didn't show.

"He should be here," the receptionist informed Nancy. "His name's on the afternoon worksheet for the fifth floor."

"Thanks. I'll see if I can find him."

Nancy searched the fifth floor from end to end, going through the east and west wings several times. At the nurses' hub, she asked if anyone had seen him.

"Yeah, just a few minutes ago," a young R.N. answered. "He was called to Room five fifty-three."

Nancy hurried to Room 553. Peeking inside, she saw an elderly man napping in the hospital bed. There was no sign of David.

Back at the nurses' station, the same young nurse flagged her down. "He was just here! I told him a reddish blond candy striper was looking for him, and he said he'd find you."

Well, then, where is he? Nancy asked herself. She prowled the halls several more times, but

David Baines wasn't around. Could he be avoiding her?

Nancy punched the Up button on the elevator. When the doors slid open, however, she changed her mind, and took the stairs instead. She couldn't find David Baines on the seventh floor, but Dr. Rayburn might still be in his office. Of the two, Dr. Rayburn seemed more likely to tell Nancy what he and David had been discussing. Nancy rapped on the gray door to Rayburn's office. There was no answer, so Nancy let herself inside. Dr. Rayburn's secretary wasn't at her desk; apparently she'd gone home for the day.

This time the door to Dr. Rayburn's inner office was open a crack, and Nancy knocked again. "Dr. Rayburn?" she called, but without much hope. The door swung open wider. The room was empty, but a navy blue sports coat hung on the brass coatrack.

He must be coming back, Nancy thought, so she hovered in the doorway between Dr. Rayburn's inner office and his secretary's anteroom. To pass the time, she let her gaze travel over his medical diplomas and awards.

"Medical school in Boston," she murmured. "Well, that certainly doesn't have anything to do with Saint Louis." Maybe her theory about David Baines was all wet.

It was a quarter after six before Nancy gave up her vigil. She returned to the lobby, but there was no sign of Ned.

"Oh, Ms. Drew," the evening switchboard operator said, reading Nancy's name tag. "There's a message for you." She held out a pink slip.

Nancy took it from her hand and read: "Meet me at the administration building. Will be late. Ned."

Nancy walked down the corridor to the side exit door, pushed the bar, and stepped into the dusky evening air. The parking lot security lights were just flickering on.

The administration building was west of the hospital. Nancy walked along the sidewalk, then cut across the parking lot to save time. Her steps echoed on the pavement. She thought she heard the scrape of a sole behind her.

Glancing back, she let her gaze sweep the surrounding cars. A red Porsche was parked in the northwest corner of the lot. Baines's car!

Nancy hesitated, biting her lip. Ned, she decided, was going to have to wait. Turning, she hurried toward the gleaming red car. It was the latest style and year. "Must have cost him a fortune," she thought aloud.

Suddenly a gloved hand jerked Nancy off balance. Before she could yell, she felt a hand clamp over her mouth! Her arms were wrenched behind her back. Stunned, she immediately struggled, but her attacker was strong. He held her in a bone-crushing grip.

"Stay away from the hospital, Nancy Drew," a man's voice snarled viciously in her ear. "Unless you want to end up in the morgue!"

Chapter

Ten

NANCY KICKED BACK HARD, connecting with the man's left shin. Her attacker yelped with pain but kept dragging her toward the bushes near the dark corner of the parking lot.

Nancy twisted and fought, her heart pounding wildly. Her arms were held so tightly she couldn't free herself. The man was strong but slender. His voice sounded somewhat familiar. If only she could get a look at his face!

"Hey!" someone yelled from near the administration building.

At the same moment Nancy bit down on her

attacker's hand. "Help! Somebody help me!" she screamed when he let go of her mouth.

The sound of footsteps came pounding toward them. Her captor didn't wait. He threw her to the ground. Nancy hit the pavement and a loud groan escaped from her as the heels of her palms skidded against the asphalt. She scrambled almost instantly to her feet. Her attacker was zigzagging among the parked cars. Nancy ran after him, but by the time she got into gear, he was just a memory.

She stopped in the center of the lot, panting. Doubled over, she drew several long breaths, willing her heartbeat to slow down.

"Are you all right?" a voice asked.

"Yeah. Fine." She straightened up to see a worried-looking man in a lab coat standing beside her. "Thanks. He, uh, got away."

"You'd better come back inside the hospital and report this, miss. Have you still got your purse? This parking lot's getting dangerous!"

Nancy smiled an agreement. She let her would-be rescuer think this was just a random mugging, but she knew better.

Ned was pacing the hospital lobby when she returned. "Nancy! Where were you?" Seeing her torn dress and scraped palms, he asked, "What happened? Are you all right?"

"I'm fine," she assured him. "I was just on my way to the administration building to meet you when a guy attacked me from behind."

"What guy? What do you mean, the administration building? I got a message you were going to be late."

Nancy blinked. *"You* got a message *I* was going to be late?"

He nodded. "I picked it up here at the front desk."

Nancy turned to the two people at the desk. "Both messages were just dropped on the desk," the receptionist informed them when Nancy asked. "That's how it's done. People just pile them up and we route them to the right person or office."

"Someone wanted you to be outside alone," Ned said grimly to Nancy. "He meant to attack you!"

"I know," Nancy answered in a low voice, pulling Ned toward the door. When they were out of earshot of the others, she told him about her attacker's warning. "Ned, I'm not positive, but I think the guy who grabbed me was David Baines."

"Baines!"

"His voice was just a growl, but it sounded familiar. I got a look at him as he was running away. This guy had David's slender build and dark hair. It could have been someone else, I suppose, but I think it was David."

Ned's gaze narrowed. "Let's get out of here. We can pin Baines down tomorrow. I just want to get you home safe and sound."

Seeing that Ned was worried, Nancy agreed to wait until the next day to talk with Baines. They walked outside together in silence. Ned's car was parked near the largest dorm. As they approached it, Nancy stared ahead. Just visible far across the parking lot was a red Porsche.

"I'm sure that's David's car," Nancy said, pointing it out.

Before Ned could answer, they both noticed a brown-haired woman in a white lab coat as she walked down the sidewalk toward them, her head bowed. "Is that April?" Nancy asked Ned, peering through the gloom.

"If it is, we're saying hello. Then we're making tracks out of here. Agreed?"

"It *is* April," Nancy said, slipping from Ned's arms. "April!" she called, hailing her down.

April barely raised an arm. She walked over to Nancy and Ned in silence. There were tears glittering on her cheeks. She wiped at them and said in a trembling voice, "Trevor—is—with—*Suzanne!*"

Nancy appealed silently to Ned, who said softly, "April, I think Trevor's just reacting out of anger. He cornered Nancy this morning and wanted to know why you were so upset with him last night."

April stared at Nancy. "You told him what I said?" she gasped.

"I'm sorry—I had to," Nancy admitted. "I don't believe Trevor did anything wrong, but I have to consider every possibility."

"It doesn't matter." April sighed. "If he loved me, he wouldn't have gone back to Suzanne."

"I don't think he's really gone back to Suzanne," Nancy said.

"Oh, no?" April dug inside her purse for a tissue. "Then how do you explain the gold necklace Suzanne showed me when I ran into her in the cafeteria? It was a present from Trevor! That's a pretty expensive gift from someone who supposedly doesn't care about her!"

Nancy's lips parted in surprise. "Who told you Trevor gave it to Suzanne?"

"Suzanne did."

"Maybe she's lying. She struck me as the kind of person—"

"Thanks, Nancy. Really. But I don't want to talk about it. My father just died, and I'm still in shock. I can't take this, too." She drew a sharp breath through her teeth, exhaling it slowly. "I've asked the med school for a few days' release from classes, and they've given me a leave."

"What are you going to do?" Nancy asked, worried.

"I don't know. Maybe I'll leave town for a while. I need some time away to take care of my father's affairs and to put things in perspective. Thanks, Nancy, for all you've done." She managed a crooked smile and shook hands with Nancy and Ned. Then she walked into her dorm without a backward look.

"What do you make of that?" Ned asked as they headed to his car.

Nancy shook her head, climbing into the passenger seat. "It's a mess," she admitted.

They circled the hospital, and Nancy glanced toward the emergency room. A familiar figure was standing just inside the glass door, outlined against the light. "Ned!" Nancy cried excitedly. "Stop the car. That's David Baines! Now I'm sure he's the guy who grabbed me!"

Baines's hand was on the door, but he was talking to someone just out of sight.

"Ned, he's getting away!" Nancy cried as she leapt out of the car. David's silhouette was no longer visible. She ran to the emergency room, yanked open the door, and glanced both ways.

David was standing near the corner of the corridor, staring down the hall. There was a flurry of activity near the far end. Paramedics were bringing people in on stretchers. But the person David had been talking to was long gone.

"Is that the guy?" Ned asked, coming up behind Nancy.

Hearing him, David glanced back. His eyes widened when he saw Nancy hurrying toward him.

"I'd like to talk to you," Nancy began, but David was already moving toward the door.

"Yeah, well, I don't want to talk to you. I'm busy."

"Wait a minute, pal," Ned ordered, grabbing hold of the orderly's arm. David tried to pull free, but Ned's grip was too tight.

"Let go of me!" he demanded.

"In a minute," Ned said calmly. "Nancy has a few questions she'd like answered first."

"I don't have to talk to you! I'm calling security."

"Go right ahead," Nancy said coolly. "I'd like to speak to them, too. You see, someone attacked me a little while ago in the parking lot. I should report it."

David's eyes narrowed. "What's that got to do with me? I didn't do it."

His quick denial only strengthened Nancy's belief that David had indeed tried to drag her toward the bushes. But until she had real proof, she couldn't accuse him outright. "Didn't the nurse on five tell you I was looking for you earlier?" she asked him. "I get the feeling you've been trying to avoid me."

David glared at Ned's hand on his arm. "What do you two want?"

"Information," Nancy answered instantly. "I heard you were expelled from medical school in Saint Louis."

"So? I just got unlucky, okay? Since when is that a crime?" He sneered.

"Dr. Gerard Shaw was on staff at the medical school hospital in Saint Louis. And he was also consultant to the medical board of examiners."

"So?" David repeated. But his face drained of color. Bingo! Nancy thought with satisfaction.

"I don't have to listen to this!" David declared suddenly. He started struggling in earnest, and Ned practically had to pin his arms behind his back.

"You blamed Dr. Shaw for your being expelled," Nancy pressed. "That's right, isn't it?"

"Look, the old guy stuck his nose in where it

didn't belong. It had nothing to do with him! But those jerks at the hospital asked for his advice. They *listened* to him. And he didn't know anything about it!" With a supreme effort of will David jerked himself free and lunged for the door.

"Didn't know anything about what?" Nancy demanded, pushing open the door after David.

"Want me to tackle him?" Ned asked tersely.

"No, wait—"

Backing across the parking lot, David yelled, "You're way off base, girl detective! I didn't kill Dr. Shaw! But I know who did. And why!"

"Who?" Nancy asked, hurrying after him. "David, *who?*"

Headlights flashed at the edge of the parking lot. An engine revved. Nancy was so intent on David, she barely noticed. But David did. Slowly he turned his head, lights pinning him in their white glare.

"Nancy!" Ned called from behind her, panicked.

She glanced up. Roaring toward her and David was an ambulance! It screamed through the parking lot. Nancy dived to the right and rolled, her shoulder slamming into the curb.

She heard a shriek of terror. Glancing back,

she saw a flash of red and white. The ambulance was bearing down on David.

"David!" Nancy screamed.

To her horror, the ambulance hit David head on, tossing him like a rag doll up and over the hood. His limp body crumpled to the ground on the other side!

Chapter

Eleven

D AVID!" NANCY YELLED AGAIN.

She stumbled to her feet as Ned raced past her. The ambulance ripped by, careening around the corner, tires squealing.

David lay unconscious on the pavement. Nancy checked his breathing as Ned ran back to the hospital for help. She tore off her candy striper apron and wrapped it around him for warmth.

Within minutes a group of people had gathered around the scene and several paramedics appeared with a gurney. They lifted David carefully onto the gurney and wheeled him straight into the emergency room.

Ned touched Nancy's elbow. "This is a matter for the police. Whoever was driving that ambulance wasn't fooling around. He tried to kill David!"

Nancy nodded. "And David said Dr. Shaw was killed. That means we've got a murderer who's attempted to kill more than once."

"Including the attacks on you," Ned reminded her grimly.

Nancy nodded in response, wondering when the killer would take the opportunity to strike again.

Two hours later Nancy and Ned had explained everything to the chief of staff. Reluctantly, he called in the police. David was placed in intensive care and was still unconscious when Nancy and Ned were ready to leave.

"A concussion," Dr. Clemmons, the resident on duty, told them. "Possible ruptured spleen and a number of fractures."

"Will he be all right?" Nancy asked.

Clemmons was noncommittal. "His vital signs are stable."

Nancy and Ned walked back toward Ned's car. "It's kind of late for dinner," Nancy pointed out.

"Yeah." Ned sighed. "I've got some studying to do before I turn in."

"Should we forget about dinner?" Nancy suggested.

"Only if you promise to make it up to me." Ned kissed her, then grabbed her hand and steered her toward her own car.

"Promise," Nancy said.

He waited until she was safely behind the wheel and the doors were locked. Then he pointed at her and repeated, "Promise," in a voice that said there would be no backing out later.

The phone call woke Nancy from a deep, dreamless sleep. She opened one eye, checked her alarm clock, and groaned. "Go away," she told the ringing phone even as she groped to answer it.

"Is this Nancy Drew?" a young woman's voice asked.

"Yes, it is." Nancy yawned. It was only 5:30 A.M.

"Nancy, this is Emily Richards from the emergency room. I wanted to catch you before you left for the hospital. I realize this is short notice, but would you mind working from three o'clock to eleven today? Today's Friday, and we're always a lot busier in the afternoon and evenings on weekends. It would really help me out."

"Sure," she agreed, realizing she would have the entire morning to work on the case. "I'll see you this afternoon."

Nancy hung up the phone and yawned again, drawing her pillow over her head. She closed her eyes, but sleep eluded her. Who had tried to run David down the night before? How had the would-be murderer gotten hold of an ambulance? And did David really know who killed Dr. Shaw?

Flinging back the covers, Nancy climbed out of bed. She took a quick shower, dressed in faded jeans and an oversize cream-colored sweater, tied on her sneakers, and hurried downstairs.

Nancy called the River Heights police station and left a message for Detective John Ryan. They'd both been involved in a case Nancy called *Circle of Evil,* and even though they'd been working at cross-purposes, Detective Ryan had eventually admitted that Nancy was a talented investigator.

While she waited for some kind of answer, she did some thinking. The key to David Baines's involvement in this case had to be his expulsion from medical school. He'd turned completely white the night before when she brought the subject up. But did his grudge go deeper?

Nancy reached for the phone again. She dialed April's number at the dorm. The line rang so many times Nancy decided April must have left town, but April finally answered. "Hello?" she answered, her voice tired.

"Hi, April. It's Nancy. Sorry to bother you so early," Nancy apologized, "but I wondered if you could help me."

"Sure. How?"

"Did you hear what happened to David Baines last night?" April said no, and Nancy told her about the accident. April gasped, and Nancy said, "I need to find out more about David. I think he knows something."

"How can I help?"

"I need to know why he got expelled. Is there any way you can find out? Maybe from someone your father knew at the hospital in Saint Louis?"

"Well, Dr. Grafton's still there, I think," April said. "He's a friend of my father's. Or was." The line went quiet.

"April?" Nancy hated pushing her, but she really needed her help. "Would you mind calling Dr. Grafton and asking him about David?"

"I don't know what good it'll do, but I'll try."

"Thanks, April."

As soon as Nancy hung up, the phone rang. "Hello?" she asked into the receiver.

"Nancy Drew?"

She heard the smile in Detective Ryan's familiar voice. "Hi, there," she said. "As I recall, you once said you'd be happy to work with me on a case again."

"What kind of case?" he asked.

"Well, it's a little complicated. I need to do a background check on someone. His name is David Baines, and he's a patient in the hospital at Westmoor University Medical School. He works there, but last night—"

"He was mowed down by an ambulance. I've got the file right here, Nancy. Hospital security's guarding him against another attack. What specifically do you want to know?"

"Well, I'm working on a theory," she admitted. "I'd like to know about his bank balance."

"That's classified information," the detective warned.

"I know, but David seems to have a lot of unexplained money. He drives a Porsche, but he works as an orderly. Unless he has another job, I don't see how he can afford that kind of car."

Detective Ryan seemed to mull that over. "What do you think he's involved in?"

"When I know more, I'll tell all," Nancy countered, smiling to herself. Detective Ryan always tried to get her to reveal more than she was willing to tell him.

"Okay. Will you be home today?"

"I'll either be here or at the hospital." Nancy gave him the emergency room number.

"I'll call you," he promised.

The morning was passing quickly, so Nancy decided to get to the hospital. She changed into her candy striper outfit, grabbed her purse, and headed for the door. Just then the phone rang. Detective Ryan! Nancy made a mad dash for it.

"Nancy, is that you?" It was April.

"Right here. Have you got something for me?" she asked excitedly.

"Well, maybe. I'm not sure. I got in touch with Dr. Grafton."

"And?"

April hesitated. "Dr. Grafton wants this kept strictly confidential, but David was expelled for dangerous negligence. A patient died because David gave her the wrong medication. My father helped make the final decision to expel him."

"The wrong medication?" Nancy repeated, her pulse hammering. This was sounding increasingly familiar!

"The patient's husband threatened to sue the hospital. Nancy, Dr. Grafton told me something else, too. Dr. Rayburn worked at the same hospital. And he was one of the doctors who helped get David expelled!"

"Dr. Rex Rayburn? Chief cardiologist at W.U. Med School? *That* Dr. Rayburn?" Nancy asked, surprised.

"Small world, huh? Dr. Grafton says Dr. Rayburn was only there a short time."

"What was the name of the patient who died?" Nancy asked.

"Treadway. Anna Treadway," April answered. "She died of cardiac arrest. David took it upon himself to administer medicine to her even

97

though he was just a student. She died as a result. The evidence was pretty clear."

Nancy whistled. A beep sounded in her ear. "April, I've got another call coming in. I'll talk to you later, okay? And thanks. Thanks a lot." Nancy touched the receiver, disconnecting April and connecting the incoming call. "Hello? Drew residence."

"Hi, there, Nancy," Detective Ryan's voice greeted her. "You were right on the money with Baines, so to speak. The guy's bank balance has a few extra zeros."

Nancy was elated. "How many extra zeros?"

"He's got thousands just sitting in a checking account. Now, where do you suppose that money came from, Detective Drew?"

"I'll let you know when I figure it out," Nancy said with a smile. "I owe you one."

"Since I'm being generous, here's one more item of interest: we found the ambulance that hit Baines. It was abandoned down by the river. No fingerprints. Officers are checking into how it was stolen. So far it looks as if someone just lifted the keys and took it."

Keys again. That someone must be fairly well connected to the hospital to be able to pull off a stunt like that, Nancy thought. She thanked the detective and hung up.

Nancy drove straight to the hospital, parked

near the emergency room door, and strode up the walkway. Running footsteps sounded behind her. Nancy whipped around, half expecting more danger. But it was Suzanne Welles coming across the parking lot.

"Nancy!" she cried, waving her arm. "I just saw you drive in. I've been looking for you all morning!"

"You have?"

"Yes." Suzanne slowed down, her fingers lightly touching the gold necklace encircling her neck.

"That's beautiful," Nancy remarked, eyeing the necklace.

"Trevor gave it to me," she answered proudly, as if she'd been waiting for Nancy to bring up the subject. "Nancy, I've been thinking about what you said the other day. About someone setting up Trevor. That's why Dr. Shaw's body is missing, isn't it? Whoever stole it must know an autopsy would show that Trevor is innocent."

Nancy regarded her silently, waiting for her to get to the point.

Suzanne hesitated. "I have an idea who the body snatcher might be."

"You do?"

She nodded. "April Shaw."

"April!" Nancy was taken aback.

"I know on the surface it doesn't seem possible, but think about it," Suzanne went on hurriedly, before Nancy could respond. "She could have killed her father. She hated watching him suffer. She as much as said she couldn't wait until his suffering was over. And now I'm convinced that she only pretended to love Trevor!"

"Suzanne," Nancy protested.

"She used him," Suzanne went on, her jaw tightening angrily. "She needed someone to throw the blame on, and she used Trevor. Have you seen April cry any real tears over her father's death? No! Nancy Drew, if you're looking for a murderer, look no further than April Shaw!"

Chapter

Twelve

OH, COME ON, SUZANNE," Nancy said. "April loves Trevor. They've been engaged for months, since long before Dr. Shaw came to visit her."

Suzanne lifted her chin. "I notice you don't deny that she could have been involved in a mercy killing."

"I only agree that she wanted her father's suffering to end. That's a long way from murder."

"Not that long."

They were at a stalemate. Nancy looked into Suzanne's dark eyes, wondering if her accusations had any basis in truth. A tiny seed of doubt

grew inside her. April was an emotional wreck—
of that much Nancy was certain. April had been
very composed after her father's death—
unnaturally so, Nancy had thought at the time.
Could her emotional state now be caused by
guilt?

Nancy left Suzanne and went into the hospital.
It was almost two. Shaking her head clear of
Suzanne's allegations, Nancy used the lobby pay
phone to call April. "Hi, April. It's Nancy. I've
been thinking about a few things and wondered if
you could help me again. I'd like to know more
about what happened to Anna Treadway in Saint
Louis. Is there any way I could get my hands on
some old records? I have a hunch that what's
happening now must relate somehow to that
tragedy."

"I could call Dr. Grafton again," April said
doubtfully. "He might be willing to let you see
the files."

"Tell him about what happened to David. We
don't want any more 'accidents.'"

"Okay, Nancy."

Nancy hung up, lost in thought. She gasped
when a hand suddenly grabbed her arm.
"Trevor!" she exclaimed, whipping around.

"Sorry to frighten you. I couldn't help overhearing. You were talking to April, weren't you?"

His handsome face was set and serious. Nancy could no more read his mind than she could Suzanne's. "Yes, I was."

A muscle in his jaw flexed. "How is she?"

"Okay, I guess. She's trying to put the last few days in perspective. They've really taken an emotional toll." When Trevor didn't respond, Nancy added lightly, "I saw the necklace you gave Suzanne. It's beautiful."

"The gold necklace?" Trevor asked blankly. "Suzanne showed it to you?"

Nancy nodded. "And she showed it to April, too."

"What! But I gave that necklace to Suzanne years ago. It was a birthday gift." He looked stunned. "You don't think April believes I gave it to Suzanne recently!"

"As a matter of fact, that's exactly what she thinks," Nancy replied, deciding to use the opportunity to clear up some facts. "Trevor, what's going on between you and Suzanne? Could you be using her to get back at April?"

Trevor opened his mouth, then clamped it shut. He strode away without answering. Nancy realized she didn't have time to follow him. It was time to show up at the emergency room.

The afternoon passed quickly; as the head nurse had said, Fridays were really busy. Ned appeared at five o'clock, ready to leave. "The week's seminar is over," he said, smiling. "Now I've got to decide if this is the kind of work I want to do. You know, I really should take you on a tour of some of the labs and classrooms before we leave. All you've seen is the hospital. This place is huge. I even got to see one of the refrigerators where they keep organs for transplants."

Nancy made a face. "I think I'll pass on that. Besides, I have seen more than the hospital. I've been to the administration building."

"I wish you were off duty," Ned said wistfully. "You could make good on our dinner date."

"Too bad I'm stuck here until eleven," Nancy said, disappointed.

A voice laughed behind her and Nancy turned to see Emily Richards. "You can go if you want," she said, smiling. "It was really unfair of me to ask you to change your schedule. You're not even employed here."

"But I thought you were shorthanded."

"We are, but it's really nurses we need. I've managed to find some who want to earn overtime pay. Don't worry, Nancy. I've got enough candy stripers. Go enjoy yourself."

"So where do you want to eat?" Ned asked, once he and Nancy were in the corridor outside the emergency room.

Nancy untied her candy striper apron and pulled it over her head. "Ned, I know you've heard this before, but I'd like to stay at the hospital a little longer. I want to try to see David. He's our strongest link in this case."

Ned considered. "Well, okay. As long as you make it up to me later."

She smiled. "Maybe over dinner we can brainstorm about where Dr. Shaw's body could be."

Nancy and Ned headed for the third floor. It wasn't hard to find David's room. A gray-suited security guard stood outside the door, his beefy arms folded across his chest. Just looking at him made Nancy's hopes sink. He didn't seem the type to bend the rules even a little.

Nancy hovered at the corridor juncture, turning her back on the guard so he wouldn't get a good look at her.

"What do you want to do?" Ned whispered in her ear.

"I don't know, but I've got to get in there somehow. If only I were a doctor, or something," Nancy murmured, thinking aloud.

"Well . . ." A gleam of mischief entered Ned's eyes. "You *can* be a doctor for a while. At least you can fool people into thinking you are."

"How?"

Ned led her toward the elevator. "Follow me."

He guided her to a locker room next to the operating rooms. "Check out the lockers," he told her. "Some aren't locked. On our tour I noticed some of the doctors left their lab coats hanging up."

"Ned, you're wonderful!" Nancy cried, pushing open the door.

The fourth locker produced results. Inside was a white lab coat with a lapel pin attached. Nancy slipped it on and met Ned in the outer hall.

"Dr. Marcia Smythe," Ned read, when she rejoined him in the hall.

A pair of glasses were nestled in the coat pocket, and Nancy stuck them on her nose after she pulled her hair back. "Do I look old enough?" she asked anxiously.

"Not really. But the hair and the glasses help." They headed back to floor three. "I'll keep a lookout at the corner of the corridor in case you get in," said Ned. "If anyone comes, I'll create some kind of distraction to give you time to get out."

"Wish me luck," Nancy murmured, straightening her shoulders.

"Luck," Ned said softly. "And be careful."

Nancy strode purposefully down the hall, glancing around. Two doors down from David's room, a gurney covered with a sheet was waiting outside an open door. The rest of the doors were closed. Only she and the security guard were in the corridor.

Nancy's heart was pounding in double time, but she hid her nervousness behind a tight smile. "If you'll excuse me," she said, pulling open the door to David's room with authority. She looked carefully at the guard. Would her disguise work?

The security man simply nodded and let her pass. With a silent sigh of relief, Nancy let herself into the room. She slipped the glasses back into the coat pocket.

The room was dimly lit. Light from the outside parking lamps filtered in through the blinds. David lay on the far bed, a bandage around his head, one side of his face bruised and scraped. He was tossing restlessly under the covers.

"David," Nancy whispered, glancing nervously over her shoulder to the door. "Can you hear me?"

"Doctor . . . Rayburn . . ." he muttered.

"No, it's Nancy Drew," she said swiftly, touching his arm. "You were talking to me outside the emergency room last night. Do you remember?"

His eyelids fluttered open. He seemed to focus on her. "The ambulance," he mumbled.

Nancy nodded encouragingly.

David licked his lips. "It was in Saint Louis . . . She was dead. . . ."

"Anna Treadway?" Nancy asked quickly.

A small sound escaped David's throat. "Not my fault. Not my fault—it was an accident—Dr. Shaw . . ."

"How did it happen?" Nancy asked. "How did the accident happen?"

David sighed deeply and seemed to sink into a deeper sleep. His breathing became slow and regular. His eyelids closed.

"David?" Nancy whispered. "David?" Outside the door she heard cushioned footsteps coming down the hall. Anxiously she searched for a place to hide. But the guard already knew she was in the room!

Nancy heard Ned's voice outside, speaking loudly. "Hey, I'm lost. Can you tell me where ICU is?"

Nancy's heart nearly stopped. He was warning her!

Gathering all her courage, Nancy swung open the door and strode into the hall as if she owned the place. A nurse was standing next to Ned, holding a tray of small white paper cups. The patients' evening medicine. She glanced up at Nancy, her brows raised as she brushed past and entered Baines's room.

The gurney Nancy had spied in the hallway was now standing just inside a room with an open door. Nancy glanced back at Ned. To her dismay she saw Dr. Clemmons just rounding the corner! She had to get out of sight before her cover was blown!

Nancy's eyes darted wildly in all directions. Nowhere to hide. Turning into the open room, Nancy stopped short. An orderly was making up one of the beds. A patient lay on the other bed, asleep. Nancy pressed herself against the wall, heart thudding. Where could she hide?

The gurney.

Without another thought, she lay on the gurney and pulled the sheet over her head.

"You're Nancy Drew's friend, aren't you?" she heard Dr. Clemmons demand loudly.

"That's right," Ned answered.

"Well, where is she? You were with her a little while ago."

"She's not here."

"Who do you mean?" the security guard asked.

Nancy's heart sank. Here it comes.

"I mean a red-haired girl who doesn't know how to obey hospital rules," Dr. Clemmons said angrily. "We're talking about a patient's life! If I find she's inside this room, I'll make certain she's removed from this hospital!"

Nancy drew a quiet, shallow breath. Seconds later, she nearly jumped when Ned whispered near her ear, "Nancy?"

"Can I help you?" The orderly who had been tidying up the room asked.

Nancy froze.

"I, uh, was just looking for a friend," said Ned.

"No one here." The gurney suddenly lurched away from the wall. Nancy had to fight back a gasp. To her horror, she realized the orderly was pushing her out of the room! "Excuse me, I have to take this body down to the morgue."

The morgue?

"Er, *this* body?" Nancy heard Ned ask.

"Yeah, buddy. You got a problem with that?"

Nancy nearly choked as the gurney was pushed from the semidark room to the brightly lit hallway. The wheels clattered and squeaked as she felt herself being pushed in the direction of David's room!

"A red-haired girl?" the guard was repeating thoughtfully. "Reddish blond hair?"

"Is she in there?" Clemmons demanded. Nancy heard a flurry of footsteps. Grimacing, she realized Clemmons wasn't going to wait for an answer. He was heading straight into David's room.

There were more footsteps. The gurney stopped short. Nancy realized the jig was up.

"All right, Ms. Drew." Dr. Clemmons's voice boomed with suppressed anger. "You're coming with me! The chief of staff won't appreciate your having gone against direct orders!"

Chapter

Thirteen

Nancy counted her heartbeats and waited for Clemmons to yank the sheet back.

"What are you doing, Dr. Clemmons?" a female voice asked.

The nurse! Nancy realized with relief. That's who Clemmons was addressing, thinking she was Nancy!

"I—I—" Clemmons sputtered, confused.

The gurney lurched into motion again. Nancy felt herself being wheeled away from David's room. She had to hold back her laughter as she heard Clemmons's embarrassed apology.

"Hey!" Ned called, his footsteps falling into step beside the orderly's.

"Get lost, buddy," the orderly growled impatiently. "Go make a nuisance of yourself somewhere else."

Nancy was thinking fast. When she felt the wheels turn the corner, she threw off the sheet. The orderly, a young man with red hair, shrieked.

"Miraculous recovery," Ned said with a grin, grabbing Nancy's arm.

They dashed down the hall to the stairway and took the stairs at a run. Halfway to the first floor Nancy collapsed in a fit of laughter. "Did you see the orderly's face?"

"Yeah." Ned grinned. "But you should have seen Clemmons's face when that nurse walked out of David's room! He turned bright red. Did you get a chance to talk to David?"

"No, but he was mumbling in his sleep. He brought up Saint Louis again. The key to the mystery's got to be what happened to Anna Treadway."

Ned thought for a moment. "Do you suppose David moved Dr. Shaw's body to cover up the fact that he'd killed him? He could have stolen Sam's keys and removed the body."

"That means he killed Shaw for revenge, but it

113

doesn't explain where the body is now. And it doesn't explain who was driving the ambulance that ran David down."

"Who else do you think could be involved in this Saint Louis business?" Ned asked.

Nancy reflected for a moment. "Well, maybe Dr. Rayburn. David did say something to him about Saint Louis outside his office, and April said Rayburn worked at the same hospital. He might have a grudge against David, too."

"It'd have to be a pretty serious grudge to give him a motive for killing them," Ned reasoned.

Ned was probably right. "What about someone connected with Anna Treadway?" Nancy suggested, looking for an alternative. "I mean, she was killed. Maybe one of her relatives blamed David and Dr. Shaw for her death. April told me Treadway's husband threatened to file a malpractice suit."

"Well, whoever's behind all these incidents is in pretty tight with this hospital. Could one of Anna Treadway's relatives be employed here?" he asked.

"I'll check it out." Nancy frowned; she felt very frustrated. "But why would one of her relatives want to frame Trevor? It keeps coming back to that. And why involve the hospital at all? If someone wanted to get rid of David or Dr. Shaw, there are a lot easier ways to do it than at the hospital." Ned opened the door to the first floor as Nancy continued. "I need more information about what happened to Anna Treadway. I'm going to call Detective Ryan to see if he can help me."

Nancy was heading for a pay phone when Trevor walked into the first floor lobby. He seemed a little embarrassed at seeing them. "Seminar's over, right?" he said to Ned, not knowing what else to say. "So how did you like it?"

"Okay, I guess. Although I'm glad it's you in the anatomy lab, not me."

"Detective Ryan's not in this evening," a female voice told Nancy. "Can someone help you?"

But Nancy wasn't listening. Her thoughts were buzzing. Anatomy lab! she thought excitedly. Dr. Shaw's body wasn't in the morgue, but it had to be hidden in a cold place! "Uh, thanks, no," she managed to say into the phone before hanging up.

"Nancy, I need to talk to you," Trevor said, sighing. "I've been such a jerk. I shouldn't have kissed Suzanne," Trevor went on. "You were right. I was just mad. I mean, how could April think I killed her father! I'm a doctor, for crying out loud. I would never do anything like that."

"April's just upset," Ned said.

115

Realizing they were both looking at her, Nancy surfaced. "Do you think April could have performed a mercy killing herself?" Nancy asked Trevor.

He looked incredulous. "No way!"

"Suzanne thought she might be capable of it."

Trevor's eyes sparked with fury. "I'm beginning to see Suzanne would do anything to hurt April. What an idiot I've been!"

"You're sure April's innocent?" Nancy asked.

"Absolutely." Trevor's face was serious. "April loved her father. She hated to see him suffer, but she would never have ended his life. She cared for him too much."

Trevor's words rang with sincerity. Nancy smiled. "I believe you," she admitted. "I never really took Suzanne's accusations seriously, but I wanted to hear how you felt. What about Suzanne? Could she have murdered Dr. Shaw? As a way of putting the blame on you?"

"That's reaching even farther. Suzanne would never jeopardize her career that way. Her work is too important to her. A lot more important than *I* ever was," Trevor added.

"So who did it?" Ned asked.

"I'm not sure," Nancy said slowly, "but I think I know where to find Dr. Shaw's body."

"I can almost hear the gears turning in your

head," Ned said, grinning. "Out with it, Ms. Drew."

"You're the one who keeps talking about the anatomy lab." Nancy laughed. "Isn't there a dissecting lab in the classroom building? And doesn't the medical school use cadavers in anatomy class?"

"Well, yes," Trevor answered. "But we only work on authorized bodies."

"But an unauthorized body could be hidden among the cadavers, couldn't it? Isn't there some kind of cold storage place where cadavers are kept?"

"Well, sure, there's a freezer, but—"

"That's right!" Ned snapped his fingers. "A huge walk-in freezer. The classroom building used to be the old hospital. The freezer there is right next to the dissecting lab!"

"There are cadavers in the freezer," Trevor admitted. "But I'm sure it's been searched."

"The search has really only taken place at the hospital," Nancy reminded him. "And it would be a simple matter to change the name on a body. No one would be the wiser."

Trevor nodded, blinking rapidly. "That's true," he said with dawning amazement. "Nancy, you're right! Listen, I'm still on duty, and I've got to check on one more patient before I take a break. Give me a few minutes and I'll meet you at the freezer."

"Ned and I'll wait for you there," said Nancy. "We'll need you to identify Dr. Shaw's body."

Trevor nodded. "Okay. I'll be there in about twenty minutes, maybe a little longer if I run into a snag or two. I can't afford to mess up on my duties right now, or I'll be suspended." He turned, then hesitated, glancing back. "Want me to call security?"

"Let's wait to see if my theory pans out," Nancy suggested.

"Right." Trevor tried to smile.

Nancy and Ned hurried to the nearest exit. Ned guided her across the campus to the classroom building, which housed the anatomy lab. It was in the oldest section of the school, an ivy-clad brick building with poor lighting. Just thinking about the task in front of them had Nancy looking over her shoulder.

"Think we're being followed?" Ned asked, glancing around suspiciously.

"I don't know. This building's a little creepy. Didn't you say something about tunnels under it?"

"Yeah, they run from here to the hospital. It's a great way to move bodies without upsetting visitors."

"That's how our body snatcher did it, then,"

Nancy declared. "He must have moved the body through a tunnel from the hospital to the anatomy lab. Which floor is the lab on?"

"Third. I checked after April quizzed me the other day."

They hurried upstairs. Nancy caught the smell of formaldehyde as soon as they pushed open the door to the third floor.

"It's right down here," said Ned, indicating a door with Anatomy written across its pebbled glass window.

"It's locked," Nancy said, trying the handle.

"Should we just wait outside?"

Nancy nodded, and they stood quietly outside the door. Nancy's thoughts were on David Baines. "David could have moved the body," she muttered. "Maybe he murdered Dr. Shaw and was afraid the autopsy would prove it."

A slight noise from inside the anatomy lab interrupted Nancy's thoughts.

"What was that?" Ned asked softly.

"Someone's in there!" Nancy whispered. She quickly pulled her lock-picking kit from her purse and quietly worked the lock with a slim metal tool. The tiny clicks she made sounded to her like pistol shots in the dead quiet of the hall.

Seconds later the knob turned noiselessly in her hand. Pressing a finger to her lips, she squeezed inside the room. Row upon row of tables filled the enormous classroom. A thin light glowed beneath a far door.

Ned's hand clamped down on her shoulder. "Stay here," he mouthed to her. Nancy vehemently shook her head, but Ned ignored her. His running shoes made no noise as he crept across the linoleum floor. Nancy had little choice but to watch him steal toward the far door. Someone needed to stand guard.

At the end of the room, Ned touched a finger to the door. It swung in, unlatched. He gave Nancy the thumbs-up sign, then disappeared inside.

Nancy chewed on her lower lip. Minutes dragged by. She stole a glance at her watch every thirty seconds. Where was Trevor? Why hadn't Ned returned?

At the end of fifteen minutes Nancy couldn't stand it any longer. She left her post and tiptoed hurriedly to the door Ned had pushed open. Another classroom lay beyond, lit by a row of ceiling lights. Nancy's heartbeat quickened as she moved forward.

She cautiously glanced around that classroom's door frame. A giant metal door stood at the end of a short hallway. The freezer! Nancy moved toward it and pulled back the latch. It clicked loudly and the door creaked open.

With a glance inside Nancy knew she had found the place where the cadavers were kept.

Thick translucent plastic sacks hung from hooks. But Nancy barely noticed. Because directly in her line of vision lay Ned, sprawled on the cold wooden floor. And a pair of hands covered by surgical gloves were pushing his limp body inside a huge plastic sack!

Chapter

Fourteen

N ED!" NANCY SCREAMED, racing forward.

The hands jerked back. Then Nancy heard a clatter and running footsteps. She reached Ned as a man dressed in surgical greens slipped behind a tall stack of boxes.

Nancy checked Ned for a pulse and realized he was breathing steadily. Then, quick as a cat, she leapt to her feet and began to chase the assailant. The huge freezer was filled with stacks of hospital supplies. Nancy spotted her quarry at the end of a long row of boxes. "Stop!" she yelled.

The intruder half turned toward her. Nancy charged forward. Now there were barely ten feet between them. In a flash, Nancy grabbed his sleeve before he could slip away. She held his right arm, trying to see his face. His mouth and nose were covered by a surgical mask and he wouldn't turn her way.

"Nancy!" Trevor's voice called from the other end of the freezer.

"Over here!" she yelled. At that moment, the man jammed his left elbow into her stomach, knocking the wind from her. He threw her down and zigzagged through the rows of boxes back toward Trevor!

"Trevor," Nancy called weakly, trying to warn him.

Racing footsteps echoed through the refrigerator. Boxes crashed to the floor.

"What the—" Trevor said, but his words were cut off. Nancy heard a groan; then the footsteps receded through the classrooms. She heard the click of a latch.

The door! Nancy thought with fear, staggering to her feet. All three of them were locked inside the freezer!

She hurried toward Trevor, cold air flooding into her lungs. When Nancy found him, Trevor lay in a heap. Luckily there was a latch on the inside of the door. It turned easily in Nancy's hand, and she breathed a sigh of relief as the door opened. Far ahead Nancy heard the intruder's footsteps disappearing. She propped open the door with a box.

"Trevor, are you all right?" Nancy asked anxiously, gently slapping his face.

Trevor shook his head and sat up, looking around dazedly. "Did you see him? He slammed into me before I got a chance to do anything."

"I didn't see his face. Come on, we've got to help Ned."

Trevor followed after Nancy. Ned still lay unconscious on the floor. Trevor bent over him. "His eyelids are fluttering. That's a good sign. Quick, help me carry him out of here. We've got to warm him up. Be careful with his neck. I'll take his shoulders; you take his feet."

Nancy was glad Trevor was there. He immediately got down to business. By the time they carried Ned to the warm classroom, he had begun to come around. "Nancy," he mumbled.

"Shhh," she said.

"Lay him down here," Trevor said, settling Ned on the floor. He yanked a penlight out of his coat pocket and examined Ned's eyes. "You look all right, my friend," he said seriously, running expert fingers around Ned's head. Ned winced. "But you've got a nasty bump at the base of your skull."

"Where'd he go?" Ned demanded, trying to sit up.

"He's long gone," Nancy said. "Are you okay?"

"You'd better get over to the hospital and have a thorough examination," Trevor told him.

Against his protests, Trevor and Nancy helped Ned toward the door. He assured them he could walk on his own, but Trevor was reluctant to let him make the trek by himself.

"What do you want to do?" Trevor asked Nancy.

"Get Ned to an examining room, then find Dr. Shaw's body."

"You guys go and look for the body," Ned ordered, leaning against the doorjamb. "I'll be okay."

Trevor glanced at him. "I could make a quick check and meet you both at the hospital."

"I don't want to leave you here alone, Trevor," Nancy said, worried.

"Go, Trevor," Ned insisted. "I can wait."

"Okay, I'll be right back." Trevor went back inside the freezer. Nancy waited with Ned, glad to see color slowly return to his cheeks.

"Stop looking at me as if I'm an invalid. I'm fine, I tell you. Who was that guy? All I saw was a green mask."

"Well, it wasn't David Baines, but it was a man. Our mysterious Mr. X. I'll bet he's the same person who ran David down in the ambulance.

And I'll bet David was blackmailing him—that would explain David's hefty bank balance."

"Blackmailing him for what?"

Nancy shook her head. "I don't know. If it has to do with Anna Treadway, then it's got to be someone who—" Nancy sucked in a breath. "Oh, I've been so blind! Ned, I think I know who's behind this!"

"Who?" Ned asked, just as Trevor came striding toward them.

"It's there!" Trevor said excitedly. "Dr. Shaw's body is there under another name. I recognized it because the name on the body was that of a patient who died here months ago. There's no way they'd still have the cadaver."

"I think our mysterious Mr. X was trying to move the body," Nancy said.

"Then we've got to call security," Trevor said. "There's a phone at the end of the hall. I'll stay here while you make the call. When the security guards get here, I'll tell them to take Dr. Shaw's body to the pathology lab in the basement of the hospital building. You take Ned to the emergency room. I'll meet you there later."

"I tell you I'm fine!" Ned said again, but Nancy steered him out of the room.

Just as they were disappearing into the hallway, Trevor called out, "Would you phone April? Let her know her father's body's been found."

"Sure," Nancy yelled back. Spying a telephone in the hallway, she and Ned quickened their steps.

"Okay, Nancy, spill it," Ned said. "Who do you think stole Dr. Shaw's body?"

She grinned. "How does Dr. Rayburn grab you?"

"Rayburn! Why Rayburn?"

They had reached the phone, so Nancy shook her head and dialed the reception hub. She asked for several security guards to be sent to the anatomy lab at Dr. Trevor Callahan's request. Ned waited impatiently for her to finish.

"All right, give," he said when they reached the first floor and headed back across the gloomy campus to the hospital.

"Rayburn was a doctor at the Saint Louis medical school. He was also partially responsible for David getting expelled."

"But what has that got to do with killing Dr. Shaw?"

"I'm not sure—yet. After all, Shaw and Rayburn were on the same side. But I think Rayburn's the connection. He knows something. Maybe something he wants buried."

"What are you going to do now?"

"Go to Rayburn's office," Nancy said determinedly as they walked into the emergency room. "There's something I have to check out."

"I'm coming with you."

"No way." She half pushed him down the hallway. "This man needs a doctor," she said, as one of the emergency room nurses looked up inquiringly. "I'll be back," she whispered to Ned as another candy striper came toward him with a warm smile on her face and a clipboard in hand.

Trapped, Ned muttered, "Traitor," out of the side of his mouth.

Nancy headed straight for Dr. Rayburn's office. When she found the door locked, she wasn't surprised. With her lock pick, Nancy let herself into the secretary's front office and then into Rayburn's inner office.

Inside, the blinds were drawn, but she didn't dare turn on a light. Instead she pulled her penlight from her purse and flicked on the small beam of light.

Rayburn's mahogany desk was an antique. Rows of locked drawers ran along the front. Nancy painstakingly jimmied the lock on each one and searched quickly through the sheaves of paper within. Finally she unlocked a slim drawer near the top and found a medical file inside it. She placed the folder on the smooth desktop and began thumbing through the papers. Nothing.

She was replacing the file when she noticed that the back of the drawer moved slightly. Pushing against the wooden slat, she realized it was a drawer divider. Elated, she removed the slat and found another file behind it. When she opened it, a single piece of paper fluttered onto the desktop.

It was a typewritten demand for ten thousand dollars, and a threat. The words jumped out at her.

Pay by Thursday unless you want to face a very messy malpractice suit. You know who I mean. I've got a Porsche to pay for, remember?

The note was unsigned, but Nancy knew it must have been from David Baines. Blackmail! she realized excitedly. That explained David's fat bank balance. But Rayburn involved in a malpractice suit? What *did* David have on the man?

Nancy quickly replaced the file and relocked the drawer. She sat for a moment in utter silence, thinking hard. Through the blinds, the outdoor security lights glinted in streaks on Dr. Rayburn's framed certificates. With sudden insight, Nancy jumped to her feet and ran the beam of her flashlight over Dr. Rayburn's Boston medical diploma.

"So that's it!" she murmured, focusing on Dr. Rayburn's printed name.

Nancy quickly closed the door to Rayburn's

office behind her, crept through the secretary's room to check the hall, then slipped into the hallway and softly locked the outer door behind her. Now she had all the facts!

She was on her way back to the emergency room to meet Ned and Trevor when she thought about Dr. Shaw's body. She hurried to the elevator and punched the button for the basement. Once she made certain that Dr. Shaw's body had been moved and was now secure and safe in the pathology lab, she could rejoin Ned.

The basement was deserted. The overhead fluorescent lights buzzed faintly as she walked down the corridor. Nancy's heartbeat fluttered. Her every nerve was on edge.

The door to the pathology lab was standing wide open. As Nancy glanced inside, her heart jumped to her throat. Slumped on the floor were the bodies of two security guards—the guards who had just brought the body here! She rushed forward, stunned, then stooped to check their pulses. They were alive, but out cold.

Through another door she saw a man in a white coat sprawled across a counter. Nancy ran forward. He, too, was breathing but unconscious. His sleeves were rolled up, and she could see a small red mark on his forearm. So that was how the intruder had knocked them out so easily. They'd been jabbed with a hypodermic needle!

Hearing a familiar squeaking, Nancy spun around in time to see a draped gurney being pulled through a low door at the far end of the room. Nancy raced toward it. Ahead was a long narrow hallway. The tunnel, she realized. Dr. Shaw's body was being stolen again!

Chapter

Fifteen

S TOP!" NANCY SCREAMED. "Stop!"

A man in green surgical gear glanced backward. The same man who had attacked her in the anatomy lab! Nancy caught a glimpse of familiar scowling black eyebrows just as he thrust the gurney toward her with a mighty shove.

Nancy dodged, but the gurney hit her hip, knocking her against the wall. The sheet slipped to reveal a body. It must be Shaw. Her quarry took off at a run. Without further hesitation Nancy raced after him into the old tunnel.

The ceiling grew lower. The floor sloped down

beneath her feet. The lighting was weak and shadowy. As she progressed farther, the tunnel grew narrower and less well tended. Though the walls and floor were concrete, Nancy could smell the faint dank scent of earth. She wished she'd told Ned and Trevor she was going to the pathology lab. She could use a little backup.

She was certain now that she was following Dr. Rayburn. Should she just give up and go for help? Though the eerie tunnel made her a little nervous, she wasn't willing to turn back. Who knew what Rayburn would do next? She had to stop him.

As a precaution, she tore off some of the hem from her lab coat. She tied a thin strip to one of the metal light protectors and pinned Dr. Marcia Smythe's nametag on it. If Ned came down this tunnel, he'd know she'd been here.

Thirty feet later, the tunnel forked in two. Nancy paused. Kneeling down, she pressed her ear to the cold concrete. Faintly, down the tunnel to her right, she heard the impact of hurried footfalls. She tore off another strip from the coat, marking the passage.

Nancy picked up her pace. If Rayburn reached the end of the tunnel before she did, she might never find him. He obviously knew these tunnels and buildings intimately.

Straight ahead of her, a wooden door blocked her exit. She strained but was able to pull it open. To one side, a flight of stairs led up. Her sense of direction told her she was beneath the medical classroom building.

Climbing the stairs, Nancy reached a landing and another door. It was warmer here. She cracked the door open and saw she was in an unfamiliar basement with huge, dusty insulated pipes running beneath the ceiling.

Nancy stepped forward cautiously. She heard a sound behind her. She whipped around in time to see those same dark eyebrows and steely eyes. Hands clamped around her arms, but Nancy was quick. She twisted free, snatching off the man's mask.

"Dr. Rex Rayburn," she said coolly. "How come I'm not surprised?"

"Because you're too diligent for your own good," he said. "Sorry, Ms. Drew."

Rayburn grabbed her, and a second later she felt the prick of a needle. Panicking, Nancy struggled free of his grasp. "But you underestimated me. I've got too much to lose. You must understand."

Nancy glanced in horror at the tiny puncture mark on her arm.

"Just a sedative," he told her. "Until I can

come up with a better plan. I must admit, you really caught me off guard." His expression was more concerned than angry. "I really wish things could be different, but I'm afraid you know too much."

Nancy opened her mouth, hoping to try to reason with him, but her tongue suddenly felt thick and woolly. Dr. Rayburn's face dissolved into a watery pool.

She felt his hands catch her as she crumpled to the floor.

The light hurt Nancy's eyes. She squeezed them shut and turned her head. She raised an arm, only to have it fall back limply.

Memory returned in a cold rush. Dr. Rayburn!

She forced her eyes open. She was lying on some kind of table in a room with cinder-block walls painted a dull beige. Her head ached. Squinting, she saw there was a bright lamp directly above her.

She was lying on an operating table!

A tinkling noise caught her attention. She turned her head in the direction of the sound. Dr. Rayburn was busying himself at a stainless-steel portable table.

Nancy's heart lurched. What was he planning?

It took all her energy and willpower to force

her limbs to move. Fighting back a groan, she rolled onto the floor. Her legs were jelly.

"Oh, no, Ms. Drew." Rayburn was beside her in two quick steps, grabbing her arm and helping her to her feet. "You can't leave."

"Where am I?" Nancy's tongue slurred.

"This is the operating room beneath the medical classroom building. It isn't used much anymore except by students, and generally they don't work on live subjects. But every once in a while . . ."

Dr. Rayburn put her back on the table. This time he strapped her down, making certain her hands and feet were securely restrained. "The facilities are still quite good," he went on, "if a bit isolated."

She saw him connect the tubes that were hanging from the wall into a machine near her head. He flicked a switch, and there was a faint hissing sound. Then he turned back to the table, snapping on a pair of plastic gloves. Nancy's head was clearing. She twisted against the leather bands. "People know where I am. You'll never get away with this!"

"Oh, yes. I'm afraid I will." One hand reached for the gas mask attached to the machine.

Anesthesia! Nancy realized in horror.

"I truly am sorry," he said again, advancing on

her with the mask. In his other hand he held a deadly sharp scalpel!

Nancy's terrified gaze fell on the surgical knife. It glinted menacingly in the intense light, poised above her head. In another second Dr. Rayburn was going to operate. On her!

Chapter

Sixteen

NANCY THOUGHT QUICKLY. Her only chance of survival was to stall for time. Ned and Trevor would eventually find her. The two security guards and the pathology man would awaken and sound the alarm. Maybe they already had. Then they would follow the trail she had left.

"April told me you used to work in Saint Louis," Nancy said conversationally, keeping her eyes averted from the knife. She couldn't show fear. She couldn't let him know she was buying time. "You knew David Baines and helped get him expelled from medical school."

Rayburn didn't answer. But he didn't continue either.

"Since I'm going to die, do you mind if I make a few guesses as to what really happened?" asked Nancy.

"I don't have much time, Ms. Drew."

"Anna Treadway, a cardiac patient, died because of gross negligence," Nancy said quickly. "The wrong medicine was prescribed. David was to blame, but he wasn't the only one."

Rayburn shook his head vehemently. "It was David's fault, not mine."

"It *was* your fault. You made a mistake. A big mistake. One that would have justified a malpractice suit and maybe even cost you your license. But you blamed it all on David."

"No." Rayburn was clearly agitated. "That's what Shaw thought, but he couldn't prove it."

His admission made Nancy realize she was on the right track. "Maybe not. But Dr. Shaw knew you were to blame. He worked with you at the hospital in Saint Louis." Nancy paused, playing a hunch. "He'd seen you make mistakes before."

"No!"

"It was his recommendation that got you thrown off the staff there. I saw the name on your Boston medical certificate. It was altered to Rayburn. What's your real name? Rayburne?

You took off the last *e* to keep anyone from digging into those years in Saint Louis!"

Rayburn's face turned deep red. "But you won't be around to prove any of this, will you? It's all allegation!"

"Dr. Shaw had proof that you were tossed out of the Saint Louis hospital. That would have opened an investigation into your qualifications. People would have checked more thoroughly into your background."

Rayburn sucked air through his teeth, clutching the surgical knife in a gloved hand. "Shaw was a meddling old fool. He almost recognized me the night he was brought in. I couldn't take the chance he would remember me. I'd been so careful to change my records. Do you think I could have gotten a job anywhere with that black mark against me? As it was, I had to settle for this mediocre hospital, where one cursory background check was enough to convince them I was an excellent doctor!"

"I would hardly call W.U. Med School a mediocre hospital," Nancy said.

Rayburn snorted in disgust. "Well, it's nothing like where I should be. And I didn't kill Anna Treadway! Baines fouled that up all on his own."

"Baines was doing your job for you. He wasn't even qualified to administer medicine. You told him what to do, then let him take the blame." Nancy regarded him seriously. "But you killed Dr. Shaw yourself."

Rayburn closed his eyes, his lips a thin line. For a moment Nancy wondered if she'd pushed him too far. She tugged against the leather bindings and felt one foot slip loose about an inch. Her pulse leapt. If she could just keep him talking a few more minutes!

"I didn't want to kill Shaw," Rayburn admitted, "but I had to."

"How did you do it?"

"I injected air into one of his veins. It caused an air embolism—a bubble. When the bubble reached his heart he had a massive heart attack. It was quick."

Nancy could scarcely believe her ears. If only she had this confession on tape!

Rayburn waved the scalpel, and Nancy said quickly, "David Baines followed you to River Heights."

"That's right. The little blackmailer!" Rayburn spat viciously. "But he'll pay for that."

"He knew who you were and demanded money in return for his silence. That's how he could afford to buy a Porsche." Nancy twisted her left arm, stealing a quick glance at her wristwatch. How long had she been here? Where was Ned?

"There's one thing I'm curious about: why did you pick Trevor to frame?"

Rayburn sighed. "Poetic justice. He was going to be Shaw's son-in-law. I couldn't believe it when April Shaw—*Shaw's daughter*—was accepted to medical school here. I didn't make the connection for a while. She was just another student. And then I overheard her talking to Trevor one day, telling him she wanted to be as great a doctor as her father. I had to check it out."

Nancy could well imagine Rayburn's panic. "You took Trevor under your wing so you could keep track of what was going on with April."

"It was just possible Shaw would never know about me," Rayburn continued. "But then he came to River Heights and became a cardiac patient. *My* department."

"So you planned to kill him. You used some of Trevor's old standard orders, changed the dates, and stuck the new patients' names on them—effectively ordering the wrong medicine and making it appear as if Trevor had blundered. Under the guise of friendship, you ruined Trevor's reputation so that when Dr. Shaw died, everyone would blame Trevor. Even April."

Rayburn didn't deny it.

"Even worse," Nancy added softly, "you endangered other patients' lives."

"Ms. Drew, you don't understand. We're talking about the end of my career. My life! I would never have been able to start over again. Too many people would know."

Nancy didn't remind him again about the lives he'd jeopardized in his selfish pursuit of personal goals. His hands were shaking violently. He was fast losing control. She couldn't afford to antagonize him further.

"You should have taken my earlier warning to heart," Rayburn said sadly.

Nancy cautiously moved her right foot, trying to wiggle it free of its bonds. "You mean the first time you knocked me out with a hypodermic?"

He nodded. "I put you in the stairwell. I was going to push you down, but unfortunately I could hear other people coming. Then, when you and your boyfriend showed up at the anatomy lab, I knew I had no choice. I was going to have to dispose of you one way or another, but first I had to get Shaw's body out of the hospital. I'd been trying to move him for days, but security was everywhere, searching for him."

"How did you move him from the morgue?" Her right foot was free! Keeping eye contact with Rayburn, Nancy worked on the left.

"That was easy. Those morgue employees are as regular as clockwork. I lifted keys from the attendant, made a duplicate, then waited for Shaw's body to arrive. When the attendant went on his break, it was a simple matter to roll the body out of the morgue and through the tunnel. The pathology personnel barely glanced at me."

"What if you'd met someone in the tunnel?"

Rayburn shook his head. "Let's not think about that unpleasant scenario."

"What made you decide to run down David?" Nancy asked.

"That was your fault. You were getting too close. You were pressuring him. The paramedics had just brought some patients into the emergency room. There was a lot of confusion. The ambulance keys were available, so I took them. I was going to follow David, but then *you* stopped him! Don't you see? I had to run him down." He paused, frowning. "I wish he'd been killed outright. I'm going to take care of him as soon as I'm through with you."

"You can't get away with this," Nancy said calmly. "I talked to David. He mentioned your name in connection with Saint Louis. Security's looking for you already."

Rayburn laughed derisively, as if indulging a dull child. "If that were true, those security men wouldn't have been taken by surprise when I anesthetized them. Soon I'll help them search for the mysterious body snatcher I followed through the tunnel. I suppose that's when we'll—uh—learn of your unfortunate demise, Ms. Drew. Now I think we've talked long enough, don't you?"

Smiling regretfully, he tightened his grip on the scalpel, aiming it at Nancy's throat.

Chapter

Seventeen

Nancy struggled violently, straining at her bonds. Rayburn grabbed her shoulder. The scalpel was poised above her throat. She screamed and bucked. Both feet were free! Swinging her legs, she connected with Rayburn's hand, sending the knife singing through the air. Rayburn howled in surprise. He lunged forward, but Nancy gave him a quick, sharp kick. He spun around.

She jerked her hands furiously, trying to break the leather bindings. Rayburn staggered forward and she kicked out, landing a glancing blow on his left shoulder. His face registered surprise. She twisted her arm, pulling her wrist free, friction burning her skin.

"You can't do this," Rayburn warned.

"Watch me," Nancy muttered through her teeth. She fought to loosen the binding on her other hand, poised to fight off another attack. Rayburn, changing course, turned toward the surgical cart. Out of the corner of her eye Nancy saw him grab another scalpel. With a cry of frustration, she managed to free her other hand, propelling herself off the table at the same time.

Rayburn stuck out his leg, tripping her. Nancy went down and began to crawl frantically forward. He grabbed her leg. She saw the knife slice downward. Twisting, she slammed her foot against his head. The knife hit the floor with a harmless ping.

"You can't—get away—" Rayburn panted.

Nancy was scrambling to her feet, prying his fingers from her leg. Her flailing arm hit the I.V. stand. She pulled it over, slamming it onto Rayburn's back.

Chest heaving, she searched the room for an exit and spotted a pair of swinging doors in the far wall. She ran as fast as she could, slamming against them. Her bones jarred. The doors were locked with dead bolts high out of her reach!

Rayburn's footsteps were right behind her.

Nancy whirled around, her back to the doors, her heart racing.

"I warned you, Ms. Drew," Dr. Rayburn said with a shake of his head. Nancy searched wildly for another avenue of escape.

He stopped a few feet in front of her. "There's no way out," he said, reading her mind.

Think! Nancy willed her brain. Her gaze raked the room. There were weapons galore—every kind of surgical device imaginable. But Rayburn was right; there was no escape.

She crept sideways as he advanced, keeping a small counter between them. The surgical table stood across the room in front of her. Tubes stuck out from the wall and curved snakelike toward the anesthesia machine.

Rayburn stopped, two feet away on the other side of the counter. "I am sorry," he apologized.

"Right," Nancy said. "I can see how sorry you are." She gauged the distance between them. Edging to the right, she watched as he did the same, keeping her trapped behind the counter. He pulled a long rubber tube from his pocket and wound it casually around one hand.

"Strangulation?" Nancy asked, eyeing the tube.

He took a step nearer. Nancy backed up until her heel connected with the wall. Rayburn took a step to the left, watching her closely. Nancy didn't move. He took one more step.

Now! she thought, leaping toward her right. Rayburn lunged forward, his hand narrowly missing her sleeve. Nancy ran to the surgical table. Rayburn's footsteps clattered behind her.

She grabbed the closest anesthetic mask. Rayburn's arm snaked around her waist, yanking her back. Gas was escaping. With all her strength she twisted around, forcing the mask down over Rayburn's face.

He fought like a tiger. His knee connected with the operating table and he stumbled, flailing. Crack! His head hit the floor. He lay dazed.

Nancy strapped the mask to his face, then stepped away from him. She counted the seconds. Fourteen—fifteen—sixteen . . . How long did this anesthetic take to work? Rayburn's head slowly moved back and forth. Twenty-two. Twenty-three—twenty-four . . . Was it seconds or minutes? What kind of anesthetic had she given him? What if it was straight oxygen? She might be helping him more than hindering!

Nancy didn't wait to see. She ran for the door, searching for a stool to stand on.

"Nancy!" a muffled voice called from outside.

"Ned!" she yelled back. "The door's locked. Wait! I'll get it open!"

"Are you all right?" he shouted anxiously.

Nancy spied a small stool and dragged it toward the door. She climbed up on the stool and unlatched the dead bolts. Ned and Trevor stormed in as one. A swarm of security men followed. Seeing them, Nancy slumped against the wall.

"Nancy! Are you all right?" Ned's arms encircled her.

"I am now," she admitted shakily, laying her head on his shoulder.

Trevor was leaning over Rayburn's prone form. "Wow," he said, examining the gas line. "You knocked him out with nitrous oxide. Laughing gas!"

"He knocked himself out. Will he be all right?" Nancy asked anxiously.

"Sure." Trevor chuckled. "We could leave the gas on and give him a nice rest, though. He might be easier to handle."

"Come on," Ned said gently, his arm supporting Nancy's shoulder. "You can tell me all about it on the ride home."

"After we inform the authorities," said Nancy.

"After we inform the authorities," Ned agreed.

"And so that's all there is," Nancy said later that night, seated cross-legged on the Drews' den couch, munching on a sandwich. Ned, Bess,

George, Trevor, and April were in chairs around the room. They all looked at Nancy with wonder.

"I'm so glad you weren't hurt," April murmured, snuggling closer to Trevor. It was clear that the misunderstanding over Suzanne had been resolved. "When Dr. Grafton told me my father had always suspected Dr. Rayburn was to blame for Anna Treadway's death, I got really worried."

"Your father just didn't have proof," Nancy said.

Ned took a bite of his own sandwich, chewing thoughtfully. "When you didn't show up at the emergency room, Trevor and I went down to the pathology lab," he explained. "We found the security men and the lab attendant out cold and the door to the tunnel open. Trevor called for backup, and we started down the tunnel. I saw the piece of coat you left and the name tag, so I knew we were on the right track." He glanced at Nancy's sandwich. "You still owe me a dinner," he remarked teasingly.

Nancy laughed.

Bess's blue eyes were wide circles. "An empty operating room? A crazed doctor? Nancy, it's just like the movie we saw! Creepy!"

"No wimpy heroine, though," George said with a grin.

"He wasn't actually crazed," Nancy corrected.

151

"He just had his priorities confused. He didn't seem to understand the seriousness of his actions. It was Rayburn who took the Deverly file, of course. He was trying to pin all the blame on Trevor, just as he did to David in Saint Louis." Nancy shook her head. "He kept apologizing, hoping I would understand that everything he did was necessary."

Trevor's gray eyes were grateful. "Thanks, Nancy. For everything you've done to help me."

"Help *us*," April corrected.

"How's David?" Nancy asked. "Is he going to be okay?"

Trevor nodded. "He came to while you were fighting it out with Rayburn. He's admitted that he sent you and Ned the fake notes so he could get you out in the parking lot alone. When he grabbed you, he only meant to scare you. Apparently he was afraid you were getting too close to the truth and that you might dry up his blackmail source: Rayburn!" Trevor smiled. "I understand a Detective Ryan is taking his formal statement."

"Detective Ryan!" Nancy laughed. "He'll never forgive me for getting into so much trouble."

"He called to say he's coming by tomorrow," Ned told her. "He wants to hear the whole story from you."

152

"Well, I'm never going near a hospital again," Bess declared. "It's not safe!"

"Oh, I don't know. I'd trust Trevor and April any day," Nancy said, smiling. "How about you, Ned? Have you decided to go into hospital administration?"

He wrapped his arms around Nancy, squeezing her in a bear hug. "This time I have to agree with Bess. I'll stick to plain old business administration. Working at a hospital is more dangerous than being a detective!"

Nancy threw an arm over her eyes in an exaggerated faint. "But you saved me, you strong, handsome male."

"Wimpy heroine," George groaned.

Everyone broke into laughter.

OVER
THE EDGE

Chapter

One

"Nancy, watch where you're going!" With a shudder, Bess Marvin glanced at the waves dashing against the rocks below the cliff road and squeezed her eyes shut. "You're going to get us killed."

Nancy Drew, hands competently gripping the wheel of the rented jeep, shot a quick look at her friend. "Calm down, Bess," she called into the sea breeze that was blowing her hair back from her face into a red-gold halo. "I'm in complete control."

"Yeah, come on, Bess," George Fayne said from the backseat. "Relax." Leaning forward, she touched her cousin Bess's arm. "Open

1

your eyes. The Oregon coast is one of the most beautiful in the world, and you're missing it."

Bess just shook her head and yanked her floppy khaki hat down over her eyes. She slid even lower in her seat. "If we're going to die, I don't want to watch it happening."

"Sometimes I don't understand you," George said, shaking her head. "Only a couple of hours ago we were in a plane that was five miles up in the air. You weren't scared then. But now you're terrified because we happen to be a few hundred feet above the ocean waves."

"And rocks—don't forget the rocks," Nancy teased.

"Stop it, you two," Bess wailed. "You're not being fair. Anyway, a plane's different. You're closed in, in a nice comfy seat, with someone bringing you food—" She paused to sigh, a smile on her face. "That cabin attendant was adorable, wasn't he?"

"Now, that's the Bess I know and love." George grinned.

George caught Nancy's eye in the rearview mirror, and they exchanged knowing smiles. Bess could be on an arctic iceberg and still manage to find a cute guy.

George and Bess were cousins as well as best friends, but they were complete opposites. George had short, curly dark hair, dark eyes, and the long, toned body of an athlete. Bess

2

was blond with a short, curvy body and a two-track mind—boys and food.

"Okay, I'll admit this is a fairly gorgeous place," Bess said, forgetting her fears long enough to raise the brim of her hat and peer around. "But I'll still be glad to get off this road. How much farther to Club High Adventure?" Then she added with a low mutter, "As if we need more adventure after this!"

"Not too far," Nancy assured her.

"Hey," George said, "for a few minutes there I almost forgot we're here on a case." She made a sweeping motion toward the pine- and alder-covered hills that rose sharply to the left of their jeep. "I was only thinking about getting on my hiking boots and tackling these mountains."

Bess glanced at Nancy with a small, worried frown. "Do you think it's going to be a dangerous case?"

"It doesn't sound all that serious. And it'll probably take only a day or two to clear up." Then she laughed. "But how many times have I said that, and then it's turned out to be just the opposite?"

At the age of eighteen, Nancy had established herself as a world-class detective. As the daughter of a well-known criminal attorney, Carson Drew, Nancy received many cases through her father. This one at Club High Adventure was no exception.

Marva Phillips, the daughter of an old college friend of Mr. Drew, had called him about the problems she was having with the club she had inherited at her father's death three years ago. Mr. Drew suggested that Nancy was just the person to help find a solution to the death threats Marva's guests had been receiving.

Although no real attempt had been made against anyone, Marva was afraid that her business would be ruined. On the phone she pointed out to Nancy that there wasn't a guest in the world who would voluntarily visit a resort where there was the possibility of being killed.

Nancy had agreed that the sooner she got to Oregon, the better. So after some hurried packing, Nancy, Bess, and George had boarded a plane to Portland, Oregon.

"Well, I sure hope we can find out who's sending the threats and fast," George said. "That way we'll have time to enjoy ourselves. Just looking at that brochure Marva sent you makes me drool. A resort totally devoted to wilderness sports, like rock climbing and kayaking and spelunking—" She closed her eyes and leaned back. "Now, that's my idea of heaven."

"I'll tell you what activity I think sounds like heaven," Bess piped up, checking her windblown hair with the aid of a pocket mirror.

"The evening barbecues with dancing under the stars." She cocked her head to one side. "Do you suppose they have a cute dancing instructor?" She shook her head at her own question. "Never mind. I'll find someone. Maybe a personal trainer. I'm glad I brought my new striped leotard—"

"I don't mean to interrupt," Nancy said, laughing. "But do either of you see a sign?" Nancy had downshifted and slowed the jeep to almost a crawl. The high hills to their left had fallen off into a thickly wooded ravine. "Marva said there'd be a sign to mark the entrance. But I don't see a space even wide enough to be called a driveway."

As they rounded the next bend, Bess pointed excitedly. The sign read: "Entrance to Club High Adventure." Nancy smiled and turned the jeep onto a narrow lane.

The gravel road climbed through a series of tight turns. Lush walls of overhanging trees on either side almost blocked out the sunlight. At ground level and nearly choking the road, light green ferns mixed with rich, dark rhododendrons, whose branches were almost solid with huge pink flowers. Nancy had to shift the jeep down to first.

"Talk about a wilderness getaway," Bess commented. "I almost expect to see Big Foot jump out from behind a rhododendron."

5

"You never know," George said. "This is the northwest. And if there really is a Big Foot, this is his stomping ground."

"Thanks. I really needed that." Bess groaned at George's joke. "How much farther, Nan?"

"Not too far, I hope. I'm glad we went for the four-wheel drive," Nancy said as their jeep bumped along the narrow gravel road.

"Yeah," George said. "We'd never make it if we'd listened to Bess and rented that red sports—" She broke off as they took the last steep turn. Suddenly they were out of the woods and at the top of the cliff.

Ahead of them lay a gentle sloping meadow, in the middle of which sat a cluster of buildings. Rising behind these were steps of increasingly taller hills, which finally led up to the high coastal mountains.

"That must be the main lodge," Nancy said, stopping the jeep long enough to take in her surroundings. She was pointing to a long, low contemporary structure of redwood and glass that sat at the edge of a sparkling crater lake. There were three small sailboats on the water, tacking into the breeze.

"Hmmm—that looks great," George said, watching the boats. "And it's one sport where I don't need lessons."

"Yeah," said Bess with a snort. "Along with karate, deep-sea diving, bicycling— Hey,

6

check that out," she exclaimed. She was pointing almost directly overhead. "What kind of kite is that? It's huge."

Nancy stopped the jeep. The three girls hopped out and looked up to see a large yellow kitelike object floating above them.

"It isn't a kite, Bess," George said when she got a good look. "It's a hang glider. See, there's the pilot."

The glider had circled so that now they could see a white-helmeted figure hanging below the glider's sail. The pilot was holding onto a bar similar to that on a trapeze.

"That's the control bar," George explained, pointing.

"Now, that's something I'd really like to learn how to do," Nancy said with enthusiasm.

"Definitely," George agreed.

"What's definite," Bess said with a shudder, "is that you two are insane if you want to try anything that dangerous."

"Aw, come on, Bess," George coaxed. "Nothing could be better than flying on your own steam."

"You know what my idea of fun is," Bess retorted. "A pool, a bronzed hunk, and— Hey, that's pretty weird, the way that guy's flying that thing. What's he doing, anyway?"

"I don't know. Maybe some new kind of maneuver." George was frowning.

The glider had stopped making its wide, lazy

circles, and was instead stuttering with short jerks in midair. All at once, the yellow material began to ripple and then flap in the wind, as the glider rocked back and forth.

"Nancy!" George grabbed her friend's arm. "Doesn't it look like that guy's in trouble?"

As she spoke they watched the pilot frantically maneuvering the control bar, first pushing, then—apparently realizing that was the wrong move—pulling it back against himself. As he did, the glider's nose dipped, the flapping stopped, and he appeared to be in control again.

"Whew," George said. "He's okay. Boy, that was scary. For a second I thought he was going to cr—" She stopped talking, mouth open.

The glider had once more come to a shuddering stop. This time, though, before the pilot could do anything, it started to fall, spinning toward the ground just in front of them.

"He *is* crashing!" Bess screamed.

Chapter

Two

WE'D BETTER SEE what we can do to help," Nancy said, already running.

Bess didn't move at first but watched in horror as the glider crashed in a crumple of aluminum tubing and gaily colored material.

Seconds later all three of them had reached the crash site. Nancy was afraid they might be too late to help. The pilot wasn't moving, and the fall had jarred his protective helmet loose. As Nancy knelt beside the still form of the pilot, she saw a spill of shiny auburn hair surrounding the pretty face of the now unconscious young woman.

"That's no guy!" Bess said, stating the obvious. "Do you think she's going to be okay, Nancy?"

"There's no blood that I can see," Nancy said over her shoulder to her friend. "But she's out cold." Nancy ran her hands along the girl's arms and legs. "Nothing seems to be broken. Still, I think you should take the jeep and go for help, George."

"Looks like help's on the way." Shielding her eyes from the glare of the sun, George was looking up the road at a dark green minivan that was barreling toward them.

With a spatter of gravel the minivan skidded to a stop. The driver and his passenger were already out and running before the loosened gravel had a chance to settle back into place. Both were dressed in what Nancy decided must be the club's unisex uniform for staffers: khaki shorts and dark green polo shirts.

As the young female passenger dropped to her knees beside the fallen woman, Nancy recognized her as Marva Phillips—there was no mistaking the elfin face and cap of honey blond hair. She'd seen a photo of Marva in the club's brochure. There'd also been a photo of her companion, from whose tanned features and sun-streaked light brown hair Nancy recognized Marva's assistant, Gil Forrest.

"Oh, no!" Marva cried out as she saw the injured woman's face. "It's Lisa Gregson."

Marva seemed to be speaking to no one in particular as she blurted out, "Is she—is she—"

Nancy started to answer. But before she could, Marva had leapt to her feet and was facing the driver of the van. "What kind of lousy instructor are you, Gil?" she yelled. "This is all your fault. How could you have allowed this to happen? Lisa's hurt—maybe dead." Marva nervously put a hand to her mouth. "Oh, this is awful—just awful."

"She's not dead," Nancy said in a voice loud enough to get the club owner's attention. "But she is injured and could have a concussion. A doctor should examine her as soon as possible."

At that moment Lisa's eyes fluttered open. "Wh-what happened?" she asked weakly. Then her eyes focused and she looked past Nancy to Gil. "I don't understand. Something was wrong with the glider. . . . wouldn't respond to . . ." She winced suddenly, obviously in pain. "Ouch, that hurts," she said after touching the side of her head.

"This young lady's right," Marva said, meaning Nancy. "Lisa should see a doctor. Maybe we should take her to the hospital in Newport."

"No!" At the suggestion Lisa had jerked up to a sitting position. "The last thing I want is to go to any hospital." Gil was supporting

11

Lisa, his arm about her shoulders. "I'm all right," Lisa insisted. "I just have a little headache. That's all."

"Well, if you're sure . . ." Marva appeared to hesitate. "All right. But we're going to call the club doctor and have him check you over, just to be sure. In the meantime, you've got to take it easy." She turned to Gil. "We'll drive her to the infirmary." She paused, then gave a little shake of her head. "Gil, I'm sorry I snapped at you," she said in a lowered voice. "We'll talk about this later."

Gil's reply was a cold shrug as he helped Lisa to her feet.

Marva turned to speak to Nancy. "Thank you for your help." She put out her hand. "I'm Marva Phillips. I own Club High Adventure." She nodded her head in Gil's direction. "And this is my assistant, Gil Forrest."

Nancy smiled. "I'm Nancy Drew, and these are my friends." She introduced Bess and George, then suggested they ride back to the club together. "It would be a good chance for us to talk," Nancy added.

Marva managed a wan smile. "I'm so glad you're all finally here. And, yes, I think it'd be a good idea for us to ride back together." She glanced at Gil. "Can you handle Lisa by yourself?"

"I can manage," Gil answered curtly.

Nancy couldn't help noticing the unhappy

frown that slipped across Marva's face as Gil held his arm longer than necessary around Lisa's waist.

"Oh, Marva." Lisa smiled at her sweetly, then allowed her head to drop weakly on to Gil's shoulder. "Would you mind stopping by my cabin to let my roommates know I'm all right? I was supposed to meet them for lunch. Now that I'm going to the infirmary, I don't want them to worry."

"Sure, Lisa. I'll be happy to do that." Nancy could see Marva was barely able to keep her eyes off Gil as he helped Lisa into the van and went around to the driver's side. Finally, as Gil drove off with Lisa, Marva turned back to Nancy.

"I can't tell you how glad I am to see you," she said again. "Especially after this accident."

"After all the threats, do you think this really was an accident?" Nancy asked as she stepped over to the damaged glider and began to examine it. But since she didn't know much about hang gliders, she wasn't sure what to look for.

"I hate to think it could have been deliberate," Marva said as she watched Nancy. "But it is possible. Lisa *was* the first to receive a threat."

"But it could have been an accident, couldn't it?" Bess had picked up Lisa's helmet and was handing it to Marva.

"Yes, but Lisa's had some experience. And, despite what I said to Gil, he is one of the best hang-gliding instructors around."

"What Lisa said about the glider not responding makes me wonder," Nancy said thoughtfully as she stood back from the glider. "I think you should send someone out to see that no one touches this glider until Gil can look it over. I'd like his opinion on whether or not the glider was sabotaged."

"I'll do that," Marva agreed as the four walked to the jeep and climbed in. "Let me show you to your cabin. We can talk afterward."

Marva directed as Nancy drove. "Take the road that cuts to the left, past the clubhouse," she said as they drove past the main complex.

Gil had parked the minivan and was helping Lisa from the front passenger seat. A crowd of curious guests had gathered.

"I honestly hope she's as fit as she looks," Marva commented drily. "I know it's insensitive of me, but if anything is seriously wrong with her, my insurance could easily be canceled. And her father is the kind of man who would sue me for everything I have."

"What kind of insurance company would cancel a policy because of one accident?" George asked. "That's what insurance companies are for."

"Not when one accident is coupled with

everything else that's been going on here," Marva said. "Oh, Nancy, you've just got to help me. I'm already at my wit's end. And after this"—she gestured to Lisa hanging onto Gil's arm—"I just don't know what to do."

"That's why I'm here," Nancy assured her. "To do whatever I can to find out who's behind these threats. I won't leave until I do."

Marva smiled a little and relaxed enough to point out a tiny flowered meadow and stream where, she said, deer came to drink every evening. Nancy was only a little surprised that Marva could go so quickly from being proud and confident to being on the verge of tears. The threats were clearly taking their toll on her.

They continued on the road several more yards to an area of individual redwood-and-glass cabins, perched in the middle of dense woods but still within a hundred yards of the rocky coastline. Marva directed Nancy to pull up in front of the third one.

"Every cabin has its own special view," she explained as she helped them with their luggage. "Yours looks out over the mountains. The one next to you"—she pointed to a cabin just visible between the trees—"looks onto that deer-grazing area. That's Lisa's cabin. Her roommates are Sara Lakin and Kirsten Peterson. Oh, that reminds me. I'll have to tell them about Lisa as soon as we're finished."

Marva didn't look too eager to break the news to Lisa's roommates about her accident. But she shook herself and tried to smile as she let Nancy, Bess, and George into their cabin.

Inside, the girls' cabin was a subtle combination of luxury and comfort. Two roomy bedrooms, each with its own full bath, opened onto a living room with a cathedral ceiling and stone fireplace.

"This must be the VIP cabin!" Bess exclaimed, dropping her yellow duffel bag on the cream-colored carpet. She plopped down on one of the two turquoise couches that flanked the fireplace. "All I need now is something to eat. It seems like hours since we had breakfast. And with the time change, it's way past our lunchtime."

With the smile of a proud owner, Marva turned to Bess. "There's a minikitchen behind the entertainment wall." She motioned to a freestanding wood-paneled section of wall that held a large TV, VCR, stereo, and enough video and audio cassettes to keep anyone happy for a year. "There's a refrigerator stocked with soft drinks and fruit, and there are plenty of munchies in the cabinets."

"Super!" Bess jumped up. "Anyone besides me want anything?"

"Something tall and cold sounds good," George said.

"Make that two"—Nancy turned to Marva —"three?" Marva nodded. "Would you mind filling us in before you see Lisa's friends?"

"Not at all," Marva said, perching on the arm of one sofa. "The sooner you know all the details, the sooner you can get started."

While Nancy and George sat down on matching armchairs, Bess went into the kitchen. She was back quickly with a tray of sodas and a plate of crackers and cheese.

"When did these death threats start?" Nancy asked, trying to be as gentle as possible. "And how many have there been?"

Marva thought for a moment. "Actually the first one was right after Lisa and her friends arrived. I think hers was the first. At least she was the first person to come to me about it."

"Tell me," Nancy said, "did any of your guests leave suddenly before then? Without explanation? Or did you notice any one of them acting particularly nervous?"

"I really don't remember." Marva nervously ran a slender hand through her short cropped hair. "But I think that's because so many other things were going wrong. Besides, it's not unusual for a guest to leave at a moment's notice. A lot of them are famous or important and their schedules are always changing."

"You mentioned other things going wrong. Like what?" Nancy asked.

17

"Oh, I don't know," Marva answered with a thoughtful frown. "I guess they're just the usual things that only go wrong when you're short of money." Marva ticked them off on her fingers. "The sauna heater went out. A guest left the water running in his tub so that it ruined the entire carpet in one of the cabins. The door to the walk-in freezer broke so that it can't be opened from the inside. The part is on order, but it's taking forever to get here. One of the kitchen help quit because he was accidentally locked inside for a few minutes." She laughed bitterly. "If it's not one thing, it's another."

Nancy nodded sympathetically. "I can see that."

"Also, my financial situation is not that great," Marva went on. "Which is, as I explained on the phone, why I can't call in the police. If anything leaked to the press about the threats, I'd have a hard time getting new customers, or managing to convince the old ones to come back. That would be the end of Club High Adventure."

"I understand," Nancy said reassuringly. "Now tell me about the threatening letters. You mentioned each was different, but maybe there's a pattern."

"If there is, I can't see it. But I have them in my office if you want to take a look." Marva went on, absently picking up her glass and running a finger down the side, making a mark in the frost. "Lisa's was a note. Just three words, written in regular ballpoint pen. 'You will die.' What's so upsetting is that the note was on my personal club stationery."

"How do you think the writer got to your stationery?" Nancy asked. "Do you keep it where a guest or employee could get to it?"

"No. It's expensive. I keep it in my desk drawer."

"So either a guest ran across it while riffling through your desk," Nancy mused, "or an employee knew about it." She shook her head. "Too early to tell."

"Strange," Marva said thoughtfully. "Until now I hadn't considered whether it was a guest or an employee. I guess I didn't want to think about it too hard."

"What about the second one?" Nancy prompted. Bess and George were also listening attentively at this point.

"Sara got that one. A couple of days later. She came back from the club pool and found an eight-by-ten photo of herself taped to the mirror in her bathroom." Marva drew in her breath sharply as she remembered. "Someone must have taken it without her noticing— there was a heavy, black X scratched through her face."

"Oh, that's awful," Bess exclaimed, putting down a bit of cracker and cheese she'd been about to pop in her mouth.

"How about that other girl—Kirsten?" George jumped in with a question. "Did she get one, too?"

Marva nodded. "The very next day. She goes for a long run every morning before breakfast. When she picked up her Walkman one morning she found a strange cassette in it."

Bess leaned forward, eyes wide. "What was on it?"

"The voice was disguised, muffled so it was impossible to tell if it was a man or woman," Marva said. "But the message was clear enough. 'Keep an eye on your friends, or you might find yourself in serious danger.'"

"Wow!" Bess rolled her eyes.

"Hmmm. I think we've got a creative criminal to deal with." Nancy chewed on her lower lip. "You mentioned there were several threats when we talked on the phone. That's only three."

"Yes. The others were mostly notes that turned up in the guest cabins." Marva paused. "Every time the guest who found one swore they'd locked the cabin before leaving."

Nancy nodded, storing away this bit of information.

"Larry Quinn—he's a businessman from

Portland—got the most recent one last night. I didn't see it, though. He just told me about it."

"Wouldn't he show it to you?" George asked.

"He said he threw it away. He thought it was a stupid prank by someone who gets his kicks trying to frighten people. Like someone who makes obscene phone calls."

"That's one possibility," Nancy said.

"Gil agrees with him." Marva glanced down at the third finger of her left hand where a diamond sparkled. "Gil's my fiancé, you know."

Nancy thought that for someone who was engaged, Marva was smiling a little unhappily. She hadn't known Marva and Gil were engaged, but she'd certainly noticed Lisa flirting with Gil.

"Gil sees the threats as just one more thing that's going wrong. He's trying very hard to convince me to sell the club." Suddenly she balled her fists and said firmly, "But I refuse. I won't give up."

Marva stood up. "I really should get going," she said. "I have to get back to work, and before that I have to stop in to see Sara and Kirsten."

"I think I have enough to go on for now," Nancy said.

"Let me know if you need anything," Marva said. She walked across the living room, then stopped at the door. "And Nancy," she said, "thanks for coming."

"You're welcome," Nancy answered. "Don't worry, Marva. We'll catch this person." Marva gave Nancy a hopeful smile and let herself out.

"I like her," Bess said positively, after Marva left. "And I think whoever it is who's leaving those death threats is one true creep."

"It doesn't necessarily have to be a guy," George said.

"Right," Nancy said absently, obviously lost in thought. Setting down her glass, she stood up, suddenly alert. "I'm going to get right to work after I unpack and take a quick shower."

As Nancy stood under the shower's warm spray, she went over what Marva had told her. One fact stood out in her mind—the threats had been left in locked cabins. That, along with the theft of Marva's personal note paper, made Nancy decide to concentrate on the employees first.

After toweling dry, Nancy slipped into a pair of denim shorts and a striped soccer shirt. Then she laced running shoes on her feet. Standing before the mirror, she gave her shining hair a few quick strokes. The first thing to do, she decided, would be to go to Marva's office and check through the personnel records. Perhaps she would find a clue that would help her narrow the possibilities.

Nancy stepped into the living room. There

she found a note Bess and George had left her, explaining they had gone for a short walk to explore the club.

Nancy had just put the note down when a piercing scream came from the woods outside the cabin. A moment later there was a sharp knock on the front door, which burst open before Nancy could get to it.

Marva stood there, her face pale beneath her tan. "Larry—Larry Quinn—there's been an accident. . . ." Her voice shook. "I—I think he may have been killed."

Chapter

Three

QUINN? KILLED?" Nancy quickly stepped to Marva's side and put her hands firmly on Marva's shoulders. "Where is he? What makes you think he's dead?"

"Because he's not moving," Marva cried, fighting back tears. "And he's so pale." She looked frantically at Nancy. "He was hardly even breathing when I left him."

"Where is he?" Nancy tried to get Marva to calm down enough to get some answers. "Where did you leave him?"

"On the cliff trail." She pointed out through the living room's sliding glass door. "There's a trail in back of the cabins that leads to the main complex. Larry was right in front of me. He was walking along, and then the next second he seemed to lose his balance. He fell. He—he hit his head." Marva shook her head, as if to rid herself of the terrible sight.

"Marva, listen to me." Nancy shook Marva by the shoulders. "His injury may not be as bad as you think. In any case, we have to get to him." She looked Marva in the eye. "Pull yourself together and show me where he is."

Marva nodded. "You're—you're right." The color had slowly returned to her cheeks. "I'll show you. Come on." Turning, she sped out the door, Nancy at her heels.

The spot where Marva had left Larry Quinn wasn't far—just beyond Lisa's cabin. Nancy didn't know what she'd find when they got there, but she was glad that help had arrived ahead of them.

Two young men in club uniforms were lifting Larry Quinn onto a stretcher. There were some bruises on his face, and a nasty-looking cut over his left eye was still bleeding. But as he was carried along the trail, Nancy saw that Quinn was breathing easily. It looked as if he'd survive. According to one of the young men, a guest had called for help.

After they'd gone, Nancy saw Marva biting at her upper lip, tears welling up in her eyes.

"Oh, Nancy, I feel horrible about this. *I* should have been the one to get help, not some guest. It was my responsibility." A tear spilled over and slid down her cheek. "I don't know what's happening to me. I'm falling apart. Two near-fatal accidents in the space of a couple of hours. It's too much. The death threats are coming true." She covered her face with her hands.

"Marva, I know how worried you must feel." Nancy put a comforting arm around her shoulders. "But you can't break down now. You have to help me."

"Help—you?" Marva lowered her hands to stare blankly at Nancy. "How?"

"I want to know exactly what happened. You said Quinn was right in front of you, and that he seemed to lose his balance. Do you think he might have tripped on something?"

"Ummmm . . ." Marva frowned, obviously trying to remember the details. "No. It was more like his feet suddenly went out from under him. If it had happened a few feet farther on, he might have gone over the cliff. The trail narrows and it's a straight fall of eight hundred feet. But what I don't understand is why Larry Quinn was on this trail alone. It's clearly marked that no one should take it alone—except staff. It is quite dangerous in spots."

Nancy nodded. While Quinn was being carried away, she had noticed the signs warning guests away from the trail.

"It could be as simple as Quinn losing his balance because of his shoe soles," she told Marva. "Or maybe a pebble slid on the ground. Show me where he fell. I'd like to check out the spot for myself."

Marva pulled herself together enough to point Nancy to a piece of the trail ten feet away. Nancy walked slowly in that direction, her eyes fastened to the ground. It was a dirt trail, solidly packed from people walking over it. Nothing looked suspicious until she reached the place where Quinn had lost his balance. There, the dirt appeared to be loose.

Looking around her, Nancy found what she needed—a stout stick. She began to dig. A few seconds later she looked up at Marva. "I think I've found something."

"What is it?" Marva had joined her and was peering at the hole Nancy had dug. "I don't see anything."

"Here. These three round rocks." Nancy poked at the stones she'd uncovered. "They're not very large, but if I'm right, they were big enough to do the job. I'd guess someone deliberately dug them up, then replaced them and added a thin cover of dirt so that anyone stepping on them would slide just enough to lose their balance." And possibly go right over the cliff, she thought.

"You're saying it definitely was not an accident, then?" Marva turned wide eyes toward Nancy. "Someone was deliberately trying to kill Larry?"

"Well, give him a scare at least," Nancy said cautiously.

"What are you going to do now?" Marva put her hand on Nancy's arm. "You've got to hurry and solve this mystery. All those people who've received threats—their lives are in danger, too."

"I'd like to start by taking a look at the actual notes," Nancy said.

"Good idea," Marva agreed, nodding. She seemed to have finally regained her composure. "Let's head over to my office."

Forty minutes later, Nancy and Marva were sitting in Marva's office. Nancy was sitting on a sofa across from Marva's desk, with the notes scattered around her. She held up the defaced photo of what was probably a pretty Kirsten Peterson and looked at it a last time. Then Nancy got up, picked up the evidence, and set it back down on Marva's desk.

"I thought if I saw these"—she waved a hand at the pile of crumpled notes—"I'd find a lead. But they're not telling me any more than you already have."

After seeing the disappointed look on

Marva's face, Nancy added a hopeful note, "But, look, sometimes I'll see something and not actually realize where it fits in until much later. It was still a good idea for me to go through these." She smiled, trying to give Marva some encouragement.

Marva was about to answer when the door opened and Gil Forrest walked in. After acknowledging Nancy's presence with a quick hello, he turned to Marva.

"Thought you'd be glad to know the doctor's given Lisa a clean bill of health," he said impersonally. "Nothing more than some minor bruises. Apparently the ground was soft enough where she landed, and even though her helmet came off on impact, it did protect her head. But he suggested she stay the night in the infirmary to get some rest."

"That's good to hear," Marva replied, clearly scanning Gil's eyes for some sign of emotion. "I'm relieved Lisa wasn't seriously hurt. But how about Larry Quinn? How's he?"

"Larry?" Gil stared at Marva in confusion. "What about him?"

"He had an accident. He was hurt. Badly." Nancy noticed an edge creeping into Marva's voice. "If you were really at the infirmary, like you said you were, you must have seen him. That's where Josh and Ken took him."

"Well, I didn't *just* come from there," Gil

said, frowning at the way Marva was treating him. "What happened?" He looked from Marva to Nancy.

"Actually, *accident* would be the wrong word to use," Marva went on. "He almost went off the trail."

"There were some loose rocks on the trail," Nancy explained. "He lost his balance, slipped, and hit his head on a rock. That's really all we know right now."

"Just how bad is he?"

"I don't really know," Marva admitted. With a shaking hand she picked up the phone. "I'm not even sure if he got to the infirmary safely. What's wrong with me? I should have called." She punched out the infirmary's number.

"If he's up to it, I'd like to talk to him," Nancy told her.

Marva answered with a quick nod.

Nancy tried to overhear the conversation, but Marva kept her voice low. From what she could tell, however, it didn't look good.

"Well, he's going to be all right," Marva said with a sigh after she had hung up. "But Dr. Hill said it is fairly serious. He wants to take Larry to the hospital in Newport for X rays. And he wants him to spend the night—just in case."

Swiveling in her chair, she faced Nancy. "I'm sorry, but Dr. Hill said Larry wasn't in any shape to talk. Not now. Maybe tomorrow."

"I'm sorry, too," Nancy replied. "He might have been able to give me a clue."

"Clue?" Gil lifted his eyebrows. "Come on, Marva. Aren't you letting this get out of hand? I think you're overreacting. Some jerk with a warped sense of humor sends a few guests fake death threats. Then there're a couple of accidents. And you're building it up into some kind of murder plot."

"Gil!" Marva's voice was shrill, her eyes glittering with the beginnings of real anger. "You don't understand—"

"No!" Gil held up a hand, stopping her. "You don't understand, Marva. Club High Adventure is devoted to risky sports. That's what we're all about, remember? We've had accidents before. And we'll probably have them again."

"I know all that, Gil. And I still say I'm not overreacting. These 'accidents' are different." She leaned forward in her desk chair and stared hard at him. "The problem I see is that you're not reacting at all."

"Marva—" Gil tried a soothing smile.

"Stop that, Gil." She pointed a finger at him. "Stop treating me as if I were one of your pretty little students who can't tell the difference between up and down. What's happening here should be as obvious to you as it is to me—and Nancy." She nodded once in Nancy's direction. "Those threats weren't the work of some sick prankster. They're real." She slapped her desktop with the palm of her hand, sending papers scattering. "Real!"

"Marva, calm down, please," Gil pleaded.

"Oh, you can be so dumb at times, Gil." Glaring at him, Marva cried out, "How many accidents have to happen before you realize that this is serious? There's someone here at the club—right here—who's either trying to destroy me by destroying the club's reputation, or is a homicidal maniac. These accidents—whatever you want to call them—are enough to convince me."

"I—I— Oh, I don't know what to say anymore, Marva," Gil said with resignation. "I think the best thing I can do is leave you alone to cool off. When you want to talk quietly about this, let me know." Turning, Gil stormed out of Marva's office.

"Oh no," Marva moaned. Her fury disappeared when Gil left, and she collapsed back against her chair. "Maybe I should just give up. Do what Gil wants me to do. Sell the club. Perhaps if I went away all this would stop and the guests would be safe."

"Marva, I know you can't mean that," Nancy said gently. "This place *is* you. With you gone, Club High Adventure could never be what you've made it. Giving it up won't accomplish anything—you've got to see this through."

Watching her reaction, Nancy saw Marva's inner strength begin to return. Finally Marva took a deep breath and shook off what was left of her panic.

"Thanks for the pep talk, Nancy," she said. "I guess I needed that. I just wish Gil felt the same way. But in time he'll come around, I'm sure." She straightened in her chair. "I'm making you one promise. No matter what happens, no one will force me out. Not even Gil Forrest!"

Chapter

Four

NANCY SAW by the set of Marva's jaw and the fire in her blue eyes that her resolve was genuine. Nancy decided that with Marva once again in control, it was time to get on with her investigation.

"I'd like to take a look inside Larry Quinn's cabin," she told Marva. "I may be able to find the note he said he threw away."

"Of course," Marva answered. "I'm sure he'd understand. You'll find his cabin on the other side of yours from where Sara and Kirsten's is."

Turning away from her desk, Marva walked

over and opened a wall cabinet. Rows of loose keys hung on individual hooks, with cabin numbers printed above each one. Marva reached in and took a key from the number 8 hook. She frowned slightly. "Strange. There should be two spare keys here, and there's only one."

The small detail didn't escape Nancy's eyes. "Who else might have taken one?" she asked.

"I can't think of anyone." Marva shrugged. "Well, maybe Larry lost his, and Gil gave him the other spare. But normally when that happens, Gil lets me know."

"Um-hmm." Nancy nodded. "But what if our local joker decided he needed to take a look in that cabin as well?" Reaching down, she picked up and pocketed the key Marva had placed on the desk. "If so, I hope he didn't find what he was looking for."

Nancy said goodbye to Marva, who returned determinedly to work. In the hall just outside the office, Nancy found Gil. He was staring moodily out of a window. Nancy paused to talk to him.

"Sorry to disturb your thoughts." Gil jumped at the sound of her voice. "Did you get a chance to check out that damaged glider?" she asked when she had his attention.

"Not yet." He gave her an annoyed scowl.

"If you recall, I had a few things to do, like taking care of Lisa's injuries." Then he hesitated. "I, uh, had some other things to take care of," Gil explained limply. "But don't worry. I'll get to it soon."

"Good." Nancy looked at him evenly. "The sooner, the better," she told him before walking away toward the main door.

Leaving the complex, Nancy headed for the cabin area along the cliff trail. Although the loose rocks had probably been removed by the groundskeeper, she knew that walking the path would give her a better picture of the event.

As she walked, Nancy thought the trail didn't even seem to be that dangerous. It was quite wide where it traced the cliff edge, and there was a retaining wall. The worst the trail could do was scare someone who was afraid of heights.

When Nancy reached the final bend before turning off for Quinn's cabin, she found her way blocked by a large, burly man. He appeared to be in his midfifties, and was obviously in excellent physical condition. He was nearly a head taller than Nancy's five feet, seven inches, and at least a hundred pounds heavier. And all of it muscle, Nancy thought, lifting her face to stare into eyes that glowered back at her.

"Excuse me," she said, attempting to pass.

"What are you doing on this trail?" the man demanded. "Didn't you see the red marker on the tree at the trail head? Guests aren't supposed to use this trail alone. It's too dangerous."

"Sorry, I didn't realize," Nancy said. No use broadcasting who she was. People would find out in their own time.

She noticed the man had on the dark green shirt of a staffer. "Next time I'll make sure I'm not alone," Nancy said placatingly.

Hearing her apology, the man lost his forbidding look. A smile crossed his face. "Just don't want to see any of the guests get hurt unnecessarily." He put out his hand. "My name's Al Hunt, by the way. I'm the rock-climbing instructor. Call me Uncle Al. Everyone else does."

"Okay." She shook his tanned and callused hand. "I'm Nancy Drew. You can call me Nancy."

"Nice to meet you, Nancy." He smoothed his short, graying hair. "I'm sorry for the gruff way I came across just now. Accidents like today's tend to make us a little extra cautious."

"I understand." Nancy smiled back at him.

"Well, I've got to get going. Glad to have you with us." As he started past her, he added,

"Come to one of my classes. You look like the type to enjoy rock climbing."

"Thanks. I'll try to make time," she called after him.

Passing behind Lisa Gregson's cabin a moment later, her thoughts turned to the pretty teenager who had so narrowly escaped serious injury. She wanted to question the girl, but the doctor had ordered her to stay in the infirmary, so Nancy would have to wait until morning. Still, there were Lisa's friends, Sara and Kirsten.

Nancy made a quick decision to put off checking out Quinn's cabin and turned onto the path that led to the front of Sara and Kirsten's cabin.

Nancy's knock was answered by a girl with shiny black hair, cut in a short feathered style that emphasized her deep-set, jade green eyes. Tinted contacts, Nancy observed.

"I'm looking for Sara or Kirsten," she explained after introducing herself.

"Kirsten's not here. I'm Sara." The girl didn't invite Nancy to come in. "I'm just on my way over to the pool to meet someone." She glanced at a slim gold watch on one wrist. "Could you come back later? I really don't want to be late."

A guy, Nancy was willing to bet. With her high-heeled purple sandals, matching lavender string bikini and robe, Sara looked more like she was on her way to meet a date than taking a dip in the pool.

"This won't take long," Nancy promised. "Only a couple of questions. I'm trying to find out more about Lisa's accident. Could you tell me about the threat she got?" Nancy hoped this would stir Sara into asking her inside, but Sara stood her ground.

"Look, I said later, okay?" A slight frown marred Sara's otherwise pretty face. She tapped a polished red nail impatiently against the doorjamb. "I don't have anything to say to you. Nothing that could help. Why don't you wait until you can talk to Lisa? Ask her about it."

Sara pulled the cabin door shut and started to walk past Nancy.

Nancy decided to try another tactic. "Sara," she said, reaching out for the girl as she tried to pass her. "I'm only trying to help. You may think you don't have anything to say that would help me figure out what was really behind the accident, but you might be surprised. If we could just go inside, sit down for a few minutes—"

"Look. You don't know Lisa Gregson. I do." Sara yanked her arm free. "That crash was no accident." She started down the cabin's stairs, leaving Nancy standing there.

Nancy watched the girl as she took the steps

awkwardly and stumbled along the redwood-chip path in her high heels.

Sara Lakin is completely out of her element here at Club High Adventure, Nancy thought as she made her way in the opposite direction toward Quinn's cabin. I bet she'd prefer being at a luxury resort having her nails wrapped and going to parties. So what is she really doing here? Nancy stored the question away with the other pieces of the puzzle she'd collected so far.

Using the key Marva had given her, Nancy let herself into Quinn's cabin. It was similar to hers, except here the color scheme was earth tones, browns and dark greens accented with cream-colored couches and chairs. The living room was neat. A half-filled coffee cup on the counter of the tiny kitchen was the only clutter.

The bedroom was also tidy, except for the unmade bed. A gray suitcase sat squarely on the luggage rack. Through the open door of the bathroom, Nancy could see an organized array of toiletries.

There was nothing there to show that Larry Quinn's behavior in the past few hours had been anything but that of a normal guest. And to Nancy's practiced eye, it was fairly certain that no one else had searched the cabin before she'd arrived.

Especially since this is still here, she thought excitedly, bending to retrieve a wadded piece of paper from the wastebasket beside the dresser.

After smoothing the crumpled sheet of yellow lined paper, she read the message. It was in block letters, written with blue ballpoint pen. "Leave the club today and you'll live. Stay and you'll die."

Whoever was behind this wasn't beating around the bush, Nancy thought as she folded the paper, stuffed it into a pocket of her shorts, and returned to the living room.

Taking one last look around, she pushed open the sliding glass door to the sun deck and stepped out.

Unlike the cabin she shared with Bess and George, this one backed up to a rocky cliff. The far end of the sun deck was supported by long wooden stilts buried into the cliff face. Nancy relaxed for a moment. Taking a deep breath of the tangy salt air, Nancy walked to the railing and leaned against it, letting the sun warm her head.

Far below, sea lions basked on the offshore rocks. Overhead, sea gulls swooped and called to one another in a chorus of noisy screeches.

Closing her eyes, Nancy tilted her face up, warming it in the sun. Club High Adventure could be a very appealing vacation spot, she thought.

As Nancy was basking in the sun, something hit her, hard, against her back.

Nancy's eyes flew open. She felt herself being lifted up and over the side of the deck! She was falling, spread-eagle, with nothing between her and the sharp rocks forty feet below!

Chapter

Five

TUCKING HER KNEES into her chest, Nancy
did a tight roll and threw her arms straight up
over her head. Clawing with her right hand,
she reached out and closed her fingers around
one of the upright bars supporting the railing.
She tried not to look down at the waves
crashing below her.

Tears sprang to her eyes as her shoulder was
wrenched from the bone-jarring stop she'd
made. But she hung on and swung like a
pendulum from her right hand.

She was safe for the moment. She tried to
catch her breath, but how long could she hold
on before her fingers and shoulder gave out?

Even worse, wouldn't the person who had to have shoved her try to finish her off?

Nancy listened for footsteps on the deck above, but none sounded. Nancy's shoulder was hot with pain.

She thought for an instant about calling for help, but knew that any cries of hers would be lost in the screeching of the gulls. Their noise must have prevented her from hearing her attacker approach.

She was hanging facing away from the house. Quickly, before she could consider the additional pain, she threw her body to the left and grabbed another upright support with her left hand.

It was now a simple matter of inching up, hand over hand, until she reached the top rail.

Nancy used all of her strength to pull her body upward with her left arm until she could grab for the next higher bar. Before she could lose her momentum, Nancy grabbed for the top and last bar with her right hand.

With a final heave, Nancy shimmied up and over the railing and finally collapsed onto the deck. Except for the throbbing in her shoulder, she knew she was okay.

Nancy's instincts told her that the time it had taken to pull herself back up had also given her attacker the chance he, or she, needed to escape. Still, Nancy searched the cabin—just in case. Picking up the poker from the fireplace for protection, she crept through the rooms, looking behind every door and in the shower. The cabin was empty.

More determined than ever to get to the bottom of the mystery, Nancy hurried back to her own cabin. Her "accident" had left her aching and disheveled. She wanted to clean up and change into fresh clothes.

Bess and George were there to greet her. Bess had been to the pool and was now wrapped in a yellow terry robe, toweling her hair dry.

Looking up and seeing Nancy come through the door, she stopped drying her hair and rushed to her. "Nancy," she cried. "What happened? You're a wreck."

"I'll second that," George added from the doorway of their shared bedroom. "Looks like you were on the wrong end of an argument."

"Yeah, I never got a word in," Nancy joked grimly. Flopping down on one of the couches, she told them what had happened. "Of course I didn't get a look at who pushed me," she finished.

George shuddered. "I could have been walking right by there when it was happening. I got back from a hike along the trails only a few minutes ago."

"Did you see anyone on the path in front of Quinn's cabin? Anyone at all?" Nancy asked.

"Nope. Only a couple so wrapped up in each

other that they practically bumped into me before I could get out of their way." George shook her head. "No one else."

"Probably whoever it was slipped through the trees, instead of using the path. Someone who knows his way around very well."

"Does that mean you've already got some idea who's behind all this?" Bess asked expectantly.

"Just the start of a theory," Nancy replied. "But it's a long way from being complete. Right now, we don't really know anything definite about what happened to Lisa Gregson or Larry Quinn."

"What's the plan?" George asked. "What do you want us to do?"

"Nothing right now, George. What I have to do next, I have to do alone."

"Well, if you're not going to let us in on your plan, at least be careful," Bess admonished.

"Yes, Nan, watch yourself," George echoed her cousin's concern. "Whoever is making the threats must know you're here to investigate. He already tried to kill you once, and he's sure to try again."

"I know," Nancy said, her blue eyes serious. "And, believe me, I don't intend to be such an easy target again."

Because it was getting late, Nancy changed her mind about showering and putting on fresh clothes. She took only enough time to go into the bathroom and wash her hands and face.

A few minutes later, after knocking to make sure no one was in Lisa, Kirsten, and Sara's cabin, she deftly picked the lock on their door, and slipped inside.

Remembering Sara's outburst that "the accident was no accident," Nancy wanted to find out more about the girl.

It wasn't difficult figuring out which bedroom belonged to Lisa Gregson. A gold necklace with her first name etched on its pendant was tossed on the dresser. Stuck into the edge of the dresser mirror was a color snapshot of Lisa and a good-looking boy, who would have looked even better if he hadn't been scowling into the camera lens.

Nancy pulled open each of the three drawers in the dresser and found only piles of expensive clothes jammed in every which way. Apparently, Lisa came from a wealthy family and had absolutely no respect for the designer fashions she was able to afford.

Finally, in a drawer of the bedside table Nancy hit pay dirt. She found a half-finished letter, dated the night before. Nancy scanned it.

My adorable Roy,
I can't tell you how much I miss you. I have your picture where I can look at it

constantly. I wish I could reach out and touch you as easily as I touch the photo. I hate my father for making me stop seeing you. He just doesn't understand how it is with us. He never will. I just know it. But I have a plan that is going to make him sorry—really sorry.

The letter ended there. Nancy replaced it carefully. Searching further, she discovered a clipping and a picture from a newspaper. She picked it up to look at it closely.

The photo was blurred, but Nancy was fairly certain the girl in it was Lisa. She was handcuffed to a police officer, as was a boy. Even though he had his free hand over his face, Nancy recognized the boy from the other photo. He and Lisa were about to step into a police cruiser.

The caption under the photo read, "Lisa Gregson, daughter of prominent real estate businessman Greg Gregson, was arrested for shoplifting today. This is the second time in three months for Miss Gregson."

It looked like Lisa didn't lead a typical teenage life, Nancy thought, tapping a finger against the worn edge of the clipping. Could she be the one behind the threats? What did she mean about making her father sorry? Could the letter to her boyfriend mean that the accident that day—

A noise interrupted her thoughts. It was the faint sound of a key being turned in the front door. Either Sara or Kirsten had come back to the cabin. Nancy was about to be caught breaking and entering.

Trying not to make any noise, Nancy placed the clipping back into the drawer, then slid it shut. She glanced around, looking for a way out.

The window—but it was too high and too small.

Nancy looked desperately for another escape route. She was about to slip out of Lisa's room when she heard the front door open. Footsteps crossed the entry and were heading her way.

Nancy was trapped.

Chapter

Six

So what did you do?" Bess asked, eagerly leaning forward across the dining table. She kept her voice low so the other guests wouldn't hear.

"Yes, how did you escape without being found out?" George added quietly.

Nancy stopped buttering a roll to answer. "I'd figured out Lisa didn't share a bedroom. So it was pretty good odds that whoever was in the living room wouldn't come into Lisa's room. So I just hid in the closet, and when I heard the other bedroom door close I sneaked out and left the cabin by the front door."

"You've got guts." Bess speared a cherry tomato, dipped it in dressing, and popped it into her mouth. "It's a good thing you're the detective, and not me. I would've panicked and tried to think up some unbelievable story for her roommate. Guess I don't have the stomach to be an investigator."

"No, your stomach is too busy consuming food," George teased her cousin.

"And is this food good," Bess answered, not at all bothered by George's remark. "As far as I'm concerned, Nan, we can take forever to solve this case. When I'm not working, I'll lie around the pool and eat."

"And get fat," George added under her breath. "Maybe you should consider doing a little jogging."

"Uh-uh." Bess shook her head. "You know jogging's not my thing. But maybe a little after-dinner dancing might be beneficial." She smiled at the retreating figure of a six-foot-tall hunk who had just passed their table.

"Back to the case," George said in a low tone, looking around to make sure there was no possibility of being overheard. "Do you really think it could be Lisa Gregson who's behind all this?"

"I'll say this much." Nancy took a sip of her ice water. "I consider her a definite suspect. She's a girl who's apparently desperate for attention. And desperate people do desperate things."

"But hold on," George argued. "Unless she had an accomplice, how could she have been in Quinn's cabin, pushing you over the railing, and be in the infirmary at the same time?"

"That occurred to me," Nancy replied. "I called the infirmary before dinner. No one was there, except Lisa, during that time. Even the nurse had stepped out for a little while. So Lisa doesn't have an alibi. She could easily have left, gone to Quinn's cabin, and returned without being seen. Especially if she went through the woods."

"But what about Lisa's accident?" Bess asked. "I can't believe anyone would stage an accident like that on purpose. She could have been killed."

"We still don't know if the glider was tampered with," Nancy said with a shrug. "Lisa has had some experience with hang gliding. So it's possible she could fake a problem that only *looked* dangerous." Nancy reached for the salt.

"Anyway," she went on, "I'll know more tomorrow. On my way over here tonight, I stopped and signed up for a hang-gliding lesson early in the morning. I'll talk to Gil Forrest about the damaged glider then, too. He should have had time to check it out."

"I should take the class with you," George suggested. "I could keep my eye on Gil."

"I've already signed you up," Nancy answered her friend with a grin.

"Well, that's fine for you guys. But I'm going to stay on the ground where it's safe," Bess said. "Now, for tonight, I want to stop thinking about the case and start dancing."

Bess shoved her chair back and stood up. "I think I see my partner now," she said mischievously.

Early the next morning Nancy and George were standing, along with five other students, at the top of a gentle slope at the far end of a meadow. Gil Forrest was talking to them, a row of gliders behind them. Their multicolored sails were bright against the green grass.

The students all wore standard orange jumpsuits. Nancy cradled her helmet in her arms as she listened to Gil introduce them to the sport of hang gliding.

"First, let me assure you that there is nothing complicated about this sport. There are successful twelve-year-old hang-glider pilots. And good gliders don't have to have a lot of strength." Gil glanced in the direction of one of the more petite students.

"But the wings," the petite student spoke up. "They're so huge. How are we supposed to carry those things?"

Gil grinned at her. "The ground maneuvering of what is essentially a large kite—with about a twenty-two-foot wing span for women, and a twenty-six-foot span for guys—can be a bit of *fun* to get used to at first." There were a couple of groans. "But, I promise"—Gil held up a hand—"it's easier than you'd believe. And once you're in the air, you'll be very glad you have all that sail to play with."

"You just said the magic word," a good-looking blond guy yelled out. "When do we get to do that? Go into the air? I thought you had to jump off a cliff, or something. But I don't see one around here."

"Whoa!" Gil smiled. "We're not going to do any jumping off cliffs for a while. You'll need a few lessons under your belt before you tackle that sort of thing."

"Then what do we do?" the blond guy yelled back with a grin. "Just run and jump into the air and hope we take off?"

"You've got it," Gil told him and grinned back. "And since you're so smart, I'm going to let you go first. Come up here with me and we'll get this harness on you."

There was some easy laughter as the boy swaggered boldly up to Gil. "What's your name?" Gil asked.

"Drake Reynolds."

"All right. And thanks for volunteering, Drake." There was another ripple of laughter before Gil went on. "Now, remember, there's nothing difficult about this sport. There aren't many rules. But you want to avoid breaking any of them—"

"Because then you'll crash," a student at the edge of the group interrupted. "Just like Lisa Gregson did, right?"

"We don't know what happened with Lisa," Gil replied in a subdued tone. Nancy noticed a muscle twitch at the corner of the instructor's mouth. Then he recovered smoothly. "But you're right," Gil said. "Ignore the rules, and you *will* find yourself in trouble."

Gil began helping Drake into a harness made of the nylon webbing Nancy recognized as being similar to those used by parachute jumpers.

"One of the first rules," Gil was saying, "is to make sure your equipment—both your harness and glider—are in good condition."

Nancy watched and wondered if Lisa had thought about this before she'd taken off on her last flight.

"Now let's talk about getting off the ground," Gil said. "What makes the glider sail like it does is the wind. When the air flows over the top of the wing surface, the sail creates a vacuum. The air flowing under the wing pushes the glider up as it tries to fill that vacuum."

"That's interesting," George said to Nancy. "I'm going to remember that when we fly back home."

"And the glider is constructed," Gil continued, "so that you can get into the air with minimal wind speed. You're going to be doing just what the Wright brothers did when they first began playing with the idea of flight.

"After you've put on your harnesses and attached yourself to your gliders, you're going to run down this slope and allow the wind to pull you up into the air. You won't be that far off the ground this first time, but it'll seem high enough for most of you." He patted Drake's shoulder. "Even for you, I bet."

"I'm ready." Drake raised a fist into the air. "Let's go for it!"

"All right. Let's go over and hook you up." Gil led Drake and the others to the waiting gliders.

When they had regrouped, Gil went on. "Now to learn how to stay up when you want to stay up. It has to do with the way you maneuver your glider." He put his hand on a large triangle of aluminum tubing fixed to the bottom of the glider. "This is your control bar. Push it forward and the nose lifts, pull it back and the tail lifts, shoving the nose down—"

"Why would you want to push the nose down?" someone asked. "I thought you wanted to stay up."

"Give me a second more and I'll explain why," Gil said. "Remember that wind that is keeping you aloft? Well, if you tilt your nose up too far your glider will stall. In order to get that airflow back, you'll have to tilt your glider's nose down." He paused. "Ignore that rule, and you'll drop like a rock."

"Oh, boy," the small girl spoke. "That does it for me. I've decided to skip this sport." She sat down cross-legged on the grass. "You guys go on without me. I'm sticking to commercial jets."

"That's all right, Vicki," Gil said. "This sport's not for everyone. Anyone else who wants to drop out, please do. Don't feel as if you have to prove something by staying in." He waited, but no one else said anything.

"Okay, we're almost finished." Gil nodded. "You land by using the stall. But you do it only when you get close to the ground. You don't want to crash, you want to land. Simply glide down to the ground, pull your nose up at the proper moment, and there you are—back on good old solid earth."

At the end of her first hour of practice, Nancy discovered she had a real knack for hang gliding. It had taken her only a couple of false starts before she managed to maintain a short but successful flight. She was even able to make simple right and left turns by shifting her body as it hung in a free position in the harness.

"I really love this sport," she told Gil as she slid out of her jumpsuit. "I guess it's about as close as you can get to feeling like a bird."

"Yes—free." Gil agreed with her, and Nancy felt she was in touch with the real Gil—the man Marva loved. "I love it, too." He took the jumpsuit and helmet from her. "You really should keep taking lessons after you go back home. Maybe join a club."

"I think I'll do that—"

"Hey, Nan." George had hurried up and was interrupting. "I don't mean to rush you, but if we're going to make that rock-climbing class at Devil's Rock, we'd better get a move on."

"Okay," Nancy said, lacing up her last hiking boot. "We'd better go." She looked up at Gil. "I wanted to talk to you about the damaged glider. Did you have a chance to go over it?"

"I did. But what I found has me a little puzzled. I can show you now, if you want. Then I can drop you off at Devil's Rock."

The three of them piled into the club van and soon pulled up in front of a utilitarian-looking building behind the main complex.

"So this is all that was wrong?" Nancy asked, running her hand over the small bend in the frame of Lisa's glider. "I would have expected more."

"The thick grass absorbed most of the shock of the landing. There's only that slight damage in the tubing of the leading edge—where you're feeling now." He shook his head. "What disturbs me is that there shouldn't be any bends there at all. The glider came down on its keel, the other end."

"You think this was done deliberately?" Nancy asked, pointing to the broken spot.

"Well, I can't say for sure." He ran a thumb thoughtfully down the side of his face. "But it's possible. And whoever did it knew what he, or she, was doing. Because there's just enough damage to affect the control but not enough that an experienced pilot would have too much difficulty saving himself." He paused. "Or herself. Remember, Lisa Gregson's logged a lot of time hang gliding."

"Right." Nancy nodded thoughtfully. Then, shaking her head, she said, "I guess we'd better get going."

Back in the van, Gil headed for the foot of the mountains. "That's Devil's Rock," he said, taking one hand off the wheel to point. "Over there."

"I can see how it got its name," George said, peering through the windshield.

Half a mile ahead of them a four-hundred-foot-high dome-shaped rock loomed bare against the dense forest of the mountains behind it. Natural ledges on the otherwise sheer granite front formed an evil-looking devil mask.

"It looks like a dangerous climb," Nancy commented.

"Well, it can be. But any serious climb has its dangers."

"It doesn't scare me," George said bravely.

"Here we are." Gil slowed the van to a stop. "This is as close as we can get by road. That trail over there will take you up the side to the top. Normally the class meets down here, then goes up together. You're a few minutes late, so they've probably gone on ahead."

"We're both in good shape," Nancy said as she pushed down on the door handle. "I don't think it'll take us long to catch up."

"Hope you enjoy the class." Gil leaned over to pull the door shut after they got out. "Uncle Al is a good instructor. He'll teach you everything there is about rock climbing."

With a wave at the departing van, Nancy and George turned and started up the trail. The climb was steep and after several minutes the two had to pause to catch their breath.

"So, what do you think?" George asked, leaning back against a warm rock. "Do you think Lisa could have sabotaged her own glider?"

"It looks bad for her, doesn't it?" Nancy remarked, bending down to tighten the laces on her hiking boots. "But the glider could have gotten that small dent another way, too. Maybe when it was loaded into the van, or taken out. Lisa could have forgotten her preflight check." She straightened up. "It was pretty tough to spot. Gil had to show me where it was."

"I don't know," George argued. "I say Lisa did it herself, to get attention."

"But we need some hard evidence before we decide," Nancy replied. She reached over to pat George on the arm. "If you've got your breath, let's go. We have another lesson before the day's over."

George laughed and took the lead. "Right, boss," she said.

After ten minutes of rough climbing, Nancy and George reached the top. When they got there, they found a class of eight students grouped about Uncle Al, the bear of a man Nancy remembered from the day before.

They were standing on the top of Devil's Rock in the middle of an open area, about the size of a basketball court. All around them was a panorama of ocean, mountains, and forest.

Uncle Al was demonstrating the various types of knots used by rock climbers. As Nancy and George quietly took their places at the back of the group, Nancy noticed the instructor didn't have everyone's attention. A couple of guys were punching each other good-naturedly, obviously enjoying some private joke.

"They'd better cut that out," George whispered to Nancy. "If Uncle Al were glaring at me the way he is at those two, I'd be shaking in my boots."

"I don't blame him," Nancy muttered. "This isn't exactly the safest place in the world to horse around."

Uncle Al had stopped his demonstration in midsentence.

Flinging away the rope he'd been using, he stared openly at the two guys. Then without warning he lunged at them, startling Nancy and the others.

Still moving, Uncle Al reached out a muscular arm and grabbed at the nearer, and smaller, of the two. The short guy nimbly stepped aside, and Uncle Al's elbow caught the bigger boy in the shoulder. Al's blow sent him way off balance.

A girl screamed, and Nancy and George watched, horrified, as the beefy teenager lost his footing, teetered, and flapped his arms. Almost in slow motion, the boy started to fall backward over the edge of Devil's Rock!

Chapter

Seven

PUMPING HIS MUSCULAR ARMS, the boy managed to throw his weight forward and land sprawled on his stomach across the hard rock surface. He was breathing in ragged gasps, and Nancy saw the color had drained from his face, leaving it a pasty gray.

From the student, Nancy looked to where Al Hunt stood, also breathing hard. He kept staring at the boy until he was sure he was all right. Was that a look of fear Nancy saw in Al's eyes? He must have realized that he had overreacted and that his mistake could have been fatal.

With a shake of his bearlike shoulders, Uncle Al pulled himself together. Walking over to where the student was sitting, the instructor held out his hand.

"Sorry, son," he apologized in a controlled voice, as he helped the boy get up. "Didn't mean to be quite so physical there." He paused. "But it looked like you two were headed for danger. The top of this rock is slippery and it's no place for anyone to act like a six-year-old."

The young man was on his feet now, looking both embarrassed and angry. "We weren't doing anything wrong," he mumbled.

"Well," Uncle Al answered, "I don't take kindly to students who don't pay attention when I'm trying to teach them something that might just save their lives." He had turned his attention from the boy and was talking to the entire group.

"Okay, okay." Nancy saw the student's face had gone from white to red and his eyes were narrowing in anger. He looked as if he was more than ready to lose his temper over being made an example for the rest of the class. "I get the message. You want our undivided attention. You got it, *Uncle* Al."

"Cool it, Ron," his friend advised, seeing how upset he was. He put a hand on the young man's arm. "The guy's just doing his job. Why don't we just sit down and let him do it."

Al had picked up the demonstration rope and was explaining the fundamentals of rappelling. The two young men sat down on a rock outcropping near where Nancy and George were standing.

Despite Al's warning, Nancy found herself listening to their whispered conversation rather than paying attention to the demonstration.

"I don't think that old guy's playing with a full deck," Ron growled. "That was a really crazy thing he pulled on us. He could just as easily have pushed me over as kept me from falling."

"Drop it, will you." His friend was starting to sound annoyed. "It's over. Your problem is that it's just beginning to dawn on you what a jerk you made of yourself in front of everyone."

Ron folded his large forearms across his chest. "Not everyone," he said.

"You bet," his friend answered. "Especially Vicki Kirk. Look—forget it, and she'll forget it. Keep it up, and she'll really know you're a jerk. Take it from me."

"Well . . ." Ron hesitated. "Okay, maybe you're right." Nancy was relieved when the two finally fell silent and turned their attention back to Al, who was beginning to notice their chatter again.

Still, Nancy could hardly wait for the lesson

to be over so she could talk to George about Al's tantrum. It seemed out of character to her.

After an hour of practice in the basic rock-climbing techniques, the class started back down the trail. Nancy and George hung back to bring up the rear. With no one to overhear them, Nancy voiced her concern about Al's strange behavior.

"That really was crazy, the way he acted with those two guys," Nancy said.

"Maybe he's just nervous and jumpy because of what's been happening lately," George suggested.

"Or maybe there's some other reason," Nancy said, frowning.

"Are you adding him to your suspect list?" George asked.

Nancy slowed down to negotiate a steep part of the trail. "I don't think there's any connection between him and Lisa Gregson," she said, holding on to a thin pine tree for support.

"I don't see one either," George admitted.

They had reached a plateau where both girls stopped to take in the view. Nancy's mind turned back to the case.

"But we don't know for sure yet," she said.

"What's the next move?" George asked as they continued down the trail.

"A soda," Nancy laughed. "After all these lessons, I'm thirsty."

"Sounds good to me," George answered. "And I'll bet we find Bess waiting for us."

The two girls made their way back to the main complex and out onto the club's terrace café. Sure enough, Bess was there.

"You never quit, do you?" George asked as she sat down. Just before Nancy and George arrived, Bess had been saying a cheerful good-bye to yet another six feet two of tanned muscle.

"Actually," Bess said, pouting, "I was working on the case. Jed—that's his name—was telling me that Gil and Marva have been having problems for a long time now."

"What kind of problems?" Nancy asked, after she gave the waitress her order. "I know they've been under a lot of pressure lately, what with everything that's been going on at the club."

"Yeah, Bess," George added. "I'll bet that's what Jed, or whatever his name is, meant."

"No, it wasn't," Bess insisted. "I know because I asked him how long it'd been going on. He's known Gil for a while. He said Gil and Marva have always had problems. We even laughed and talked about how for some people that's what a relationship is all about." Bess smiled, obviously going over the conversation again in her head.

George and Nancy exchanged a look. Nancy

didn't think Bess's news was all that significant or important to the case. Except, she thought, that it might give Gil a motive.

Nancy got up. "Sorry, guys, but I have to get going."

"What's up?" George asked.

"I want to go over the employee files before lunch," Nancy said. "I have a feeling I'll find something in there that'll give us a few more pieces to the puzzle."

"You sure you don't want us to come along?" Bess asked halfheartedly.

"No, Bess," Nancy laughed. "You keep asking Jed those questions. Let me know if you find out anything else."

George chuckled. "Since you don't need us, I think I'll take a swim. It's getting hot."

Nancy and George left Bess in the café, and strolled over behind the back of the main complex to where the swimming pools were. They split up, George heading over to the Olympic-size pool, Nancy walking down a short path to the complex's back entrance.

Opening a screen door, Nancy found she was in a long hall, off of which several doors opened into what must have been offices and storage areas.

She had gone no more than a few steps when she heard the sound of angry voices drifting out of one of the rooms. She was sure it was

Gil and Marva, and it sounded as if they were having some sort of lovers' quarrel.

Nancy thought she should turn around and leave quietly so they wouldn't think she'd been eavesdropping, but something about the desperate tone of Marva's voice made her stay in the hall. As their voices grew louder, Nancy inched closer to where they were coming from.

"No, Gil, I won't do it. I won't, I tell you—never." The pitch of Marva's voice rose higher and higher until she sounded hysterical. "Not for you, *not for anyone!*"

"You've got no choice, Marva," Gil answered in cold fury. "You should do what I'm telling you to. Sell the club. Sell it, or I'll—"

"Do what?" Marva screamed back.

For a long moment the only sound that reached Nancy's ears was that of ragged breathing from the other side of the partially open door.

Then Nancy heard Gil and Marva scuffling, followed by a barely stifled sob from Marva.

Nancy was about to burst in on them when she heard Gil's voice raised in anger.

"I won't take much more of this, Marva," Gil cried out.

Marva's only response was another racking sob.

"Sometimes I could just kill you!" Gil shouted.

Chapter

Eight

NANCY STARTED to rush inside when Gil came storming out, almost knocking Nancy down. After giving her an icy look, Gil marched off.

"Marva?" Nancy turned from Gil to peek into the room. "Are you okay?" she asked.

Marva glanced around, startled. "Oh, Nancy." She began to cry all over again.

"I'm sorry, Marva," Nancy said, trying to console her. "I'm sure he didn't mean it."

Marva wiped the tears from her cheeks, then seemed to pull herself together. "You heard?"

Nancy explained that she was on her way to

find her when she overheard their fight. "I almost left but stayed because I got worried."

"It's okay." Marva sighed. "I'm sorry you had to hear the stupid way we were both acting." She made a disgusted face, then she looked over Nancy's head, unable to meet her eyes. "We're both under a lot of strain," she said hesitantly.

"I know you are," Nancy answered kindly.

"Gil really has my best interests at heart," Marva said, trying to smooth over the fight. "He's so worried about me that he ends up yelling." She gave Nancy an unhappy little smile. "Gil loves me, and I love him. That's really the bottom line," she said as they walked from the room into the hall.

Marva stopped and turned to Nancy. "You were looking for me?" she asked. "For a minute there, I was so wrapped up in my own problems that I wasn't thinking. Did you need something?"

"Actually I was on my way to your office. I was planning to spend a little time going over your employee records." She glanced down the hall toward the kitchen, where the staff was busy getting ready to serve the noon meal. "But I didn't realize how late it was getting. I suppose it can wait until after lunch."

"I'll be in my office," Marva said. "And thanks for looking out for me," she added. "I can't tell you how much I appreciate what you're doing."

"All in a day's work," Nancy joked as she and Marva parted.

Before returning to her cabin Nancy made a quick detour to the infirmary. She wanted to check on Lisa, but she learned from the nurse that Lisa had been dismissed a couple of hours earlier. Nancy used the phone there to place a call to the hospital to find out about Larry Quinn's condition. It was worse than she had expected—during the night Quinn had slipped into a coma.

Back at her cabin, Nancy worried about how serious the case had gotten. Quinn in a coma, Marva and Gil fighting, and still no clues about who could be responsible for terrorizing Club High Adventure. Without a lead, Nancy couldn't prevent worse things from happening.

While she was changing into white cotton slacks and a red knit shirt, Nancy heard Bess and George return. She went out into the living room to greet them. Maybe if she talked out the case with them, they'd see something she'd missed.

George ran past Nancy into the bedroom. "I'll just be a minute," she said to Nancy. "Can you wait for me to change?" Nancy nodded. Bess, looking fresh and pretty, poked her head into the living room. "You want a soda?" she asked.

"Sounds good," Nancy answered distractedly, curling up on one of the couches.

"Well, now I know everything there is to know about kayaking," Bess announced as she handed Nancy her drink. She plopped back on the other couch. "Jed told me all about it, and I positively love it. It's a super sport."

George stepped out into the living room, wearing red running shorts and a striped yellow-and-blue rugby shirt. "What's up, Nan?" she asked. "You look preoccupied."

"I was thinking about the case," Nancy answered. "There's so much that doesn't add up."

"Like that business up on Devil's Rock, you mean?" George asked.

"How about filling me in?" Bess said. "What about Devil's Rock, wherever that is?"

Nancy realized she hadn't told Bess earlier about their morning's activities. She went over what had happened, ending with the incident with Uncle Al and the two students.

"Wild!" Bess's eyes went wide. "This Uncle Al sounds crazy to me. What do you think, Nan? Do you think he could be the one behind the threats? I mean anyone sending those notes has got to be a little crazy."

"I don't think the man's insane, Bess," Nancy said. "I do think he did overreact to those two guys fooling around. That doesn't make him crazy. Besides, what motive could

73

he have that would make him send threats to the guests?"

"Okay, then we're back to Lisa." Bess nodded. "Because of what you said about the glider being sabotaged."

"She is still tops on my suspect list," Nancy said. "But there's more here than just a spoiled rich girl throwing what amounts to a glorified temper tantrum. What about Quinn's accident? And the attack on me?" Nancy pulled thoughtfully on a strand of hair. "If only I could talk to Quinn."

"Why not?" George asked. "Why don't you go to the hospital? It's not that far to Newport."

"I can't for one good reason. He's unconscious. He lapsed into a coma last night, and the doctor has no idea how long it'll be before he comes around—if ever."

"If ever?" Bess stared at her. "But that's horrible. That means Quinn could end up being the first real murder victim. Oh, I hope he doesn't die."

"I hope not either," Nancy replied. "For Marva's sake as well as his own." Then Nancy told Bess and George about the argument she'd overheard between Marva and Gil. "Marva swears Gil only yells at her because he loves her so much and he hates seeing her miserable. He really wants her to sell out and let someone else take over the problems—"

"Gil loves Marva?" Bess blurted out. "Oh, wow, is that a joke! The only person that guy loves is himself. He thinks he's God's gift to women. Haven't you noticed how he flirts with everyone? Just now as I was passing Lisa's cabin guess who I saw locked in a very serious kiss with Sara Lakin?"

"Gil?" Nancy and George both said at the same time.

"You got it. Mr. Wonderful, himself," Bess replied.

Nancy thoughtfully rubbed the side of her glass with her finger. "This case gets more complicated by the minute. Let's get going."

After lunch Nancy decided to pay a visit to Lisa Gregson. She wanted a chance to talk with the young woman—alone.

"I recognize you." Lisa smiled at Nancy as she opened the door. "You were there when I came to—after the crash."

"That's right." Nancy returned the smile. "I hope you're okay now."

"Oh, sure, I feel great." Lisa fiddled with the doorknob. "Do you want to come in?"

"Yes, I'd like to." Nancy stepped through the open door before Lisa could have a chance to change her mind. Crossing directly to a chair near the fireplace, Nancy sat down. "Actually I'd like to ask you a couple of questions about the accident. And about something else as well."

"By something else, do you mean the threat I got?" Lisa asked candidly as she sat down opposite Nancy. "Marva told me you'd want to question me about it. Did you happen to see my note?"

"Yours, and I saw Sara's picture and heard about Kirsten's tape."

"Brrr—" Lisa said. "Really creepy stuff, don't you think?" She shuddered involuntarily.

She's really upset about the death threat she received, Nancy thought. Or else she's a very good actress.

"I mean, who would want to do something like that? Other than Sara and Kirsten I don't know anyone here."

"I don't suppose you recognized the writing on the note?"

"No. It was only those three words. And it was printed."

"Probably someone trying to disguise his— or her—writing," Nancy said, watching for Lisa's reaction.

"Do you really think it could be a woman?" Lisa asked, slightly taken aback. "All this time I kept thinking it had to be a guy. I never thought about it being a woman. But I guess it is possible, huh?"

"There's no reason it couldn't be a woman." Nancy went on. "Now, about your accident. I have to be honest and tell you that because the damage to the glider is minor, I think you could have done it yourself. Especially because Sara made a comment that made me think you'd be capable of doing it."

"What?" Lisa's mouth dropped open and she stared at Nancy. "What are you talking about?"

Nancy explained that she knew that Lisa was having problems with her father. How she found out she kept to herself. "So, you can see how it looks to me, Lisa. Setting yourself up to have an accident is a good way to hurt your father."

"Oh, really! And what is Sara supposed to have said?" Lisa snapped.

"I don't want to cause trouble between you and your friend," Nancy apologized. "But when I asked Sara about your accident, she was evasive—she didn't want to talk at first. Then she said that if I knew you the way she does, I'd know the crash was no accident. So, you see, putting all that information together led me to believe—"

"Oh, you're so *wrong* it's not even funny!" Lisa yelled. She jumped up and began to pace the room. Then abruptly she stopped and balled her hands into fists before turning to face Nancy. "You're way off base, Nancy Drew. Yes, I hate my father. And I'd love to see him as unhappy as I am now. But there's no way I'm going to hurt myself in order to do that. You can trust me on that score, Ms. Detective."

"All right, Lisa." Nancy decided to back off a little. "I believe you." For some reason, she did. The girl's reactions seemed honest.

Lisa appeared to calm down and sat down opposite her again. "Look, I'm really scared about all this," she said. "And I want whoever is doing these horrible things caught. I promise I'll do anything I can to help. Whatever you want to know, I'll tell you."

"Good," Nancy said. That gave her an opening to ask Lisa about Sara and Gil.

"And about Sara's comment," Lisa went on before Nancy had a chance to ask. "Well, she was about as far off as you. And I don't understand that. She knows me, and should know I wouldn't do something stupid like crash my glider." Lisa shifted nervously on her chair. Nancy guessed she was deciding whether or not to say something more.

Nancy waited.

"Lisa," Nancy prodded. "There's more, isn't there? You can trust me."

A long pause followed before Lisa finally spoke. "The thing is, Sara's really not been herself since we got here and she met Gil Forrest. She has a huge crush on him. Everybody knows he's engaged to Marva, but it doesn't seem to matter to her. She's so jealous I bet she blames *me* for letting him take me to the infirmary."

"Hmmm . . ." What was with Gil, anyway? Nancy wondered. If he really loved Marva, what was he doing fooling around with Sara? If he didn't, why was he pretending he did? "Thanks for talking with me, Lisa." With a smile, Nancy rose. "You've been a big help."

"Poor Sara," Bess said sympathetically after Nancy told her what she'd learned. "I can understand how she must feel. I've fallen for a rat or two myself."

"I thought about it as I walked back here," Nancy said. "I think that Gil might have been playing around with Sara because he was so mad at Marva. He'd just had an argument with her. If Sara's got a crush on him, the way Lisa claims, and she happened to throw herself at him at the right—or should I say *wrong*—time . . . ?"

"I think you're being too nice," George countered. "If a guy I was engaged to pulled a stunt like that I'd never forgive him."

"I wonder how Marva would react if she knew what was going on?" Bess speculated.

"I was wondering that, too," Nancy said.

But before I can solve Marva's problems, I need to figure out what Gil is up to, Nancy thought. And there's no better place to start than with Sara's other roommate.

Loud rock music blared from loudspeakers in the aerobics class where Nancy found Kirsten. A passing instructor had pointed her out to Nancy. "She's the tall one in yellow."

"Thanks." Nancy turned her attention to watching the naturally athletic girl. Kirsten's light brown hair was plaited into a single French braid that bounced against her back as she moved energetically to the final bars of the song.

Nancy watched as Kirsten walked toward the locker room, a towel draped around her neck.

"Excuse me, Kirsten." Nancy ran a couple of steps to stop the girl. "I'm Nancy Drew. Marva Phillips has asked me to look into the threats you and the others have been receiving. Would you mind talking to me for a few minutes?"

"If I can shower first," Kirsten replied easily. "I'm sweaty, and I don't want my muscles to stiffen."

Nancy quickly filled Kirsten in on the conversation she'd had with Lisa. The girls were standing in front of a mirror where Kirsten was replaiting her hair. "I don't enjoy prying into other people's private affairs, but I want to know what you think of Gil Forrest. Considering what is happening with Sara," Nancy added knowingly.

"Well, I agree with you about keeping my nose out of other people's business," Kirsten said, staring rather pointedly at Nancy in the mirror. "And I don't see how Gil's kissing Sara could be tied into the threats we got."

Kirsten stopped braiding a minute, thinking, her arms still up by her head. "There *is* something I do know about him, though, that might have some bearing on the threats. Now that I think about it, he *might* be the one sending them. I haven't told anyone about this, but I guess I'd better tell you." Kirsten dropped her arms and led Nancy to a quiet corner bench.

"What is it?" Nancy asked eagerly.

"Well, last week I went to Marva's office, looking for her, but only Gil was there. He looked really upset. He was holding a letter, and his hand was shaking. I don't know why I didn't just turn around and leave—you know, because he might have been embarrassed with me there—but I didn't. Something about the way he looked made me feel sorry for him. So I asked him if there was anything I could do."

"And?"

"Well, he obviously wanted to talk to someone." Kirsten shrugged. "And I happened to be there."

"Go on." Nancy felt she was on to the first real clue in the case.

"He showed me the letter he was holding. It was from a businessman, someone named Roger Coleman. This Coleman had made a really good offer to buy Marva out. I saw the figure on the letter, and it was a lot of money. Gil was upset because Marva had turned the offer down—cold."

"He actually told you all this?" Nancy asked.

"I know it sounds weird." Kirsten nodded. "I'm practically a stranger, and there he was telling me all that personal stuff. But he was so mad at Marva that he lost control. Maybe he was mad enough to send those threats to the guests. You know, to scare Marva into accepting Coleman's offer after all."

"Uh-huh," Nancy said, thinking. "Tell me, Kirsten, do you know anything about this Roger Coleman?"

"Just from pictures and reputation. He's a broker who goes around buying up businesses that are about to fail. I've heard my father mention him. My father's a business broker, too. But nothing like Coleman. Coleman has a reputation for being ruthless. He does whatever he has to to get what he wants." She stood up. "I really should get going."

"Of course," Nancy replied.

The two walked outside the complex together. A gray BMW was pulling up to the main building.

"I don't believe it!" Kirsten whispered to Nancy as the driver stepped out. "This is like ESP. We were just talking about him, and there he is. Roger Coleman himself."

Nancy watched as the man paused to glance around, spotted the two of them, and stepped over quickly.

Coleman was tall, with dark good looks. Probably in his late thirties, Nancy judged. Dressed in neatly pressed tan slacks, a plaid blue silk shirt open at the collar, with a well-tailored, raw silk sports jacket over it, he looked like the TV image of a go-getter tycoon.

"Afternoon, ladies." Coleman spoke in a low, pleasant voice with the hint of a western drawl. "I'm looking for Marva Phillips. Can you tell me where I might find her?"

"I'm not sure," Nancy said, "but she could be in her office." Coleman thanked her and left.

"What do you think, Nancy?" Kirsten asked with a backward glance at the businessman's retreating figure. "Do you think Marva's changed her mind and is going to sell? If she does, she's going to be a very rich woman."

And even if Gil Forrest doesn't love Marva, Nancy thought, if he marries her, wouldn't he be a very rich man?

Chapter
Nine

Nancy was walking away from the main building, thinking about Gil and the offer to buy Club High Adventure, when Roger Coleman came back out the front door. Seeing Nancy, he waved and started talking.

"Well, Ms. Phillips wasn't in her office. I asked at the front desk if they knew where I could find her. Nothing! Zip!"

"Sorry," Nancy replied, adding a polite shrug. "I was only guessing."

"At least you tried to help. The person at the front desk just wanted me to leave my name. Said she'd let Marva know I'd been asking for her." He shook his head in disbelief. "Isn't that incredible?" He suddenly grinned good-naturedly at his own situation. "Where'd they think I dropped in from? Someplace down the street after a quick taxi ride? It took me close to forty minutes to drive here from the airport, most of it on that impossible cliff road."

"Forty minutes?" Nancy recalled the hour and a half drive she and her friends had made from Portland.

"Oh, not a commercial airport," he replied, seeing her confusion. "A little private strip up north of here. The closest one that'll accommodate a jet. I flew the Lear up from L.A." His explanation didn't even sound like bragging, Nancy thought. He said it the way anyone else would say he'd taken a bus.

Despite what Kirsten had told her about Coleman, Nancy found herself liking him. He was both easygoing and debonair.

"Was Marva expecting you, Mr.—uh—" Nancy didn't want to let on she knew his name.

"Now I'm the one being thoughtless. I'm Roger Coleman." He put out a capable-looking hand for her to shake.

"My name is Nancy Drew." She wasn't surprised by his firm grip. "Was Marva expecting you?" she repeated.

"I hope not." Coleman grinned. "I don't let people I'm doing business with know I'm coming. I like to pop in. Surprise 'em. I get better results that way."

"I have to admit I've heard of you, Mr. Coleman," Nancy said. "Now I think I understand how you earned your reputation."

"Please, call me Roger," he said in a warm tone. "Now, as for my reputation, I don't apologize for my ability to make money. Nothing wrong with that. Just as long as it's fair and profitable for everyone."

Nancy laughed at his candor. "Good enough," she agreed.

"And I've got to admit I know who you are, too. Just your name," he added. "Gil told me Marva was asking a Nancy Drew to help her with those threats. I hope you can get this mess cleared up before I become the new owner."

"From what I understand"—Nancy looked directly into his clear gray eyes—"Marva decided she's not going to sell."

"Oh, that was just her first answer. I never pay attention to first answers. At least not if it's a no." He looked around, as if appraising the club. "I've decided that I want to own this place. And I believe I have an offer she isn't going to refuse—if I can find her to make my offer."

Glancing over Coleman's shoulder, Nancy said, "I think you're about to have the chance. Here she is now."

The club's green van had pulled up behind

the BMW. Marva and Gil got out. Nancy noticed that Gil didn't seem even vaguely surprised to see Coleman. In fact, his expression told her that he was not only happy to see the businessman, but might actually have been expecting him. As for Marva, the grim set of her features was evidence enough that she wasn't happy to find Roger Coleman on her property.

As the two came toward Nancy and Coleman, they had a quick exchange of words. Gil was saying something to which Marva was emphatically shaking her head no. But a second later he stopped and touched her arm. She nodded yes this time.

Gil was the first to speak, suggesting cool drinks at a quiet poolside table. He invited Nancy to join them.

"Thanks, but I'll pass," Nancy replied. "If you're not going to use your office for a while, Marva, I'd like to go over those files we discussed."

While Gil, Marva, and Coleman went off, Nancy headed for Marva's office. It took her only a short while to locate the personnel records. After pulling the folders, she sat down at Marva's desk, stacking the files next to her.

She read through the files of everyone, even part-time clerical help. She couldn't eliminate anyone. The lengthy application forms included letters of reference, résumés, health insurance forms, and miscellaneous letters and notes. Nothing seemed out of place in any of them. With a sigh, Nancy closed the cover of the folder belonging to Uncle Al and set it on top of the tall pile she'd already finished.

After rubbing her tired eyes, she reached up and stretched. She'd been at it for two hours and absolutely nothing had come of it.

One more to go. With a sigh, Nancy opened the folder and began to read.

Five minutes later she closed the cover, nodding once to herself. She'd actually found something that might just relate to the case.

Getting to her feet, Nancy began to pace—and think. She suddenly realized she hadn't known much about Gil Forrest before reading his file, only the few things Marva had told her about him.

The two had met on a bicycle tour of Europe when they were in college. Marva had gone to Oregon State, while Gil had attended college in the Midwest. Apparently, Gil had approached Marva a year earlier and asked her for a job, and she had offered him the one as her assistant.

But it was what had happened in Gil's life between their first meeting and his coming to work for Marva that was so intriguing. It was all there in his files.

Nancy sat down again and picked up Gil's folder. His résumé showed that after graduating with a degree in business administration, Gil had moved to Seattle, where he'd gotten his real estate broker's license. He'd gone to work for a large firm, dealing in luxury resort property. With his good looks and persuasive personality, he must have cleaned up, Nancy decided. Why had he made the switch from a fast-paced existence in a large city like Seattle to a life of teaching hang gliding here in the wilderness?

Maybe that was why Gil was so interested in Roger Coleman's offer. If Marva accepted and they married, he'd have access to all that money. Maybe he wanted to get back on the fast track and become a tycoon like Coleman. Marva's money would be his bankroll. It was certainly a strong enough motive if, indeed, it turned out that Gil was behind the threats.

Satisfied that she'd learned as much as she could from the files, Nancy left the office, turning out the light and making sure the door was locked. She didn't hear the footsteps moving quietly behind her. Suddenly her vision was cut off as a hood was pulled over her head.

Nancy tried to scream, but a hand covered her face, shoving the coarse material against her nose and into her mouth. Barely able to breathe, she felt herself being dragged down the hall.

Just as suddenly, the hand was gone from her face. Nancy was pushed against a cold, hard wall. She lost her balance, stumbling to her knees.

With a sense of foreboding, she heard the slam of a metal door behind her. Then a lock clicked home.

Nancy pulled the hood from her head. Her heart sank when she realized what had happened. Someone had thrown her into the kitchen's huge, deep freezer. And she was locked in!

Chapter

Ten

NANCY STARED at the heavy door, which was white with frost. Her first thought was to unlock the door, then get out and chase down her attacker.

Almost instantly, she remembered what Marva had said about the freezer door needing to be fixed. The inside latch was broken. Anyone unlucky enough to be inside when the door was closed would be trapped. At least until someone came along and opened it from the outside. And no one would hear her screams since the thick-walled room was soundproof. No doubt her attacker was well aware of these facts.

How long could she be trapped before someone discovered her in there? Any amount of time could be too long, Nancy realized as she felt the cold settle around her.

With sudden dread Nancy remembered the dinner dance that night wasn't taking place until nine o'clock! That meant that a lot of the crew wouldn't even be on duty yet. Nancy could freeze to death long before anyone came and found her.

A shiver ran up her spine—not from fright, but from cold. Her light cotton slacks and knit shirt were no protection from the damp, frigid air. She rubbed at her arms to try to warm them as she looked for something—anything —that would help her escape.

Nancy was thankful for one thing— the freezer light didn't automatically go out when the door was shut. It would have been even worse if she'd been locked in the dark.

Maybe she could find something she could use to jimmy the lock open. Nancy quickly inspected the contents of the freezer. But there was nothing she could use to escape with. Only rows of shelves with neatly stacked boxes of vegetables and wrapped foil packages—probably cuts of meat.

Two sides of beef hung at the back of the small room. She studied the hooks they were suspended from. Was there any way she could use them? Not a chance, she decided, turning her attention back to the shelves.

With a hand that was beginning to shake from the cold, she picked up one of the rectangular foil packages. It was rock hard, shaped almost like a brick. What if she pounded on the door with it? Surely someone would hear her if she beat on it long enough.

But that was the problem. How long could she hold out? How long would it be before anyone heard her? The freezer was in a hall behind the kitchen, all by itself. No one would come back there unless they specifically wanted to get into the freezer.

Discouraged, she was about to put the package back on the shelf, when her gaze fell on a small round dial near the door. The thermostat. It gave a temperature reading of zero degrees. Nancy remembered something she'd learned about freezers—the door will automatically unlock if the thermostat stops working.

All I need to do is make sure it's not working, she thought, with sudden hope. And I have the perfect weapon right here in my hand to make sure it's not.

Moving quickly to the thermostat, she lifted the frozen package and hit the glass cover of the dial hard. It didn't crack. Apparently the glass was thicker than she'd judged. Throwing her weight into it, she hit the dial again. Still nothing. Frustrated, Nancy began hammering at it. By now her numbed fingers were barely working and her hand was beginning to stick to the frozen package.

It took several more hits before the glass on the thermostat suddenly shattered in several places at once. Listening carefully, Nancy heard a muffled click as the outside lock was released. She was free!

George and Bess were both ready to leave the cabin by the time Nancy returned. But after one look at her, the other girls demanded to know what had happened.

"I definitely don't like it," George said, after Nancy had told them about her time in the freezer. "This makes twice someone has tried to kill you. And we have no idea who could be responsible. It's no secret what you're doing here. The entire staff knows, and most of the guests. Don't you think it's time to call the police?"

"I agree," Bess said, putting her hand on Nancy's. "This thing isn't worth risking your life for."

"I admit it's dangerous," Nancy said, "but

that must be because I'm getting close to the answer. Besides, I promised Marva I wouldn't call in the police yet."

"Didn't the doctor have to report Larry Quinn's accident?" Bess wanted to know.

"No. Because it was just that—an accident. There was no foul play as far as anyone knew." She assured her friends that she'd be more careful and would stay on the alert from then on.

"You promise?" Bess said.

Nancy gave a decisive nod of her head. It was only then that it dawned on her that her two friends were already dressed for the dance that night. "Is it that late already?" she asked. "I thought dinner wasn't going to be until late."

"Oh, it's not," Bess replied. "But there's some early entertainment planned out by the pool. George and I thought we'd go over."

"But we won't now," George added quickly. "We'll stay here with you."

"Don't be silly," Nancy said. "You don't have to baby-sit me. You guys go ahead. I'll be fine. In fact I think I'll take a nice long, hot bath and thaw out. I feel a little like some of those slabs of beef in the freezer." She gave a little laugh.

"Well . . ." George hesitated.

"Go. Please." Nancy smiled. "Actually, you can do a little sleuthing for me."

"Like what?" Bess asked.

"I'd like you two to keep your eyes open. Notice if anyone acts strange. You know, if someone's where he shouldn't be—that sort of thing."

"You got it," George promised.

"And don't be too long," Bess added as they were leaving. "Or we'll start worrying and come back for you."

Remembering that locked doors were no barrier to a determined criminal, Nancy propped a chair under the knob before she relaxed into her scented bath bubbles. She focused her thoughts and went over what she knew of the case so far.

Lisa Gregson was no longer a suspect as far as Nancy was concerned. Nancy was convinced that Lisa's problems had nothing to do with the club crime.

Sara Lakin had a serious crush on Gil, or so Lisa said. That was backed up by what Bess had seen. Though that might make Sara want to see Marva have problems with Club High Adventure, Nancy could not picture the high-strung brunette carrying out any of the recent attacks.

As for Kirsten, she was athletic and

probably strong enough to have pushed
Nancy over the railing of Quinn's cabin and
dragged her into the freezer, but she had no
motive.

Marva's original thought still offered the
strongest motive: that someone was out to
destroy the club's reputation, probably to get
Marva to sell out. The obvious people who
came to mind were Marva's fiancé, Gil, and
Roger Coleman.

Although Nancy found the wealthy tycoon
charming and friendly, he did have a reputation for being ruthless in business. And even
though he'd just arrived that afternoon, he
could easily have had someone working for
him.

Could that someone be Gil? There could be
a tie-in between the two men. Gil had been a
real estate broker before coming to work for
Marva. He'd dealt with expensive properties,
and Roger Coleman's occupation was buying
up expensive properties.

Gil had access to the cabins and other areas
of the club. That was important. Also, he
would have known about such inside details as
the broken freezer door.

There had to be something she was missing.
Some connection.

I'd better hurry up and find out what it is,
Nancy thought. Because whoever started out

only making threats was now taking serious risks.

"Risks that are putting your own life in danger, Nancy Drew," she said to herself.

There'd been two attempts on her life already. The next one could very well prove fatal.

Chapter

Eleven

Nᴀɴᴄʏ ᴘᴀᴜѕᴇᴅ in front of the bedroom
mirror for a last-minute check. Partly to take
her mind off the frustrations of the case, she'd
put on one of her favorite outfits—a full
flowered skirt teamed with a pale green scoop-
neck top. The green set off the red-gold high-
lights in her hair.

Satisfied, she slipped her feet into high-
heeled sandals, picked up her light cotton
sweater from the bed and left the cabin.

Dinner was just being served when Nancy
entered the dining room. She slid into her
chair as a waiter was putting an iced fruit cup
at her place. Nancy smiled hello at Bess and

George and at the other five guests at their table.

The normally casual dining room had been transformed into a romantic fantasyland. Blue linen cloths covered the otherwise utilitarian pine tables, and arrangements of wildflowers and baby's breath sat in the center of each table.

"Great, isn't it?" Bess said happily. "And did you notice? There's going to be a live band." She nodded in the direction of the French doors that ran the length of the dining room and overlooked the pool and veranda.

Nancy turned to look and saw two young men in matching silver jackets checking the sound system, while another band member removed a guitar from its case. "Hope they're good," she commented, when a movement in the shadows on the veranda caught her eyes.

It was Roger Coleman, talking animatedly with Al Hunt. Why was Coleman still here? Nancy wondered. Considering the cool reception he'd received from Marva that afternoon, he should have been back in Los Angeles by now. Also, what was he doing having an engrossing conversation with the rock-climbing instructor?

Intrigued, Nancy shoved her chair back and stood up. "I see something I want to check out. Be right back," she said in an undertone to Bess and George, and hurried from the room.

Bess looked at George. "Where do you suppose Nancy's headed?"

George shot a worried look after Nancy. "I wonder if we should go after her? I mean with all that's been going on, I'm not sure we should let her go off by herself."

"I agree," Bess said. "But wouldn't it look kind of funny if we all went rushing out? It might just draw the wrong person's attention."

"You're right." George nodded. "Nancy should know what she's doing. But if she's not back in five minutes, I vote we go after her."

Nancy had wound her way through the maze of tables to the far end of the room where the French doors opened onto the veranda. By the time she'd made it outside, however, the two men were no longer in sight. Too bad. She'd really wanted to overhear what they'd been saying. She promised herself to keep an eye out for them.

As people finished eating, they drifted from the dining room out onto the veranda. The band had begun to play some light rock as background music. Bess and George had gone down to the end of the pool to get closer.

Nancy stayed by herself, lying back on the chaise longue and enjoying the rich velvet sky punctuated with millions of tiny stars.

"Beautiful, don't you think?" a warm masculine voice said from close behind her shoulder, startling her.

"Oh, Mr. Coleman—" Nancy sat up quickly. "Hello!"

"Roger—please." He smiled as he sat down beside her. "I thought we were on a first-name basis."

"I'm curious—Roger," Nancy said. "I was wondering why you're still here."

"You mean you expected Marva to demand that I leave and not come back? That would have been a little dramatic, don't you think? Actually we got along quite nicely when we talked this afternoon. I think we understand each other."

"You do?" Nancy asked. It hadn't looked that way to her. Things must have changed after she left.

"Yes. Marva kindly suggested I stay the night and get an early start in the morning. Seems at this time of the year, the fog comes up off the ocean early and banks against the cliff. Driving on the coast road can be rather dangerous." The corners of his mouth lifted in a wry smile. "I suppose she didn't want to think about going to sleep and waking up tomorrow morning to find out I'd been killed."

Standing, Coleman put out his hand. "The band seems to have switched over to the kind

of dance music my feet understand. Shall we?"
Nancy agreed. What better chance to keep an
eye on him?

They hadn't been dancing long before one of
the guys from her hang-gliding class cut in on
them. She lost track of Coleman as she danced
with several other young men.

Then, after two or three more numbers,
Nancy found herself in Gil Forrest's arms.

"Having a good time?" he asked politely.

"Yes, thank you," she replied, but she was
feeling distinctly uncomfortable dancing with
him, considering what she now knew about
him.

"I wanted to talk to you alone," he said,
moving skillfully to the beat of a slow dance.
"This seemed to be as good a way as any."

"Does that mean you don't want Marva to
hear what you have to say to me?"

He nodded. "I decided to tell you exactly
where I'm coming from. That way, maybe, you
won't go snooping around and foul up my
relationship with Marva. Maybe you won't tell
her things that would only hurt her. After all,
I'm not perfect. No one is. But that doesn't
make me a crook."

"Where exactly *are* you coming from, Gil?"
Nancy tilted her head so she could look directly into his eyes.

"I admit I want Marva to sell the club to
Coleman. She doesn't need all the grief the

club's been giving her lately. And Coleman's offer is far too good to pass up. It would make her a wealthy woman."

"Which in turn would give you access to a lot of money," Nancy concluded, giving him a hard look. It was as good a time as any to test her theory.

"Yes. It would," Gil replied evenly. "I'd be dishonest if I said I didn't care about money. I do. But I want you to know I love Marva. Money or no money."

The music ended, and Gil thanked Nancy for the dance. She couldn't dismiss from her mind the fact that Gil still had one of the strongest motives of any suspect on her list. But he had sought her out to try to make his position clear. If he were behind the threats, would he be so open about his feelings?

As Nancy was trying to work out the logic behind Gil's behavior, Marva appeared.

"I was watching you dance with Gil," she said. There was a troubled expression in her deep blue eyes. "What were you two talking about? You looked so serious."

Nancy hesitated. How much of what Gil had said was really necessary to pass on to Marva?

"He wanted to convince me that although he is all for you giving up this club," she said, choosing her words carefully, "he would never do anything drastic—like sending those threats to scare you into selling out."

105

"Poor Gil. I hope he doesn't think I suspect that." She jerked her head toward Nancy. "You don't think that, do you? Because that would be ridiculous. Gil loves me."

"Yes," Nancy said kindly. "He told me that, too."

"Nancy, I know that Gil's behavior hasn't been the best lately. But I wish you'd put it down to the strain we're all under—" Marva paused, and a puzzled expression came over her face.

Nancy followed Marva's eyes and saw that she was staring toward the main building.

"What is it, Marva?" Nancy asked.

"Something very strange," Marva answered. "There's a light on in my office." She turned to Nancy. "I was in there only a while ago, making a phone call. I distinctly remember shutting off the light as I left. And I also remember locking the door."

"Could it be Gil?" Nancy asked.

"Uh-uh." Marva shook her head firmly. "I know where Gil is. He wanted to do some last-minute work on a couple of the gliders before tomorrow's class. He's in the work-room."

"Then I think we'd better investigate." Nancy jumped up. She called out to George that they were going to Marva's office.

It took only a few minutes for the two to

enter the building and make their way down the hall toward Marva's office.

While they were still only a few feet away from the door, Nancy held up her hand to stop Marva. "The light's out now," she said in a whisper, pointing to the dark crack at the bottom of the door. "Whoever was in there has probably gone. But maybe not. Let me go first."

Slipping out of her high heels, Nancy picked one up and held it with the sharp heel pointing out. Good weapon in case I have to defend myself, Nancy thought. Then she crept the last few feet toward the closed door. Putting her hand on the knob, she turned it and pushed the door open at the same time. She reached in to snap on the light.

"Oh no!" Nancy gasped as the light flooded the room, showing papers strewn everywhere, furniture knocked over, and shards of broken glass littering the floor.

Someone had ransacked the place.

Chapter

Twelve

NANCY, WHAT IS IT?" Marva cried out. Rushing to the open doorway to stand beside Nancy, she stared into her office, but didn't move. "Who could have done this?"

"What I'd like to know is *why?*" Nancy asked as she entered the room and stepped over the papers that had been scattered everywhere from the open file drawers.

She bent to retrieve some that were lying just in front of her. As she straightened up, Nancy glanced at the wall over the couch. Marva had a collection of framed photos hanging there—mementos of past club guests, famous people who'd visited the club, friends, and family. It wasn't these Nancy saw. Her eyes were drawn to a pale square on the wall where a photo had been but wasn't now.

"Marva." Nancy turned to face her. "Did you take a photo off this wall recently? I think one is missing."

"Excuse me?" Marva looked up from the mess to the wall. "No, I didn't. Someone else must have taken it down." A frown creased her forehead. "You don't suppose it was the person who broke in, do you?" Marva asked, puzzled. "It was just an old photo of my father."

"Your father?"

"Yes—well, not only my father. I was in it, too. Along with some of the guests who were here that day."

"Do you have another print?"

"No, I don't think so." The loss was just beginning to sink in. "Oh, Nancy, I don't even have the negative. I'll never be able to replace it. And it was a favorite of mine." Marva looked wistfully at the spot where the photo had been.

"Marva, tell me—those guests, can you remember who they were? What did the photo look like? Exactly."

"Let me think. . . ." Marva leaned against the desk and tried to remember. Finally she raised her head to look at Nancy.

"Strange, isn't it, how you can look at something every day, but then, when it's gone, you have trouble remembering the details?"

"I know." Nancy nodded her agreement. "But please try. I have a feeling it's important."

"Basically it was a picture of my father, taken when I was about seven. My father and I and a group of guests went hiking up to Devil's Rock. Someone took a photograph of all of us when we got to the top."

Nancy thought for a moment. "Do you remember anything else about the photograph? Who in particular might have been in the group?"

Marva shook her head. "You know—at that age all the guests were just so many adults to me. In the photo, they were just figures in the background. I never really paid much attention to them. Sorry, Nancy."

"It's okay," Nancy said. "Maybe the photo will turn up," she added. She gestured to the papers Marva had been clutching in her hand. "Can you tell what papers are missing?"

"Oh, it's impossible," Marva said, waving them in frustration. "I'll have to spend hours sorting them out. But I did notice one thing. This empty file folder is one I kept on Roger Coleman's offer to buy the club."

"Hello," a male voice sung out.

At the sound of the voice, both Nancy and

Marva swung about to see Roger Coleman standing in the open doorway.

"I saw the light on in here and thought I might catch you before you went—" He broke off to stare at the wrecked office. "What happened here?"

"A break-in, obviously," Nancy replied.

"So I see. Someone certainly did a thorough job," Coleman commented.

"What was it you wanted to see me about, Roger?" Marva spoke up.

"I thought we might have another chat. Since I plan to leave first thing tomorrow morning, I knew there wouldn't be time then. Just a few minutes. *Alone,"* he said emphatically, with a polite smile in Nancy's direction.

"This is hardly the time for a business talk," Nancy said, feeling protective of Marva.

"That's all right, Nancy," Marva told her. "Actually, this might be the perfect time for Roger and me to talk."

Nancy was reluctant to leave. But it was apparent that the two of them wanted privacy.

When she walked out of the building, she found Bess and George waiting for her. The band had left, and only a few stragglers from the party hung about, chatting by the pool.

"Hi!" Bess linked her arm in Nancy's. "We knew you were in talking to Marva and decided to wait."

111

"We thought it would be better if we all walked back to the cabin together. Safety in numbers, you know," George said.

"What would I do without you guys?" Nancy linked her arm with George's. "I want to hear anything you have to report about the party, and then I'm going to fill you in on the latest with Marva."

Bess reached for another cookie. Dipping it into her milk, she paused before bringing it to her mouth. "So I guess I'm a failure as a spy. I didn't learn a single thing that might help, Nan. Sorry."

The three were curled up on the couches in the cabin, a nearly empty package of cookies on the coffee table. A cozy fire crackled in the fireplace, taking the night chill out of the air.

"Ditto for me," George said. "What do you suppose anyone wanted with the papers on Coleman's offer?"

"I'm not sure," Nancy said. "But I can't help thinking his showing up just at that moment, right after we found the office ransacked, was too well-timed."

"You mean he might have been the one who did it?" George asked.

"Or he hired someone to break in for him," Nancy said. "Maybe he was hanging around waiting for Marva to discover the chaos. Maybe he hoped she'd be so upset that she'd cave in and sell him the club."

Nancy put an unfinished cookie down on her napkin. "Of course Gil might have done it. Marva said that he'd told her he was going to the workroom, but that could have been a lie. It could even have been Uncle Al." Nancy explained that she'd seen Coleman in deep conversation with the climbing instructor. "He could work for Coleman."

"Okay. So it all seems to come down to Coleman," George said in a positive tone.

"But Nancy told us how nice he is," Bess argued.

"Bess, how many times has Nancy been involved with a criminal who *seemed* nice at the start, then ended up being a pure rat?" George asked.

"Okay. Coleman's the bad guy." Bess tried to stifle a yawn, then gave up. "Case solved. I'm going to bed." She stood up and stretched. "See you guys in the morning. Good night."

"Hold on a minute, Bess." Nancy stood up. "You're going to have to put off bed for a little while. Right now, I need you to come with me."

Nancy handed her two friends their sweaters and started to lead them toward the front door.

"Where are we going?" George asked.

"I want to take a look in Uncle Al's cabin. Maybe I'll be able to find something that will tell me if he's working for Coleman," Nancy said, ignoring Bess's sleepy protest. "Let's go, you two."

There was a light showing through the blinds as they approached the cabin. George touched Nancy's arm. "He's in there. We can't break in now."

"Not necessarily," Nancy replied in a low voice. "Maybe he left the light on. Wait here, I'll check."

A couple of minutes later Nancy was standing on the porch motioning to her friends. "Just as I thought," she whispered when they had joined her. "It's only a night light." Nancy soon had the door open.

"If anything, this guy is too neat," George complained after the three had searched through the cabin. She stood in the center of the living room, hands on hips. "This place is like a motel room. I can't believe anyone really lives here."

"You're right," Nancy agreed. "There's nothing personal here. No plants, no books or magazines, no photos or letters."

"You're wrong about photos." Bess spoke up from where she knelt by the fireplace, poking through the ashes. "Crazy. But he seems to prefer burning them."

"What do you mean?" Nancy hurried over to Bess's side. Kneeling, she reached in and pulled out a partially burned photo.

The half that was left showed a kind-looking man, his arm out, holding hands with someone. The seven-year-old Marva, Nancy guessed, but she couldn't be sure because all that was left of the little girl was a small, slender arm and the tiniest glimpse of a kid's sneaker. In the background some hikers were sitting and resting, their faces mainly out-of-focus blurs.

Nancy handed it to Bess and George. "I'll bet you anything this is the photo that was taken from Marva's office tonight," she said. "But why would Uncle Al want to destroy this old picture?" she asked, almost to herself. It just didn't make any sense.

"Isn't that the trail to the top of Devil's Rock?" George asked, tapping the photo with her finger.

"Probably. Marva did say that's where it was taken," Nancy answered, looking at the photo again.

"Hmmm—maybe Uncle Al's got a thing about that place," Bess joked. "You know, Devil's Rock. Evil stuff. All that."

"Bess, this isn't the time to be—"

"I don't think it's smart for us to hang around here much longer," Nancy interrupted. "This photo's only half burned. Maybe Al was in the middle of destroying it. Which means he might be on his way back right—"

A heavy tread made the front porch creak. All three girls turned toward the sound and held their breath. Three more steps in quick succession proved for certain that Al Hunt had returned.

Chapter
Thirteen

Nᴀɴᴄʏ ᴘᴏɪɴᴛᴇᴅ. George was the first to follow her direction and move toward the bedroom and the low window to safety outside. Bess, her eyes round and staring, was rooted to her spot, but she finally budged when she heard the jingle of keys.

Nancy was right behind Bess on her dash to the bedroom. At the last second she veered off and darted into the open kitchen directly opposite the front door.

She dove for cover behind the counter just as she saw Al Hunt standing framed in the doorway. Since he didn't make a move toward her, Nancy could only guess he hadn't seen her.

It was foolish to stay, but she had to have a solid piece of evidence. Still hunkering low, Nancy saw what she needed—a glass on top of the counter beside the sink.

Before she could grab it, Nancy saw Al's feet moving toward her. Nancy was ready for him. He might have the advantage of size, but she had the advantage of surprise.

Nancy held her breath, waiting for the right moment. Several seconds passed. Nancy kept her eyes on Al's feet from around a corner of the counter. Then, for some reason, Al stopped short of the counter and turned toward the fireplace.

Peering out from behind the counter, Nancy watched as he picked up the poker and disturbed the ashes. Checking to make sure the picture was all burned, Nancy thought. Satisfied that it was destroyed, Al headed for the bedroom.

When she saw he had closed the bedroom door, Nancy darted back across the kitchen floor and snaked her hand up to retrieve the solitary glass.

Still keeping an eye on the bedroom door, Nancy walked softly across the living room, casting one last look at the fireplace. There was a lot about Al Hunt she didn't know, Nancy thought as she silently let herself out the front door.

Once outside, she stared at the glass in her hand. With any luck there'll be some good prints on this, she thought as she looked around for Bess and George.

"There you are," she heard Bess whispering from the darkness. "Over here."

Nancy's eyes adjusted to the night and she turned to where she'd heard Bess's voice. Then, out of nowhere, George appeared at her side.

Nancy grabbed on to George and dragged her over to where she'd heard Bess's voice coming from. The three of them quickly stole away from Al's cabin.

"Excuse me for asking," George said to Nancy when they were a safe distance away and heading toward their own cabin, "but we're out in the boonies, here, remember. Just where are you planning to have those finger-prints checked?"

"Tomorrow morning we'll take them into Portland," she said.

"We?" Bess asked. "Listen, Nancy, after tonight's little escapade, I'm not sure I like this case." Bess had been chattering the whole way back from Hunt's cabin about what could have happened if they'd been caught.

"Calm down, Bess," George said. "Nancy

needs our help, and she's going to get it. Besides, what can happen in Portland, far away from Club High Adventure?"

Bess rolled her eyes, then sighed. "I guess you're right."

"That's the spirit," Nancy said, laughing.

They had reached their cabin. "I think we should all get a good night's sleep," Nancy said, yawning. "We need to be as alert as possible for what we have to do tomorrow. See you in the morning."

"All right, now give." Bess wadded up the wrapper from her sausage-and-biscuit break-fast sandwich and stuffed it into the jeep's litter bag as they roared down the highway toward Portland. "I'm ready to listen."

"Me, too," George said, gulping the last of her orange juice.

"I didn't realize what the case was really about until we found that photo in Uncle Al's cabin."

"But why do George and I have to go to Portland with you?" Bess had dug into her tote and was now putting on fresh lip gloss. "It doesn't take three of us to take a set of prints to the police."

"I'm going to drop you two at the library. I'd like you to read old newspaper stories from the time that Marva's mystery photo was taken.

Since Marva was about seven, that would make it eighteen years ago."

"What are we looking for?" George asked.

"A link. Anything that might have happened at the club eighteen years ago to make Al Hunt destroy a picture," Nancy explained.

"I don't get it," Bess complained. "What link could there possibly be?"

"I think it can involve only one person. Only one person has been connected with the club for the past eighteen years."

"Marva!" Bess gasped. "But what's the link? You can't believe she's behind these attempts on people's lives."

"No, I honestly don't think that, Bess." Frustrated, Nancy drummed her fingers against the steering wheel. "I don't know what to think."

"What about Larry Quinn?" George asked. "Do you think he might know who tried to kill him?"

"I don't think so," Nancy said. "I'm pretty sure he did consider his threat as only a childish hoax."

"Someone did try to kill him," George pointed out.

"But it wasn't necessarily Quinn that the killer was trying for. He should never have been on that trail in the first place. Uncle Al told me that trail is only for staff members and guests if they're with a staff member. Marva was right behind Quinn when he had his accident—"

"Which could mean that the *accident* might have really been meant for a staff member. It might have been set for Marva," George concluded, thinking out loud.

Bess spoke up excitedly. "Also, Marva likes to hang glide. So Lisa's accident could have been meant for Marva, too."

"And then again . . ." Nancy shrugged. "It could all be a smokescreen. I don't know. There are still too many unanswered questions."

Once they arrived in Portland, Nancy dropped Bess and George at the public library, then drove to the police station. She had called that morning and spoken to Detective Claudia O'Keefe, describing what she needed and giving her father as a reference.

Inside the one-story building, Nancy told the desk sergeant who she was and almost instantly an attractive, auburn-haired woman in her early thirties came out to greet her.

"It's a pleasure to meet you," O'Keefe said, shaking Nancy's hand. "Chief McGinnis back in River Heights said you're quite a detective."

Nancy smiled. "Well, I've solved a few

cases." She handed O'Keefe the glass she had found in Hunt's cabin. "Here's the evidence I told you about."

"Let's hope we can get to the bottom of what's happening up at Club High Adventure," O'Keefe said, taking the glass. "I just wish Ms. Phillips had asked for our help earlier. But better late than never. Come back later and I'll let you know what, if anything, I've been able to come up with."

Nancy thanked O'Keefe and left the station to help Bess and George in their search at the library.

"I've had it," Bess complained wearily, an hour after Nancy had met them at the micro-film readers. "I've skimmed so many articles my eyes are crossed."

"I'm ready to call it quits, too," George said, looking up. "I haven't run across a single . . . Wait a minute," she cried loud enough to annoy three people at a nearby table. "Nan, I think I've found something."

George pointed at the screen on which a portion of a newspaper page was projected. "Take a look at that."

Nancy's eyes scanned the article. Then she read the fine print under a headline. "Eighteen years ago this month," she said, thinking out loud.

"What is it, Nancy?" Bess asked, leaning over Nancy's shoulder.

"Something that can't be just a coincidence, Bess," Nancy said, and she read the caption out loud:

" 'Gruesome Murder at Club High Adventure, on Top of Deadly Devil's Rock.' "

Chapter

Fourteen

BESS BENT OVER her friend's shoulder to get a better look at the microfilm screen.

George slid out of the chair, letting Nancy take her place. "Here, sit down, you can see better."

After skimming the first few lines again, Nancy began excitedly to read the story aloud.

Seattle computer entrepreneur E. Raymond Jensen was killed in a 190-foot fall yesterday morning during an ascent of Devil's Rock, a popular climber's landmark eighteen miles south of Newport. Jensen's business partner, Alden Hunsfield, has been arrested on suspicion of murder. The 43-year-old entrepreneur may have been pushed to his death.

Lincoln County Sheriff's deputies have Hunsfield, of Britebyte Corporation, in custody. The two men had been vacationing at Club High Adventure, a luxury resort catering to lovers of risky sports.

An eyewitness to the fall was the club owner's seven-year-old daughter, whose name is currently being withheld.

"If the little girl hadn't seen the whole thing, we would have written this off as just another climbing accident," Sheriff Mike Parker said.

Jensen and Hunsfield were scaling the final cliff face before the summit when the young witness says she saw Hunsfield loosen a piton holding his partner's safety line. Hunsfield, according to the girl, then attacked Jensen, causing the victim to plummet to a ledge nearly 200 feet below.

Hunsfield has denied the charges, claiming that the piton was coming loose under the strain of Jensen's weight and that he was trying to save the man when he fell.

"Marva Phillips!" George and Bess chorused in unison. "The little girl was Marva."

"It says here that the murderer's name was

Alden Hunsfield," Nancy added. "Does that sound familiar? Alden Hunsfield and Al Hunt sound too much alike to be a coincidence."

Quickly Nancy wound the microfilm forward. "There's got to be more on this. Something about the trial. What happened—" The spool of film had ended.

"Here—this is the next one in order," George said, yanking a spool from the pile beside the machine.

Nancy inserted the new spool, and the three friends leaned forward. "Here's something," Nancy exclaimed. "This article mentions the results of the trial. Hunsfield was convicted of murder, but the charge was reduced to second-degree. Which means he could be paroled by now."

"But if Uncle Al's really this Alden Hunsfield, what's he doing back at the camp?" Bess wanted to know. "That's really stupid."

"Haven't you heard?" George answered her. "The criminal always returns to the scene of the crime."

"Only if he's got unfinished business," Nancy said in a grim voice. "If Hunsfield is Hunt, he's at the club for only one reason. To get revenge against the one witness who sent him to jail. And that explains why he burned the photo—he and his partner must have been in it." She leapt up. "There's one way to know if the two men are one and the same."

"The fingerprints," George cried out.

"Right!" Nancy grabbed her purse. "Come on. Back to the police station."

Nancy left Bess and George in the car as she hurried inside to see Detective O'Keefe.

"Hope this information helps. It came in over the FAX line from Washington, D.C., just a few minutes ago," O'Keefe said, handing Nancy the report.

Nancy glanced over the sheet of paper and nodded grimly. "I think you'd better get some officers up to Club High Adventure—fast. This man is a murderer, and I think he's about to become one again." She filled O'Keefe in on the details.

The detective agreed with Nancy's theory and told Nancy she'd have several cars on their way immediately.

"The prints matched," Nancy said to Bess and George as she climbed into the driver's seat of the jeep a few minutes later. "There's no doubt. Uncle Al is Hunsfield."

"Nancy," George said. "I just remembered. Al's taking a class of advanced climbers up Devil's Rock this afternoon, and I heard Marva say she was going to join them."

"When is the class?" Nancy asked, shooting a glance at her watch. "It's one-forty now."

"Oh no!" George exclaimed. "The class is supposed to leave the clubhouse at three.

That's only an hour and twenty minutes from now."

"But it's an hour-and-a-half drive back to the club," Bess said, her eyes wide in despair. "We'll never make it back in time."

Nancy reached for the ignition key and switched it on.

"We have to," she said, quickly throwing the jeep into gear. "It's the only way we're going to stop a second murder from taking place on Devil's Rock!"

Chapter

Fifteen

EVERYTHING'S CLEAR NOW. Marva's been Al's intended victim all along," Nancy said, pulling away from the police station.

"Do you think we can make it?" George asked, worried. "Most of the trip is along that mountain-coast road. And we can go only so fast."

"Don't forget those awful rocky cliffs," Bess moaned. "Isn't there a different road we can take? Something quicker? Something safer? Like this nice, wide freeway?" She made a grab for the metal roll bar as Nancy whipped the jeep up the on-ramp and into the afternoon traffic.

"I wish we could," Nancy called over to Bess, the wind stirring her hair around her face as she maneuvered the jeep into the fast lane. "But there's only one way to get back—the coast road."

"Do me a favor, Nancy," Bess shouted over the rush of wind. "Make your next case one back in good old River Heights. It's safer there."

Forty minutes later Nancy left the west-bound freeway to take the winding mountain road over which they'd driven hours earlier.

The road dipped and climbed, swung back and forth in sharp curves as it followed the natural line of the terrain. Fortunately the jeep was the perfect vehicle for rough driving, and Nancy handled it expertly. The road was nearly deserted. Encountering ar occasional slow-moving log truck, its long trailer loaded with huge redwood trunks, Nancy would bear down on the horn until the driver pulled over enough to let them slip by.

"We've got to be near the coast road by now," George said with an anxious glance at her watch. "We don't have much time to get there. We're really cutting it close."

"I think I can smell the ocean," Bess said in a hopeful voice. "I remember that huge grove of pine trees up there on that ridge." She pointed to a sharply rising hill just in front of them. "Look, Nan. Is that smoke? Do you think it's a forest fire?"

Nancy looked away from the road long enough to see what Bess was talking about. "Oh no. I don't believe it."

"What?" George leaned forward from the backseat. "What are you talking about?"

"Fog." Nancy pointed to the thick white mist sliding between the trees and slipping down the side of the fern-covered hill. "Let's hope it's just a patch that we can get through in a hurry."

By the time they'd topped the ridge, then made their way down the other side in first gear, the fog was so thick that their headlights couldn't penetrate more than a few feet in front of them.

"All I can do is follow the line in the center of the road and just keep creeping along until the fog clears." Nancy clenched the wheel, her voice heavy with frustration.

All three sat on the edge of their seats, as if peering hard into the blinding white mist would help get them through it faster.

Nancy was not able to drive the jeep faster than ten, sometimes fifteen, miles an hour. Other cars came at them on the other side of the road, crawling along equally slowly, their headlights blurred halos.

"Maybe they'll cancel the climbing class,"

Bess said hopefully. "I mean they wouldn't go rock climbing in this stuff, would they?"

"Devil's Rock is a lot higher than this ground fog." She paused. "Wait a second, I think it's lifting now."

"You're right," George said, brightening. "And, look, there's a car without any headlights on. We must be nearly out—" She abruptly stopped talking as the jeep slid suddenly out of the fog. Ahead of them the road lay clear, the sun bright overhead.

"All right!" the three chorused at once.

"Let's move it!" Nancy called as she clamped her foot down hard on the gas pedal.

Bess didn't even shut her eyes when Nancy took the bends around the cliffs of the coast road at high speed. She was as eager as the other two to get there.

"I just hope we've made it in time," Nancy called out as she slammed the jeep to a halt in front of the main building several minutes later. Leaping out, she raced toward the front door.

"Tell me," she asked the girl at the front desk, "has the rock-climbing class left for Devil's Rock?"

"I'm sorry, Ms. Drew." The girl looked up casually from the romance novel she was reading. "But, yes, they've already left. But you're not able to take that class, anyway. It's advanced—"

"You don't understand," Nancy broke in firmly. "And I don't have time to explain. Just tell me, how long ago did they leave?"

"Nancy, hi." Gil's voice reached her ears as she felt him touch her arm. From the tense set of Nancy's face, he must have been able to tell something was wrong. "Marva?" he asked with slight dread. "Has something happened to her?"

"Not yet—I hope," Nancy replied, purposefully controlling her tone. "But we've got to hurry to prevent something from happening to her." Taking his arm, she pulled him, running and filling him in at the same time.

"And I think he intends to kill her at the same place where he murdered his partner," she finished at the jeep. "Is there a way to get up there, other than the hiking trail? A way I could drive the jeep?"

"I don't know—" Gil scowled. "Yes, I do remember. There's an old fire road that goes up the back of Devil's Rock, but I don't know what shape it's in. It might be overgrown—" He stopped. "What are we waiting for? Let's get going!"

"You'd better stay and show the police how to find that fire road." She pulled open the door and hopped in.

Bess and George were sitting inside, waiting for her. Nancy turned the key and ground it into gear as Gil gave her directions. A few seconds later they spun out, heading for Devil's Rock.

Gil was right, she thought as she reached the fire road. There was barely any resemblance to a real road left—just the bare bones of one as it wound up the steep, rocky hill. Nancy shifted into first and kept her foot steady on the gas. The thick brush was hood-high in several places. Still, they were making better time than if they'd tried to catch up with the class on foot.

They had nearly reached the top when George, who was leaning out the passenger side to guide Nancy, yelled a warning. "Watch out, Nancy. You're about to hit—"

Crunch! The sound of metal scraping and tearing was followed by silence as the jeep's engine sputtered and died.

"—a big rock," George finished lamely.

Nancy tried the ignition. Nothing. The jeep was out of commission. She paused long enough to consider the situation, then pulled on the hand brake and put the gearshift lever into first, so the jeep wouldn't roll back down the road. Leaping out, she started at a run up the final stretch, George and Bess right behind her.

The sight that greeted Nancy as she reached the top sent adrenaline shooting through her.

Marva was about to rappel, or climb down, over the side of the cliff.

"Marva, stop!" Nancy screamed as loud as she could. Half-running, half-flying, Nancy dove toward Marva, grabbing for her.

She managed to get ahold of Marva's hips and pull her back to the safety of solid ground.

With a surprised grunt, Marva wrestled herself free from Nancy's protective hold. "Nancy, what's wrong? Have you gone crazy?"

It was then that Nancy spotted the crucial instrument of Al's plan. She saw that Marva's carabiner—the metal ring used to hold her safety rope—had been filed nearly in two. If Marva had attempted to rappel down the face of Devil's Rock, the carabiner would have snapped under her weight. Marva would have fallen to her death.

Before she could point that out to Marva, Nancy saw Al rush at her. Hunt knocked Nancy to the ground hard. As she gasped for breath Nancy saw him slip a safety line around his waist. A second one hung around his neck.

In front of Nancy's horrified eyes, Al grabbed Marva. Before she had time to react, he pulled her rope off and slipped the second rope over Marva's head and down to her waist, cinching it tight. Dragging the frightened Marva with him, he headed for the edge.

"He's going to kill her!" Bess yelled in terror.

They watched, frozen, as the crazed man plunged headfirst over the face of Devil's Rock, taking Marva with him.

Chapter

Sixteen

WITH BESS'S SCREAM still echoing in her ears, Nancy pulled herself to her feet and rushed to the side of the cliff to look over.

Seventy or eighty feet below her, she could see Marva struggling with Al Hunt. They were locked together on one of the wide rock ledges that formed the devil's face.

As she watched the two figures scuffling below her, Nancy knew what the desperate killer was considering next.

Al Hunt had jerked Marva's safety rope back over her head and was trying to wrestle the young woman to the edge. Nancy had to

138

get down there before he succeeded in pushing Marva to her death.

Nancy caught sight of the first safety rope that had been around Marva's waist and now hung free. It was bouncing against the cliff face. The rope still had to be secured to something at the top, Nancy thought. Yes, there it was, anchored securely to a large, solid boulder. Maybe she could rappel down to Marva.

Turning to the group of students who were now clustered at the edge watching the scene below with horrified fascination, Nancy took control. "Can someone show me how to use this rope to get down to that ledge?"

At first no one answered. The ones who had heard her just stared at her as if she were crazy. A slender boy of about seventeen finally answered her. "Look, if you have to ask us, you don't have any business trying to rappel down any cliff."

"Jerry's right. You'd only kill yourself doing it," a girl behind the boy spoke up.

Just then, another boy—one of those who'd never taken their eyes off what was happening below—yelled out, "Did you see that? Old man Hunt has really flipped out. Someone's got to save Ms. Phillips before she's history."

Nancy was feeling desperate. I've got to *do* something, she said to herself. I can't just stand here and let Marva die.

139

"Maybe if someone ran for help," the boy named Jerry suggested. "I could do it. I'm in track at school."

"There isn't time for that," Nancy blurted out. "We've got only seconds, at best."

"Nancy! Look!" A yell from George got her attention. "Up there!" George was pointing overhead. "Maybe that's help."

Bending her head back, Nancy shielded her eyes to look up in the direction George was pointing. Not far above, one of the club's hang gliders was circling the rock.

"It's Gil!" Bess said excitedly. "He's come to rescue Marva." She waved up at the hang-glider pilot. "Way to go, Gil!" she called.

Nancy held her breath as she watched Gil expertly manipulate the glider. Nancy guessed what Gil had in mind. He was going to attempt a landing on the ledge!

All the others were watching now, riveted to the colorful glider. A sudden flash of light from the ledge below made Nancy look down. With a sinking feeling of horror, she realized the flash had been the sun's reflection off the barrel of a gun. A gun Al Hunt had leveled at Gil.

Helplessly, Nancy watched as the killer fired once, then fired again. The first shot must have missed Gil. But the second one found its target. A small patch of red appeared on Gil's right shoulder. Gil flinched, and his hands jerked on the control bar. The glider's nose shot up too sharply, and it lost the lift—the crucial pressure of the wind under the sail—needed to keep it aloft. The sail began to flap dangerously.

A girl beside Nancy screamed. "Ohhhh—no!" Gil's body had sagged into his harness, his head drooping to one side. It looked as if he was losing consciousness.

"He's going to crash," Jerry said with a sharp intake of breath.

Just as it seemed Gil was going to take a dive, a sudden gust of wind caught the underside of the huge sail, billowing it up. The glider evened out on its own. Another gust sent the glider toward the top of Devil's Rock, in the direction of Nancy and the others.

"Catch it!" Nancy yelled as she ran to the center of the ledge. They had to intercept the runaway glider—it was their only hope!

Nancy's action triggered Jerry and George to run with her. They caught up with the glider and its unconscious pilot as it was about to sail on past them. Jumping easily, they grabbed the glider's frame and pulled it to them.

Down below Marva had managed to wedge herself between a large boulder and the cliff face. Having lost all connection with reality, Al Hunt was rocking the boulder back and forth like a man possessed. Soon he would reach his prize.

"Now what?" George asked as she helped

her friend unhook Gil's harness and ease the injured man to the ground. Bess knelt beside him, tearing away his shirt to examine the wound.

"I guess it's up to me now," Nancy replied. "Gil did say I was a natural at this sport. It's as good a time as any to find out if he was right."

"Nancy, no!" George implored. "Please don't do this—you've never taken one up before. You could make a fatal mistake!"

"I'll try not to," Nancy answered grimly. "Now help me turn this thing around so it's facing the edge."

"But what about the harness?" George asked. "Don't you need that? I'll get it off Gil."

"There isn't time," Nancy said as she and George, with the help of the two boys, lifted the glider and turned it. "I don't need the harness to fly. It's only a fancy safety belt." She gestured at the control bar—a triangular piece of aluminum tubing that was nearly five feet high at the center. "I'm going to stand on the base. I'll use my feet to push it back and forth, instead of my hands."

"You're crazy," George told her simply. "But I guess nothing I say is going to stop you."

"Right," Nancy said to her friend. "Wish me luck." Hefting the glider, Nancy ran toward the edge of the cliff and jumped off, swinging her feet up onto the crossbar sail and sending her soaring out over the valley.

Nancy had to crouch slightly because she was taller than the top of the tubular triangle. She used the weight of her body to bank the glider so she could head back toward the face of the huge rock.

Peering down at the ledge, what she saw made her cringe inside. Al Hunt had now caught sight of her. His arm was raised, and he had her dead in his gunsight.

Determined that she was not going to give him the chance to get off a good shot, Nancy went straight for the attack.

Aiming the glider at the ledge, she pushed the nose down. Diving straight for the burly climbing instructor, she tried to make her body as small a target as possible by crouching very low.

Marva, who had been momentarily forgotten by Hunt, saw her coming. As Hunt's attention was drawn to Nancy, Marva kicked out at his gun. She managed to knock it from his hand, where it hit the ledge and slithered across the slick granite out of his reach.

Good move, Marva, Nancy said to herself. Swiftly taking advantage of the situation, she raised herself up, then pushed the control bar forward as hard as she could. The glider's nose lifted and went into stall.

143

Its colorful sail flapping in protest, the glider descended, with a jolt, onto the ledge.

But the ledge wasn't wide enough for the glider, Nancy realized in horror. Slowly it began to inch backward, Nancy with it. Both would plunge to the valley floor, hundreds of feet below.

Bending her knees, Nancy sprung forward, as the glider began its final dizzy descent, and landed almost directly on top of the astonished Hunt. Before he could recover his balance, Nancy aimed a high karate kick at his jaw. Hunt went over backward, striking his head against a boulder. He lay still, his eyes closed.

"Is he—" Marva asked, slipping out of her hiding place.

"Dead?" Nancy bent over the man, feeling for his pulse at the base of his jaw. She looked up at Marva. "Just out cold. He'll be around to stand trial."

"Oh, Nancy!" Marva shuddered a sigh of relief. "I don't even know how to begin to thank you. You saved my life."

"Well, I can think of one way," Nancy replied with a glance at Al Hunt. "Help figure out how to get us down from here before he comes to."

Then Nancy heard a very welcome sound. Police sirens were echoing off the mountains around them. They really would be safe now.

Chapter

Seventeen

THAT WAS a pretty foolish thing you pulled, miss," the young detective said to Nancy. But his eyes expressed his admiration. "I don't think I'd be ready to launch myself into space —with only one lesson, you said?"

"I'm sure you do more dangerous things than that all the time," Nancy replied graciously. "I'm glad it's over."

"So am I." Marva breathed happily. "I'm happy to be down and away from that man." Her glance took in Al Hunt as he was being led away. "This time I hope he's locked up for good."

Hunt halted and turned to face the girls

145

when he heard Marva talking about him. His eyes were unfocused and wild looking. Nancy thought to herself, the man really is crazy—just as Bess had suggested the criminal behind these terrible acts must be.

"If it wasn't for you, Miss Private Snoop," Hunt spat, "no one would have guessed it was me who was sending those death threats—and setting up all those nice little accidents." His face cracked in an evil grin. "I should have hung you up with the frozen meat when I had the chance."

"How—how could you have pretended to be my friend when all the time you hated me?" Marva asked, bewildered by the change in the man she had considered almost as close as a real uncle.

"Easy." The mirthless grin was replaced by a snarl. "It was because I did hate you so much, and still *do*. You were a horrible little brat who sent me away to rot in jail." His eyes narrowed into slits. "But it gave me a lot of time to think up my revenge. And I almost succeeded this time—next time . . ."

"Come on, you!" The officer pulled on Hunt's arm. "You've done enough to this lady. You can shut up now."

As Marva and Nancy watched, the man who'd brought terror to Club High Adventure was led to a waiting squad car.

* * *

146

"You know, I still can't put the two men together in my mind," Marva said later that evening when they had all gathered in the lounge to discuss the case. "I can't believe that the awful man at the trial when I was a little girl is the same man I knew and counted on as a friend for the past three years since my dad died."

"That was the whole idea," Nancy said. She stretched her arms and legs, feeling relaxed now that the case was closed. "The death threats and accidents to the other guests were only meant to confuse things so no one would suspect you were the intended victim. I can't say for certain, but I don't think he honestly meant for the accidents to the guests to be deadly."

"How about Quinn?" George asked. "I mean, sure, we heard that he came out of his coma this afternoon. But he could have just as easily died."

"I still think that trap was meant for Marva," Nancy replied. "That trail's not for lone guests. He shouldn't have been there at all. So it was a matter of his being in the wrong place at the right time."

"And poor Lisa," Bess commented. "She's such a mixed-up kid. It probably didn't help that we all thought she sabotaged her own glider."

"Well, I believe she's going to be fine,"

Marva said, surprising them with her confident tone. "We had a little talk. She admitted that her father's sending her here was a good idea. I think it's helping her get over that boyfriend. And she's ready to go back and try to work things out with her father."

"Oh, I'm glad about that," Bess said. "I really like her."

"You know, it's funny," Marva mused. "I kept thinking that it was someone who was trying to ruin me so I'd sell the club."

Gil, who was sitting beside her, his arm in a sling to protect his injured shoulder, looked guilty when Marva said that. "I'm really sorry I ever tried to convince you to sell," he said. "I know you love the club. And I'll remember that from now on. I promise."

"I admit that's what threw me off at first," Nancy said. "I thought it was someone trying to scare you into selling as well. I was positive that was the motive. It was only after we found that partially burned photo that I realized I'd been on the wrong track all along. That's when I decided the motive was personal."

"And since the photo was found in Al Hunt's cabin . . ." George shrugged expressively.

"It had to be him," Bess finished.

"Well, I'm just glad the club's reputation is

safe now," Marva said happily, and snuggled up closer to Gil.

"Yeah," Gil said, dropping a kiss on the top of her head. "I'm glad, too. After everything that happened this afternoon, I realized I've come to think of the club as home. I just might even end up loving it as much as Marva."

"Well, you'd better," Marva said jokingly, and kissed Gil back. "After all, we're going to be spending the rest of our lives here." She turned to Nancy. "Gil mentioned this afternoon that it would be nice if we ran it as a married couple. So I'll be exchanging this engagement ring for a wedding band. And he'll be exchanging all his other girls for just one—me."

"Marva, how wonderful," Bess exclaimed. "When?"

"Soon," Gil said. "The sooner, the better." He squeezed Marva's hand. "Then we're going on a nice long honeymoon. I think we could do with a vacation."

"Oh, that's funny." Bess giggled. "A vacation from a vacation resort."

After the collective groans had died down, Marva asked, "But how about you three? Can you steal a few days before you go back to River Heights?"

At Nancy's nod, she invited them. "Then please spend it here at the club as my—our—guests," she said with a quick grin at Gil.

"You'll get to know the club for the wonderful place it really is."

Nancy and George exchanged delighted glances. Despite Bess's small moan of protest, they agreed that Club High Adventure could be the perfect place to spend a few restful days.